Shades of Violet

also by
Hallie Lee

The Shady Gully Series
Paint Me Fearless
Wolfheart

For a list of Who's Who in Shady Gully? visit
https://www.hallielee.com/whos-who-in-shady-gully

Shades of Violet

The Shady Gully Series
Book 3

HALLIE LEE

WordCrafts Press

Shades of Violet is a work of fiction. Names, characters, businesses, places, events, locales, and incidents are either the products of the author's imagination or used in a fictitious manner. Any resemblance to actual persons, living or dead, or actual events is purely coincidental.

Shades of Violet
Copyright © 2023
Hallie Lee

ISBN: 978-1-957344-54-6

Cover design by Mike Parker

Published by WordCrafts Press
Cody, Wyoming 82414
www.wordcrafts.net

For my precious daughter, Bree

"Someday when the pages of my life end,
I know that you will be one
of the most beautiful chapters."
~Anonymous

Thursday

As we merged onto the Bluegrass Parkway, Lexington, Kentucky, grew farther and farther in the rear view. I felt comfortable there, where blue and white flags jutted from the windows of Volvos and Corollas alike, and University of Kentucky license plates identified long-haired millennials and old-school curmudgeons as members of the Big Blue Nation.

A rambunctious group of gray-haired ladies crammed into an old-school Cadillac honked as we sped past. I dipped my head respectfully, acknowledging the blue Wildcat paws painted across their cheeks. When they spotted my own well-worn UK cap they beeped again in solidarity.

"They look happy," Petey remarked from the driver's seat.

I didn't even have to look at him. I could hear the amusement in his voice. "They are. Because we won last night." I added smartly, "As usual."

"Yes indeed." Again, with the playful teasing. "Another road trip saved by a masterful offense." When I risked a glance, he rewarded me with his singularly mischievous grin, and as usual, I endured an embarrassing spark of heat as it flamed across my cheeks. "Are you okay?" His eyebrows stitched in concern.

"Yeah. Just sleepy." I slid lower in the seat of his Ford truck, tugging the brim of my hat down to conceal my ragged emotions. "I'm just gonna rest my eyes."

He grunted, clearly baffled, but after a few minutes he became distracted and turned his attention to the road. Holding Petey's attention was never easy, but at least now I had a chance to study him undetected.

I let my imagination go wild as his long, slender fingers caressed the steering wheel with nervous energy. I admired the jaunty angle of his chiseled profile as he passed a sluggish truck carrying horse fencing. His light brown hair was disheveled, due in part to our early morning departure from Lexington, but also because he was careless with his appearance.

He was serious in other ways, however, and that earnestness presented itself in the form of a fresh tattoo on the wrist of his left arm. He brushed his fingers along the cuff of his shirt, tentatively shifting it to expose the cross. Nothing fancy, beautiful in its simplicity, the basic black cross suited him perfectly.

Unaware of my scrutiny, or so it seemed, he positioned his arm precisely along the steering wheel. My gaze naturally drifted to the deep, black ink glistening in the morning sun.

Despite my anxiety over the trip to Shady Gully, the cross seemed to momentarily ease my worry. While Luke and Bella's wedding would surely be a joyous event, it would also mean going public with our secrets, and with that unveiling would come the inevitable showdown with my mother.

There would be disappointment. There would be repercussions.

But the longer I stared at Petey—and the symbolic cross on his wrist—the consequences of our uncovering drifted farther away, and the sleep that had eluded me for so long fell over me in a heavy wave.

A wave that lasted all the way from Memphis, Tennessee, to Tuscaloosa, Alabama.

"Hey, you gonna sleep forever?" Petey stirred me playfully. "I could have kidnapped you and hauled you to another country by now."

I rubbed my eyes, squinting as I tried to make out the interstate sign.

"Did you know you snored? That honker of yours was so loud a couple of eighteen-wheelers tooted back."

"Funny." I pushed myself higher in the seat and stared out the window, trying to get my bearings.

"Seriously. We're almost to the border."

"Of Mexico?" I started a grin.

"Who's funny now?" He finished it. "No, Scarlet. To God's country. Louisiana." In one fluid motion, he struck his blinker and curved into a gas station. After he hopped out of the truck, he raised his arms in a languid, graceful stretch. The black cross along his wrist maintained its shimmer even in the sagging sun. We'd been on the road most of the day.

"Where are we?" I grumbled, still searching for proof that we weren't in Tijuana. "I'm starving."

"We're close." He yanked his Wildcat Blue pullover over his head. "Time to change."

I managed to catch the duffel bag he tossed, while trying not to stare at the dips and contours of his lean, wiry physique. Aware of the wardrobe requirement, I *tsked*, and headed to the restroom.

"Hey, Ruby," he hollered from the rear of the truck, once again citing any color under the sun other than my actual name. Still shirtless, he unscrewed the Big Blue Nation license plate holder, replacing it with one of purple and gold. "What do you think?" The numbers were the same, but the gaudy contraption in his hands sported a growling tiger.

Before I could think of a suiting retort, his shaggy head dipped back in laughter. Powerless then, I merely watched as he reveled in his joy, his hazel eyes crinkling as they found mine. And lingered there. "We'll get some boudin balls and andouille up ahead."

"Qui, mon cher," I answered in French, offering up an exaggerated cajun inflection.

Once I'd changed into shorts and my Louisiana State University jersey, I found him waiting for me in the truck with bottled water and a caramel apple pop. "Oh, my favorite." As I ripped open the wrapper of the sucker, I inspected his Fighting

Tiger T-shirt. "You're looking very purple. And gold. Not sure it complements your eyes as much as Wildcat blue."

He scoffed and reached behind his seat. "I got you a gift." Rather than waste time presenting it to me, he retrieved a purple and gold LSU Tiger cap from the bag. "When in Rome…" As he removed my battered, blue baseball cap, my thin, baby-fine hair tumbled out. He tucked each stray strand carefully into the new cap, and then purposefully weaved my ponytail out the back. "Much better." He appraised me. "That's what I'm talking about."

Before I could fixate too long on the way his fingers felt moving along my scalp, he'd geared the truck into action and pointed it in the direction of *God's country*. Within moments his face relaxed.

We drove on. Mostly in silence. Occasionally he'd inject one of his entertaining reveries, sometimes with a grin, sometimes a wink. We traded glances often. Like we had some kind of secret. Which of course, we did.

As the interstate brought us closer to central Louisiana, his frenetic drumming on the steering-wheel picked up a notch, and his right leg twitched so much it threw off the cruise control. Unable to contain himself, he reached for his phone.

"I wouldn't," I cautioned. "Not yet."

"It'll be fine." The inflection in his words made it seem like a question.

I shrugged, wary.

"Mama," he said when she answered. "What's for dinner?" Pleasure danced along his edges.

I could hear her squealing on the other end of the phone. Thrilled. Happy. *Surprised.* How I loved her. The sound of her voice brought me pleasure as well. But I knew it wouldn't last.

"Oh no, Mama." I watched as his tone changed, became guarded. Regretful even. "I was joking. We're not—"

Aunt Desi hardly paused, her excitement intensifying the pitch of her endless questions. "Why? Where are y'all now? When will you be here?"

"Uh…uh…" He struggled, a heavy shadow stealing his happiness. I read the anguish in his manner, understood the guilt as the very cross on his wrist convicted him. "It's…well. The traffic…"

When this man with the light inside him looked at me in desperation, I did what I had to do. What he *couldn't* do.

"Aunt Desi!" I said into the speaker. "We're just leaving the Bluegrass State now. We're on our way, but we won't make it until tomorrow."

I lied for him.

After he said goodbye to his mother, we passed the exit ramp to Belle Maison and Shady Gully, merging instead onto I-12, headed south. To Baton Rouge.

"Thanks, Jade," he said finally.

"Any time," I muttered with a heavy heart, reminding myself how important it was to keep our plan to ourselves. For now, anyway.

A lot would depend on what happened in the next few hours.

Chapter One

Temperamental Thespian
Lenny

My wife was beautiful. Undeniably stunning. Even prettier than when she was in high school. I knew this because I was around then, hanging on her every word, doing her bidding, and yes, occasionally walking on the proverbial eggshells.

Well, maybe more than occasionally. Perhaps my role could better be described as buffer-of-random-drama, and while this may seem a low-reward-high-risk position, it was a cakewalk compared to my current pickle.

What had I been thinking? I'd told my gorgeous wife of over thirty years that she was as cute as a bug-in-a-rug as she cut and arranged flowers. This as she sat slumped over the kitchen table, flustered and discouraged, surrounded by a battlefield of massacred lilies and amaryllis.

Neanderthal move. And with all my experience. Granted, the compliment could have gone either way, but I'd nailed my own coffin when I'd laughed.

Another rookie blunder.

In one emotional sweep, Desi had burst into tears and sent the flower carcasses flying onto the floor, pruning shears, stem cutters, and all. Mary Ann and Ginger, our cocker spaniel and papillon respectively, had immediately run for cover. Ginger, being the drama queen she was, had unfurled an impressive squeal for effect.

Of course, the temperamental thespian was fine, but Desi

had collapsed into another round of crying at the notion of murdering her beloved dog.

Good grief. I deserved to be quartered and butchered, just like the ill-fated flowers.

"Did you see what I did, Lenny?" She raked her hands through her chin-length hair. "I can't do anything right. What is the point of me?" She marked me expectantly.

Tricky territory here, and I didn't like my odds.

"Is that her squealing? Go check, Lenny. What if she's bleeding?"

It was then I realized the persistent yapping belonged not to Ginger, but to Desi's phone. The blinking screen trumpeted the caller as *The Prodigal Son*, a contact Luke had mockingly created for his younger brother, Peter.

I presented the phone to Desi like a member of the royal court, hoping for his imminent pardon. "Look. It's for you. It's Petey."

Desi reached for the phone, her mood immediately lightening. I listened as she quizzed Petey as to his arrival, puzzling over menu items while gathering cast-off flowers from the floor. After a pause, her expression changed again. "My sweet Violet! I can't wait to wrap you in a hug. I've missed you."

"When are they getting here?" I wanted to know.

Desi waved me off, single-mindedly prattling on with Violet. "That's wonderful. Y'all think about what you want me to cook. Okay then." Desi's eyes finally landed on me. "Drive safe. We can't wait to see y'all."

Once she hung up, she bent to scratch Mary Ann and Ginger under their chins, thoughts of nearly skewering them long forgotten. "I think I'll do a gumbo tomorrow. I'll need to get chicken thighs."

"So, what did they say?" I pressed. "I take it they're arriving tomorrow?"

"Yes," Desi answered, distracted. "You know Petey likes dark meat. Oh, and okra. Do you think Sprite will have some at the Quick Stop? Probably not. They're not even in season yet."

"Give me a list," I said. "If Sprite doesn't have okra in one form or the other, I'm sure Charlie Wayne will have some stashed in the freezer at the Cozy Corner."

Desi glanced across the kitchen, clearly dismayed as fragments of once vibrant lilies littered the hardwood floor with pollen.

Before her disquiet resurfaced, I fired up the tea kettle. "A little cup?"

"No. I don't need the caffeine. But maybe the herbal. The lemon vanilla." As I set about making her tea, her manner softened, and I thrilled at the feel of her arms encircling me from behind. "You're so good to me, Lenny."

I stirred a teaspoon of sugar into her tea. Handed it to her. "Why wouldn't I be?"

"Because I'm a mess. I think I've overloaded myself. I'll be glad when Robin gets here."

"Did Violet say when she was coming?"

"No. Violet and Petey both seemed a little rushed. Probably in the middle of traffic." Desi sipped her tea, a smile relaxing her face. "But Robin told me on the phone the other day that she and Sterling were booking a flight ASAP. Who knows? They might even beat Petey and Violet here."

Robin and Desi had been best friends since junior high, and their bond had only grown stronger over the years, despite a season of lies and rumors that nearly ruined their relationship. Individually, they were amazing, but together, they formed a fearsome matriarchal force.

Because of their connection, our children had grown up thinking of one another as cousins. Luke, Petey, and our daughter Micah, had grieved along with Robin and her twins, Sterling and Violet, when they lost Dean to cancer seven years ago.

Seven years, I thought. Hard to believe my buddy had been gone that long.

I shook off my melancholy, determined to cheer Desi up. "You know, you could just hire someone to do the flowers for the shower. Isn't that what most people do?"

Desi harumphed. "Luke doesn't want me to spend too much money."

"That's ridiculous."

"It is. But that's not the point." Desi raised her eyebrow indignantly. "Meadow's lack of involvement is unnerving. She doesn't seem interested at all. If she is, she hasn't indicated it to me. I don't think anything makes her happy."

"Desi…"

"I'm serious. She's the most miserable human being I think I've ever known."

I matched her eyebrow raise with one of my own. "You should tread lightly with Meadow. She's Bella's mother—"

"Exactly. And Bella told me herself that her mom wasn't really,"—Desi raised her fingers in air quotes—"into weddings."

"Well." I chose my words carefully. "Can you blame her?"

Desi sighed, as Meadow's unfortunate past discouraged any further grumbling. "I suppose you're right," she said finally. "And Lord knows Micah isn't the ideal maid of honor either. That girl, I don't know where her head is these days."

Desi set her mug on the table with a thump, reminding me I was supposed to be cheering her up. Not troubling her. I watched as she retrieved the broom, and manhandled her frustrations against the hardwood floor. "I can't believe I ruined all these flowers. The wedding will be here before we know it." She glanced at me through a veil of lashes. "I can't understand why Bella and Luke are in such a rush."

"You can't?" I grinned. "Really?"

"I just don't know how I'm going to get everything done."

"It'll get done. Robin is on her way, and you two will pull off a wonderful shower. And then a beautiful wedding. Meanwhile, I'm going to hire a florist."

"But Luke said—"

"I don't care what the mayor of Shady Gully said," I quipped. "He's not the boss of me. We have the money, and we're going to give him and Bella a nice wedding. End of subject."

When Desi allowed a tiny smile to escape her lips, I took the broom.

"If you say so." But she didn't look convinced. And even worse, tears once again puddled at the corners of her eyes.

I swallowed back a beleaguered sigh. And then did what most any man would do in the situation. "Why don't you give me a list? I'll pick up the chicken and hunt down some okra for the gumbo. And whatever else you need me to get. Or do. Or…"

She eyed me suspiciously. "You're not going to go to that silly store, are you? With everything going on? With Petey and Violet on their way?"

"It's not a *silly* store, Desi. It's my store. It's where I work."

"Where you work? Honestly, Lenny." Desi huffed as she pulled open a kitchen drawer, angrily retrieved a notepad, and began furiously scratching items onto it with a pen. "You don't need to work. I don't know why you're doing this. You finally got away from that horrible oil rig in the Gulf of Mexico."

"Desi—"

"The one that nearly destroyed your back, by the way."

Desi's vexed tone drew both Mary Ann and Ginger from their plush doggie beds. They warily closed in and assessed the situation, ready to rally behind their queen and rumble if necessary. Unfortunately, the *clickety-clicks* of their dancing toenails seemed to exasperate Desi further.

"Don't be that way, honey. It makes me happy. I want you to be excited for me."

"I thought you enjoyed tooling around art galleries with Robin and me. When did that stop being fun? And reading your whodunnits? When did that stop being enough?"

"You know I love traveling with you and Robin. Going to art galleries. Seeing your mom's paintings celebrated."

"Apparently not."

After Dean died, Robin had used some of their vast wealth to showcase Sunny's paintings at exclusive art studios across the country. For Desi, the act of honoring her mom's talent helped ease the pain of their estrangement, as well as cope with her sudden and tragic death from an overdose.

"I'm just saying you don't need to work so hard. Mama's Giclee prints have made us plenty of money."

"I'm aware." Giclee prints were digital prints made on canvas with an inkjet printer, and not only had they sold well, but they allowed Desi to keep Sunny's original paintings.

And me to quit my back-breaking job on an unforgiving oil rig in the Gulf of Mexico.

Thanks for the reminder, honey.

After a quick glance at Ginger and Mary Ann, who guarded the heels of my beautiful, undeniably stunning wife, I took the errand list and headed out to do her bidding.

Usually, a leisurely ride through Shady Gully lifted my spirits, but not today. I couldn't understand why, with all the progress and prosperity over the last few years, Desi would be so unhappy. There was so much to look forward to, with Luke and Bella's upcoming wedding, with Petey's returning home to Shady Gully, and with Micah...

Well, there *was* Micah. But still, she would be alright, and her aimlessness wasn't anything new. And it didn't explain Desi's random emotional outbursts. Or her tears. So many tears. I sighed, resolving to drag my thoughts away from my troubles at home.

I passed Nails and Thread, the town's hottest new business, amazed by the overflow of cars in the parking lot. The way women flocked to nail salons never ceased to mystify me. Granted, Sigourney Sky was one of The Creek's most talented entrepreneurs, and a gifted seamstress, but coaxing her loyal alterations customers from across the creek, while simultaneously enticing Shady Gully's women with pedicures and manicures, and then providing all those services in one beautifully designed cottage smack dab in the center of town was brilliant strategy.

Sigourney hired and trained young women from both across the creek and Shady Gully proper. Not only did this create jobs, but it contributed to healing and unity. Hard to believe that just over two years ago protests and violence had consumed our small town. Besides a bridge collapse and considerable damage to property across the creek, two churches had burned, and tensions between the communities had escalated.

Things had greatly improved since, largely in part to Luke, who'd become mayor of Shady Gully shortly after it incorporated.

Luke was a uniter. As was Sigourney. Frankly, the only downside for her and Nails and Thread was her next-door neighbor, Dolly, the owner of Dolly's Diva Dome. Since Dolly did hair, the location made sense in that women could park and get their whole beauty regimen done in one shake. Dolly was a challenge though. She had issues, to put it mildly.

As I approached the four-way stop sign, a figure lingering at Sprite's gas station and general store caught my attention. Located on one of Shady Gully's four corners, Sprite's Quick Stop bordered a cluster of Bradford pear trees and azaleas. Between the foliage and the individual's oversized hoodie, I couldn't make out much more than his distinguishing gait. Something about it looked vaguely familiar.

When an insistent honk dragged me from my puzzlement, I realized I'd dawdled at Shady Gully's four-way stop too long. I turned my attention to the irritated driver at the adjacent stop sign.

Meadow. Speaking of challenges.

I offered a friendly smile, a pleasant nod, and raised my hand in a chipper wave. After all, we'd be family soon. She scowled, her expression pulsing with each spin of the dome light atop her mail car. Feeling ridiculous, I lowered my hand, and signaled her ahead.

Despite the scowl, Meadow was beautiful. Stunning even. Like Desi, but in a different way. While Desi was petite, with dark eyes and a trendy, highlighted haircut, Meadow was tall, statuesque, green-eyed, and wore her long, dark hair straight down her back.

Refusing to budge, we played the awkward you-go-no-you-go routine to excruciating embarrassment. All the while Meadow maintained her scowl. The distinct grimace reminded me a lot of her Uncle Wolfheart, and I wondered if she'd learned it from him.

Regardless of what I'd told Desi, I feared Meadow was irreversibly broken. Taken advantage of at a young age by an older man, Meadow had carried the bruises and scars of that experience her whole life.

If you could consider lovely Bella a bruise. Or a scar. Feisty enough to make her way in a resistant community, Bella's bright personality and spirited nature had been enough to enchant Luke, my painfully serious son.

After another sharp honk, Meadow shook her head in exasperation. Her scowl inched downward another notch. This time, without hesitation, I put my foot on the gas and turned right at the four-way stop. Best to keep things friendly.

After all, we'd be family soon.

So much for the uplifting spin around Shady Gully. Just as I'd dodged Meadow's perturbed glare, my eyes landed on Shady Gully's biggest eyesore. Despite all the progress upon incorporation, it seemed Shady Gully could do nothing about the likes of JJ Wheeler.

An unseemly sort, Wheeler and his scraggly beard and man-bun had taken up residence on one of the corners of the four-way stop, right where Jesse's church had burned during the protests. In fact, it now appeared as if JJ had expanded onto James's lot, which was where the second church had caught fire.

Apparently, without even opening their mouths at the pulpit, Jesse and James, the estranged twin preachers of Shady Gully, had managed to bring shame to the town in the form of JJ Wheeler.

There were a couple of different versions going around as to how Wheeler had gained possession of Shady Gully's most prime piece of real estate, but I suspected it was a combination of both.

The first was that James was holding off on rebuilding his church because he wanted Jesse's lot. His plan was to build one big church, thus keeping his brother off the pulpit for good. Meanwhile Jesse, who was in and out of rehab after setting his brother's church on fire two years ago, refused to sell. Probably out of spite.

The second version was that their sister, Dolly of Dolly's Diva Dome, somehow persuaded her sickly daddy to take matters into his own hands. Now, everyone around Shady Gully knew Brother Wyatt, who had once been a formidable preacher himself, was on his death bed, so there was speculation that Dolly's hands were the ones taking matters.

Enter JJ Wheeler. And his big tent. And his barbeque. Ornery as all get out, JJ had stolen Charlie Wayne's business at The Cozy Corner in one fell swoop. JJ had filled his ice chests, fired up his grills, and danced about like he was cuckoo as he mixed up his secret sauce. He was an absolute spectacle, his tent a monstrosity, and the enticing smell of his ribs taunted the whole town.

Charlie Wayne had been furious. "This is my territory," he'd argued. "And no trailer trash with an updo is gonna prance around and steal my customers."

The battle had waged for weeks now, and each week the results were the same. Known for being cantankerous himself, Charlie Wayne and the Cozy Corner were part of Shady Gully's history. They were legendary. And now, thanks to a cackling psychopath with a man bun, they were nearly bankrupt.

I rolled my window down as I passed JJ's tent. Resisted the smell of his tantalizing barbeque. Denied the grumbling in my stomach.

The lunatic rubbed his tummy and beckoned me with an obscene gesture.

Although my foot tapped the brakes and my fingers twitched for the right blinker, my eyes remained stiffly ahead.

Woefully, I continued toward my silly store.

Chapter Two

Not On Your Life, Mrs. Cleaver
Meadow

I fumed at the stop sign while my daughter's soon to be father-in-law, Lenny, went through the motions of being polite. Seriously, just go already. Hoping I could scare him into movement, I set an edge to my glare.

Finally, he paled and turned right on Shady Gully's four-way stop. "Great," I muttered when I realized we were going in the same direction.

Something about Luke's parents made me want to tear out my hair. If I had to listen to Desi ask one more time, *What do you think, Meadow? Wouldn't this be a lovely color for the bouquets?* I'd scream like a banshee.

"Uuuuugrrrrrr!" My exasperated grunt bounced within the confines of my crappy car. I furiously pounded the steering wheel, sending a pile of JCPenney flyers tumbling to the floorboard. Perfect. Gathering and reassigning those would delay me another fifteen minutes.

No, Desi, I think coral is an ugly color. I think the flowers are ugly. And I think it's all a big waste of time and money, but since you have plenty of both, just knock yourself out and leave me out of it.

Unfortunately, my lack of interest only seemed to spur her on.

What about the bridal shower, Meadow? Does it bother you that it's so close to the wedding? I know it's not usually done that way, but honestly, it's the best time for our extended family in Kentucky to get here… Yada, yada, yada.

I have no clue, Desi. We don't have bridal showers on The Creek. Speaking of that, do I really need to be there?

On and on it went.

I'm sure Petey will want to throw Luke some sort of bachelor party. How about we girls take Bella on a road trip to celebrate?

Not on your life, Mrs. Cleaver.

But nothing deterred Desi. And if it wasn't her, it was Bella.

My daughter had been angry with me lately, accusing me of not caring about the wedding. Of disapproving of Luke. Truth was, I *didn't* care about the wedding, and Luke, all things considered, was a fine enough fellow. Now, would I have preferred Bella marry a nice young man from The Creek? Sure, but when had I ever got what I wanted?

And why was it necessary to rub my nose in it all? Just because Luke's parents were footing the bill for the big event, was I expected to fall to my knees in gratitude? Fat chance of that.

"Watch it!" I screeched as Mr. Cleaver drifted ahead of me, hesitating and wobbling like he wanted to pull into JJ Wheeler's barbeque tent. He corrected just before I rear-ended his truck. I swore as he headed straight past the post office and turned left into his hardware store.

Lenny's Tool Shed.

I guess they'd buy up all of Shady Gully before long. Soon it would become unrecognizable. They'd call it progress. Prosperity. I'd call it something else.

JJ Wheeler leered at me, grabbed his crotch as I passed his tent. I stretched my arm out the window and shot him the bird. He laughed.

If Dolly's intent had been to annoy her outlaw-preacher brothers while they fought over land, leasing the corner to this cat showed some creativity. As much as I detested her, watching the town spin over Wheeler was entertaining as all get out.

I saw Bella's name flash across my phone as it vibrated. I groaned, dreading more wedding talk. I'd almost rather my Uncle Wolfheart's face flicker across my screen. At least then I could serve back salty comments when he urged me to be nice, to join in, and to be happy for Bella.

"Hello." I clicked on Bella's face.

"Mama, hey. What are you doing?"

"Delivering mail." I turned right, my tires crunching along the gravel parking lot of Sacred Heart Catholic Church. After securing my earphones, I grabbed a larger than usual stack of mail and stuffed it into the office box before Father Patrick carried his jolly self out to chat a spell.

Seeing as how the other two churches burned to the ground a few years ago, Sacred Heart had turned into a welcome hub for displaced Christians looking for a home to land.

"Guess what?" Bella was happy.

"What?" I waved off the cheery red-headed priest as he made for the door.

"Violet and Petey are driving in. They're going to be here tomorrow!"

"Well, that's nice." *And so it begins*, I thought, my body filling with dread.

"And Aunt Robin and Sterling are flying in too. It's really happening, Mama. I'm actually going to be married, and I'll be the mayor's wife. Doesn't that sound unreal?"

I couldn't decide which annoyed me more. The fact that Bella had adopted the *Aunt* when referring to Desi's best pal, Robin, or the idea of my daughter being part of the political establishment of Shady Gully.

"Mama?" Bella groused. "What's wrong? Why aren't you happy?"

"I'm thrilled."

Bella huffed in response to my sarcasm. "Whatever. Anyway, we're going to have a big party when they all get into town. Kind of a pre-shower celebration. It'll be fun."

Father Patrick caught my eyeroll, and quickly picked up his step, no doubt assuming I needed spiritual assistance ASAP. I hurriedly pulled out of the parking lot before his chubby legs could reach me.

"Desi was going to make gumbo, but now she's thinking it would be easier to do burgers. She wants to keep it simple. What do you think?"

I turned right, moving along to Bella's future husband's pet project, the Shady Gully Recreation Center. A bit over-the-top, in my opinion, as the place was so big it often took two trips to drop off the ridiculous mass of bulk mail and packages.

"Mama?"

"Huh? What?" My jaw clinched. "It's getting late, Bella, and I've still got more deliveries."

"Desi has a lot going on too. With all the preparations for the shower. And the wedding." A drawn-out pause. "But I guess once Aunt Robin gets here, she'll have help."

I winced. Both from Bella's passive aggressive comment and the strain of hauling a heavy box of printer paper into the Recreation Center.

"Okay, whatever," Bella eventually said. "Will you at least come to the party? Or is that too much to ask?"

I could practically hear Uncle Wolf's cautionary warning. *Resist, Meadow, resist.*

But I ignored it. "I'll check my schedule."

"Funny." Bella's voice cracked. "Seriously, Mama. I want you to be there."

Guilt swept through me then, causing me to lose my balance and drop the awkward box just steps before reaching the mail bin at the Recreation Center. As the box hit the ground, the rubber band on a cluster of flyers snapped, sending them flapping across the parking lot. "Bella, I've got to go."

"Mama—"

After hanging up, I dodged around the parking lot of Luke's beloved Recreation Center, randomly retrieving flyers promoting his father's new business. I felt like a fool. The good news? Lenny's Tool Shed was offering ten dollars off a fifty dollar purchase. Swell.

As resentment and frustration ballooned inside me, angry,

incoherent curses spewed from my mouth. Once I finally stuffed the miserable flyers into the mail bin I returned to my car, cranked up the dome light, and continued with my mail route.

My phone chimed with a schedule alert.

Great. Now I was going to be late picking up my date, who was quite literally the only other person in Shady Gully who shared my testy, blasé attitude over Bella's impending nuptials.

The Shady Gully Fire Department sat alongside the sheriff's substation, which nestled next to Sprite's Quick Stop on the corner of the four-way stop. Located pretty much in the center of town, the fire station looked as established as if it had been there for decades. The only thing that gave it away was the shiny, new fire truck sitting outside.

And the gangly twelve-year-old Creek boy hosing it down. When I pulled in, he gave me a super cool tilt of the head. I matched his super cool head tilt with one of my own. We were quite the pair, he and I. Two years ago, he'd been a lovestruck adolescent pining away for Bella, while I'd been a thirty-eight-year-old cynic holding a grudge against the world. Not much had changed since then. Except he'd grown taller and more awkward in puberty. And maybe a little more in love with Bella.

"Hey," he turned off the hose, "I still gotta dry." As he reached for a stack of towels, I marveled at the expanding muscles along his back and shoulders. Maybe one day he'd find an actual girlfriend and get over Bella.

"I saw her at Sigourney Sky's earlier," he grumbled. "With that ridiculous white dress. What a waste of time."

"Throw me one," I sighed, hauling myself out of the car and catching a towel. "I don't have all day, Littlefry."

"Shhh." He flitted his eyes from me to the firehouse.

His given name was actually Littlefire, but the boys on The Creek had teased him with the Littlefry tag. Regardless, his moniker had evolved into Fireman over the last two years, partly because he loved putting out fires, and partly because he'd set one that burned down a church.

Of course, his arsonist tendencies weren't known to everyone, and those of us who did know kept it close. Nevertheless, Fireman had atoned for his wrongdoing, and would likely serve his community as a real fireman one day.

Raucous laughter spilled from the firehouse as Sheriff Rick and one of his deputies strolled outside, both chuckling over something amusing. The sheriff tipped his hat. "Howdy, Meadow."

"Sheriff." I moved my hand in a circular motion, buffing the body of the fire truck to a pristine cherry. "What's so funny?"

"Just a little back and forth between agencies." He snorted. "I reckon this year Quietdove will get a Christmas card from the precinct in Jackson, Mississippi."

"Lubbock, Texas, too," griped Deputy Quietdove. "What do I look like? The NCIC?"

I had no clue what they were going on about.

"Hey, Quietdove." I snapped my fingers, hoping to draw them out of their bizarre cop humor. "Are you headed back to The Creek?"

He looked at his watch. "Getting close."

"Cool." I tossed the rag to Fireman, telling him tersely, "I'm outta here. You can ride back to The Creek with him."

"Chop. Chop." Quietdove eyed Fireman. "I'm not far behind."

Although Quietdove hailed from across the creek just as we did, he was often accused of divided loyalties. Assimilation was one thing, but becoming a sheriff's deputy was another altogether. While the accusations didn't seem to faze him, the strikingly handsome thirty-year-old was a bit of a mystery.

"Are you volunteering at the fire station on The Creek tomorrow?" he asked Fireman.

"Yep. I'll be washing their truck too." He grinned. "Redflyer said he'd let me drive it out of the garage."

The sheriff raised an eyebrow. "That's a lot of truck for a little—"

"I'm almost a teenager now."

The sheriff popped an orange taffy into his mouth. "Yep. I

reckon you'll be filing for social security shortly thereafter." He underhanded a grape candy to the boy. "You know your probation period for that, uh, for that little incident, is over now. You could take a break and be a kid. While you still can."

Fireman appeared genuinely perplexed. "Why would I wanna do that?"

The sheriff shook his head, directing his attention my way while Quietdove picked up a rag to help Fireman along. "You doing okay, Meadow?"

"Just fine." I moved toward my car, finding Sheriff Rick's desire to chat annoying. He was probably being friendly because he assumed I was in good with Luke and his family. No doubt trying to get the low-down on Robin's ETA.

Everyone in town knew he had the hots for Robin, who'd lost her husband to cancer several years ago. From what I heard, the two were almost an item now, but maybe not if he didn't know her traveling plans.

"How's Wolfheart doing?"

I shrugged. "He's good."

"I guess he's busy working on his toast for the wedding. He was pretty keyed up about it last time I saw him."

News to me. But then again, anything wedding-related was news to me.

I grimaced, done with the chit-chat. I mock saluted and pulled out of the fire station, taking a right and heading toward The Creek. I glanced back one last time at Fireman and Quietdove, merrily scrubbing away at the big red truck.

Assimilators, the both of them. They were just like Bella.

The kid would be fine. He was a hard worker, ambitious, and shadowing part-time at the new fire stations would do him good. He'd follow Quietdove's path and wouldn't give a hoot what the die-hard Creeks thought about him.

On the surface, Creeks were like everybody else. We wore the same clothes. Ate the same food. Read the same magazines. Other than where we lived, and our unusual names…

Well, we had prettier hair maybe. And awesome green eyes. Except for Bella. Her eyes were blue.

Bella was living proof that I'd once been fool enough to think I could assimilate. Oh, how I'd wanted so desperately to belong. To escape life on The Creek. And for a time, I'd believed I could.

My blue-eyed prince had told me he loved me. And he'd made love to me like he loved me. He'd told me *I* was beautiful, and that *we* could have a beautiful life together. I'd bought into the fantasy and had soon begun to picture myself as a mover and shaker in Shady Gully. Much like Bella does now.

Having him by my side had made all things possible. So unlike anyone on The Creek, he'd carried himself with confidence, with assurance, and without fear of consequences. As long as I was with him, I'd held a share in his poise and certainty. His optimism.

I'd trusted him. I'd clung to the illusion.

Until I hadn't.

Until his wife got suspicious, and he'd tried to hide me, as if he were ashamed of me. As if I were trash and needed to be discarded. Suddenly, consequences came into our conversations. Fear and consequences began to define us.

Bella defined us.

He no longer acted with assurance. With confidence. He began to carry himself with doubt. And when *my* reality stripped *him* of all the things that made him secure…he'd fled.

Poof.

Just like that, my blue-eyed prince, my ticket to a better life, vanished.

Over the years, I'd come to think of him as a character, like a hero in one of my romance novels. Or like in a movie, when the strong, blue-eyed soldier rescues the beautiful, green-eyed damsel in distress.

He'd been a false deliverer then. And now, he was nothing more than a phantom. A ghost. A reminder of my long-ago, shameful belief in fairy tales. I'd been a fool then, but no more.

I'd never be like Quietdove. Or Fireman.

Or Bella, whose future portended a grievous parting from The Creek. In many ways she'd already taken her leave.

I mean, really…who even heard of *bridal showers* on The Creek?

Chapter Three

Flip-flopped Character
Violet

Friday

We sat across from one another at a hole-in-the-wall café in Opelousas, Louisiana, nothing but a caddy of ketchup, mayo, and mustard between us. His normally sunny face pulsed with disappointment, and unfortunately for me, the server's disposition was no more hopeful.

"Did y'all decide yet?" The gloomy, middle-aged man checked his watch. "Sunny side up or over easy?"

"Just a little more time," Petey replied amiably.

The guy impatiently tapped his pen against his pad. His expression clear. *They're eggs, man, don't overthink it.*

"We'll decide soon," I offered, nixing my craving for pancakes, which would likely send Mr. Salty Server into a rant. Once he returned to his position behind the counter, I turned to Petey, whose uncharacteristic sadness broke my heart. "You'll rebound. You always do."

He shrugged. "I don't know. What if it's a sign? What if God's trying to tell me—"

"Petey. It could have been a sign, yes. But it could also have been a test. Since when do you back away from a challenge so easily?"

He shook his head, his shaggy bangs even more unruly than yesterday. "I don't understand. I was so prepared. I was on top of the world. I was going to blow that crowd away. Instead, I nearly collapsed in a sweat-filled-tear-soaked disaster."

"Maybe you over-prepared? And if I'm being honest…"

He raised his hazel eyes attentively. "Go on. What?" He fidgeted with the condiment caddy.

"The Petey I know and—" I hung back, rewording. "You don't normally use phrases like *top of the world* and *blowing crowds away.* That doesn't even sound like you."

His eyes widened.

The brooding server returned, hovering over us with an impatient sigh. "Sunny side up," Petey responded without taking his eyes off me. "Sausage."

"Toast or—"

"Biscuit."

"And for you?" Mr. Congeniality turned his fractious gaze on me.

"I'll have the same," I said, all hopes of buttery pancakes drenched in syrup now completely doused. "Except Bacon. And toast." I took a deep breath and met Petey's hazel stare. "Maybe you were too focused on impressing Timothy rather than delivering the message."

He released the condiments, and slowly placed his hands flat on the table. "You're right. I'm a fraud."

"I'm not saying—"

"You don't have to." He mooned over the tattooed cross on his wrist, sulking. "And beyond that, I *did* let Timothy down. After all the strings he pulled to get me that gig."

"Gig? Really?" I scoffed. "Is that what you're calling a jam-packed auditorium of religion students at LSU these days? You need to listen to yourself, Petey." I stared hard at him until he finally lifted his hands from the table and raked them through his hair. "If it was a test, I'm pretty sure you failed." I lowered my eyes, surprised by the harshness in my tone.

Just as a text sounded from my phone, the glum server slid our plates of eggs across the table, disappearing before I could ask for a coffee refill. "Just because you panicked during your first preaching"—I made air quotes—"sorry, *gig,* doesn't mean you're a fraud. It just means your motivation was faulty."

When Petey wouldn't meet my eyes, I feared I'd gone too far.

Eventually he picked up his fork and gored his sunny side up eggs. "That's why I like you, Olive. You don't sugar coat. You're straight with me." But he didn't seem happy about it.

Still, I pushed on. "Timothy believes in you. He knows what you're capable of, and he knows your motivation is ultimately noble." I picked up my empty coffee cup, moving it toward my lips. "He also knows you're human. I bet if you talked to him, he'd tell you he's been right where you are."

Petey held my gaze, scrutinizing me to the point of discomfort. And then he turned his head, signaling Mr. Personality, who seemed to be staring despondently into space. "Sir? Could we get another cup of coffee for the lady here?"

The waiter snaked over, already bored with us. As he topped off my cup, I noticed the slightest tremor in his hands, and I was certain Petey had registered it as well.

"How's your day going so far?" Petey asked him with genuine interest. As he studied the dejected man, he flashed him a smile, and not just any ole smile. When Petey turned his exceptionally captivating grin on, the impact resonated.

"Fantastic." The downcast server rolled his eyes.

Whoa, that was a first.

While Petey tirelessly engaged the joyless man, I glanced at my phone, skimming a text from my twin brother, Sterling.

```
Mom and I are boarding our
connecting flight to Char-
lotte. After that, we're
Louisiana bound!
```

I was in the process of texting him back when another one bounced onto my screen. A big wide-eyed-smiley emoticon followed by three question marks.

```
Did you get good news at LSU???
```

"Look, man," the wrung-out server scoffed at Petey, "I'm not religious. You're wasting your time."

"That's okay," Petey said. "And you're not a waste of time at all, but if you'll talk to me, I'd really like to pray for you today."

Sweat beaded the man's forehead, and his agitation increased as he glared down at Petey. "That's what I hate about you people. You're so damn pushy."

The server angrily glinted at me as another text dinged my phone, but Petey remained unshaken. Assured that he was in his element and had things under control, I excused myself to go to the restroom.

Once enclosed in the privacy of a bathroom stall, I texted Sterling a long, detailed response. I reread it, delighting in the last four words of my text.

`Couldn't have gone better!`

When I reentered the café, I found the morose server sitting quietly across from Petey. Their heads were bowed and Petey's eyes were closed. His lips moved rhythmically. I immediately recognized the image of him deep in prayer.

True. Noble. Sincere.

What surprised me was the sight of the beleaguered man he was praying over. The unpleasant server clung to Petey's hands, leaned into his words…and sobbed into our plates of barely touched eggs.

Sometimes you just never knew.

I stood back, allowing them their privacy, certain that the debacle at LSU was the last thing on Petey's mind now.

As we drew closer to Shady Gully, I tried talking to him about the troubled server from the café. Although his mood was lighter, Petey was hesitant to share too much. It was an ethical issue for him.

"It's not my story to share, Lilac." He winked, flashing his cocky, back-to-Petey grin. Honestly, his use of every color on the spectrum other than my actual name was amusing at best, baffling at worse.

"Well, for what it's worth," I offered, "I think you helped him. I'd say you did fairly well for a fraud." I winked.

He acknowledged the tease with a lackluster chuckle. "We'll see. I hope so." He merged into the lane toward Shady Gully. "I gotta tell you though, when he finally opened up and shared his heart with me, I was overcome. To think he'd trust me, of all people, with that kind of pain. It was raw. Heartbreaking. I honestly didn't know what to say to him. A regular ole run-of-the-mill platitude just wouldn't do."

"But?"

"But God took over, and He gave me the words. He gave me the strength to embrace this man's grief. Not for me, but for him. It was a humbling experience."

I nodded empathetically, allowing Petey's introspection to sit for a spell. Soon we drifted into an easy silence, one that took us the rest of the way to Shady Gully.

Once we passed Shady Gully High School, Petey opened his window and draped his arm along the edge, on the ready to raise it in a frisky wave. Eventually we rolled to a stop at the fabled intersection at the center of town.

"Ah, one of the most consequential questions a Shady Gullian must face each day," I joked. "Which way to go?"

"Well," Petey launched into his tour guide routine, "you've got Sprite's Quick Stop on your right. Charlie Wayne's Cozy Corner on the left. My brother's Auto Body Shop is over yonder to the right. And to the left—"

"What is that?" I squinted.

"I think the bigger question is *who* is that? And what is that smell?"

Despite the abundant growth in the community since the destruction two years ago, neither Jesse's nor James's churches had been rebuilt. Rather, some bearded fellow wearing flip flops and a greasy T-shirt occupied a corner of the four-way stop. With nothing but a tent over his head and a cluster of grills at his feet, the strange man danced to the tune of a song only he could hear.

"It smells like ribs." My stomach growled on cue.

Petey took a left at the stop sign and parked in front of the slapdash tent. He then summoned his most irresistible smile, the one that made old ladies giggle and young boys stand taller. He presented it to the flip-flopped character with great pizzazz, fully expecting the usual response. "Howdy. Nice day, huh? I'm Peter."

The odd squatter worked up an elaborate loogie and hocked it within an inch of Petey's feet.

"Whoa." Petey stepped back, undaunted. "It sure smells good. What all you got there?"

When the man cleared his throat again, I yanked Petey backward, afraid that the second flying spit ball would hit its intended target.

"Nothing for the likes of you." The nutter flashed a lascivious grin at me. "But the lady, well, I reckon she can have whatever she wants."

"I'll have a couple of those baby backs," I said without hesitation, suddenly ravenous.

"Name's JJ." He slapped a few ribs into a Styrofoam serving box, throwing in a piece of cornbread with a wink. "JJ Wheeler." When I reached for the box, JJ pulled it back. "That'll be twenty bucks." He eyed Petey.

"Twenty bucks? Are you nuts?"

"Right. My bad. Cornbread is extra. Twenty-five." He handed me the box after Petey paid him. "Y'all come back now, ya here?" JJ cackled like a mad man.

"Unbelievable," Petey muttered, incredulous, as we walked back to the truck.

"I know," I said around the food in my mouth. "I should have eaten my eggs this morning. You have to taste this." I handed him the second rib. "I've never tasted anything so good."

Petey's eyes widened as he bit into it. "Oh…wow." Barbeque sauce pooled at the corner of his mouth. "Wow. I mean, really—"

"Stop right there!" A bellow sounded from across the road. Charlie Wayne shoved his coke bottle glasses up his nose and glared at the both of us. "Drop that rib, Petey! Drop it right now."

Petey glanced at me, still chewing. Deliberating. I could tell he was thinking about taking another bite. Charlie Wayne slammed the order window at the Cozy Corner and stalked across the road, pointing his finger at us. "If you eat one more bite, I'm telling your daddy."

Petey held firm to the rib.

Charlie Wayne practically growled. "And your mama."

The rib fell to the grass.

"Prodigal son," Charlie Wayne muttered. "What a disgrace."

JJ Wheeler, who was probably a decade younger than the closing in on sixty-year-old Charlie Wayne, narrowed his eyes at the long-time owner of the Cozy Corner. Somehow, he maintained eye contact while picking up a can of lighter fluid. He squeezed a healthy stream of the flammable into a smoker already lined with charcoal. "Just gotta light 'er up again. Ain't nothing but a thing."

The zany man grinned.

Charlie Wayne exuded frustration as he stalked back to his order window at the Cozy Corner, where nary a customer waited.

Petey's eyes bent in confusion. "Are you sensing a little tension around here?"

"A tad."

"Time to go buy some hardware, Raven."

Micah, hunched over the counter by the cash register, barely looked up as the chime announced our entrance. "Welcome to Lenny's Tool Shed."

"Ma'am," quipped Petey. "I'm looking for a thirty-amp breaker and a gardening claw."

"Gardening supplies are on aisle three, and we've got fifteen, twenty, and thirty amp breakers next to the grounded outlets on aisle ten."

"Holy moly, Magenta," Petey side-eyed me. "We've officially entered the twilight zone."

Micah slowly raised her head. "Petey! Violet!" It took two

seconds for her to reach Petey and a half second to leap into his arms. "Y'all are here! I can't believe it!" Micah's feet didn't reach the ground once Petey picked her up. Like her mama, Micah was tiny, and I usually felt like an Amazon around her, but when she beat a path to me and wrapped me in a huge embrace, I giggled like a schoolgirl. "I missed y'all so much," she said through happy tears.

"We missed you too." I hugged her back. "You look great."

Micah always wore trendy, stylish clothes and applied her make up with the skill of a YouTube diva. With her petite frame and perfect blonde highlights, she was, in truth, adorable.

"Dang," Petey ribbed her, "you actually sound like you know what you're talking about. Ground outlets? Breakers? How'd that happen?"

"What do you mean? We grew up around this stuff. Remember, Daddy taught us how to count with lug nuts?"

"Yeah, but still, this is a stretch for you, isn't it? What happened to the dental hygienist job? Remember—"

"I know, Petey. Mom and Dad paid for my school and all that jazz." She turned back toward the cash register, where she'd been tallying sales numbers. "I like this better. And besides, Daddy needs all the help he can get."

"What happened to Daryl and Bubba? I thought Dad's buddies were pitching in?"

Daryl and Bubba had graduated with both Petey's parents and mine and last I heard worked at Luke's Auto Body Shop.

"Daryl's been doing a lot of the new construction around Shady Gully. He used to do that years ago," Micah explained. "He's pretty talented. Who knew? Anyway," she went on, "Shady Gully is booming with new businesses and new subdivisions, so he's pretty busy lately. Hey, have y'all seen Nails and Thread? The cute little cottage?" Micah looked pointedly at me. "We have to go there."

"And Bubba?" Petey steered Micah back to his question as he swiped a taffy from the candy bowl.

"Those are only free to Sheriff Rick." Micah slapped his hand away. "Bubba opened up this morning." She raised a perfectly shaped eyebrow. "Because I try to avoid that if possible."

"Need your beauty sleep, huh, sis?"

Micah rolled her eyes. "Bubba rotates back and forth between here and Luke's auto body shop. Helps out when he can."

As Micah rambled on, I perused a few of the aisles, impressed with the lay out, the homey feel, the freshly brewed coffee, and—"Oh wow, is that a popcorn machine?"

"Yep," Micah said. "My idea. And *it's* free." She flicked Petey a look, prompting him to give her a quarter for the taffy. "I've learned that hardware is to guys what eyeliner is to women."

When she looked at me for confirmation, I shrugged, utterly clueless when it came to girly things.

"You know, guys can come in here and browse for hours and never get bored," Micah explained. "Kind of like us at Sephora."

"Oh yeah," I said vaguely as Petey flashed me an amused look.

I handed him a bag of popcorn. Munched on one of my own.

"Hey," Petey asked Micah. "What's up with the hairy guy on the corner? Looks like he's using both Jesse's and James's lots. He's got Charlie Wayne all riled up."

"JJ Wheeler?" Micah chuckled. "He's Dolly's idea of annoying her brothers, I guess. I hear she figures it will shame them into coming to an agreement as to who gets to build a church."

Petey and I exchanged glances, and I watched as he leaned into the topic. "Maybe they should sell to a third party? After what happened two years ago, Shady Gully might do well with a fresh start."

"Maybe. But they'll never sell. And folks are doing fine. Either streaming Timothy's online service from Kentucky or going to Mass at Father Patrick's."

A chime at the entrance interrupted Petey's next sentence as Uncle Lenny's voice bellowed throughout the whole store. "Well, lo and behold, look what the Kentucky holler dragged up."

Petey moved toward his dad, enveloping him in a heartfelt

embrace. It was hard to say whose eyes misted the most, the father's or the son's. "You're looking great, old man," Petey said. "And this place, it's amazing. Despite the staff."

"Funny." Micah returned to her calculator.

"And Violet." When Uncle Lenny opened his arms, I fell easily into them. "As beautiful as ever." I savored the fatherly hug, as his embrace was the most like my dad's, and his love the closest I'd ever come to my father's. He seemed to realize this, as he held the hug for several long, blissful moments. Even when he released me, he maintained his steady grip along my shoulders.

"How's Mom?" asked Petey.

"She's…good. She'll be thrilled to know y'all made it." He glinted at me. "And you'll be glad to know that *your* mom and Sterling are on their way from the Alexandria airport."

"Oh." My heart thrilled at the thought of seeing my brother… and plunged at the notion of facing my mother.

"Why didn't you go with Mama to pick them up?" Petey asked his dad.

"Well…" Uncle Lenny hesitated.

With growing dread, I realized *why* before Micah even opened her mouth. "Actually, Sheriff Rick went to get them, and Bubba said he was very chatty about it when he stopped in for coffee this morning."

An awkward, heavy silence filled the atmosphere, and the only thing that diluted it was the sound of the door chime.

"Bella! Luke!" Micah's voice rose as she swiveled toward the door in delight. "Look who's here."

Petey grinned as he set eyes on his big brother. "There he is. The mayor of Shady Gully."

And while the sight of Luke and Bella pleased me immensely, it was the last face through the door that made my heart soar.

Lose Something?
Lenny

Watching my sons jab playfully back and forth roused my soul. Both were tall, with similar builds and hair color. Luke wore pressed pants and a neat, button-down shirt, while Petey looked as if he'd dressed in his truck. Luke's eyes were dark, like Desi's, and Petey's hazel eyes matched my own.

Even though they hadn't seen each other in months, they horsed around like they had when they were boys. Luke's earnest expression revealed careful strategy whereas Petey's spontaneity reflected his fun-loving attitude.

"Come on, Mr. Mayor," Petey jested, circling his brother as he sparred. "Surely you got more than that."

"Nope." Micah mindlessly stuck an ink pen behind her ear. "Nope. Nope." She hurried around the cash register with a sense of urgency. "That mutt is not allowed. Sorry Bella, you know I love you, but that troublemaker stays outside." She pointed at the door, just as Luke used the diversion to tousle Petey's hair and claim the shadow boxing victory.

"Come on, Micah," Bella pleaded. "Duchess wants to meet Petey and Violet."

"Last time you let her in she ran off with a whole pack of Phillips flat head screwdrivers." Micah looked pointedly at me. "That's sixteen dollars and ninety-nine cents you'll never see again, by the way."

Ignoring Micah's outburst, Bella used a leash to lead Duchess into the store. "I'll watch her, I promise. And you can put the screwdrivers on our tab."

Bella was a younger version of her beautiful mother, Meadow. The spitting image really, except for her striking blue eyes and her…well, her delightful personality. Musically inclined and blessed with the voice of an angel, Bella was beloved locally for her stirring voice and her gift for worship music.

Luke flashed with amusement as he watched Bella unclip Duchess's leash, and then envelop both Petey and Violet in a welcoming hug.

I exchanged glances with Micah, who eyed the rescue dog suspiciously.

"How's school going?" Bella asked Violet. "You must be a doctor a hundred times over by now. How many degrees do you have anyway?"

Violet shrugged and seemed suddenly uncomfortable. When she shot Petey a furtive glance, he quickly changed the subject.

"Hey, come here, girl." Petey knelt, beckoning Duchess over. "What kind of doggie are you? Just looking at you makes me smile." Duchess seemed to prance especially for Petey then, her tongue lolling playfully. "You're funny."

"She's a Shiba Inu," Violet said. "They're an ancient breed native to Japan." She ruffled Duchess's thick red and white fur, and the little rabble-rouser flashed a toothy smile. "They're little dogs with big personalities."

"I'll say." Micah snorted, unmoved by the dog's goofy grin.

"They've very agile, and they love to run and hike," Violet went on. "And they do very well with rough, rugged terrains. Like mountains." Violet seemed to relax the more she spoke about the dog. "And yeah, they're known for their mischievousness."

"That totally makes sense." Bella glanced at Luke. "Duchess loves to run all over the woods along the creek. And I guess she is a tad rambunctious. We got her at the animal shelter after someone returned her."

"Figures," Micah quipped.

"I think she ate the owner's hearing aid or something," Luke said. "I admit she's a bit of a challenge, but Bella will be moving in soon"—he grinned sweetly at his bride-to-be—"and I'll have reinforcements then."

Micah tracked Duchess as she wandered toward the auto parts aisle, her tail twirled and vigilant.

"She kind of reminds me of a husky," Petey remarked. "Or an akita."

"But she has a foxlike face," Violet mused. "It's almost wolfish in its alertness."

"Yeah. It is, isn't it?" Bella's voice resonated with the lingering effects of grief. No doubt recalling the brutal murder of her grandmother two years ago, as well as that of her beloved wolfdog, Hania, who'd died trying to protect her.

As the silence stretched, heightening the moment, Luke set a sympathetic arm along Bella's shoulders.

"Well," Petey nudged Violet, "I guess we best be headed to the house. See how Mom's doing. How's the gumbo coming along, Dad?"

I cleared my throat, drawing quick attention from the lot of them. "About that. I know you had your heart set on gumbo, son, but after y'all called yesterday your mama started fretting. She's overwhelmed with the bridal shower coming up this weekend, and—" I stopped, not wanting to slight Meadow and risk offending Bella. "Anyway, how about we just do burgers on the grill? Would that be okay?"

"Well, sure." Petey narrowed his eyes, concerned.

Micah drew her head from the steady reconnaissance on aisle five. "That doesn't sound like Mom. What's wrong?"

Luke, the most sensitive and intuitive of our children, marked me knowingly. Fortunately, he didn't challenge me in front of the others. "Actually, on my way here I got flagged down by a, well, let's just say a concerned citizen. He suggested something that could be helpful to us tonight."

Petey muttered. "Uh-oh."

"Right." Luke speared him with feigned outrage. "According to this citizen, an egregious act of betrayal occurred earlier at the four-way stop—"

"Betrayal? Are you kidding?" Petey guffawed. "That's a bit strong."

"He alleges that unlawful barbeque ribs were marketed, bought, and then"—he eyed Petey and Violet—"consumed at said incident."

Petey pointed to Violet. "It was Rose here's fault. She should have eaten breakfast." I chuckled at Petey's endless and colorful substitutions of Violet's name.

"The citizen suggested in order to make amends," Luke continued, "he'd be willing to host an event, and graciously provide the food, which of course we would pay him for."

"What did you do?" I asked Petey, entertained despite it all.

"I, well *she*," he again pointed to Violet, "ate a rib."

"Oh my gosh." Micah's swoon resounded somewhere between aisles three and four. "JJ's ribs are so good."

"I know, right?" Bella agreed. "His brisket is amazing too."

When the door chime sounded, we all turned in unison. "Oh, look everyone," Petey said, "it's our concerned citizen and most generous host."

In walked Charlie Wayne, glowering behind his thick-lensed glasses. "Don't get smart with me, you little reprobate. I remember you when you were nothing more than a twinkle in your daddy's eye."

Violet and Bella laughed, and then made their way to Micah and Duchess as the muffled sounds of a dust-up emerged from aisle three.

"Did you get my message?" I asked Charlie Wayne. "From yesterday?"

"I did. I got what you asked for in my truck." Charlie Wayne turned to Luke. "Seriously, how long are you going to allow that spectacle at the four-way to continue? That buffoon and his dilly-dallying smack dab in the center of town is a disgrace.

I won't be voting for you in the next election, *Mr. Mayor*, that's for sure."

Luke had run unopposed in the last—or Shady Gully's first—mayoral election, and up until now, he'd been the town's golden boy.

"Charlie Wayne," I said, "don't worry. Luke will get it resolved. Won't you, son?"

"You can count on me, Charlie Wayne," Luke confirmed. "I've got an attorney looking into it. The fact is, what Wheeler's doing may not even be legal. If he's selling a product, it stands to reason he'd need a permit."

"I don't know." Charlie Wayne shook his head, woebegone. "If Dolly set this in motion, I suspect she did her homework. About as conniving a woman as I've ever known. Close tie with Claire, o'course."

Claire, who ran Shady Gully's post office, and was frequently and unfavorably referred to as Cruella of the Post Office, had without a doubt stirred her fair share of pots.

Charlie Wayne continued to brood. "I could use a show of support, is all. And a prime-time demonstration of that support might help." He sowed his dejected expression throughout the room. "Might make up for all the traitors in your family."

Before I could take offense, Luke responded with mayor-like diplomacy. "Absolutely. And Mom will appreciate the break. Won't she, Dad?"

Aware of Petey's scrutiny and growing worry, I nodded my consent.

"Alright. I gotta go." Charlie Wayne pushed his thick glasses up his nose. "I probably got a customer."

Petey squinted out the window, dubious.

"I'll walk you out." The chime dinged behind us as I followed Charlie Wayne to his truck. He handed me a plastic bag chock-full of every southerner's vegetable of choice. "I thought you said you were gonna plant some okra." He indicated the bag. "Frozen is all I got."

"I did. Built a greenhouse behind the store. I wanted to surprise Desi, but they aren't quite ready yet." I dangled the bag, holding his coke-bottled gaze for an extra beat.

"Something on your mind, Lenny?"

Charlie Wayne and I had known each other for many years, and we'd seen a lot of drama for a town this small, which is why I was loathe to open this particular can of worms. But I went ahead and popped the top anyway. "You're right in the middle of town, Charlie Wayne. Got your order window facing Sprite's gas station."

"So?"

"Just curious if you've seen anybody different lately."

"Well yeah, Lenny." He tilted his head toward the four-way stop. "That loon with the lady hair. Turned up like a bad burrito and now he's trying to steal my business with his fake food." When I looked at him quizzically, he scoffed. "Probably brimming over with hormones and antibiotics and such."

I highly doubted Charlie Wayne knew the distinctions of food laden with harmful ingredients, but I appreciated his point. "I guess I mean somebody different, but familiar."

He eyeballed me, genuinely stumped. "You alright, Lenny? You been drinking? Or maybe smoking that stuff Wolfheart used to sell across the creek?"

I sighed. Charlie Wayne was right. "I'm fine. I'm sure it's nothing. Forget I even said anything."

"Stop! Daddy, quick!" Micah hollered from the door of the store. "Grab the mutt!"

As a red and white mist flashed past his truck, Charlie Wayne's chin dropped. "What the…?"

"Duchess." I clapped my hands. "Come here, girl!" She paused, I'll give her that, and even whipped her expressive head in my direction, but then she made a mad dash toward the post office, a twelve-dollar set of jumper cables dangling from her pesky mouth.

Luke whistled, hot on her trail, followed by a frantic Bella and a focused Violet. Petey, however, stayed behind to enjoy his vantage point from the door of the hardware store. "Incredible!" He cackled. "That dog has some moves! Classic bait and switch."

Amid all the shouting, chasing, and assorted pandemonium, a beat-up black truck put-putted toward us from the four-way stop. An olive-skinned arm casually unfolded itself from the driver's window, signaling a lackadaisical turn in the general vicinity of the post office. The dilapidated vehicle, almost legendary at this point, nestled to a slow stop between the public mailboxes and Charlie Wayne's Cozy Corner.

Wolfheart, always long and lean, now sported a touch more silver in his blue-black hair than in the past. After he leisurely extricated himself from his truck, he casually reached into his pocket and gestured to the canine renegade.

Duchess promptly trotted over to Brad Wolfheart, the former bad boy of Shady Gully, and released the jumper cables at his boots. After letting go with an enthusiastic (and oddly piercing) cry of sheer pleasure, the naughty prankster gobbled up the offered treat.

Duchess's eyes then flattened into joyous slits to meet her perfectly arched lips, forming an adorable half-moon of happiness. She then gazed up at Wolfheart and beamed.

Wolfheart didn't need a leash to lead Duchess back to Bella. Rather, the well-muscled mischief maker trotted behind him willingly. I wasn't surprised that Wolfheart had the power and charisma to charm the beast into submission. He tended to do that with humans also.

Of course, the doggie treat hadn't hurt either.

Wolfheart lifted a speculative brow at Bella as he presented her with her runaway dog. "Lose something?"

"Uncle Wolf!" She squeezed his wiry waist appreciatively. "You saved the day."

He seemed unmoved, and a little reserved amid the numerous

characters in my family. He handed Micah the jumper cables, which she carefully inspected. "They look sellable. Thanks."

When a customer pulled into the parking lot, the younger generation followed Micah back into the hardware store. Struck by the uncharacteristic sense of purpose in my usually aimless daughter, I let out an involuntary *Humph* of bewilderment.

"She seems comfortable on her journey." Wolfheart's musings were often like that; heavy on tone and nuance, deeply philosophical, and sometimes hard to understand.

Charlie Wayne gawked at Wolfheart, trying to find either an agenda or a punchline. Finding neither, he stalked off. "Tell Desi to call me about tonight. I'll have everything ready." He added over his shoulder. "Bring your checkbook."

We watched as Charlie Wayne drove the mere ninety-nine yards to the Cozy Corner. He honked as he passed the post office on the right, and even waved cheerily. Charlie Wayne never did anything with cheer, but the act gave him an excuse to avoid JJ Wheeler's mockery on the left.

Wolfheart chuckled. "Good times, indeed."

"I'm glad you're having fun."

He frowned. "What's wrong, Lenny? You've got all your kids together. Your son is getting married in a little over a week. You're a lucky man."

I followed him to his truck, where he let down the rusty tailgate and pulled an ice chest to the edge. I half hoped he'd pull out a cold beer, but I knew better. Wolfheart had turned over a new leaf many years ago, and even when he was the dastardly devil of Shady Gully, I'd never seen him take a drop of alcohol.

Sure enough, he pulled out a can of cold tea. Cold tea. For real.

"Chai?" he asked. "Sadly, it's not authentic, but it'll do."

"No thanks. I'm trying to quit." I dug out a bottled water, twisted the cap. "So, the shindig tonight is going to be at Charlie Wayne's."

"At the Cozy Corner? Is Desi okay with that?"

"You know, at this point, I think she will be. She's feeling very…" I resisted going into detail with Wolfheart. For a number of reasons. One of which was I didn't want to spotlight Meadow's lack of involvement in the wedding. After all, she was his niece.

"It'd be nice if Meadow took more of an interest." He sipped his chai. "It's something she will regret," he contemplated. "But Robin's arrival will lift Desi's spirits, spur her energy."

Sometimes I puzzled over this mysterious bond Wolfheart had with my wife. Certainly, I knew all about what happened that fateful night all those years ago, when a flirtation between Desi and Shady Gully's own Rhinestone Cowboy, Adam, came dangerously close to crossing a line. Because of Wolfheart's presence, and his unrecognized sense of morality, the odds went in my favor.

He proved that night that he was a friend to me. Not just to Desi, but to me.

And yet, sometimes I felt incapable of connecting with Desi the way he did. Not because of anything untoward, but because of my own limitations. As hard as I tried to please Desi, it seemed nothing I did would ever be salve enough to assuage the damage that had been done to her as a child.

And yet, Wolfheart's reserved, taciturn demeanor seemed to speak to her in a way my words couldn't. I didn't begrudge him this. I was truthfully grateful to anyone who could ease her pain.

"I'll try to get Meadow to come tonight." He chugged his tea, staring deeply into the can. Perhaps searching the tea leaves for answers. "But she handles her pain differently than Desi." He scrunched the empty can tightly between his fingers.

"She's been through a lot," I said. "I'm sure she's hurting."

"No, Lenny." Wolfheart tossed the shriveled can into the bed of his truck. "Meadow is consumed with rage."

As I watched Wolfheart's old truck scutter toward The Creek, I congratulated myself on my patience. While Charlie Wayne had dismissed my query regarding an odd stranger in Shady Gully, Wolfheart, I was sure, would have pressed for more information.

If I'd told him, he would have wanted details. He would have suggested we bring in Sheriff Rick and his posse of deputies to scour Shady Gully, The Creek, and all the surrounding areas.

Quite simply, if I'd shared my concerns with Wolfheart, he would have propelled the situation with the kind of passion he'd used to crush the tea can, and like Meadow's rage, it would have been all consuming.

Chapter Five

Yucking It Up
Meadow

I waved to Sprite, the little squirt who sat on the high stool in the big window of his gas station and general store, Sprite's Quick Stop. He smiled. I glared. Didn't want him to get the wrong idea. Like I was happy or friendly or anything.

The gesture had been more about my shift ending, and my relief upon seeing Claire steer her new Ford Explorer in the direction of her home. In Cruella Claire's absence, I'd be able to close out my delivery log in peace.

Sure enough, when I unlocked the crowded mailroom, I found myself alone. Hallelujah, as Bella and Uncle Wolf would say. "Hot damn," I said aloud, preferring my own version of exclamation.

After plowing through Cruella Claire's rainbow of posts-its and sorting through tomorrow's deliveries, I lit a cigarette. Partly out of spite, but also because I craved one. It had been a long day. I'd had to endure the sight of Uncle Wolf and Bella yucking it up with Desi's clan at the hardware store. Maybe *yucking it up* was an exaggeration. Uncle Wolf didn't yuck it up with anyone. Ever. Still, they'd looked *very* cozy. Almost *familial.*

I groaned aloud, tidying up and finally locking the post office behind me. I removed the spinning dome from my car, tossing it into the back seat with the stray bubble wrap and assorted boxes. Finally, I pointed my ride in the direction of The Creek.

Unfortunately, when I stopped at the four-way, I noted two

oddities. One, the barbeque man with the Farrah Fawcett hair was asleep in his lawn chair, and two, Dolly stood on the porch of the Diva Dome flapping her arms in the air. All out fluttering like a Vegas show girl with fake angel wings. Geez.

My heart jumped inside my chest. I nervously glanced in the rear-view mirror, and then all around the four-way stop. Surely, she'd been signaling someone else. *Someone who hadn't slept with her husband.*

What to do? I decided I would keep going straight as if I were headed across the creek. I'd pretend I never saw her.

Seriously. I could count on one hand the number of times I'd spoken to Dolly. In fact, less than one hand. Zero fingers even. I'd *never* spoken to her. Not once. And yet, there she was, waving at me like we were long lost sorority sisters.

Staring straight ahead, I accelerated at the stop sign. Creek, here I come. I took a long puff of my cigarette. Home sweet home. But then—my cursed brain started needling me. What if that weirdo JJ Wheeler wasn't actually asleep? What if he'd croaked?

"Agggrrrr," I grunted aloud, slamming my hand into my steering wheel. I winced as hot ashes flickered across my legs. Maybe I'd stop at the substation and tell Sheriff Rick to send the coroner. Even though JJ Wheeler was persona non grata, I'm sure he'd eventually get around to it.

But Dolly's fried-blonde-pigtails continued to beckon in my peripheral. Begrudgingly, I turned my car around, and headed back toward the Diva Dome.

My own breathing sounded loud in my ears, ricocheting around my car at an irregular pace. The gravel crunched under my tires as I pulled to a stop between the Diva Dome and Nails and Thread. Even though Sigourney Sky was a traitor, there was a slight possibility she'd try to save me if Dolly tried to murder me and dissolve my body in perm solution.

"Hey." Dolly bounced to my car, smirking like we were besties. Her shorts were short, her lashes were fake, and her pig tails screamed middle-aged-lady-trying-too-hard. And naturally, now that I was closer, I determined that the ingrate JJ Wheeler was merely asleep, and not dead. A shame.

Meanwhile, Dolly's surgically stretched eyes twinkled with barely contained delight.

I strategically positioned my cigarette just in case I needed to defend myself.

"Hey," she repeated in a breathy voice.

"H-hey." I uttered my first words to Dolly. To Mitch's wife. It seemed off. Why *now*?

"I didn't have any mail today?"

Was she serious?

"I just thought I'd check."

My gaze drifted to Wheeler, who greeted Shady Gully with an exaggerated yawn after his nap. I watched as he stretched to the sky and then swooped down to touch his toes. He finished up his yoga routine by bending at the waist and dramatically shaking loose his lavish locks. He looked up, winking at me as he twisted his mop into a messy bun at the nape of his neck.

"Uh…were you…expecting something?" I mumbled to Dolly.

"Yes. Well, I don't know." The Cheshire grin made her eyes crinkle into slits, the fake black eyelashes jutting out like insects.

I know. It all made sense now. I must have died, and this was hell. I guess I should have paid attention to that fancy Kentucky preacher Uncle Wolf and Bella always went on about. Tommy? Timothy? Tiger?

It was then that I detected movement behind Dolly.

The door scraped against the wood as it opened, and dusty brown cowboy boots clonked lazily onto the porch. From the cowboy boots, my eyes traced upward to the jeans, and landed on a familiar western belt buckle.

I watched, enthralled, as the man behind the exaggerated western adornments lowered his long, tall body into Dolly's rocking chair.

My breath hitched as I eyeballed the signature cowboy hat, the reddish hair, and the amused grin. Shady Gully's one and only country crooner had returned. He winked, acknowledging me with a tip of his hat.

Dolly's short shorts rose a little as she twisted in his direction. "Oh," she gushed. "You remember Adam, don't you?"

Well, well. Giddy up, Shady Gully.

Seeing Dolly up close disquieted me. Stirred up an extra salty cocktail of anxiety.

Despite Uncle Wolf's fixation on Desi, it had been the blonde Dolly that had been *my* obsession for as long as I could remember. When I'd fallen in love with her husband, I'd set out to learn everything I could about the irreverent diva. As a quiet, innocent looking fourteen-year-old, I'd easily lifted a few old yearbooks from the school lobby, and those old annuals soon became my coursework.

Each evening after my chores, I'd scrutinize Dolly's old photos, staring into those squinty mascaraed eyes. Desperately searching for…what? A flaw? A secret?

She'd had fried blonde hair even then, and a fake smile that never reached her eyes. And most importantly, she'd had Mitch by her side. Her in her skimpy little cheerleader outfit and him in his blue and white Wildcat football uniform. Number 32. His blue eyes dazzling as they bounced off his blue football jersey.

I'd cast my hopeful theories to each and every picture, trying to gage their level of affection for one another.

Was it my imagination, or was Dolly's grip around his waist a tad clingy?

Was there a note of nonchalance in Mitch's posture as he posed next to her at Homecoming?

On and on I studied, practically memorizing the images plastered throughout the pages of Shady Gully's high school yearbook. Of course, Bella's soon-to-be mother-in-law (Ms. Homecoming Queen herself) was featured in a number of photos as well, but her reflection was tame and naïve compared to Dolly's.

Never far behind Desi was her bestie, Robin, always hovering along the edges as if she could garner some of her friend's charisma. Funny, these days Robin was the self-assured woman of power, while Desi seemed restless and unsettled.

Things would likely get worse for Desi and Lenny now that Adam was back in town. Perhaps the Rhinestone Cowboy had returned to throw his hat in the ring again. According to Uncle Wolf, he'd courted Desi hot and heavy, even after she'd married Lenny and had three kids in tow. Whether their affair was ever consummated, one would never know, but the way he'd high-tailed it to Texas afterwards sure made it seem that way.

While Adam still hadn't achieved country music fame, his affairs and homewrecking status were indeed legendary. Why, I wondered, after all this time, would he return to Shady Gully? What were he and Dolly up to? Were they an item? Or did they just want it to seem that way?

As I approached the bridge dividing The Creek and Shady Gully, I lit a cigarette and tried to shake off the drama of the day. The original bridge, which had been nothing more than rotted boards glued together with bubble gum, collapsed two years ago amid a season of violence and upheaval. Even now, as I crossed the swanky new construction Luke and Sheriff Rick had commissioned, I experienced the visceral terror from that day all over again.

The ripping pain spilling from my head wound, Bella's screams as the murderer of my parents pursued her across the dilapidated bridge, and finally, the crackling of rotting wood and concrete as it spiraled into the snake and alligator infested creek below.

The ride across the new bridge today was perfectly smooth. Nary a bump, jangle, or clank to be heard. My future son-in-law called it a truss bridge. He explained, in painful detail, how it was constructed with iron, steel, and reinforced concrete. To me, it looked like a cluster of triangles slapped together by a four-year-old, but Luke insisted those triangles were skillfully welded, and that the new bridge was sturdy. And safe.

Luke always emphasized the *safe,* as if his memories of that day were as deeply disturbing as mine. I'd never forget the extravagant—and frankly, ridiculous—ribbon cutting ceremony at the creek's edge upon the opening of the new bridge. The way the reserved, buttoned-up kid had looked down at Bella, his eyes brimming over with fierce affection.

The sight of his raw emotion shattered me. *So that's what love looks like,* I'd thought.

Luke had said that day that the new bridge would never again be known as a means to divide or separate The Creek from Shady Gully, but rather to connect and unify it.

Sorry, Luke, I guess we'd have to agree to disagree on that one.

There was no better place to sort out the iniquities of Shady Gully than from the vantage point of my mama's front porch along the creek.

The woods, thick with pine, cypress, and maple trees, emerged from a carpet of duckweed and viney ground cover. Spanish moss swathed the trees, creating a hazy umbrella guarding either side of Mama's shanty. The creek waited beyond that, and sometimes late at night, just as the cicadas grew weary of their concerto, one could detect the trickle of the creek as it flowed passed my little home.

I was finally able to think of it as home now, despite the atrocities that had raged within these walls two years ago, namely the heinous beating and murder of my mother. Bella's grandmother. Uncle Wolf's sister. And of course, the murder of our beloved Hania, Mama's great Spirit Warrior, who'd fought for her until his end.

I set the framed picture of the great domesticated wolf along the railing of the porch, setting it beside Mama's picture and an older one I'd discovered of my father while sorting through her personal items. Dropping into my favorite porch chair with a sigh, I took a sip of wine and then set the glass alongside my shrine to the past.

As the sky dusked and the shadows mounted, I settled in for my nightly vigil along the creek. I'd just lit a cigarette and unscrewed an empty water bottle for the ashes when my uncle's black jalopy *putt-putted* down my dirt driveway.

Since he could track his way along the swamp blindfolded, he didn't bother with headlights at this point. His long-booted legs stepped out of his truck, and I noted both the care he'd taken with his dress and the powerful musky scent emanating from his person.

His eyes traced mine all the way onto the porch, and then landed on the wine and the picture frames lining the railing. "I see the gang is all here." He lowered himself into his favorite, broken-in rocking chair.

Too tired to engage his passive aggressive remark, I asked, "What is that Poo-Foo juice dripping off you in puddles?" My upper lip curled. "It's a bit much, don't you think?"

He said nothing, his vivid green eyes instead seeking and settling on the gallant Hania. I noted the faint shudder as it ran through him. Even now, after two years, he still grieved my mother and her heroic protector.

Our silence mounted beneath the cicada's steady rant.

"I came to pick you up." He eyed me critically. "Are you ready?"

"Pick me up? For what?"

He glanced at his watch. "The party. You know, for your daughter? And her soon-to-be husband, Luke?"

"You're mistaken. That party is to celebrate the homecoming of the great, prestigious, and savior-of-all, Robin. The rich and—"

"Meadow." His tone was sharp. "Get dressed. Come with me. You're the mother of the bride."

The very words scraped along the fragile edges of my psyche. "Whatever," I snorted. "I wish you'd stop saying that." When his disappointed gaze swept over me, I said through gritted teeth. "I'm not going to this ridiculous shindig tonight. I'll go to the stupid shower though. Okay? Are you happy now?"

He shook his head, lingering over the photograph of my saintly mama, Peony. The intensity of his gaze suggested the two of them were pondering my failings. I cleared my throat, a shade unnerved.

"No. I'm not happy," he said finally. "I'm at a loss with you. I don't know how to reach you. I thought after what happened"—he tilted his head at Mama—"you might eventually find your way. An experience like that changes you."

I took a long, hard drag from my cigarette. Stopped short of blowing the smoke on him. He stood and stared into the swamp for an extended moment. "You still have the gun?"

"Of course. Why?"

"Just that you're out here alone." He glinted at the pictures on the railing. "And they can't defend you."

"I don't need anyone to defend me, Uncle. You know I'm a bad ass."

"Yeah, right." He shuffled down the steps. Looked around. "No strays?" He meant the assorted dogs, cats, chickens, rabbits, and random critters that my mama regularly nurtured.

"I think they've all found their way to your place now."

He took a few steps toward his truck, then stopped. "You ever see Crazy Tom out and about? You know, while you're delivering mail on your route?"

"You mean, Tom, the old pervert? Desi's stepdad?" When he nodded, I added. "I heard he's got Alzheimer's, and his new wife, Wanda, has her hands full. I haven't seen him though. Why?"

"Just thought I saw him shuffling around a few days ago. Seemed off."

"What's the matter, Uncle? You worried he's gonna go after your girlfriend again?" His green eyes sparked. I'd have been wiser to blow cigarette smoke on him. Mentioning Desi in a derogatory way always tweaked his disposition. And yet, I pushed, keen on revenge for his mother-of-the-bride comment. "What happened to all that forgiveness you and Bella are always speaking of? Isn't that the kind of stuff your preacher-man online espouses? Surely, you can forgive an old man for petting his pretty little step-daughter a trillion years ago—"

I'd miscalculated, and his harsh expression turned into a furious slash.

Even after fifty-eight years, my Uncle Wolf found new ways to evoke terror in a single scowl. He stalked to the truck.

When he turned, even the symphony of cicadas seemed to pause anxiously. "You break my heart, Meadow."

Much later, after the brooding darkness of nightfall had snuffed out all traces of dusk along the creek, I traipsed inside to return my beloved pictures to their proper place. Naturally, that place of reverence was a beautiful bookshelf handmade by my uncle.

Potted herbs decorated the shelves as well, all especially planted and nurtured by him, as he'd inherited the same healing touch with herbs as my mama. The scant stars blurring through the window led my gaze around my shanty, and my weary eyes bounced from one of my uncle's generosities to another.

Replaced lighting. Repaired windows. Remade furniture. He'd done it all. He'd given of his time and his limited resources to remake this Ground-Zero-of-Terror into a cozy home for me. If not for my anger, I'd almost feel ashamed.

My thoughts drifted to the festivities in Shady Gully, by now in full swing with song, laughter, food, and wine. As I rinsed the muted red smears from my wine glass, I stared at the specks of the cork as they slid down the drain. The filthy, gray ashes I'd dumped into my water bottle followed, the sludge probably a reflection of the cloudiness mounting in my own lungs.

My jaws clenched as I considered my evening intake of cheap wine and cigarettes, while on the right side of Shady Gully they happily celebrated my own flesh and blood. *Unjust,* I thought, coddling the notion of betrayal and disrespect.

My beautiful Bella, who would be unable to resist the adoration, wouldn't give my well-being a second thought. And Uncle Wolf, who had once held my welfare in the highest regard, had now also abandoned me to join with them.

An unbidden, begrudging tear slid down my cheek. I was here, cast aside, in a hell of my own making. I hated them all. I hated myself. Ah, but I didn't see a way out. The die had been cast all those years ago when Mitch and I had made our choice. To love rather than surrender to a judgmental society's rules. Sure, there'd been an age difference. Sure, he'd been married, and yes, he'd been a guidance counselor at school, counseling me on my difficulties at home. My struggles with Madhawk, Mama's live-in boyfriend, who'd ultimately destroyed us all.

I dragged my fists across my damp cheeks, stalking back to the bookshelf that housed the picture frames. I reached for the one showcasing Hania, the honorable beast who'd always been loyal to me. I flipped the frame on its back and fumbled with the clasps along the edges until I found the picture behind it.

Mitch. From the yearbook, in all his glory, his cocky grin flashing at the photographer. I'd cut Dolly out of the photo long ago, choosing instead to imagine it was me.

Carrying the worn photo onto the porch, I sat quietly in Uncle Wolf's rocking chair, trading my hopeless reality for my fantastical notions. If only Mitch had been the age he was in the photo when we'd met. It would have changed everything.

If only.

Instead, while my family yucked it up in Shady Gully, I remained alone, squinting at the red eyes of some desperate critter in the woods. I imagined that my lover was out there, that he'd come all this way to claim me and to rescue me from my loneliness.

Despite it all, I'd do it over again. If only he knew that.

I surveilled the woods and the creek beyond, relaxing into my reverie.

I could almost feel him out there.

Chapter Six

They Ain't That Dirty
Violet

"Check it out." Petey pointed, his expression giddy and wide-eyed. "Ole Charlie Wayne strung colored lights all around the Cozy Corner."

"I see that." I grinned, always finding Petey's jovial manner infectious. Still, doubt tugged at me as we traipsed through the gravel parking lot toward the venue. While Petey's personality attracted—and enjoyed—attention, mine was better suited to deflecting it.

"He even set up a game for horseshoes." Luke managed to point to the stakes in the ground without letting go of Bella's hand. "Care to make a wager, PeePee?"

"Game on, brother. I'm the master of the horseshoe. Right, Hazel?" Since he knew I was anxious about encountering my mother tonight, Petey winked playfully, trying to lift my spirits. He turned to his soon to be sister-in-law. "Bella, I apologize in advance for the whupping I'm gonna lay on your fiancé."

As Petey continued to tease Bella and Luke, I turned to find myself face to face with one of the chief threats to my anxiety. One particularly tall and very mustached threat.

"I reckon Charlie Wayne's trying to make a good impression," Sheriff Rick said, his wacky mustache taking on a life of its own as it loomed large over his lips. "Say, Violet," he turned to me, "your mama told me you just picked up another degree." He smoothed his khaki pants awkwardly. "She sure is proud of you."

Why, oh why, did my mother's *boyfriend* feel the need to tell me how impressive I was? And how proud my mother was of me? As if he knew her better than I did.

"Ain't got much book learning myself, but hats off to you, young lady."

For a moment I thought he was actually going to remove his cowboy hat. I smiled gratefully when he didn't. Unfortunately, he misjudged my smile for encouragement. "What's this latest one? Your mama said it was some kinda masters."

I desperately searched the growing crowd for my brother but spied only random Shady Gullians like Claire from the Post Office and her friend and fellow pot stirrer, Old Man Chester. "Yes," I answered in a clipped voice. "I received a Master of Science degree in clinical research."

It was then my mother spotted us talking. I could see her eyes widen clear across the venue. Unfortunately, my small window of escape had passed, as she made a hasty path toward us.

"Well, that's mighty fine. Mighty fine," the sheriff went on. "I reckon you'll cure cancer shortly."

His remark sucked the oxygen right out of the air. I quite literally felt my heart drop. Illogically, I glanced at the gravel beneath my feet to see if I'd find it there, misshapen and deformed, pumping faintly under the cruelty of the mustached man's words.

Just as my mom approached, Petey miraculously appeared at my side. How did he always know when I was close to unraveling? He intercepted her with one of his irresistible smiles. "Hey, Aunt Robin." He gathered her up in a giant Petey-sized hug. "Snazzy spectacles. Are those vio—" Petey stopped, wrinkling his brow.

"They're purple." Mom perched higher on her tiptoes to show off her new glasses. "Aren't they cool?"

The sheriff, tall to Mom's tiny, beamed down at her with total adoration. She took his adoration, and raised it with affection. Sorry, but it was all too much. The *cool* purple eyeglasses. The doe-eyed looks at Mr. Mustache. The over-the-top animation. All of it disgusted me.

"How are ya, Sheriff?" Petey surprised the sheriff with a hearty pat on the back. "Hanging in there lately?"

"Doing okay," he said, flashing at my mother. "And getting better by the minute."

I stifled an eye roll. Or at least I thought I did. Evidently my effort had been unsuccessful as my mother looked wounded. Great, now guilt piled onto my already frazzled nerves. Rather impulsively, I blurted, "Petey and I visited Daddy's grave today."

Mama flinched. The sheriff's mustache stilled. Petey's mouth fell open.

Once he recovered, Petey explained. "It was earlier. Before y'all made it in from the airport."

"Oh." Mom nodded, her gaiety now firmly extinguished.

Amid the hush, we all turned and awkwardly scanned the crowd. Immediately, I locked on to another menace, this one gorgeous, with raven hair and a buxom figure. Petey's ex-girl-friend, Tammy Jo, looked on-point as she chatted up his parents. I watched as Aunt Desi and Uncle Lenny, and even my brother, Sterling, seemed to hang on her every word.

"Where's Buford?" I asked my mother in accusation, mostly to needle her.

"He's at my place," Sheriff Rick said. "Keeping Gerty entertained."

Oh, have mercy. Now their cats were in love? I turned to my mother, slashed, "You know Buford doesn't like other cats."

"They seem to be getting on just fine," she slashed back. "In fact, Buford seems less anxious."

"And Gerty has stopped clawing the furniture," the sheriff offered kindly.

I seethed.

"Hey." Petey tugged my arm, no doubt trying to turn me away from my wickedness. "Let's go say hi to Tammy Jo."

Great.

I could feel my mother watching me, her judgement heavy against my back as we started to skulk away.

"It's been seven years," Petey whispered. "You oughta cut her some slack."

I glared at him, betrayal ripping through the empty hole in my chest. The hole where my heart had been before the sheriff had uttered the dreaded C word. And now Petey was siding with my mom? As if it mattered how many years my daddy had been gone.

He should be here! And he wasn't! Nothing about that was okay!

Distracted suddenly by the death rattle of Brad Wolfheart's old truck, I consciously set my anger on simmer and watched as he parked his black clunker next to the Cozy Corner order window. Wolfheart unfolded himself from the ancient vehicle with the grace and ferocity of a majestic lion. He held his head high as he ambled to the party alone—without Bella's mom.

I glanced at Bella, who continued to chat with Micah and Luke even as disappointment and resignation spread across her face. Luke tenderly put his arm around her shoulder in a gesture that reflected both affection and self-assuredness.

"Hey, Robin." Wolfheart meandered over to my mom with a bouquet of flowers. "Welcome home."

"Those for me?" The sheriff asked jokingly.

"Nope. Sorry, Ricky. I'd have brought rag weeds if they were for you. These are for my favorite hillbilly from Kentucky." The usually reserved Wolfheart almost broke a smile when he offered Mama an affectionate peck on the cheek. As the three of them bent their heads together, Wolfheart leaned into the sheriff, and murmured discreetly.

But Petey doggedly tugged me forward (apparently eager to get to Tammy Jo) so I missed what was said next. "Come on, Pink. Let's go mingle."

Before I turned toward Tammy the Terrific, I glanced back toward the sheriff and Wolfheart as they continued to exchange urgent conversation. The only decipherable snippet sounded like, "Where'd you see him?"

"Hey, Violet, come see," Micah beckoned as Bubba and Daryl

walked up with Duchess in tow. The rambunctious Shiba Inu brightened my spirits, even as Petey made his way to Tammy Jo and his parents without me.

"Bubba and Daryl made a bet." Micah brightened.

I turned my attention to the dippy duo of Shady Gully. Pals since childhood, Bubba's hefty frame always seemed to equalize Daryl's scrawny silhouette. "What's that?" I turned away from Petey's fading back, and toward Bubba.

"How many of those fancy degrees you got?" He smothered a beer burp. "Daryl said you got one, but I'm betting you're up to two now."

"I've got a master's degree in medical science and one in clinical research."

"Hot damn," Bubba cackled. "Daryl, I'll take another beer. And the good stuff. None of that—"

"Listen up!" Charlie Wayne rapped on a picnic table then, demanding everyone's attention. He got right to the point. "Burgers on the right. Hot dogs on the left. All the fixin's are on that table yonder. Dig in."

"Wow," muttered Daryl. "What a moving speech. Anybody got a handkerchief?"

The hearty guffaws seemed to embarrass the old curmudgeon. Charlie Wayne shuffled his feet and added awkwardly. "Welcome back to Louisiana, Robin. Congratulations Luke." He then looked pointedly at Bella over the top of his coke bottle glasses. "There's still time to run, young lady."

Everyone laughed, grabbed paper plates, and cued up the horseshoes.

Despite my unrestrained spitefulness toward my mother throughout the evening, she bounced around the crowd in good cheer. Her rosy cheeks and animated laughter grated on my nerves, and the intimate, knowing looks she exchanged with the sheriff set me on edge.

Look at them, I thought angrily, *partying and reveling only a few hundred feet from Daddy's grave*. While he rested at the tree-lined cemetery just past the now-vacant church lots at the four-way, they carried on like he'd never existed.

"Are you okay?" Micah sidled up to me. "There's wine in the ice chest. Beer is so gross."

"I'm fine." Micah's presence always had a way of easing my anxiety. We were the same age, and had grown up together, the only girls in a flock of boys. "How do you like living in the duplex?" I could just make out Luke's economy apartments positioned past his auto body shop.

"Better than living with Mom and Dad. Bella stays with me most of the time. She wants to be close to Luke, but she won't sleep at his place." She shrugged, reaching down and absently petting Duchess, apparently forgetting her annoyance with the dog. "He's got the best apartment of all. It's got a fireplace, an island bar, and a walk-in shower."

I scratched Duchess behind the ear, trying my best to ignore the sight of Petey, who was currently flirting with Tammy Jo. I caught a glimpse of the black cross on his wrist as he lightly rested it along her shoulder. I shook my focus back to Micah. "I guess he has dibs since he's the landlord."

Micah sniffed, distracted by a spectacle at the crossroads. "Is that Father Patrick? What's he carrying? Is that…?"

Duchess's ears perked as the delicious aroma of barbecue drifted closer to the festivities. Everyone turned, their noses instinctively titling upwards, perfectly positioned for optimum smelling.

"It looks like a to-go box from—"

"Hold it right there, Padre!" Charlie Wayne squared off against the jolly, red-headed priest. "What's that you got there?"

"Dang." Bubba piped from the vicinity of the horseshoe game. "My mouth is watering."

"Oh, heck yeah." Sterling made his way over to the rosy-cheeked priest. "I've heard about this barbeque, Father. I'm so down to try some."

Father Patrick's expressive blue eyes landed on Sterling. "Have some, son. I'm…uh…*down* too. While everyone goes on about the ribs, I'm particularly fond of JJ's chicken. It's absolutely superb." Father Patrick opened the box and did a happy little jig as he began setting out the barbeque. "I brought plenty for everybody."

"Uh-uh. Hold on to your collar there, Daddy-o," Charlie Wayne fumed. "And you," Charlie Wayne scowled at Sterling. "Hands off that chicken. Nice and easy now."

"But Charlie Wayne," insisted Father Patrick. "I was being charitable. It's not polite to come to a party empty-handed."

But the Cozy Corner owner wasn't buying it. In one fluid motion he swept the to-go boxes into a throwaway bag and stalked to a giant trash can spray painted with the words, *Garbage Goes Here, Moron!*

"No, don't do that," I heard someone beg. "Aw no. I can't watch."

As Charlie Wayne turned to argue the point, he slipped on a plastic cup and lost his grip on the bag in his hands. People gasped as one of the white Styrofoam boxes flipped open, revealing JJ Wheeler's coveted barbeque chicken. The saucy meat seemed to tumble to the graveled parking lot in excruciatingly slow motion.

"Dang, but that looks good." Daryl whistled.

Bubba moved quickly for a big guy. He bent his pudgy body and stretched with surprising agility down toward the gravel. "They ain't that dirty," he reasoned.

But he was too late. At the mere scent of chicken, Duchess had made a beeline for the forbidden barbeque, and in one wily gulp snatched a breast and a side of potato salad.

"No! Somebody grab her!" The gathering erupted with something that sounded an awful lot like envy.

"Save me some!" Sterling called out.

The crowd bounded after the shifty dog. A lost cause because Shiba Inus were known for both their speed and cunning. Duchess flaunted her craftiness by crawling on her belly and nestling under a pickup truck.

The partygoers had no choice but to watch as she devoured the spoils of her victory. When she was done, her eyes disappeared into satisfied little slits, and her mouth arched in a full-on grin.

JJ Wheeler could be heard from across the four-way stop—cackling in his lawn chair.

Charlie Wayne was livid.

Saturday

Sigourney Sky, the owner of Nails and Thread, floated from room to room checking on her manicurists, her facial technicians, and mostly, her customers. The woman seemed almost fluid, the way her long, wispy dress brushed along the wood floor, and her dark, wavy hair swished from side to side.

Still a little sluggish from the festivities last night, Bella, Micah, and I managed to jump to our feet as Sigourney entered the alteration's parlor. "Thank you for fitting us in so early this morning," Bella said.

"Not a problem." Sigourney's lithe figure moved in tandem to the garment bag she carried.

"It's my fault," Micah admitted. "I have my dental hygienist gig in Belle Maison this morning."

Sigourney's green-eyed gaze moved past Micah and settled squarely on Bella. "Let's have you now." She waved Bella over to the private dressing room. "Or are we waiting for your mother?"

Next to me, Micah's breath hitched. We both turned to Bella, who appeared nonplussed. "No. She said she'd come by later if she could." Bella ran her hand along the white satin fabric. "But I don't want to wait."

When the two disappeared behind the fitting room curtains, Micah's breathing seemed to relax. "Poor Bella. I feel so sorry for her."

"What's the deal? Don't she and her mom get along?"

"It's not just her mom. It's—a lot of things." She squinted at me, as if considering how much to share. Knowing her like I did, I figured there was a fifty-fifty chance she'd spill the beans.

However, she surprised me, settling into predictable territory. "Meadow doesn't seem happy about the wedding. I mean, Luke's a dweeb, sure, but he treats Bella like a queen, and he really loves her." Micah shrugged. "I'd die if my mom ghosted my wedding."

"I don't think you could tear Aunt Desi away from your wedding," I teased.

"Hard to imagine, isn't it? But lately," Micah mused, "she's different."

"What do you mean?"

"I don't know. She cries a lot. Seems sad. Depressed even."

Menopause, I assumed. An affliction that had apparently bypassed my own mother, who wore purple eyeglasses and cavorted like a teenager, which was equally disturbing.

Movement behind the curtains caught our attention. "Are you ready, bridesmaids?"

Despite my ineptness when it came to clothes, makeup, and all things girly, my heart fluttered. I stood expectantly and maybe even giggled when Micah grabbed my hand.

Sigourney swept the curtains aside in one dramatic motion, and Bella entered the parlor. The atmosphere shifted, as Bella, so poised and regal—even with her hair contained in a single drugstore hairclip—stole the breath right out of us.

Her striking blue eyes and dark hair contrasted perfectly with the white of the dress's fabric. The gown itself seemed flexible as it reformed and switched, almost as if it were designed to catch fragments of light that accentuated Bella's best features. Her eyes filled with tears as she waited impatiently for us to speak.

But we could only stare. Off the shoulder, the dress bent to the perfect contours of her figure, clung to her impressive cleavage, her tight waist, and her shapely hips. A daring slit on the left side of the dress mirrored her own bold personality. The train was graceful, lace marrying satin, the back fancy to balance the front's simplicity.

"Well?" Bella's tears begged for a response. "Tell me."

Micah leaped into her arms. "I love it."

Sigourney shooed Micah away, suspicious of her tears and makeup, worried they'd soil her exquisite creation. Kneeling beside the train, Sigourney scrutinized every inch of the dress, trolling for the slightest flaw.

"Wow." I approached slowly. Tentatively.

"I know it's not your thing, Violet," Bella said. "But—"

"Oh, Bella," I said thickly. "It's absolutely perfect."

"I know, right?" quipped Micah. "How did my dorky brother get a hottie like you? A voice like an angel and drop dead gorgeous."

As we both moved in for an embrace, Sigourney narrowed her eyes. "I have some adjustments to make. Let me get her pinned."

While I maintained my distance, Micah fluttered like a top around Bella. "Up or down?"

"Up," breathed Bella.

"Down," countered Micah.

Bella frowned uncertainly. "Well, Luke does like it down."

It took me a moment to decode their ambiguous banter. "How about…"

Everyone, including Sigourney, looked at me in surprise.

"Up," I said. "But loosely."

Sigourney Sky winked at me. "Exactly."

I blushed at her approval, this quintessential female who understood her gender and tailored her unique creations accordingly.

Distracted, I glanced at my phone twice before registering Petey's text.

> *I got some news. How much longer*
> *are you going to be?*

As I reacted, everyone spun in my direction. With pins in her mouth, Sigourney asked, "Everything okay?"

As I met her gaze in the full-length mirror, I caught a glimpse of my own awkward reflection. Amazon-woman tall. Shoulders large and wide like a swimmer. Pale. So pale. And stringy white-blonde hair that was maddening and impossible to contain.

Mama always said comparison was the devil, and maybe it was, because my spirits took a nosedive. Compared to Micah and Bella—and Tammy Jo—I was homely, at best.

"It's fine," I muttered. "Everything is fine."

As I shook off my senseless and childish insecurities, I considered Petey's text. His words emphasized the looming impact of our choices, and while my change of course wasn't official yet, apparently something significant had happened on the way to Petey's fresh start.

Ready or not, our detours of the heart were imminent, and I should be mindful of my inclination toward comparison. I needed to stay in my lane and avoid the temptation of envy, especially when it came to Micah's alluring perkiness and Bella's elegant beauty. And Tammy Jo's…well, and Tammy Jo. Period.

I would never be described in those terms. My path in life would be quite different from Bella's or Micah's. Mine would be messy. It would be difficult, challenging, and very, very complicated.

I got some news…

A jolt of panic—and thrill—shot through me.

When Sigourney and Bella disappeared once again behind the curtain, Micah and I faced one another. Horrified to find her holding back tears, I exclaimed, "Micah? What's wrong?"

She shook her head emphatically. Squeezed her eyes shut so rigidly more tears sprung from the corners. And not the happy, wistful kind, but the kind that portended fear…the kind that reflected foreboding and dread.

"Micah. Tell me."

"I can't say." She cut her eyes toward the dressing room curtains. "I *shouldn't* say."

"I think you should," I said firmly. "Maybe I can help."

"It's just that she looked so happy." Micah raked her fist across her cheek as another wave of sobs broke the surface. "Her wedding…it could be so incredibly perfect."

"Could be?"

She hesitated, clearly wrestling with something heavy. "Come on. You have to tell me."

Micah wavered. "I'm just worried."

"About what? What is it?"

She let loose with a long, belabored sigh. "Bella set something in motion. Something big, and I think she regrets it now. But it may be too late."

I frowned.

"It's bad, Violet. I'm afraid it's going to ruin the wedding. Or worse."

Or worse?

I gulped, totally blown away. Apparently, Petey and I weren't the only ones in Shady Gully with secrets.

Chapter Seven

Uncle PeePee
Lenny

Sunrise in Shady Gully was truly something to behold, and today was no different. Sheriff Rick and I sat in rocking chairs on the front porch of my long-dreamed of hardware store, Lenny's Tool Shed, and watched as the sun cut a red and pink patch across the tree line.

The chairs, chosen by Micah for their *Instagrammable* potential, were large. Extremely large. Humongous even.

"These rockers…" As Ricky strained his vocabulary searching for the precise word, his upper lip curled in distaste.

"I know. They're big."

"Big? They're enormous, Lenny. And they're also really, really *blue*. I can hardly drink my coffee 'cause the color is making me seasick."

"Micah picked 'em. Said the kids will drag their friends here, and friends of their friends, and friends of —"

"I get it. There will be heathens everywhere. Excellent."

"She said they'll take pictures in the chair and post them on instagrammable."

"I believe it's Instagram." He smirked. "Robin has an account."

I side-eyed him buoyantly. "You don't say." I savored my coffee, grateful Micah had picked up a few hours at her paying job this morning, giving me the opportunity to make the java the way I liked it. Extra strong, and without judgement. "How's that going, by the way?"

My old friend's mustache inched higher up his cheeks. "Mighty fine, I reckon. Our cats seem to get on, and we always have a lot to chat about, never a dull moment…" He paused, grinning to himself.

"And?"

He shrugged, glancing past the post office, toward Charlie Wayne's, where I could just make out the signage instructing *morons* where to put their garbage. The sheriff and I had been the *morons* putting garbage *there* well past midnight last night as the rest of the crowd dispersed after Duchess stole the bar-beque—and the show.

"That was some spectacle last night, huh?"

He nodded absently. "I like Robin's son, Sterling. We get on fine. But Violet is a hard nut to crack."

"She misses Dean."

"I do too, Lenny. He was my friend too. Heck, everybody liked him." He peered at the crepe myrtles lining the graveyard less than a hundred yards across the road. "Remember? You threw the football. I caught it. And Dean recorded it in the stat books."

We laughed easily together, embracing memories of our time at Shady Gully High. "He prided himself on being a nerdy brainiac," I said thickly. "I loved the guy."

The sheriff swallowed, his mustache pointing downward now. "I really want her to like me, is all. I'm not trying to replace her daddy. Heck, I'm not even sure Robin is ready to…get involved yet."

"Desi seems to think she might be."

He gawked at me, unable to hide the relief blooming across his face. "You don't say?" He twisted awkwardly in the oversized chair, grunting as he clumsily lowered his coffee mug to the ground. "I reckon that's good to know." Satisfied now, he turned his attention to me. "I might have a bit of scoop for you."

"Tell me. But only if it's good."

"Robin told me this morning that she found a caterer for the wedding. Some lady in Naryville who lays out a right nice spread for a reasonable fee. Comes with references, and she's available."

"That's great. It will ease Desi's mind." I chugged my coffee, relishing the caffeine as it sprinted through my veins. "I knew seeing Robin would cheer Desi up." I shot the sheriff a teasing look. "What do you mean Robin told you this *morning*? That's really early, unless—"

"Talked to her. On the phone. She's at her fancy house on Osprey Lake."

"Oh," I chuckled, a little disappointed for my friend.

"No use trying to trip me up, Lenny. I been around this old country road a few times. Speaking of which, I need to mention something that ain't so good." Done with his coffee now, Ricky slowly peeled the wrapper off a saltwater taffy.

"Let's have it." I stood, tossing the rest of my coffee over the railing of the store's porch.

"Wolfheart got wind that someone was seen in town yesterday. He said it could've just been an overactive imagination, but it was someone we ain't seen in a while."

"And who would that be?" My pulse quickened as I recalled the odd figure lurking around Sprite's Quick Stop.

"Now you can't go getting all worked up, Lenny. He wasn't sure. Said that Moonpipe or Youngdeer, or one of his buddies from The Creek, saw someone that looked like him, but they could be wrong—"

"Who?" I removed my baseball cap and rearranged it on my head.

"Old man Tom. Desi's stepdad. Who—"

"Yeah, I know what he did, but…" I forced myself to slow my breathing, wishing now Micah had opened the store this morning, and I'd been drinking her watered-down coffee instead of my fully leaded mix. "I thought he was sick."

"He is. Alzheimer's. I heard he and Wanda bounce around Shady Gully in the after hours to get food and supplies, but usually they stay to themselves."

"So, he was by himself? Without Wanda? I don't get it."

"That's what Wolfheart heard, but—"

"Where was he seen?"

"Somewhere between Luke's auto body shop and his duplex. Again, it's all hearsay. And honestly, Lenny, what can I do? Whatever Tom did, it was a long time ago, and I know it messed Desi up something awful, but there ain't much that can be done about it all these years later."

I nodded. Considered climbing back into the ginormous blue chair to nurse my agitation. "Funny. I thought I saw someone familiar the other day too."

"Really? Familiar how?"

Since my suspicions were probably baseless, I instantly regretted saying them aloud. Still, while Tom was a pervert, a nuisance, and a bitter blast from Desi's past, if I were right, Shady Gully had more to worry about than a sickly degenerate.

"Anything I need to be concerned about?" Ricky grimaced again as he twisted awkwardly in his big, blue rocking chair. "Just say the word and I'll get Quietdove on it. He's been working a lot lately with other state and local agencies. Trading information, sending things up the flagpole. He's like a human NCIC."

I squinted in confusion.

"National Crime Information Center." Ricky shrugged. "Or computer. That's what I call him. Anyway, if something is bothering you, let us put some feelers out."

I spotted Luke's truck heading our way. "No. It's probably like Wolfheart said. Just like Moonpipe and Youngdeer, I'm imagining things."

As Luke parked in front of the store, Duchess, who'd been riding shotgun, leapt over him and beat a path to Ricky and me. The rambunctious bundle of mischief nuzzled my hands, sniffing for the secret treats I kept stashed under the check-out counter inside. I patted her fuzzy head.

"Hey, Sheriff." Luke shook Ricky's hand.

"Hey yourself, Mayor. Why so glum?"

Luke glinted at Duchess but decided to table the matter as Petey drove up, braking his truck to a perfect stop beside his brother's. My youngest son trotted over, a skip in his step, his intoxicating grin evenly dispersed between the three of us. "Oh man, cool chairs. How'd I miss these yesterday?" Petey walked around the chairs, sizing them up as he cued up his phone.

"Daryl just finished them. He brought them over this morning. Micah's doing."

Luke laughed as Petey encouraged us to pose for a few pictures.

"Don't be ridiculous," the sheriff sputtered, his mustache turning aquiver.

Luke tugged me back into the chair, stretching against me like a housecat. "Come on, Duchess. Let's sit on Granddad's lap." I marveled at the new playfulness in my usually reserved son. Bella had been good for him. "Come on, Sheriff," Luke teased. "Sit on my other side."

"I will do no such thing. We're like little Weebles in these ridiculous chairs. Like something out of Alice in Wonderland. I want no part of this nonsense. We're elected officials. We've got reputations—"

But Petey had already snapped a dozen pictures, including some of the sheriff, the mayor, and the town's First Dog. "I'm gonna tag Aunt Robin." Petey cackled. "She's gonna love these."

"Tag?" Ricky looked at me, befuddled. "That don't sound good."

I shrugged, rather enjoying my boys' antics, heads bent together, chortling at the images on Petey's phone. "Did you ever find your remote?" Petey asked Luke.

Luke eyed Duchess, who'd hopped onto the other rocker beside Ricky. "Yep. She grabbed it off my coffee table and wouldn't give it back, and then she hid it somewhere. Stashed it so I couldn't find it."

"Why would she do that?" I swallowed my amusement.

"I don't know, Dad. She's bored. Lonely. Bad." Luke tapped Petey's phone. "Post that one. Anyway, I let her out to go potty last night before bed, and this morning I found it buried in the yard. I have no idea how she managed that."

"Outrageous." Ricky heaved himself out of the big blue rocking chair. "You're my friend, Lenny, but I gotta be honest, your family is weird. Thanks for the coffee. It tasted less like water today."

"I gotta run too." Petey returned his phone to his pocket. "Father Patrick asked if I'd help with the children's Bible school at church, and I'm also going to do a little counselling."

"Oh dandy," the sheriff remarked wryly.

"Yeah." Petey missed the sheriff's sarcasm. "He's overloaded seeing as how Sacred Heart's the only church in town now, what with the barbeque man and all."

"That's great," I said. "You'll be good at that." My eyes automatically drifted to his newly tattooed wrist, a keepsake from his time in Kentucky.

Luke's cell phone made us all jump, with the exception of Duchess who'd started to gnaw on the blue rocking chair. "Mayor Luke here." Luke tucked the phone under his chin while trying to distract Duchess. "Oh no, I'm sorry to hear that." Luke's eyes darkened, his expression turning somber. "What room is he in? I'll check on him later today, and I'll let Father Patrick know. I'm sure he'll want to stop in as well."

Petey, Ricky, and I exchanged looks when Luke ended the call. "Brother Wyatt had another stroke. He's at Saint John's Hospital."

"That's not good." The sheriff frowned. "He barely survived the last stroke."

Brother Wyatt, the father of Jesse, James, and Dolly, had been Shady Gully's original fire and brimstone preacher. While his Sunday sermons had become tamer over the years, his retirement had significantly impacted Shady Gully's church history.

It had set the stage for strife and cast his sons in the modern-day roles of Cain and Abel. My gaze drifted to the culmination of that spectacle on the corner of the four-way stop. "I wonder if we'll ever get a church there again."

Petey regarded me curiously. "Of course we will, Dad." Something about his certainty reassured me.

Luke inched his shoulders up in a shrug. "Who knows what will happen if Brother Wyatt passes. Jesse and James could fight over that land forever and leave the church community in limbo indefinitely."

Ricky climbed into the substation's Ford F-150. "Keep me posted." He shot Petey a cautionary look. "Not on instagrammable though."

Petey winked, moving toward his own truck.

"Hey, wait," Luke said to Petey. "Why don't you take Duchess with you? She'd make a great therapy dog."

I wondered what kind of therapy the kids would need after spending time with the canine troublemaker.

"Come on, I've got to go to the hospital," Luke pushed.

Petey, clearly hesitating, cast his arm out the window.

I took in Duchess's reddish-ginger face and her singular toothy smile, shuddering at the potentially chilling before and after images of Father Patrick's glorious church. "I don't know, Luke, maybe that's not the best idea." On the other hand, the idea of Duchess galivanting all over Saint John's Hospital seemed even more precarious.

Luke made one final plea to his brother. "Come on, Duchess wants to bond with her Uncle PeePee."

Petey threw his shaggy head back in laughter. "I don't know about that, but I know a girl from Kentucky who'd love to hang out with her today." He glanced at his phone. "If she'd ever text me back. How long does a dress fitting take anyway?"

Luke and I traded baffled looks. "No clue," we said in unison.

Petey flashed his bright hazel eyes at Duchess. "I'll text her again and have her meet us there. And don't worry, Dad, Father Patrick's stained-glass windows will survive the day."

"Excellent." Luke clapped his hands.

As soon as Petey opened the door of his truck, a full-of-herself Duchess made a quick path over and scrambled into the passenger seat.

Ricky tipped his hat from the driver's seat of his own truck. "Like I said, Lenny, weird." He waved goodbye and headed right toward the substation, while Petey hung a left on his way to Sacred Heart Catholic Church, Duchess happily riding shotgun.

"Want some coffee?" I asked Luke. "I made it."

He made a face. "Hard pass. When is Micah getting here?"

I led him inside, deciding against pouring myself another cup. "This afternoon. She's still working at the dentist's office when she can, although I don't think she enjoys it."

"She hates it," Luke confirmed. "That dental hygienist school was a bust. I honestly think she'd rather be here."

"She has been unusually engaged, hasn't she? And these promotional things she comes up with…" I trailed off, still on the fence about the big, blue rocking chairs.

"She's got good public relations instincts. Who knows, Dad, maybe this is a gateway to her real career."

Luke filled the popcorn machine with corn and oil, turned it on, and within seconds Lenny's Tool Shed smelled like a movie theatre.

"Want some?" Luke munched from a hot bag as soon as the popcorn made it out of the popper. "How's Mom?"

"She's better now that Robin is here." I reached for a handful of the salty popcorn. "Oh, by the way, Ricky said Robin found a caterer for the wedding. From Naryville, of all places."

"Really? On such short notice? That's great. Bella will be relieved. She's been feeling guilty about Mom being so stressed."

I didn't respond, as I was beginning to suspect that something other than the wedding was stealing my wife's joy. "And you, son? Are you happy? You're not having cold feet or anything, are you?"

"Not at all. I can't wait. Eight more days."

I shook my head. "You know, part of your mama's stress is the hurry of it all. She says 'the timing is all cockamamie. Who ever heard of a wedding one week after a bridal shower?'"

"She says that? Really?" He flashed with amusement. "It wasn't just that we can't wait to be married, Dad. A lot of it is about our Kentucky family, and when they could be here."

"I realize that."

"Speaking of that," Luke crumbled up the empty popcorn bag, "your son wants to go look at lots."

My heart rate picked up as I gawked at Luke. "For what? Is he moving back home?"

"Don't get excited. I really don't know. As usual, Petey was vague, but he seemed kind of keyed up. He wants to look at average sized lots in Shady Gully. I asked the usual questions—"

"Lots for a house? Or a business?"

Luke bobbed his shoulders, finding my inquisition entertaining. "He said he just wants to see what's available within three or four miles of the four-way. In every direction."

What in the world? Desi would be overjoyed to have all her kids close to home again. "You have to find him something, Luke."

"Well, he's going to have to tell me what it's for then. If he wants Daryl to build him a house, I'd suggest going out toward Piney Lake, where y'all are, or Opry Lane, or some of the other nice residential areas in Shady Gully. If he wants to start a business, he should aim for the center of town."

"Or a church?" I flashed back to Petey's confident expression about Shady Gully having another church someday. "Maybe he wants to build a church?"

"Maybe." Luke shrugged. "He's always been spiritually gifted, and I guess you noticed his tattoo?"

"I did." Petey had been in Lexington, Kentucky, interning for two years with Timothy, the charismatic pastor of North Lake Christian Church. Desi and I half suspected he'd end up settling there, in Lexington, and eventually take a role at the prestigious and popular church. "You have to find him a lot," I repeated.

"I will, Dad. But don't get your hopes up. When it comes to a church, not just any lot will do. You know how folks feel about the four-way."

"I know, and I agree. A church should stand there."

"Right. Building a church somewhere else in Shady Gully probably wouldn't work. Especially the way Jesse and James have the community so divided. Everybody wants to appear neutral, so they're more than happy to stay home and watch Timothy online."

"Or they've converted to Sacred Heart."

"Exactly. And then there's Violet," Luke pointed out. "She's in school up north, which would be another reason for him to stay and work at North Lake. It's obvious they're…into each other. Whether they know it or not."

I shrugged. "He seemed friendly with Tammy Jo at the Cozy Corner last night. But who knows with Petey. He's always been cagey about his feelings."

"What?" Luke reacted. "He has not. His feelings are all over the place. He has feelings for everybody. That's part of his problem. He loves everybody, and everybody loves him. The trick is picking someone." He swiped another bag of popcorn from the warmer.

"I don't know. I guess time will tell."

"Maybe he's hesitating because of the whole cousin thing. Even though we aren't related, we always talk like we are. You know, Aunt Robin, Uncle Dean…" He frowned. "Speaking of Uncle Dean, Violet still seems really sad. Have you noticed that?"

"Yeah, and so has Ricky."

"Sheriff Rick," Luke corrected.

I chuckled. "I don't have to call him that."

We turned as the door chimed. In walked Redflyer, the chief at The Creek's Fire Department, followed by Moonpipe and Youngdeer. "Hey, Lenny."

"Hey, fellows. What can I do for you today?"

"You got some wash and wax?" Redflyer, a tall, muscular man born and raised on The Creek presented himself with an impressive sense of purpose. "Gotta spiffy the old girl up. That storm the other night muddied up her tires."

I appreciated the way he and his crew polished their new fire truck to a shine every other day, storm and muddy tires notwithstanding. "Sure thing."

"Later, Dad." After Luke headed out, I tended to my customers.

A sense of well-being and hope flooded through me. The

idea of Petey settling down and coming home to make a future in Shady Gully brought me joy. It would do wonders for Desi as well.

Still, Petey had always marched to the beat of his own drum, and as Luke had cautioned, I'd do best not to get too excited.

My thoughts drifted to Brother Wyatt then, at the hospital and quite possibly on his death bed. A good man whose children had mostly brought him disappointment and scandal. Lord knows they'd tested the grace and mercy of most of Shady Gully.

Perhaps Brother Wyatt was tired and looking forward to what was on the other side of the horizon.

Chapter Eight

A Potion Or Something
Meadow

"I don't see why I have to do this." The mass of bursting hormones cloaked in the form of a cranky boy grumbled. "It's a waste of time. The solution is simple."

"And what might that be, oh, wise one?"

"They need to break up."

"Right. Well, I think that ship has sailed." I clicked my blinker and hung a right into the parking lot of Sacred Heart Catholic Church. Once again, I'd been elected as Fireman's personal cabby after his Granny called and claimed to be flour-deep in batter and confectioners' sugar. More likely Epson salt and liquid Drano. Granny Lacey was well known around The Creek and Shady Gully proper for her unfortunate combination of poor eyesight and horrific baking.

Wanting no part of Granny's latest baking calamity, I offered to pick up the lovesick lad and deliver him to his appointment with Father Patrick. I politely declined Granny's offer of thanks in the form of Ooey Gooey Pecan Pokeys.

She seemed relieved. In her defense, she was an old lady trying to raise a fire-setting delinquent in love with a woman thirteen years his senior. Of course, just as that love match was doomed, so were Granny's chances of ever being featured on the Food Network.

"There's Duchess." Fireman pointed to the thick, red and white dog frolicking across the parking lot. We watched as she playfully tossed some unidentifiable object—or victim—high into the air, bucking with joy as she reclaimed it and jammed it back into her mouth.

"Are those communion wafers?" I squinted.

Fireman ignored me, hopping out of the car and heading toward the heavy wooden doors of the church. "Maybe Bella's here."

"Hey, pest." I ruffled Duchess's scruff, glimpsing a soggy package of honey nuts lodged between her teeth. I watched as she quickly swallowed them, package and all. Her eyes flattened into slits as she erupted in a sassy smile.

The massive door squeaked as we entered. "This place gives me the creeps," I muttered. When Fireman looked at me in surprise, I shrugged. "Just saying."

Footsteps bounded from the direction of the vestry, and a vaguely familiar blonde nearly ran into us. "There you are!"

Duchess wagged her tail, grinned sheepishly. I'd never actually seen a dog smile until Bella discovered this mutt at the animal shelter. The blonde deftly slipped a collar around Duchess's neck and fastened a matching harness.

I blinked in amazement. Duchess usually outsmarted even the cleverest of humans, but this woman was keen and never let her eyes stray from the beast. "Nice," I said aloud.

"I'm Violet. You must be Meadow, Bella's mom?" She offered me her hand.

I shook it, feeling ridiculous as I wasn't a hand-shaker. "Yep, that's me."

"I'm one of her bridesmaids. Well, the one besides Micah. She beamed suddenly. "Have you seen her dress? We saw it at Nails and Thread this morning. It's beautiful."

And just like that, the tall, curious blonde lost me. I shifted from side to side, right there in the nave of the church. Feeling disinterested. Or ashamed and guilty? Either way, I was itching to extricate myself.

"Ah! There they are!" Father Patrick bellowed from the church offices. He entered with a cheery, flushed smile. "My little captives. How wonderful to see you!"

Captives? I thought not. "Just dropping him off. Maybe you can do something with him. Give him a potion or something."

Fireman skewered me with a glare.

"Nonsense. We'll have us a sit down right here in the pews. It'll be lovely." He directed us to the second and third pews, with a perfect sightline to Jesus. "Not very conventional, of course, us gathering for a chit-chat smack dab in the middle of the sanctuary, but if we've learned anything in the last few years, it's that convention is overrated. I don't think He'd mind." He cut his eyes toward the cross. "Do you?"

"Uh, I really can't say." I shook my head. "I mean, *stay*. I really can't stay." I resisted Fireman's spiteful tug as he yanked me into the pew beside him.

Violet, presumably trying to play an unobtrusive role in Father Patrick's little sit down, withdrew to the pew behind us with Duchess, whose expressive face monitored her closely.

"Hey, everybody!" Luke's brother practically vaulted into the pew, cornering Fireman and me. He sported a tattoo on his wrist, and while the ink looked impressive, his messy hair and casual appearance seemed incongruent with the formality of Sacred Heart Catholic Church. "Sorry I'm late. I'm Petey."

"I was just saying that Jesus frequently challenged convention," Father Patrick said. "Do you agree, Petey?"

"Absolutely. As I recollect, he often called out the Pharisees for their unbending, by-the-book rules."

"You're Luke's brother," Fireman said accusingly.

Uh-oh. This could get ugly, I thought.

"Guilty as charged." Petey removed several bags of honey roasted peanuts from his pocket. "I reckon I might as well confess to another crime. Sorry Father, but I swiped these from my dad's store this morning."

Father Patrick reached for a bag. "Shame on you, Petey. I do hope you got the spicy ones. Next to the saltwater taffy?"

"Of course." Petey passed them around, frowning as he flashed at Violet and Duchess. "I could have sworn I had at least ten bags though. Strange."

"I'll go grab us some Cokes." There was a bounce in Father Patrick's step as he hurried to his office.

I glanced at the time, mindful of my delivery route within the hour. Just before I could beg off this lame powwow, Petey directed his gaze at Fireman. "My brother tells me you saved Bella's life. He said you were a real stand-up guy."

Fireman chewed. Skeptical.

"He said you told the sheriff about the bad guy—"

"Bad guy?" I interjected out of sheer orneriness. "His name was Madhawk. The one who murdered my father many years back, then knowingly took up with my mother, only to beat her to death two years ago."

Tattoo man paused. The blonde gasped. And a chill ran through me as I looked at Jesus hanging on the cross, now pretty sure he'd have preferred a tad more convention.

"He was a bad man." Fireman studied the tattoo on Petey's wrist. "He cut me with a knife, and then tried to kill Bella. And…" He stopped, his gaze landing on me. "He put Meadow in the hospital."

Everyone pivoted in my direction. Even the dog. I said nothing, afraid the words would get jumbled in my throat.

"Wow. That was brave," Petey said sincerely. "That took a lot of courage."

Father Patrick returned with ice-cold bottled Cokes and passed them out. Fireman twisted the top. "Yeah, I guess. But I did some bad stuff too."

"You're a fine young man," the priest insisted. "All that's been forgiven."

Fireman scoffed. "Well, if that's true, why doesn't anything good ever happen to me? I never get what I want."

The whininess in his tone sparked my annoyance. He was twelve years old. He had no idea just how cruel and disappointing life could be. I pursed my lips, bit back my irritation.

"No way?" Petey leaned in. "Are you serious? *Nothing* good has ever happened to you? That's crazy! I'd be mad too."

I could see the wheels turning inside the kid's head, wondering what the crazy, shaggy haired man was up to. "Yeah. I mean, it's not fair. I have to do whatever people tell me to do, and grownups"— Fireman dumped his peanuts into his Coke—"they can do whatever they want. They always get what they want. It's not fair."

My leg twitched as I fought the temptation to hurl back. I chugged my Coke, regretted passing on the nuts.

"I'll tell you a secret, Fireman," Petey said thoughtfully. "I feel like that sometimes. Like things aren't fair. And I bet He did too." Our gazes followed Petey's straight down the center nave of the church and up to Jesus's crucified body. "But you know what I do? I talk to Him. He knows about all the things I want. He understands. He knows what I worry about, and what I'm afraid of, and He understands when I'm jealous, or when I'm mad because somebody else got what I wanted."

Fireman studied Petey.

"Yeah, it's true. See, just because I'm a grown-up doesn't mean everything goes my way. And just like you," Petey continued, "sometimes, it feels like He's not listening."

"Right." Fireman nodded earnestly. "Why do you keep talking to Him then?"

Petey's striking hazel eyes brightened. "Because He's the best friend I ever had. And He's a lot smarter than me. You see, some of the things I want real bad, well, they aren't so good for me."

"*Humph.*"

"And you know what else?" Petey patted Fireman's leg. "He's always working on ways to help me. Even when I feel like He's not listening, or like He doesn't care, He's always working behind the scenes. He does that for you too."

"Why would He do that?"

"Because He loves you. And here's the kicker—He has a way better plan for you than you do. Let me ask you this. You said you did something bad, right?"

"I set a church on fire. It was an accident, but still…"

"How much jail time did you do?"

"What?"

"A year? Two?"

"I didn't go to jail. I just helped at the sheriff's station, and when Luke got the fire stations built in town, I worked there." Fireman brightened, his childhood enthusiasm momentarily overriding his resentment. "And guess what? Redflyer let me drive the big firetruck out of the garage at The Creek's fire station."

"That's cool!" Petey exclaimed. "I sure wish I could do something like that. Let me ask you another question. What do you want to be when you grow up?"

"I'm gonna be a fireman. Redflyer said he can start paying me next summer, and I can get training at both the station in The Creek and the one in Shady Gully."

"That's awesome. I always wanted to be a fireman."

"I don't know. You're kinda skinny. You gotta drag those big hoses and all."

"True. I guess I won't get to do that." Petey sighed, waxing disappointed.

"But maybe you could do something else." Fireman finished his Coke. "You should probably talk to your friend. God. Maybe there's something you can do even though you're skinny."

Violet, who'd been quiet up until now, snorted.

"Maybe you're right." Petey nodded. "Maybe I'll be just like you, and something I've done that wasn't so good can turn into something great. Like when you set the church on fire but didn't have to go to jail. And then, ended up getting a dream job at the fire station."

"Yeah." Fireman appeared reflective. "Maybe so."

Petey glanced at me through the corner of his eye, and danged if I didn't like the guy, even if he was Luke's brother and Desi's son. "I've got an idea. We can try it together if you want."

Fireman nodded, clearly digging the Coke, the nuts, and his new, personal apostle.

"Maybe, if we try to find the good—even in things that don't seem so good—we won't feel so terrible. You want to try?"

"I don't know. That doesn't really make sense."

"Think about it like this: what if we were to do something nice for someone that made us mad? Like, here's an example." Petey looked thoughtful. "You know how Charlie Wayne is so mad at JJ Wheeler?"

"Yeah. He's jealous 'cause he's stealing all his business."

"Right. Well, imagine if Charlie Wayne cooked JJ a hamburger, and brought it over to him with a side of fries and"—Petey held up his empty bottle—"an ice-cold Coke?"

We all laughed. Even me.

"That would be really radical." Fireman giggled.

"Why not?" Petey grinned. "Let's be radical. We might find that the ones we're jealous of, or who seem to have the very things we want, aren't so bad after all. Heck, they might even have stories all their own. Stories full of unfairness and disappointments just like ours. What do you think?"

"It's worth a try." Fireman studied Petey for an extended moment. "I'm game."

As the fidgety rustle of discarded nut bags marked the end of the sit down, I was shocked to find I'd lost track of time. Luke's brother had a way about him, a humbleness I hadn't expected.

Clearly, Fireman felt the same, as he cheerfully rose and began chasing Duchess up and down the church pews, whatever angst he'd endured over losing Bella temporarily set aside.

Once Violet moved to keep tabs on Duchess, Father Patrick's gaze switched from Fireman to Petey. "Well done. You planted a seed. Now, to nurture it and pray it grows."

"He's a good kid." Petey turned to me, as if I were Fireman's mother. "Bella told me he watches Timothy online with Wolfheart sometimes."

"Who?"

"Timothy. The pastor at North Lake Christian Church in Kentucky."

"Oh," I muttered. "Right." *Tiger. Trey. Turk. Whatever.*

"I think he'll get a kick out of meeting him in person. He's way better at this than me."

"You did splendidly, Petey. Don't sell yourself short." Father Patrick added bashfully, "I must confess though, I'm a little star struck by the charismatic Kentucky pastor myself. I'm rather nervous to meet him."

"He can't wait to meet you, Father Patrick." Petey grinned at the stout priest. "You're one of the first ones he wants to meet when he gets here."

"What?" I asked, finally catching on. "The TV preacher is coming here? Why in the world would he do that?"

Violet, who led the typically rowdy Duchess over at a polite trot, looked at me in surprise. "For the wedding. He's going to marry Bella and Luke."

"Oh. That's right." I nodded. "I knew that."

My voice reeked with false bravado, and none of them would meet my eyes.

Violet left Duchess with Petey and Father Patrick, and then walked with me to my car. Her hovering made me uncomfortable, so rather than snapping at her I hollered at Fireman. "Let's go, Little Fry. I'm late!"

I narrowed my eyes at the kid as he dilly-dallied around the basketball goal at the side of the church. I grunted, my irritation mounting.

"I remember you," she said. "From a few years ago. After the fire. Or fires, I should say."

I eyed her. This was a pity chat, and I was in no mood. I could care less about who was marrying Bella and Luke, or about Bella's pretty white dress. I'd just be glad when it was over, and I could get on with my life.

"You know, weddings really aren't my thing either." The pale, gangly girl shuffled her feet. "I didn't think I'd ever be able to find a bridesmaid dress, but thankfully, Bella took pity on me and said if I could find something purple, that would be okay. I ended up having a seamstress make one."

I said nothing.

"It looks ridiculous on me, like a nightgown." Violet laughed self-consciously. "Kind of like a grape housecoat. But Bella said it was fine."

"I'm sure it's lovely." Our eyes met, and the atmosphere shifted.

Initially, I'd regarded her as a pleasant young woman. A bit too serious maybe, but full of purpose and disinclined to waste time. Or words. But now I recognized a curiosity and a depth behind her eyes that was quite enchanting. Beautiful even. It made me want to linger.

And I wasn't a lingerer.

"The truth is," I slowly sputtered, "I had no idea who was marrying Bella and Luke."

Violet nodded flatly. Without judgement. Highly attentive.

I took a long, deep breath, and despite the pinpricks of warning needling across my neck, I spoke. "When Bella was young, she was my everything. I was so protective of her, so…invested in her well-being. I couldn't imagine how I'd ever carry on when she grew up and moved away from me."

I hesitated then, gaging Violet's reaction, searching for the slightest hint of scorn. Or pity. When I detected none, I continued. "And then, honestly, I couldn't even say when or how or why, just that she began to see me differently. She asked questions and when I couldn't give her answers, she began to judge me. She became angry with me, disappointed in me, and soon, I could do nothing right."

What on earth was I doing? Was it possible that I'd been so easily inspired—or *manipulated*—by the charismatic man-boy with the tattoo that I'd spew to this young woman I barely knew? Apparently. Because suddenly I desperately wanted to share my side of the story, my version of history.

"I became nothing more than a human punching bag," I went

on. "A conduit for Bella's anger. She stopped seeing *me*. I literally became nothing more than a resource to supply and accommodate her basic needs."

Violet continued to listen intently. Not a single eye roll. Not even an exasperated sigh. I realized that unlike Bella or Uncle Wolf, she wouldn't bring our family's convoluted history to the table, and she wouldn't regurgitate all my past mistakes to shut me down. And more than anything, I wanted—I *needed*—someone to understand that I'd tried, that I'd given my daughter everything I could give…until I had nothing left to give.

"I guess at some point, I just disengaged."

"Disengaged?" Violet's sudden interruption, albeit a soft one, reminded me that I was indeed speaking, sharing, confessing…

"Yes," I said. "It had become a matter of self-preservation."

I finally stopped, suddenly loathing my vulnerability.

Despite her empathetic expression and compassionate manner, Violet was *Bella's friend*. Heck, she was one of her *bridesmaids*.

I quickly pulled myself together, reverting to the sarcastic, generally disagreeable person I was, and I looked directly into the pale young woman's eyes. Where I found no judgement and no condescension. Only compassion.

"Watch out!" The bounce of a basketball jolted us back to reality. Fireman pounced, snatching the ball just before it sideswiped Violet's rear-end. "Look." He pointed at two red pickup trucks as they pulled into the parking lot. One driven by a skinny man with spectacles, and the other by an obese man with spectacles.

We gawked as they each climbed out of their trucks and headed toward the heavy wooden doors of Sacred Heart Catholic Church.

"Is that…?" Violet squinted as the two men walked past us with their noses in the air. Not only did they refuse to speak to us, but they barely acknowledged one another.

"Yep," I said. "That's Jesse and James. Shady Gully's very own Cain and Abel."

Chapter Nine

You Are A Hick
Violet

Still reeling from Bella's mom's stirring remarks, I was reluctant to rush off even as the infamous Jesse and James stormed into the church.

"Go on," Meadow insisted. "I'm late for my mail route, and I still have to drop the kid off at the Shady Gully Fire Station."

Whether inspired by Petey's coaching or lured by the promise of the fire station, Fireman dropped the basketball and settled himself into Meadow's car. As I waved goodbye, I marveled at Bella's mother, an extraordinary woman whose straightforward personality camouflaged a range of suffering.

When I entered Sacred Heart, Father Patrick and Petey lingered in the pews, their heads bent in discussion as the feuding twins approached. Upon seeing me, Duchess leapt happily and rushed past the brothers, the spicy peanut bag dangling from her jaws like a prize. She joyfully surrendered it to me, obviously pleased with herself.

"Gentleman." Father Patrick stood, his usually cheerful demeanor forced. "I just heard about your father's stroke. I'm terribly sorry."

"Hey, there." Petey offered the heavier one his hand. "I'm Peter." While his gesture went ignored, Petey remained steadfast.

"Yeah, I know who you are. You're Mayor Luke's brother. I won't hold that against you." The man's beady eyes sunk deeper into his face. "Or maybe I will."

Father Patrick stiffly cleared his throat. "You remember Jesse. And this is his brother," he indicated the skinny brother, "James."

Despite their vastly difference carriages, I could see the similarity in Jesse and James. I vaguely remembered them from the church fires, but while James appeared much the same, Jesse had certainly…blossomed.

"Of course, I remember," Petey said. "I guess y'all are headed to Saint John's. How's your dad? Any updates?"

The skinny one, James, shook his head. "No. Do you mind if we talk?" He moved to sit on a pew. "We could sure use your counsel."

Father Patrick fussed accordingly. "Of course. Most certainly. Why don't y'all come on back to my office?" Unlike young Fireman's counsel, Father Patrick seemed inclined to settle these guests amid office supplies and filing cabinets.

James cut his eyes at Petey as he followed the priest. "I still recall the great fires of Shady Gully like it was yesterday, and I still remember the way your prayers touched the crowd." James's innocuous words didn't quite match the sarcastic inflection in his tone, making the remark seem anything but complimentary. Undaunted, Petey glided toward the offices.

Unsure what to do with myself, I hesitated. Duchess made the decision for me when she dashed ahead of Petey and Father Patrick. She stopped at the office door, turned expectantly, and marked me with her lolling tongue. "Come on, Lady Duchess." Father Patrick unlocked the door. "You're welcome as well."

"What?" Jesse huffed. "No privacy?"

"Oh no worries, Jesse, Petey is one of my staff members. I wholly trust him." Petey's eyes widened, apparently unaware of his new position in the Catholic Church. I felt my face flush as I still hadn't heard Petey's big news. Father Patrick's comments, even if in jest, now had me curious.

"And the lovely Violet is here supervising Lady Duchess, who is doing therapy work today. So, the gang's all here. Delightful, yes?"

"You bet." Petey flashed Father Patrick a perceptive smile.

"Have a seat everyone." As Father Patrick and Petey rounded

up chairs, Jesse and James did their best to ignore one another. "May I offer you some refreshment?" Father Patrick asked. "At the moment we have an abundant supply of grape juice."

I bit back a chuckle as I enjoyed the cheery priest's humor. Duchess wagged her tail, recognizing my amusement. The subtle rattle of a secreted peanut bag drew my attention as the crafty dog settled beneath my chair.

Another one?

Petey stroked her head, playfully trying to retrieve it.

"We wanted to catch you before you saw my father," James began. "Our sister has been with him all morning, and I fear she's trying to persuade him against us."

Jesse squeezed his large frame into the chair. "Ever since our mother died, Dolly babies him. With an eye to her advantage, of course. She sweet-talked him into taking control of my land on the corner of the four-way stop. That's why we have that disgraceful man peddling fast food."

"Conned," James corrected. "Not sweet-talked. And the whole reason they're in cahoots is because you refuse to sell me your land."

"Why on earth would I do that?" Jesse sneered with outrage.

James made a big show of summoning patience. "Oh, I don't know, perhaps because you set fire to my church." James turned to Father Patrick. "My brother should be in jail for arson rather than getting fat on a cocktail of SSRI therapy—"

"Well, if that's the case," Jesse sniped, "the little delinquent from across the creek should also be in jail since he set fire to *my* church. I had no other choice."

Petey, to his credit, tried very hard to sound supportive. "I have so many questions." He cut a glance at Father Patrick. "About all of this, but the biggest and most pressing question right now is how can we help your father?"

Except for the sound of Duchess's smacking, the office fell silent.

"I think what Petey is trying to say is, well…" Father Patrick searched for words. "Wouldn't our time be better spent at your father's bedside? Perhaps this is something you should all discuss as a family."

"He won't listen to us. Especially if Dolly is around," Jesse said.

"I just want you to put a bug in his ear," James reasoned. "When you see him."

"Well, I don't do bugs, boys. I'm sorry."

"I want him to understand that if Jesse sells me his land, I will build a church"—James glared at his brother—"that will honor his legacy. And thrive in Shady Gully."

Jesse's face reddened. "You are a charlatan. Your church was a bust."

"That's because your disgraceful church took up half the lot. One church should be on the four-way, and it should be mine. Or none at all."

"Well," Jesse said spitefully, "it will be none at all then."

I sneaked a glance at Petey, who stared in disbelief.

When the plastic dangling from Duchess's mouth crackled, I managed to gently remove the soggy honey roasted peanut bag. Father Patrick, looking slightly dazed, perked a little and shot me a thumbs up.

"I'm curious," Petey interjected, "this bug, that you, uh, want Father Patrick to put in your father's ear, are you seriously asking him to plead one of your cases?"

"I don't expect you to understand," James said. "By the way, just because you're dabbling in a career at the pulpit doesn't mean you get to rant superior."

"Oh, you're wrong," Petey said. "Trust me, I steer clear of pulpits."

"And he's not dabbling," Father Patrick added. "He interned with Timothy, the preacher at North Lake in Kentucky. In fact—"

"Another charlatan." Jesse's breathing became labored. "The point, and the one you need to convey to my father, is that I will make better use of that land."

James swiveled his whole body toward his brother. "To do

what? Plant marijuana? Open a liquor store? Maybe a few slot machines? Sell prescription drugs through a drive through window? You've already disgraced us enough, Jesse. The right thing to do would be to sell me your half and allow me to build a nice church for our members in good standing to return to."

"Never. And they wouldn't return to you. They're waiting for me."

And finally, Cain and Abel had reached an impasse.

Father Patrick rose. "I should be on my way to see your father. To pray with him. He's a good man. A fellow man of God, and I'd like to go and see to him now."

"He respects you." James made one final attempt. "I'm a man of God as well, and I want to build a church that will unify."

Jesse scoffed, awkwardly heaving himself out of the ill-fitting chair.

I followed suit as Petey stood.

Realizing she belonged to our pack, Duchess hopped to attention and waited expectantly. As the brothers seemed to sense their meeting had been futile, they angrily filed out of the office.

They'd almost made it down the hall when Jesse stopped. He turned to address his brother but made sure he was within earshot of Petey. "Do you remember when Dad let us baptize members of the church?"

James squinted, unsure where his brother was going.

"We baptized your mother, Désireé." Jesse looked over his shoulder at Petey. "A shame it didn't take."

James, proving he was of the same mold as his brother, added, "We should have known. Dolly said she didn't even know the Lord's Prayer during cheerleading tryouts. Apparently, she stumbled and muttered in front of everyone. Until her friend took pity."

"Disgraceful," they said in unison, as finally it seemed, they could agree on something.

"That will be all, gentlemen." Father Patrick's voice rose, his tone putting a stop to their malevolence.

As Jesse and James skulked toward their respective trucks, the air instantly grew lighter. I breathed deeply, and nudged Petey playfully, measuring his reaction to the nasty remark.

Father Patrick jingled the keys to the church van. "Thank you for joining me today, Petey. My instincts were right."

"Instincts?" Petey asked as we walked the priest to his traveling vehicle, an old van he apparently used to visit church members on occasion. "Instincts about what?"

"Why you, of course!" He paused, as if an idea had suddenly taken hold and banged a tambourine inside his head. "Perhaps we should set up another meeting with them. Explore our options. We'll be better prepared next time."

I wondered if I looked as clueless as Petey.

"I don't follow, Father." Petey helped the priest into the van, and then manually cranked open the garage door. "What options?"

"Just an inkling twisting around in this old brain of mine. It was an inkling such as this that led me to inviting you here today. Offering you a role in healing this spiritually ravaged community. As well as our little chat about the Book of Haggai."

As something—perhaps one of Father Patrick's inklings— flashed along the edges of my mind, I asked curiously, "Isn't there other land in Shady Gully? I mean, if James's motives are so noble, why doesn't he just build a church somewhere else?"

"There's land," Petey put in. "Lots of it. Luke said this morning that Shady Gully is brimming with potential."

"It is, and your point is well taken, Violet dear." The priest jammed the keys into the ignition. "But they want *that* land, and not just because it's *the* best piece of real estate in Shady Gully, but because showcasing their feud for the whole town feeds their narcissism."

"Wow," Petey muttered.

"Not only that," Father Patrick added. "The elders and former members in good standing see that corner lot as where their church belongs. I suspect a lot is riding on who wins the battle of the land."

"Because whoever gets the land…" I mused aloud.

Father Patrick sighed deeply as the van cranked to a start. "Is who they'll crown their church leader."

I squished the hook into the cricket butt-first, then handed the cane pole to Petey.

"Dang, Fuchsia," he teased. "You are such a turn on when you bait my hooks like that."

We'd stopped within a hundred yards of his parents' house with our fishing poles and an ice chest, and currently plucked ill-fated crickets from the screened canister we'd bought at Sprite's Quick Stop.

Petey tossed his line into Piney Lake and jiggled the fishing pole a few times. "We'll catch us a mess of bream and bring 'em to Mama to fry up." His face tightened at the mention of his mama, no doubt Jesse's nasty remarks still on his mind.

"So, tell me. What's your big news?"

"How'd you get to the church this morning? I must have texted you a million times."

I rolled my eyes. He was making me wait, keeping me in suspense. "Micah dropped me on her way to the dental clinic."

"Yeah. Dad made the coffee at the store this morning." He shuddered. "I smelled it even before I passed the four-way stop. How'd the fitting go?"

"Great. Bella's dress is beautiful. She had to stay a while longer so Sigourney could do some more pinning. Some more tweaking." I shoved a second cricket onto my hook, tossing my line several feet past his, hoping to show him up. Maybe impress him beyond baiting his hooks.

Petey scrutinized me for an extended moment. Almost as if he were trying to read beyond my glib account of the day's events. To Micah's troubling concerns about whatever Bella had set in motion. And to Meadow's extraordinary revelation.

I decided to keep both to myself for now, and to push Petey

to reveal his news by challenging him to one of our traditional *Say or Tell* matches. "Pick one."

"Go."

"Say my real name or tell me your news."

"No fair, Garnet." He pulled his line in, exposing the scant innards of the cricket. "Okay. You win, even though you're cheating." He glinted at me as we switched poles. "I talked to Timothy. He got a call from his friend in Baton Rouge."

"And?" I handed him the newly baited fishing pole.

"The feedback wasn't good. His friend said I wasn't ready." He sighed. "But considering how I tanked that night, I'm not surprised. Still…tough to hear."

"I'm sorry." I got a nibble but didn't react. Somehow catching a fish now seemed bad timing. "You sounded happy this morning. I thought maybe you'd heard something good."

"Well, I was disappointed, 'tis true. But God…" He turned his full grin on me. "I kid you not, just after talking to Timothy, Father Patrick called."

"Don't tell me. Something to do with that *inkling* of his."

"Yep. I'm still not exactly sure what goes on in that happy ole head of his, but he did offer me a rope. He invited me to lead some Bible studies and do some counseling."

"Right up your alley.

"That's what he said. I don't know, he's probably got something up his collar." He chuckled. "But I grabbed the rope anyway."

"That's great. So, it was a good day."

"Yeah. And the conversation with young Fireman energized me today. To be able to be straight with him, without having to worry about how I said things. You know, like getting my grammar right, or wrong, more like it. Or trying to say big words so the congregation would think I was smart or quoting scripture so they'd think I was faithful." Petey cringed. "I still can't believe I got Philippians and Colossians mixed up."

"Petey, there was a lot of pressure that night, and college kids are snooty. Even in Louisiana. And if you want me to be straight with you—"

"Always."

"Timothy didn't put that pressure on you, and neither did God. You put it on yourself." He snapped his eyes at me. "I'm serious. Timothy encouraged you to wait. He wanted you to start here in Shady Gully, with a smaller, more friendly congregation."

"Well, there isn't one around here anymore. Spending half an hour with Jesse and James was proof of that. And if not for Father Patrick, I wouldn't even have had the chance to offer encouragement to Fireman today."

"You pushed for the audience at LSU." I pulled my bream in when I felt a tug in my line. "What did you think would come from preaching to a room chock-full of self-involved, entitled millennials?"

"I thought they'd like me. I thought I could inspire them."

"They liked you."

"They thought I was a hick."

"You are a hick." I grinned. "So what?" I removed the hook from the flopping fish, tossed it into the ice chest. "Nothing you could have said would have made a difference." I went on, caught in a rush of emotion, thrilled to finally have somewhere to direct it. "It was LSU—"

"And why, pray tell, do you think I wanted to preach at LSU?"

"Because you don't do anything small, Petey. It's always gotta be—"

"Because of you." He yanked his fishing pole out of the lake and tossed it angrily onto the grass. "*For* you. So you won't be alone when you go there."

My heart pounded inside my chest. I turned away, unable to look at him, focusing instead on the bream yanking at my line.

"For a while anyway. It probably won't take you long. As smart as you are." He reached for my pole, pulled in the bream, squeamish as he tossed it into the ice chest. "So gross." He handed the pole back to me, and I killed another cricket. "Speaking of that, have you told anybody your plans?"

"I haven't had a chance. Besides, I don't really know anything yet. Not officially anyway."

"You'll hear soon. Trust me." He retrieved his fishing pole from the grass. "You should tell Micah. Start small, like you said. Or heck, be like me and go big. Just snatch your mama up in a giant hug and lay it out for her."

"Right." I snorted, irritation flaring. "The first thing people say when they see me is how I'm going to cure cancer, and how my dad would be so proud of me. Or how many degrees I have, or how smart I am—"

"Better than saying you sound like a hick."

"I'm serious, Petey. This is a big deal. Mama is going to flip. I barely found the nerve to tell Sterling, who's like an appendage to me."

"And he was happy for you, wasn't he? And your mom will be as well."

"Uggg. It's not like I get any alone time with her anyway. She's all googly eyed over that goofy sheriff."

"I like Sheriff Rick. Don't you think he looks just like Tom Selleck?"

"I'm in the Sam Elliott camp on that one."

"Whatever. The point is, you're just putting it off. I don't know what you're waiting for."

I sighed. "I don't know. Maybe I'm crazy. Maybe I shouldn't go at all—"

"You're going," Petey insisted. "You've been wanting this for years. And I…" He trailed off.

"You what?" I held my breath.

"I still want to go with you. Even though Baton Rouge didn't work out for me. That was the plan, right? We'd hang out together in Baton Rouge. Support each other. Fish a little on the bayou."

I chuckled; my heart full. "I don't know. What about Father Patrick? I'm beginning to think your place might be here. This is where your heart is."

Petey looked at me sharply, his hazel eyes flashing in confusion.

"Petey, I have a feeling Father Patrick's *inkling*, as he called it, is to use you here." I raised my finger in quotes. "To help heal a spiritually ravaged community. Isn't that what he said? Maybe that's your path."

"Maybe." He shrugged, dubious. "Maybe yours as well. Someday. Maybe."

I took his fishing pole and pulled the twitching bream onto the grass. I was afraid to look at him. "You aren't much of a fisherman, are you?" I teased. "At least of fish."

"Maybe I don't have to be." We grinned as we took in our mess of fresh bream. "You reckon Mama will fry these up for us?"

"I think Aunt Desi would do whatever her golden boy asked."

As Petey lifted the stocked ice chest in his arms, his phone slipped out of his pocket. I picked it up, along with our cane poles and canister of crickets, and followed him to his truck.

"Say," he said over his shoulder, "I talked to Luke about lots. Just for the heck of it. He got all excited. Went on about how much Shady Gully was booming. Said he'd be happy to show me what's available."

"Okay." My heart fell. "But…why?"

"Just in case. Maybe after you finish at LSU…you might want…" He trailed off. Then picked up again nervously. "I don't know. Just options."

"No. I mean, I'm not sure, Petey." I clamped my lips shut. Didn't dare look at him.

Petey sighed. "Remember when Father Patrick alluded to the Book of Haggai?"

"Sort of. Yeah." I shook my head, exasperated.

"He quoted chapter 1, verse 8 to me."

Impatient, I shook my head.

"'Go up to the hills and bring wood and build the house, that I may take pleasure in it and that I may be glorified, says the Lord.'"

"Petey. I'm not good at this like you are. You're going to have to explain."

"It's the way he said it. He was talking about Jesse and James, about all the strife, and then he was going on about how refreshing my conviction was and how it was *our* job to provide healing for the ones we shepherd—"

I stared at him. "He's encouraging you to build a church."

"I could be misreading."

"I don't think so. But I don't understand. Even he admitted that the only church the members in good standing would take seriously was one on the four-way stop."

"Right."

"But still, maybe he's thinking options. Or inklings."

"Maybe." He shrugged. "I don't even know how I feel about it." He took the remaining crickets, let them bounce their way out of the screened canister, and set the fishing gear in the back of his truck.

"I just think it wouldn't hurt to look. For the future," he insisted as he opened the passenger door for me. "Just in case."

My heart skipped into a dreamy free fall. Everything was all falling apart. Our plans. Everything.

A text shook Petey's phone then, and as he went around to the driver's side, my heart went from free fall to full out plummet.

> Got your message, Petey. I'm all
> in. Can't wait. Xoxo, Tammy Jo.

Chapter Ten

Here Honey, Try This
Lenny

Petey's truck was parked at a careless angle in the yard, and I heard Ginger and Mary Ann carrying on as soon as I opened the garage door. Granted, Petey's presence invited animated yips from most everyone he encountered, but this was something more.

The intoxicating aroma of cornmeal and freshly fried bream led me to the kitchen, where Desi's slotted spoon hovered over a fry-daddy filled with oil. "I got first dibs." I bent to pet Ginger, the yippy papillon, who bounced on her hind legs to reach closer to my face. "Hey, girl, hey." Mary Ann, a little slower—and much more reserved—waited patiently for me to scratch behind her ear. "How come nobody invited me to the party?"

Desi removed the golden, flaky fish from the grease. "I didn't know there was going to be a party until Violet and Petey brought me this mess of fish." She glanced at her watch. "You must be hungry."

"I am. I was waiting for Micah to make it back from Belle Maison. She said she'd man the fort for a while."

"Man the fort?" Robin teased. "That's incredibly sexist." She sat at the table folding trinkets into purple lace, at which point Violet tied each with a pink ribbon, and systematically checked from a list on a yellow legal pad.

"You're outnumbered," Petey said through a mouth full of fish. "I'd just go with it. And if anybody asks, I'm on their side."

I frowned. "How'd you get fish already?"

Petey winked at me. "Mom likes me best."

"Where's Duchess?" I asked. "I thought y'all had her?"

"We handed her off to Bella once she finished with the seamstress." Violet passed me a trinket bag to inspect. "Aren't they cute? They're for the shower."

"Ah," I mumbled, generally puzzled by the purpose of lacy bags, ribbons, and trinkets. "Things seem to be coming along nicely."

Violet went back to her ribbon while Petey crammed more bream into his mouth. "It's delicious, Mom. Thank goodness I caught so many." He slanted his eyes at Violet, begging for a reaction. "Must have been my expert fishermen skills." Which he didn't get.

I closed in on Desi, lightly draping my hand along her hip. "Smells good." She handed me a plate. "Thanks." I took it and sat at the table next to Petey, who fiddled with his phone while Violet looked on disapprovingly.

"Oh, these are funny." Robin chuckled as she pushed her purple glasses lower down her nose. "Where did you find these, Desi?" She flipped through a series of brightly colored cards.

"Online." Desi slid the ketchup to me as she sat down. "Here. Give them to me, and we'll find out who knows the bride and the groom best." Desi squinted at the cards, playful as she split her gaze between us. "Okay. Who's the better singer?"

"Seriously?" Petey made a face. "Luke, of course."

Everyone laughed because Luke couldn't carry a tune, while Bella, on the other hand, would likely get a recording contract one day.

"Too easy." Desi frowned. "Who's the better planner?"

"Uh…I'm going with Luke," Robin said. "He's the mayor, after all, so he'd better be."

"Who's the most romantic?"

Petey made a face. "I don't even want to think about that."

"Luke is very romantic," Violet replied. "Bella told me."

"Y'all talk about that stuff?" Petey gawked, incredulous.

"Yep," Violet answered in an unusually clipped tone. Intrigued, I cut my eyes at Petey.

"Oh," Desi suddenly grew misty-eyed, "and one last one. Who said *I love you* first?"

We switched our eyes around the table, eventually settling on Violet. "What?" she said, reddening. "She doesn't tell me *every*thing."

Petey set his phone down, leaned across the table, and grinned at her for a long moment. "Come on, Cherry. Give it up."

Begrudgingly, she confessed, "Luke."

"I knew it." Petey sighed. "Such a dork."

"What do you mean, *dork*?" Robin swatted him on top of the head with a random roll of lace. "It takes courage to be honest about your feelings. Especially romantically."

"I concur," Desi agreed, frowning at her beloved favorite son. "I'm serious. You shouldn't play games when it comes to love, Petey."

He scoffed, retreating to the sink with his empty plate. "Geez, y'all are a bit…much. Come on, Dad. Help a guy out here, huh?"

"What did you tell me earlier?" I pretended to recollect. "Oh yeah. Just go with it."

Violet dragged her nettled gaze from her mother to enjoy Petey's comeuppance. I thought, not for the first time, what a pretty young woman she'd become. The thought made me miss my friend, Dean, who would have loved nothing more than to be gathered around this table now, eating bream and playing silly shower games. "Have you been out to Osprey Lake, Violet?" I asked.

"She's too cool to hang out with her mother, Lenny." Robin carefully considered her daughter. "But I understand. It's an exciting time, and the girls enjoy hanging out together at Micah's."

"I'm here today, aren't I?" Violet snipped. "Although I was hoping to see Buford. Unfortunately, my mother dropped him off at the sheriff's. A play date of some kind, I suppose."

Taken aback by Violet's unqualified censure, I exchanged glances with Desi, who looked to Robin for direction.

"Buford and Gerty enjoy each other's company," Robin said. "I don't see the harm in it."

"Yeah, well." Petey swiped his phone, coughing awkwardly to break the tension. "I'll probably stay with Luke a few days, Mom. Maybe I can give him some pointers, keep him from being a total dork. If that's possible."

Robin's phone buzzed to the tune of "Take It To the Limit" by the Eagles. "Oh, it's the caterer. You want to talk to her?" She handed her phone to Desi, who stood and began to pace while speaking in an animated voice.

"Thank goodness you found someone," I said quietly to Robin.

"I can't believe Desi was going to try to do all the food herself. Carly, this lady from Naryville, will come out to the Recreation Center the night before the wedding and start setting everything up." We watched as Desi carried the phone into the office, moving her hands as she spoke. "She'll prep the food the next day, and all Desi will have to do is enjoy the night. She even said she'd be willing to help out for the rehearsal dinner."

"What's wrong with Mom?" Petey marked me with a serious look. Then turned to Robin. "What's going on? I'm serious."

"She's fine, Petey," Robin said. "Right Lenny?"

Unwilling to contradict Robin, I nodded, "Yeah. She's fine."

But when Desi returned from the office, she looked anything but fine. Tears seeped from her eyes, and she raked her hands through her hair in distress.

"Aunt Desi," Violet rushed over, covering her in concern.

"I just—I just can't do this."

I watched, helpless and heartbroken, as my wife slid to the floor in despair.

As usual, Robin took her place next to Desi on the couch, leaving me to perch on the hearth of the fireplace. I stared helplessly while Violet bookended Desi's other side, and Petey hovered on the arm of a chair.

"Drink this." Robin pushed a glass of sweet tea into Desi's hand. "Drink. Don't just hold it."

"I'm fine. I'm just tired—"

"Why?" Petey asked. "Why are you so tired?"

Too late to protect him from his boorish misstep, I shrank deeper into my neutral position on the hearth, dreading what would come next. Detecting the warning in my posture, Petey called on his infectious charm to save his hide. "I mean, besides all the wedding stuff, of course. Have you been to a doctor? Are you sick?"

Nicely done, son.

"I'm fine. I'm emotional, is all. And I'm sure it's nothing other than…" She and Robin traded looks. A second passed and Violet nodded in accord.

Petey and I remained completely mystified.

"Other than what, Mom? I don't get it." Good for Petey, taking one for the team.

Robin swiveled, and spoke to him slowly, elucidating each syllable with care. "It's the change, Peter."

Peter? Robin wasn't playing; she'd resorted to using his proper name to express her disappointment in him.

"The what?" Petey floundered on, like a blind hog searching for an acorn.

"It's the change of life, Uncle Lenny." Violet directed her remark to me, evidently determining Petey too thick headed to grasp the situation. "It's hormonal. It's especially difficult for women."

Petey nodded. "Oh." But I doubted he had a clue. When he muttered, "Oh," a second time, I was sure of it.

"She'll be fine." Robin massaged Desi's shoulder. "But Desi, seriously, a doctor could help find ways to alleviate some of the—symptoms. You don't need to suffer like this."

"It's an emotional time." Desi's voice grew thick. "I love Bella, I really do. It's just my baby is getting married, and I'm thinking, *well, that's it, then. What's next?* And then I think, *not much.*"

"Mom," counseled Petey, "I know the odds aren't good, but someday there's gonna be a guy dumb enough to marry Micah. Don't give up."

"I miss Sunny. And Harry. And I feel so alone…" Desi began to cry.

I dropped my head, her words stabbing me with guilt as they shined a light on my shortcomings as a husband. I didn't have time to dwell on my ineptitude though, because now Robin had dissolved in tears along with Desi, as she too had lost both her parents. "They should be here," Desi cried. "It's not fair."

When Violet cut her eyes markedly at Petey, he hopped up, wavering between the cluster of crying women and the safe zone beside me on the hearth.

Someone's phone rang then, breaking the emotional moment. "Oh, shoot," Desi groused through tears. "I was supposed to get the venue information for Carly. I need to look it up. Violet," she pointed to her office, "would you get my laptop?"

Violet hurried to retrieve the computer. As Robin answered the phone and chatted with the caterer, Desi opened her laptop. And burst into tears. She backed away a few inches, twisted her head this way and that.

"What now?" Petey muttered.

"Robin." Desi's hands flew to her face. "My computer. It doesn't even recognize me. It won't let me in."

Robin twisted the pocket of her sweater, retrieving a tube of lipstick. "Here honey, try this."

And then the two dissolved in laughter. Full on cackling. It was truly a sight to see. As Petey and I exchanged looks of relief, Desi and Robin bent their foreheads together the way they'd done in high school.

I fought back a tear of my own then.

As I headed back to Lenny's Tool Shed to help Micah close for the day, I turned right at the four-way stop. Business seemed to be thriving at JJ Wheeler's tent, while Charlie Wayne's numbers were dismal. Meaning—he had none.

The bad-tempered Charlie Wayne glowered from his order window while JJ struggled to keep up with the line forming around his grills. The grinning loon extended his spatula in mid-air and waved as I drove by.

Again, something about the folks in line nagged me. Different ages, sizes, and colors, dressed in everything from shorts to hoodies to cargo pants, and yet there was something, or someone, that sent a shiver of foreboding straight through me. I simply couldn't shake the idea that I was missing something.

The thought vanished as soon as I turned into the store and saw a couple of kids hop off the big, blue chair. They scampered toward the post office with their phones dangling at their sides. "Unreal," I muttered as the door chimed behind me.

"I brought you some fish." I placed Desi's to-go plate next to the cash register. "Micah?"

"I'm back here." She munched on a Snickers bar while moving a pressure washer on aisle seven. "We're going to have to reorder a few of these. Big Al and Thaddeus bought two last week, and Sprite came in this afternoon and bought another. He sure was chatty."

"He's quite the conversationalist when he's sipping his Sprite."

"Yep. Buzzing with his daily dose of sugar and soda."

I tilted my head toward the food. "Violet caught some fish in the lake this morning. Mama fried 'em up, saved you some."

She nibbled a tiny bite off the candy bar. "Naw. I'm on a diet."

Unlike Petey, I practiced the ole less is more approach when it came to needling Micah. I kept my mouth shut and moseyed to the cash register to peruse the day's sales. "Wow. You've been busy." I smiled as she strolled over and rested her head affectionately on my shoulder. "I agree with you about the pressure washers. Let's order a few more."

"Told ya," she teased. "I have another suggestion. Why don't we offer name brand coffee? I spoke to a vendor today. He said they'd come and set up a coffee bar for free. Wouldn't that be great? We'd kill it."

I hesitated, puzzled by the way promotion had changed over the years.

"Whatever." Micah let out an elaborate sigh. "If you want to stay in the dark ages, I won't make any more suggestions."

I considered her more closely, recognizing her usual gloom. "What's wrong with you? Did you have a bad morning cleaning teeth?"

"Of course. I always do. I hate cleaning teeth. Plus, I was late because of Bella's dress fitting, and my boss was annoyed. Bella's going to be beautiful though. Her dress is amazing."

"That's what Violet said. She and your mama and Aunt Robin were making…" I shook my head, searching. "Actually, I have no idea what they were making."

"Gift bags for the shower." Micah absently reached for a bag of chips. "I wish I could do fun things like that." Opened the bag, shook it.

"Why don't you head over now? I'm here. I'll close the day out."

She huffed again, setting the chips down. When she leaned into the crook of my arm, I recognized the gesture and pulled her closer to me. "I'm feeling very fragile today, Daddy."

"What's wrong, honey?"

"I don't know. Nothing. Everything."

Again, I decided it was better not to speak until I knew the extent of the matter.

"Mom and I got into it this morning. I called her on the way into Belle Maison after the fitting. She started in on me, telling me how I was the maid of honor, and I should be doing this and doing that."

Micah moved away just enough to peep at me while emphasizing her point. "I was like, 'Mother, I just left the fitting. And I had to get up early to do that, and then I had to go to Belle Maison to clean people's stupid teeth, and now I have to go give

Dad a break at the store.' And then she went on a rant about the *silly* store—"

"Micah, you don't have to come to the store every day."

"I hung up on her. She makes me so mad."

"You shouldn't have hung up on your mother." I stepped away, tried to inject a little sternness into my voice. "Don't ever leave things hanging with your mom like that."

"She's impossible lately, Daddy."

"Micah."

"And something about Aunt Robin—whenever she comes to town, it emboldens her. It's like she knows she's got back up. I can't deal with it."

"Micah."

Finally, she pivoted. Looked at my face.

"You need to cut your mama some slack."

Anger flashed across her face. Disenchantment. "You always side with her."

"I don't." But Micah was right. I did. "There are things you don't understand about your mom. Things about her…relationship with her mom. And—"

"Nana Sunny was the best," Micah said defensively. "I was only a kid when she died, but I remember how cool she was, with her painting and her smoking and drinking. Remember the little drinks with the lemons in them?"

"I do." And just as I'd recalled my friend Dean with such fondness earlier, I now grew melancholy over Sunny, Desi's flamboyant, fun-loving mother.

Always in my corner, Sunny's absolute belief that I was the best suitor to love and cherish her daughter had always been the biggest feather in my cap. Her encouragement bolstered me as I courted the beautiful and soul-stirring Desi.

I peered at Micah, recognizing that same beauty, and that same restlessness. Qualities rooted in Sunny, both my daughter and her mother were strong, fiery women. While Sunny and Desi had both been victimized by the same man, it brought me solace knowing that *he* would be one cross that Micah would never have to bear. However, an unnecessary break from her own mother would be a formidable cross of its own.

"Here's the thing, Micah honey," I began in a fatherly tone, "Sunny and Desi loved each other more than anything. Just as I know you and your mom love each other. I need you to trust me on this when I tell you, you don't ever, ever want to leave anything hanging with your mama. Don't hang up on her. Don't dismiss her. Even if she makes a mistake, don't reject her."

Micah considered me for a long moment, a moment broken only when the door to my silly store chimed. Before I turned, I repeated, "I'm serious, Micah. It's important."

"Lenny." Sheriff Rick's loud voice boomed behind me. "We need to talk."

Chapter Eleven

Shower Games
Meadow

Sunday

The day of reckoning was at hand. In my mind, I chanted my mantra like a prayer, *Pretend. Act. Pretend. Act.*

Pretend to be happy, pretend to be overjoyed about the upcoming ceremony, pretend to adore the mayor of Shady Gully.

Act like you've dreamt of this day for years, act like you and your beautiful daughter, Bella, are besties.

Pretend. Act. Pretend. Act.

I can put on a good show for a few hours, I thought, *even if my daughter cringed at the very sight of me.* Perhaps…and the notion was weighty…but perhaps *she* was reciting *her* own mantra: *pretend you aren't embarrassed by your mother. Act like you aren't ashamed of everything she represents.*

Pretend. Act. Pretend. Act.

Cruella Claire had recounted the events of the Cozy Corner hullabaloo so many times I almost regretted not being there. Almost. And that was only because seeing Duchess run off with the scandalous barbecue while the rest of Shady Gully looked on in envy would have been wonderfully entertaining.

Still, I'd paid for skipping the shindig, as Bella had skulked home in an exaggerated pout, and only to gather a few changes of clothes and toiletries.

She'd addressed me with a derisive scoff. "Where are my baby pictures? Or did you even bother to keep any over the years?"

I'd pointed at the end table in the living room, indicating the pull-out shelves. She'd hurriedly rifled through the photos, her face softening here and there. I'd forced myself to remain still, indifferent, although I'd longed to know which images had moved her to sentimentality.

After pocketing a few photos, Bella had crammed the box back into the end table drawer. "I'll be at Uncle Wolf's."

"I thought you were staying with Micah?"

"I am. I go back and forth." Her body had pivoted gracefully, and her long, dark hair swished as she'd walked out the door.

Afterwards, I'd sat quietly for several minutes, listening for the sound of Luke's truck. The angry squeal of tires indicated she'd been alone, as Luke would never drive so recklessly. For some inexplicable reason, this of all things, endeared him to me.

Luke was steady and reserved. Stable. Nothing like Mitch, who'd always been driven by his need to control and his random emotional outbursts. *So much for marrying someone like Daddy,* I thought.

When I was sure Bella had gone, I removed the box of photos from the end table drawer. At the top of the stack, I found several of me. Feeding her, holding her on my lap, dressing Barbie dolls while she watched beside me, wide-eyed and enchanted.

I mechanically replaced the lid on the box and returned it to the drawer. I tried not to fixate on why she'd only taken photos of my mother—her Mamaw Peony—and her beloved Uncle Wolf.

And why she hadn't taken a single one of me.

As I pulled into the Shady Gully Recreation Center the sun shone brightly to match the festivities. I immediately felt underdressed as a covey of girls Bella's age fluttered about in spring-toned dresses.

Even the sound of my clunker car seemed inappropriate and

obtrusive. I congratulated myself on bothering to take the spinning dome light off.

I tucked my red blouse into my black slacks, which had wrinkled on the drive, and swiped away a few strands of hair that had escaped my ponytail. No doubt Bella would wince at the sight of me. If not for the brief glimpse of the determined Fireman through the recreation center's full-length windows, I'd have turned and fled. But the heartbroken tyke was trying, thanks in part to Luke's shaggy-haired brother, so I had no choice but to push on.

I retrieved the small gift from the backseat and headed inside with a dreadful feeling in the pit of my stomach. Upon entering, a hostess asked my name, and directed me to the designated banquet room. Surprised to see a number of other events taking place, I marveled at the success of the thriving venue. "Right this way," the peppy hostess urged.

We passed a cozy bar where jingling glasses mixed with the sound of indistinct sports humming from a flat screen at the center of the room. "That's the Magnolia Bar," the young woman said over her shoulder. "The Azalea Room is just past this hallway. It's my favorite. Wait till you see the gorgeous views of the pond."

"Uh huh." I continued to gawk at the interior of Luke's ambitious community center. The kid's imagination erupted in the form of massive chandeliers hanging from twenty-foot ceilings. Five-inch crown molding festooned both the floors and the tops of the walls, and elaborate wainscoting adorned the main foyer.

Gorgeous murals drew the eye throughout the venue, and dapper hostesses with smiles plastered on their shiny faces dashed about with purpose. "Is this the first time you've seen it?"

"Uh. Yeah. From the inside."

"We're shutting everything down for Luke's wedding. His party will have the whole place to themselves."

"Oh. Well, the bride is my—"

"There you are!" Fireman, bursting with excitement, rushed over as he pushed a cart of glassware toward the Azalea Room.

Dressed in black vest and trousers like the rest of the staff, it appeared as if he'd taken Luke's brother's advice to a fanciful level.

"Look at you." I shook my head, astonished.

"I'll show her the way, Candace." He turned to the hostess. "I got you covered."

"Oh, bless you, cutie pie. You're our superhero today." As she pinched his cheek, he leaned into her with a widening smile.

I raised my eyebrow, noting the way he watched her back side as she returned to the greeting station. I straightened his deep purple bowtie. "Come on, *cutie pie*, let's get this over with."

I trailed behind his jangling cart of champagne glasses and assorted juices until we reached a massive double door embellished with elaborate carvings of azalea trees, gray wolves, and other foliage and wildlife unique to the region.

"Here you go." When Fireman opened the doors the sounds of giggling women of various ages hit me like a Mack truck. "What can I get you to drink?"

"Huh?" I looked at him oddly.

"Heyyyyyy, there you are!" A beautiful auburn-haired young woman wearing a pink dress rounded on Fireman and planted a wet kiss on his forehead. "Did they have—?"

"Watermelon." He proudly held up the juice. "Yes."

Several of the girls grew excited as Fireman unloaded the cart of champagne and juice, carefully lining the bottles along a banquet table decorated with pink, purple, and lavender flowers.

"Y'all have to try this," the young woman insisted as she instructed Fireman and the other male server how to mix the watermelon concoction into bubbling glasses of champagne.

"I think I'd rather have a regular mimosa," said Micah.

Fireman garnished a few of the glasses with precisely cut slices of watermelon and presented them to the women with a twist and a flourish. As he began mixing a mimosa with orange juice and champagne, Robin, Desi's pal and always the boss-lady, appeared stern. She took the bottle of champagne away from Fireman. "You're only allowed to pour the juice."

"Just put the bottle of champagne on the table," a shapely blonde suggested. "We'll do that part." As the young women dissolved into a rambunctious sequence of giggles, a high-blush spread across Fireman's cheeks.

The room smelled heavenly, bursting with the scent of bacon, spicy cheeses, and a variety of peppers. My stomach rumbled at the sight of the golden frittatas resting in warmers. Usually, my breakfast came in the form of a bar that tasted like packed compost. Despite my ambivalence over being present today, my appetite perked at the sights and aromas of the elaborate smorgasbord before me.

While Fireman poured juice and filled our plates with frittatas, I expanded my assessment beyond the food in the room. Before I had a chance to process much, I fielded an incoming mother-in-law to be and her loyal sidekick, Robin.

"Meadow, I'm so glad you're here," Desi almost sang. "How do you think everything looks? We tried to tie in the wedding colors with the violets and pinks—"

"It's beautiful," I said quickly, hoping to nip the wedding talk in the bud. Never mind that it was a bridal shower.

"How about a mimosa?" asked Robin. Serious. Matter of fact.

"Sure. I'll take one of those watermelon concoctions."

Desi surveyed the room, as if checking the measure of everyone's joy. Pleased with the levels, she turned back to me. "They're something, aren't they?"

I spied my daughter, certainly something, with her hair tied up in lavender ribbons and her head bent toward Micah's and Violet's. My daughter's face never ceased to astound me. How many times I'd been hurt over something she'd said, some slight that had crushed my heart and stolen my sleep for weeks, and then just like that she'd walk in, and my wounded spirit would light up at the sight of her beautiful face. My anger and resentment instantly wiped away with the singular curve of her extraordinary, warmly familiar profile.

I tried to catch her eye, suddenly overcome with the magnitude of this season in her life, but she appeared oblivious to my presence. I watched with longing as her face brightened, and she dipped her head back in gaiety over something Micah had said.

"When did young girls, or I should say, young women, become so gorgeous?" Desi mused. "I mean, I look around at all these long-haired, stunning females, and I don't remember ever looking like that."

Robin approached, handing me the watermelon mimosa. I took a long sip, which was actually more like a swig, but Desi didn't notice as she was too busy ogling the hotties. Feeling suddenly spontaneous, the fizz of the champagne churning in my stomach, I decided to try. I'd do it for Bella. Hopefully, she'd notice my effort. "Well, we didn't have YouTube back then, so we never learned how to put make-up on like that."

Robin fixated on her own daughter, Violet, and smiled wistfully. "Remember when Sunny did makeovers on us, Desi?"

"Yes. I can still smell the wet paint from her *Battle of Waterloo* painting."

They turned to each other then, connecting without words, leaving me adrift and awkward as I tried to decipher the nuances and language of their intimate history.

"Okay, ladies! It's time to play games." Micah hurried everyone to the long banquet table, insisting Bella position herself at the center. "You sit here. We want to look at you when you answer these questions."

Everyone laughed uproariously, while I remained clueless as to these games they spoke of with sly winks and barely contained snickers. I didn't like games. And I didn't like answering questions. This bridal shower had suddenly taken a bad turn.

Fireman, still blushing with pleasure over the abundant female attention, continued to set plates of fruit and warm frittatas in front of each of us. When Violet settled herself next to me, I swallowed back a wave of panic. Still haunted by my mortifying true confession, I found it hard to maintain eye contact with the dignified young woman.

"Hello, Meadow." Violet had donned a little makeup for the occasion, and the pale pink lipstick she wore complemented her porcelain complexion beautifully. She wore her hair in what I'm sure was meant to be a tight, no-nonsense bun, but by now it had loosened, transforming errant strands of hair in a way that only enhanced her stunning bone structure. "How are you?" Taken in by her easy and kind demeanor, I tried to put my shame and humiliation aside. "I thought you'd want to see this." She leaned in with her phone. "I took a picture of Bella's dress at the fitting."

As Micah passed out cards for the guests, I gaped at the image in front of me. Bella, standing atop a pedestal in a glowing white wedding dress. A little sound escaped my throat as I poured over the picture, intent on memorizing each and every detail.

"I'll send it to your phone," Violet said knowingly.

I nodded, incapable of pulling my gaze away. When I finally lifted my head, I saw Bella's blue eyes zero in on my own green ones, probing expectantly. I mouthed, "Beautiful."

My daughter smiled at me, and for just an instant, I saw a flash of that dark-haired little girl watching in awe as her mother dressed Barbie dolls.

"Okay, let's see how well we know the bride." Micah read from a card, "First one. Is she a dog or a cat person?"

"She's a dog person." Fireman piped from behind the serving station. "She likes cats too, but dogs are her jam." His remark evoked a round of laughter from the ladies.

"Correct." Micah checked off her card. "This one is going to be tougher. Who knows where Bella and Luke went on their first date?"

"Ooh! Ooh!" yipped a few of the girls. "I know."

"They went into Belle Maison for dinner at the fancy Italian restaurant." This from the auburn-haired girl. "I don't remember the name of it though."

"No, I don't think so." Desi cocked her head at Bella. "That's not right, is it?"

Bella shook her head, prompting the assembly to fire off a

number of other possibilities. I realized, rather regrettably, that I had no clue as to the whereabouts of my daughter's first date with her betrothed.

"I have the correct answer right here." Micah teased everyone with the card. "Y'all keep guessing."

Fireman strolled to the table, topping off the blonde's mimosa with a swish of orange juice. After setting a fresh bottle of champagne on the table, he turned to Bella. "I know the answer. You want me to tell them?"

She chuckled, clearly enjoying the attention.

"They had a picnic right here," Fireman said. "Back when it was Cicada Stadium. Afterwards they shared a romantic stroll down Hummingbird Trail." As the shower girls exclaimed over Fireman's awesome intel, he looked quite pleased with himself. Bella winked at him in the affirmative.

"Really?" demanded the blonde, shocked. "*Humph.* Well, I guess the date went well seeing as how Luke turned it into this amazing Recreation Center."

Hearty cackles abounded, including from Desi and Robin, who toasted one another.

"What is her least favorite chore?" Micah flipped the card.

"Washing dishes," Fireman muttered again while dawdling at the table.

"That's correct! Okay. Let's switch to bride and groom trivia." Micah pointed us to another card. "What's the groom's dream car?"

Fireman peered over Violet's shoulder, mumbling as he added fresh strawberries to her plate. "Probably a minivan. Or maybe one of those dorky smart Fortwo cars.."

Violet and I chuckled aloud, entertained by Fireman's participation. Whatever was fueling his gregarious remarks—whether it was a spike in testosterone or stolen sips of champagne—the kid was having a ball.

"Look at this one." Violet indicated the game card. "Who says they're sorry first? The bride or the groom?" She squinted across the table, mystified. "How in the world would we know that?"

The auburn-haired girl leaned over for the champagne bottle, a stray ringlet attractively framing her face. "My boyfriend always says he's sorry first. I taught him that early in our relationship."

Everyone laughed, and Robin nodded her agreement. "Same here, and that's as it should be."

Although Violet's horrified muttering got lost amid the gaggle of giggles, I heard it loud and clear. When I sneaked a glance at her, she'd locked hard onto her mother, full of disapproval.

"Where are they going on their honeymoon?" Micah again.

"Oh, I know," piped Desi. "They're going to Santa Fe!" The party clapped and cheered with enthusiasm as the mother-of-the-groom got a correct answer.

I dropped my head, studying the remnants of my eggs, hoping no one expected anything of me. It occurred to me I knew none of these things about my daughter. Not her least favorite chore, her honeymoon plans, or even the confidences of her relationship with Luke.

I felt like an imposter. An interloper. I shouldn't be here, mingling with Bella's people. Her friends and future family. I belonged on The Creek, where I could nurse my hurt alone. I cleared my throat and tried to smile at Violet. "I'm going to the ladies' room."

But Violet hadn't heard me, as she was so focused on her mother's long-winded and overly animated story about the sheriff. Or *Ricky*.

After I gulped the last of my mimosa, I rose from the banquet table. Focusing on my escape, I headed straight for the heavy wooden double doors of the Azalea Room. They magically parted as a shiny staff member opened them for me, and I was at once grateful to be free of the chatter and the noise.

I fumbled unsteadily along the wainscoted hall, scanning each nook and cranny for a sign that promised a restroom. I made a wrong turn and nearly crashed into a waiter who carried a tray of cheese and stuffed mushrooms to the Magnolia Bar.

"Sorry. So sorry."

"Geez lady," he frowned. "Watch where you're going."

My feelings hurt, and his ridicule adding to my pain, I set off again, desperate to flee.

"Excuse me," I gestured to Candace, the hostess at the entrance, but she was distracted as another party clustered around her desk.

Tears now came, unbidden, and I could feel myself unraveling. I swiped angrily at my eyes, mortified to see mascara staining my red blouse. I kept my head low, focusing on my wrinkled black slacks, hoping my wobbly legs would carry me to a safer place.

Not paying attention, I turned a corner too quickly—and ran straight into him.

I gasped aloud as his hands gripped my shoulders. Our eyes met. This man who'd upended my life when I'd been a mere child. This man who'd lied to my face, his blue eyes teasing with mischief and false promise. This man who'd skipped town, leaving me to fend for myself. And for his child.

Leaving me, a young, naïve woman from across the creek, right in the middle of Shady Gully's biggest scandal.

Selfish. Liar. User. Cheater.

I wrapped my arms tightly around Mitch, vowing to never let him go again.

Finally, he'd come to rescue me.

Chapter Twelve

Shower Wars
Violet

Naturally, I'd jumped at the chance to be seated next to Bella's mom, Meadow. Partly because she'd confided in me about her tumultuous relationship with Bella, but also because I thought that together, we could raise the art of deflecting attention to a whole new level.

I couldn't explain it, but I felt an affinity with the exotically beautiful woman. Like me, she'd come to the table with some solid baggage. While my luggage was perfectly vacuum-packed and stowed-away, and I had Micah, Bella, and Aunt Desi in my corner—Meadow had no one.

Sure, it was true that Micah and Bella sometimes tended to forget their wallflower of a friend—especially at social gatherings because that's where *they* shined—but Aunt Desi always, always, had my back. Always.

Except now. Now that she had her own metaphoric backpack weighted across her shoulders…and was seated on the opposite side of the table next to my mother.

Despite the lack of back-up, my overall shower forecast was sunny once I'd realized the ever-alluring Tammy Jo would not be present. Upon seeing Petey's text, I'd wrestled with resentment and confusion, and half-expected—feared—that I'd have to face her today. Whether she'd been invited or not, I didn't know, and I refused to ask.

The entertaining and bright-eyed boy from across the creek

had kept things lively for a while, but unfortunately, those stupid, and ridiculously intimate bridal game questions had led my mother into territory unbecoming.

She'd called him *her boyfriend*. The very words sent a shiver of revulsion up my spine. Not only was she way too old to have a…*boyfriend*…but her talking about it like it was *normal* was appalling. And gross.

And even worse, it dishonored my father.

As soon as I caught an earful of the disgraceful utterances, I'd nailed her with a defiant glare and practically dared her to continue. Apparently, she was oblivious to my disgust because she'd gushed on. And on. Scarecrow Robin, with her tight, skinny jeans and her perfect bob and her—good gracious—her *purple* glasses. What was she trying to prove anyway? Who was she trying to be?

Unable to snap out of my fury-fueled daze, I'd hardly noticed when Meadow excused herself from the table or when Bella repeatedly called my name. "Violet. Hey, Violet." Once I finally dragged my attention away from my mother, I turned toward Bella.

I heard the concern in her voice. "Where'd my mama go?"

"Oh. She must have gone to the bathroom," I managed.

Bella, suddenly unsettled, pushed herself from her seat. "I'll just go check on her."

I swiveled back to my bird of a mother, who'd finally stopped her adolescent ramblings. "So, he what now?" Bella's blonde friend continued to push. "What did he say about your cats being friends?"

"Oh, it's nothing." Mama hesitated, my outrage finally sinking in. "I'll tell you later."

Somewhere in the room I heard Micah clear her throat, and finally, *finally*, Aunt Desi came up behind me and placed her hands along my shoulder. "Come with me, sweet Violet. I could use some company while I powder my nose."

I stood and followed Aunt Desi out of the Azalea Room.

And that's when we heard the shrieks. And the crying. And the unmistakable sound of Bella's voice.

"Daddy!" She half cried; half screamed. "Daddy!"

"Uncle Wolf!" Bella howled. "What are you doing here?" And then her voice began to waver, taking on a pleading tone. "Daddy, wait! Don't go."

When the man known as Mitch tore down the hall of the Shady Gully Recreation Center and in the direction of the kitchen, Bella gave chase. The lavender ribbons that had been so carefully tied into her hair now drooped loosely along her back. I watched as one coasted to the floor as she disappeared behind the flapping kitchen doors. All the while her Uncle Wolfheart remained heavy on her heels.

The sheriff, who I hadn't seen until now, turned toward my mom. "Are you okay? Is everybody okay?" He lingered a moment before peeling off in the direction of the swinging kitchen doors.

"What's going on, Mama?" Micah cast a covert glance my way as she moved toward Aunt Desi. "Is he dangerous?"

"No, honey." Aunt Desi grabbed her up in a tight hug. "I don't…I don't think so."

"But how would we know?" my mother asked, wide-eyed. "We haven't seen Mitch in decades."

Aunt Desi scanned the girls from the shower, urging them to a bench in the hall along with Micah. "Why don't y'all all sit down?" She propped Micah next to Meadow, who was already on the bench, looking a little shell-shocked. "Everything is going to be just fine."

Meanwhile, my mother steered young Fireman toward the shower guests. "Would you look after them?" Appealing to his newfound magnanimity, she squeezed his shoulder. "Maybe they'd like some water?"

Just as I moved toward Meadow, who looked close to teetering off the edge of the bench, the kitchen doors burst open.

"He's gone." Uncle Lenny emerged. "He disappeared into the woods behind the pond."

"Lenny!" exclaimed Aunt Desi. "What in the world?"

I wondered, quite randomly, where all the men had suddenly come from. Had they all been lurking in the Magnolia Bar? Just waiting for the bridal shower to erupt in tears and chaos? "Quietdove and Max are on the way," Uncle Lenny said. "And Ricky's lining up some dogs. Hopefully they'll pick up a scent."

"I don't understand," muttered Meadow. "Why are they after him? He didn't do anything wrong."

Several sets of eyes lowered in tandem. Micah and I traded looks. The awkward silence only broke when Luke crashed through the entrance to the center with Petey and Sterling close behind.

"She's fine, son," Uncle Lenny said. "She's with Wolfheart and the sheriff."

"What happened?" Luke surveyed the wide-eyed faces around him, zeroing in on Meadow. Innately decent, Luke knelt at Bella's mother's feet, and spoke in soothing tones.

"Are you alright?" Petey closed in on me, his hazel eyes full of concern. *Or not.*

I bit back a flair of annoyance as he appeared to look past me. *Checking for Tammy Jo, I suppose.* "I'm fine."

As the sound of Bella's weeping echoed off the high ceilings, we all turned toward the kitchen, where Wolfheart gently led her into the hall. Luke jumped up and rushed into the arms of his bride-to-be.

Most of us averted our eyes during their poignant embrace, except for Fireman who walked in with an arm full of bottled waters.

"Reinforcements are coming," said the sheriff as he ambled in from the kitchen. The sound of pots and pans behind him confirmed that the kitchen staff had returned to their duties. "Does anybody need medical attention?"

Most of the heads in the hall swiveled toward Meadow.

Wolfheart moved toward his niece then, his gait intentional, quiet, with long purposeful strides. I'd always wondered about this man from The Creek. Mysterious, and handsome in an edgy kind of way, his dark hair brushed just below his collar. His demeanor screamed irreverent and nonconformant, the contrast sharp against Uncle Lenny's and the sheriff's buttoned up, conservative appearances.

Bella's weeping stopped at the sight of her uncle comforting her mother. "What did you do?" She stalked over to the bench and glared down at her mother. "You always ruin everything!"

"Bella," Luke urged softly, reaching for her elbow.

"No!" She shook off his touch, closing in on Meadow. "You ruined your life, and now you're trying to ruin mine. You chased him off, didn't you?"

"I didn't chase him off," Meadow said through gritted teeth. "He ran away because he saw someone he knew." Meadow pivoted, tagging the sheriff in accusation.

"We got a few reports that he'd been seen around town," the sheriff countered. "We were trying to keep a close, but respectful distance."

"See." Meadow tilted her chin defiantly. "It was *his* fault, not *mine*. But I'm sure you'll believe Barney Fife over me."

"Hey now," Sheriff Rick appeared wounded. "That's a little harsh."

"I wish you hadn't even come today." Bella folded her arms, her body tight with anger as she addressed her mother. "You blew everything! I've been planning this for weeks—"

"Bella." One word, spoken softly from Wolfheart. "I think you need to stop there."

Bella groused. But stopped.

"If anyone ruined this day for you, it was me." Wolfheart didn't seem hurried or emotional. "I apologize. Perhaps all this was set in motion years ago." He paused, as if considering the consequences of his impending remarks. "I've always thought what Mitch did was reprehensible, so when I heard he might be in town, I"—he cut his eyes toward the sheriff—"*we* decided to keep a close watch on you. We thought he might have come because of the wedding."

"What?" Meadow, incredulous, wheeled on her uncle. "How could you? You had no right. And who are you to say it was reprehensible?"

Wolfheart considered her for a long moment. "You were fourteen. He was the guidance counselor. I'm sorry, Meadow, but I can't think of a better word."

"You had no right." Meadow's hands shook. "Do you have any idea how long I've waited…" Her words slowed. Stopped.

Suddenly interested, Sterling drew closer to the conversation. "Were charges ever filed?" he asked. "Because even if they were, the statute of limitations has expired by now, so realistically, what could be done?"

"Right," Bella added, emboldened. "Exactly."

"I did what I thought was best," Wolfheart said somberly. "And just."

"Well, you shouldn't have. I know you were just trying…but you should have left it alone." Bella teared up, emotional as she moved closer to her uncle, all the while avoiding eye contact with her mother.

Steps sounded from the main foyer of the recreation center as Deputies Quietdove and Max—who was my mama's youngest brother—turned the corner. "Sheriff," Quietdove said, as Uncle Max acknowledged me with a raised eyebrow.

"Enlighten me." Sheriff Rick scrutinized them.

"We've got a team scouring the woods behind the pond. And the substation in Toulouse should be here with a few of their best dogs in"—he glanced at his watch—"fifteen minutes."

"Great. Let's prepare."

"I don't believe this," Meadow said, newly heated. "You have no right to do this. To hunt for him like he's an animal."

Sheriff Rick eyed both Meadow and Bella. "I just want to talk to him."

Uncle Lenny spoke matter-of-factly. "I'm sorry, Meadow. Bella. I don't trust him."

Desi raised her hand. "Neither do I."

"I'm sorry, Meadow." Mama nodded her agreement. "What would it hurt to have Ricky—the sheriff—have a talk with him?"

"Outrageous," Meadow muttered.

"Finally." Bella swiped a tear. "Something we agree on."

"We'll just have a conversation. In the meantime, I need you to let us know if he tries to make contact." Sheriff Rick dipped his hat with emphasis. "If you hear or see him at all, call us immediately. Okay?"

"He's not dangerous," Meadow said, her expression flat.

"Regardless, this wasn't the welcome he'd hoped for." The sheriff scanned the room. "And just for the record, I don't trust him either."

Meadow wobbled a little as she rose and moved toward the exit.

My heart lurched in empathy. Misguided as she was, she didn't deserve any of this. "Are you…" I asked. "Are you okay to get home? We can drive you—"

"Yes. I'm fine."

Quietdove offered. "I'll have a car follow you, just in case. How about that?"

Meadow sighed, resigned.

Before he and Max peeled off with Meadow in tow, Quietdove flashed at Micah, who stood next to Fireman.

"We've got plenty of daylight. We should have him by the afternoon." The sheriff turned his attention to Bella. "But I'd be mighty interested in knowing what you had planned, Miss Bella. It might help aid our investigation."

"I don't want to help your investigation."

"Come on, Bella. Enlighten me."

Luke, the mayor of Shady Gully, now found himself in the unfathomable position of being caught between the sheriff of his town and his fiancée. "Let's leave it rest for now, Sheriff."

Aunt Desi traded looks with my mother. "Come on, girls. And guys. We could use some help carting all the gifts to the cars." She turned to Uncle Lenny, kissing him on the cheek. "If you're going with the sheriff and Wolfheart, be careful. You're not as young as you used to be." She looked at Wolfheart. "Look out for him."

Uncle Lenny scoffed, and I got my second wink of the day.

"We'll box some of the frittatas," Aunt Robin said. "For leftovers tonight."

"Frittatas?" Petey grinned, trying to lighten the mood. "Oh man, did they put green chilis in them? And Monterey jack?" He nudged me, his playful, sheepish expression happy and bright. "Come on, Ebony. You know you can't resist."

And I couldn't. Petey's lighthearted optimism and hope tugged at me. Soon my annoyance with my mother faded, as did my concern for Bella and Meadow, and even my jealousy over Tammy Jo.

Long after the frittatas were eaten, and the gifts were unloaded at Luke's apartment, Micah, Bella, and I settled around her plug-in fireplace in our jammies and sipped chardonnay.

"Not the way I pictured my bridal shower." Bella looked forlorn. "The sheriff is hardcore."

"I think he's just concerned," Micah ventured. "I mean…"

"What?" Bella frowned. "I can't believe you're siding with him."

"I'm not siding with him—"

"I trusted you with this from the very beginning, and now you're acting like you wish they'd snatched my daddy up today and thrown him in jail."

"I am not!"

"He's too smart to get caught." Bella took a large swallow of wine.

"Is it just me?" I asked, attempting to deflect the rising tension. "Or does this fireplace thingy actually heat? It feels nice and toasty in here."

"It's fake. And it's almost summer, so of course it's toasty," Bella snapped. "Just say what you were gonna say, Micah."

"Think of yourself at fourteen. And then think of one of your teachers. Like, Coach Taylor? Isn't he like twenty-five or twenty-six?"

Bella rolled her eyes. "It's not the same."

I saw Micah's point, but refrained from commenting.

"I think he took advantage of your mom, is all. I tried to be supportive of your scheme to get him here, Bella. From the very beginning, you know I backed you up, but I was afraid it was going to end badly." Micah set her wine glass on the coffee table, punctuating her remark.

"Look at it from *my* point of view." Bella directed her argument to me, apparently seeing Micah as a lost cause. "It doesn't really matter what he did to my mother. It had nothing to do with me, really. I mean obviously, I was the result, but…"

"You just wanted to meet him," I said. "I sort of get it." I thought of my dad, and how my life would have been different if I'd never known him. The thought was unbearable.

"I wanted to form my own opinion," Bella said.

Micah picked up her glass. "He committed a crime. And oh, by the way, he was married. Just because Dolly is a witch doesn't make it right. What he did is just all kinds of wrong. That's all I'm saying."

While I agreed with Micah, I felt it necessary to once again change the direction of the conversation. When Bella glared at Micah, I cleared my throat. "How did you find him anyway?"

"It took a long time, which is another reason I'm annoyed with the sheriff." Bella twirled her glass. "I scoured and lurked all over Facebook. Got in good with some people who knew his family. Friended them and got close, and eventually worked up to it."

"Wow." Stunned, and a little inspired by Bella's boldness, I asked, "Did you use a fake account?"

"Yep. It took a long time too. I finally got close to someone who knew his sister, and I learned he'd lived in several states.

Moved around a lot. Arkansas, Texas, and just recently, Alabama." Bella grinned. "Alabama is where I found him."

Micah chuckled, softening. "Dang Bella, if the singing gig doesn't work out, you could be a private investigator." She looked thoughtful. "Come to think of it, maybe I could be one. Might be a fun career move."

Bella grinned, and they clinked glasses. Just like that, the tension evaporated. *Poof.*

"How did your mom not know?" I asked. "Or your Uncle Wolfheart?"

Bella shrugged. "They're not into social media. Uncle Wolf thinks it's the devil and Mama is anti-social, so it was pretty easy. Anyway, when I finally found him, and got his address—"

"You didn't go there, did you?" I asked. "To Alabama?"

"No, but we talked. Well, we messaged on Facebook." Bella looked directly at Micah. "He doesn't sound like a criminal. I really think he's changed. Of course, it doesn't matter now. He's gone, and he'll never trust me again."

"Okay," Micah proposed unexpectedly, "I'll help you find him."

Shocked, I gawked at her in disbelief. *Surely, she wasn't serious.*

"You should be able to meet him, to talk to him," Micah went on. "Without judgement."

Bella beamed. "Really? Are you serious?"

"Yes, but I want your word that if we find him and you meet him, you won't go alone."

"Cross my heart, but we have to keep my mother out of the loop. She'll ruin it all again. She's the one who's unhinged. Not my daddy."

I flinched, suddenly feeling defensive for Meadow. Bella didn't even know her father, but somehow, she found it easier to put the blame on Meadow.

Micah turned her scrutiny on me.

"What?"

She finished her wine. "Are you in? The three of us can be like *Charlie's Angels.* We'll start our own detective agency."

Bella giggled as she and Micah mimed sexy-gun-clutching poses. "I'm Jaclyn Smith. Micah, you can be Farrah."

Micah delighted. "Of course. Who else would I be?"

"Violet can be Kate Jackson since she's the tallest," Bella pronounced, turning to me with flushed cheeks. "What's wrong? Would you rather be Charlie?"

Micah and Bella collapsed in laughter. "Violet is a boss lady." Micah nodded conclusively. "But she has bigger plans. No private detecting for her. And certainly, no cleaning teeth. Or selling hardware."

"And she won't marry a politician," Bella chuckled. "Or sing—"

"She's going to cure cancer," Micah said matter-of-factly. "To honor her father. Aren't you, Violet?" When Micah brushed my leg, I recoiled.

"What?" She looked at me quizzically. "You will. I'm sure of it. I believe in you."

"And she'll win a Nobel Prize." Micah and Bella toasted. They laughed easily together again, and this made me glad.

But they didn't know me at all. They had no idea I was living a lie, or just how I was letting my daddy down…

I was so over people thinking I was so smart and had it all together.

I smiled and raised my glass. "I always liked Kate the best." I stood and struck a pose. "To Charlie's Angels."

We clinked.

Chapter Thirteen

Zombies From The Past
Lenny

Monday

Murky orange slivers of sun peeked through the plantation shutters in our bedroom. Unaccustomed to sleeping in, I rolled over expecting to see Desi snoring softly beside me. Instead I found Mary Ann's head resting on her pillow, one floppy ear bent at an awkward angle. I listened for a moment as soft, steady grunts pulsed from her chunky, cocker spaniel frame.

The sound of Desi's laughter, a rare occurrence these days, filtered down the hallway. On the heels of the laughter, quite literally, was the *clickety-click* of Ginger's steps as she shadowed her favorite person.

"Oh good, you're up." Desi smiled, handing me a cup of coffee. Ginger tracked up the wedged cushion propped against the bed, greeting me with a brief lick before pouncing on Mary Ann. "I thought you were going to sleep all day."

I sat up, chugged a healthy swig of coffee, and winced as it burned my mouth. "You're in a good mood, considering what happened at the shower."

She shrugged, sliding under the covers and scooting both the dogs to the foot of the bed. "Oh, I know. That was terrible. But this," she thrust her phone in my face, "is too good. Check it out."

I reached for my glasses on the night table and took her phone in my hands. And came face to face with JJ Wheeler.

"It's all over Instagram." Desi grinned.

On my big blue chair. Eating barbeque chicken. Mugging for the camera.

"What? It's dark. When did he do this?"

"Sometime during the night. It posted early this morning." She laughed again. While I enjoyed seeing my wife break through her doldrums, I'd have preferred not providing the entertainment. "Oh, come on, Lenny. It's funny. Micah said it's gone viral. Whatever that means."

"Good grief. I'm seriously over this guy. I should get Ricky to arrest him for trespassing."

Desi sipped her coffee, distracted by the comical way Ginger's tongue unrolled like a pink ribbon of candy when she yawned. When the precocious pup realized she had an audience, she twisted beguilingly, awaiting adulation. "He's got enough on his hands with Mitch. Robin texted me early this morning and said the dogs came up with nothing. She said Ricky is furious."

"Is he at Lake Osprey with her?"

"No, but they talked on the phone most of the night. Sterling is with her at the lake house. So, there's no funny business going on, if that's what you're asking."

"I wasn't asking."

"Apparently, since Meadow never pressed charges, there's nothing Ricky can do about Mitch. Legally."

"*Humph.*" I frowned thoughtfully.

"What is it?"

"I thought I saw him. Like around town the last few days." I sighed. "I don't know. I guess I'm getting old and nutty 'cause all of a sudden I'm recognizing—or think I'm recognizing—people from the past. Anyway, I started to say something to Ricky, but since I wasn't sure I didn't want to start a big hullabaloo right before the wedding."

"I can understand." Desi patted my leg. "The scene at the shower was bad enough. And besides, what if you'd been mistaken?"

I nodded pensively, thinking back to a time long ago. "Do you remember how he was in high school?"

"I do," she said. "I hated him on first sight. I thought he was cocky. Robin and I used to call him Macho Mitch."

"Yeah. He was like a rooster, always crowing about something, but he could never back it up. I remember whenever he felt threatened, or was called into question about anything, he'd spook."

"Like when he ran off after he got caught cheating on his wife with a student?" Desi snorted derisively. "And got that student pregnant?"

"Exactly like that." I absently stroked Mary Ann's dangling ears. "Maybe that's Ricky's plan. Wait him out. Spook him a little. Watch him mess up."

"Can you imagine what Dolly is thinking? And Meadow? Poor Meadow." Desi's brow furrowed. "I honestly wonder if it would be better to go ahead and let Bella have some time with him. He *is* her father."

I reached for my phone as it vibrated with a text. "I don't know."

"I just think given time, Mitch would reveal himself for what he is, and that might be the only way for them to ever move on."

I chuckled, returning my phone to the night table. "That was Father Patrick. He wants to *chat a spell*, his words, sometime in the next few days."

"I wonder what that's about."

"You never know with him. He inherited the gift of gab from his Irish ancestors, so it could be anything." Although, the truth was, I sensed an urgency in him lately, and I suspected the desired chat had something to do with those strong Irish convictions more than anything else.

Ginger, not to be outdone by Mary Ann, butted her aside and demanded I move my attention to her itchy ears.

"Brad told me Father Patrick drives the old church van to The Creek a couple of days a week. He likes to chat, but he also likes to inspect the cabernet sauvignon grapes he asked Brad to plant. Remember after Madhawk set his garden on fire?"

"Yep. I'm not surprised. Father does enjoy his fine wines."

"I suppose that's another Irish trait, huh?" Desi flushed.

A jolt of pleasure ran through me as I delighted in my wife's cheerfulness, so rare of late. "He's also giddy over meeting Timothy. I gather he spoke to him on the phone last night." When I scratched the soft fur atop Ginger's head, my knuckles brushed against the tips of Desi's fingers.

"He's like a groupie."

"Honestly, I think he's a little unsettled by the situation in Shady Gully lately. Between the barbeque man—"

"—and the lack of a church at the corner. And Mitch showing up."

"Yep. I suspect he has a plan." My mind raced with questions. And possibilities. "Lord only knows what he and Timothy could come up with if they put their heads together."

"I'm sure the Lord does know, and His plan will be for good."

Today my wife exuded peace and positivity, which filled my heart with hope.

We continued to nuzzle the dogs, until our fingers brushed against one another's one too many times. And then we scooted them off the bed.

As I passed the crazy man at the corner, he waved like a lunatic and rubbed his tummy, posturing like he was taking a selfie. Astounded by the growing line already forming under his tent, my annoyance escalated. Rapidly becoming Team Charlie Wayne, I resolved to rededicate myself to JJ Wheeler's very good riddance.

Besides Micah's car, there were several other vehicles parked in the lot at Lenny's Tool Shed. Patty, Shady Gully's favorite hometown paramedic, waved as she hopped into her car with a medium sized bag, and BlueJay, a friendly old-timer from The Creek, smiled as he trudged to his truck with a cage of fishing crickets and a twine of fishing string.

The store was humming as I entered, so no one noticed the chime. Wolfheart and the sheriff chatted next to the coffee machine, their heads bent together in earnest conversation.

"Are you sure it was him?" asked Ricky. "What would he be doing here after all this time?"

"I'm positive," said Wolfheart. "Saw him with my own eyes."

The sheriff grunted. "Last I heard he was in Texas. This place is going slap-dab crazy here lately. And we got a full moon coming next coupla' nights. Ain't no telling what kind of zombies from the past are gonna turn up then."

"Who?" I asked, pouring myself a cup of coffee. "Y'all talking about Mitch? Did y'all find him?"

Wolfheart and Ricky pulled their heads apart so fast they reminded me of teenagers caught in the beam of headlights on Lovers Lane. The way they each shook their heads confirmed their collusion.

"Who then? Tom?" My pulse quickened at the thought of that pervert galivanting around town, upsetting Desi.

"Not Tom," the sheriff said. "He turns up here and there like a bad penny, usually with Wanda, but I've decided he's not dangerous. In fact, word is he's soon headed for a nursing home in Belle Maison."

"Well, who then? What were y'all talking about?"

"Just…nothing. Probably a mistake." Ricky swigged his coffee and swallowed back a pucker of distaste. "You don't want this slop, Lenny. Micah made it. A danged waste of good water, if you ask me."

I looked pointedly at Wolfheart then, who raised his eyebrows, offering nothing.

They remained cagey, pivoting to Micah and Quietdove, who hung out next to the cash register, snickering and swiping their phones. No doubt getting their giggles at my expense.

The sheriff let loose with a rare grin, increasing my paranoia tenfold. He swiped a taffy from the jar at the register and crammed it into his mouth, no doubt trying to quell the taste of weak coffee. "There's barbecue sauce all over your rocking chair out there, Lenny. What do you reckon that's about?"

I *tsked*. "Something needs to be done about Mr. Man-Bun.

He's becoming an irritant." A swirl of annoyance began to threaten my blissful morning with my beautiful wife. I turned away from the lot of them and picked up a honey bun from the morning platter. I bit into it hungrily, eyeballing them both.

Wolfheart cleared his throat, changing the subject. "I don't think Mitch would be fool enough to go to The Creek, so if he's still here, I'm thinking he's hunkered somewhere close to town."

"Roger that." Ricky popped another grape taffy into his mustached mouth. "Meanwhile, Quietdove and Max have been reaching out to agencies in bordering states. Maybe that'll turn up something. If nothing else, a little insight into what our old classmate has been up to all these years."

"If there's dirt to be found, we'll find it," Quietdove echoed.

"All I need is enough to make an arrest," the sheriff reasoned as he smacked his taffy.

"Daddy," Micah called out, "you want me to load Instagram on your phone? The store has like 600 new followers. And 900 likes. It's going—"

"Viral. Yeah," I huffed. "Your mom told me."

Ricky gestured to Quietdove. "Let's saddle up, QD. We're burning daylight."

"See ya, Micah." Quietdove turned, offering me a pleasant smile. "I'll ask the guys at the fire station to come scrub the chair down for you. They don't have anything to do anyway." I'd always liked the quiet, reserved young man, impressed with the way he handled the occasional razzing from his own community.

He crossed paths with Petey and Violet on their way in, and when he and Petey fell into an amiable discussion about the New Orleans Saints, Louisiana's beloved pro football team, Violet slinked over to Micah. "Hey, Uncle Lenny," she said. "Congrats on the Instagram buzz."

"How's Bella?" Micah asked her.

As she was about to respond, Claire from the post office walked in sporting her latest hair—pink; and nose ring—fleur de lis; and wearing her usual smug expression. Micah moved to help her in the gardening department.

"So," I said to Violet, hoping to get the inside scoop, "Luke should be here soon. Are you excited to go look at land and lots?" She smiled pleasantly, but gave nothing away, and seemed relieved as Petey approached.

"What's up, Dad? You're practically…glowing." Petey chuckled. "I had no idea social media was so important to you."

Luke entered the store, his face pulling in distaste. "Your blue rocking chair is a mess, Dad."

Petey teased his big brother. "What kind of mayor doesn't follow social media? JJ Wheeler picnicked there last night. Didn't you see it on Instagram?"

Luke remained oblivious.

"Facebook?"

Still, Luke's face ran blank.

"Twitter?"

"I don't have time for all that nonsense. I work all the time." Luke launched into his usual diatribe. "The responsibilities and duties of a small-town mayor are underappreciated. I meet with councilman and constituents every day, and—"

"Okay, okay. I got it," Petey conceded. "And I appreciate that you still have time to give your brother a special real estate tour. Thanks, bro." Petey playfully popped Luke in the belly. "Hey, did anybody else get a text from Father Patrick this morning?"

"I did." Luke bobbed his head. "I'm not sure what to make of it. Interesting, huh?"

Both my sons swiveled in my direction. "I got one as well. Who knows? He keeps things lively, that's for sure."

"How's your bride-to-be?" Petey asked his brother as Claire and Micah returned with three potted plants. "Is she feeling any better?"

"Yeah, I think so. We've been hiking with Duchess a good bit lately, and Bella wants to go again before the wedding. Maybe do one along the creek. I think that will cheer her up."

"Who? Duchess or Bella?" Petey teased.

"Both. Anyway, she's looking forward to it." He turned and smiled pleasantly at Claire. "Hiya, Claire. Keeping everybody straight at the post office?"

"Always." She flashed with fake concern. "So sorry to hear about the fiasco at the shower yesterday. That must have been traumatic, huh?"

"It's all fine. Everything's fine," Luke said amiably.

"I couldn't believe Meadow showed up to work today," Claire remarked. "Usually, she calls in for anything. A headache, a hangnail…"

Luke didn't respond. He turned to Micah instead. "Hey, I need to get a heavy-duty harness and a leash for our hiking trip. Duchess hid hers. Again. Or else she ate it."

"That beast. What a troublemaker." Micah handed Claire her receipt and nodded at Luke. "We've got some. I'll have one ready for when y'all get back."

"Where are y'all off to?" Claire asked as she signed her ticket.

"I'm beginning to think that dog is smarter than y'all." Petey smoothly changed the subject.

"She is," answered Luke. "Way smarter. She steals things. Buries them outside. And she figured out how to open the back door yesterday. I came home, and she was lounging in the landscape in the back yard of the duplex."

"Shiba Inus are very smart," Violet said. "She's probably been studying the way you turn the latch and learned how to mimic it."

"Wow." Luke was incredulous. "I'll be more covert when I lock it from now on. Bella will kill me if she gets out and runs off."

"Thanks Claire." Micah waved as Claire reluctantly headed to the door. "Have a good day."

Once Claire was gone, Wolfheart moseyed over with a pack of assorted tea bags. "Impressive. A whole encounter with Claire without giving away state secrets." He paid for the tea. "Thanks for ordering this, Micah. I usually have to go all the way to Belle Maison for my chai. I haven't tried the lemon basil, so I'm looking forward to that."

Petey marveled at Wolfheart. "Can I just say what everybody else is thinking? You are one cool cat."

"And one of my best councilmen," said Luke. "Who I meet with quite often. Isn't that right, Councilmen Wolfheart?"

"Cheers to that." Wolfheart side-eyed me as he turned. "Lenny, you got a minute?"

I left the young ones gathered around the cash register and followed him outside. Shook my head in disgust as I passed the big blue rocking chair. "What's going on? You're not gonna tell me you have Mitch tied up in the swamp somewhere, are you? Using him as alligator bait or something?"

Wolfheart didn't find my joke amusing. "No. I haven't killed anybody in at least a month. I'm doing my best to cut back."

I winced. "Sorry. Bad taste."

Truth was, Brad Wolfheart was a good man with a big heart. Like Meadow, he'd had a rough beginning, and he'd battled demons most of his life. Eventually though, he'd found redemption, and then peace, and finally, he'd changed his ways.

I scrutinized him now, registering some sort of internal debate. "So, are you going to tell me what y'all were talking about?"

He sighed. "Have you seen Dolly lately?"

A dark blue truck rolled into the parking lot, braking to stop a few feet from us. Despite the bed of the truck being chock-full of Sheetrock and other construction material, it looked brand new.

"No. Did something happen with Brother Wyatt? Did he…?"

"No." Wolfheart shook his head. "Not that I know of."

"Howdy." The young man in the truck greeted us on his way into the store. He was over six feet tall and ripped, with a thick head of dark hair and a neatly trimmed beard. His eyes were blue, landing somewhere between kindness and pure mischief.

Once he entered the store, I focused again on Wolfheart. "Why? Do you think she's hiding Mitch?"

"No, I don't think she'd do that."

The spinning dome light atop Meadow's car distracted us. We watched as she slowed at the abominable tent at the corner of the four-way stop and chucked her hand out the window. One of JJ Wheeler's minions ran out a bag of food to her.

"Word is he's actually hiring," Wolfheart mused.

"So, what's up with Dolly?" I asked. "I know that's always a loaded question."

Brad Wolfheart studied me a long moment. His expression disturbed me. Filled me with concern and dread. Finally, he said, "She's got a boyfriend."

The staccato blast of a vehicle's horn drew our attention. Meadow, appearing grim and bothered, pulled into the parking lot."

"What?" Wolfheart called.

She urgently waved him over. "I need to talk to you."

"You better go," I told him. "Sounds important."

He hesitated for an extended moment, and then acquiesced, heading over to the spinning dome lights.

When I walked back into Lenny's Tool Shed, the whole lot of them—Petey, Violet, Luke, and Micah—gawked at the brawny driver of the blue truck. He tracked up and down each aisle of the store. Once done, his intense gaze landed on Micah, perched on a stool behind the cash register.

"May I help you?" she asked with exaggerated sarcasm.

"Apparently not. My friend told me y'all carried lumber here, but I don't see any. What kind of hardware store doesn't have lumber?"

"Who's your friend?" asked Luke, as usual rising to his family's defense…or at the very least, the defense of his father's hardware store.

"Daryl. He works sometimes at the auto body shop on the corner. You know it? Ain't much, but at least it's got what it's supposed to."

"Yeah, I know it," replied Luke. "I'm the owner."

Petey chuckled, reached for a few bags of popcorn on the warmer. He passed a bag to Violet, whose eyes were wide. Meanwhile Micah was spitting fire. I started to speak up, but hesitated, finding the exchange oddly amusing.

"Me and Daryl are old friends. Worked construction back in the day. Said this town was working its way into the current century, so I figured I'd ride on over and take me a gander. Right now, we're working on a remodel for"— he scrolled through his phone— "for a Mrs. Guidry. She wanted to open it up some." He glanced at Micah, who scowled atop her stool. "Guess I'll take a ride to a real town."

"We've got lumber outside by the garden section, Lame Brain," Micah said flatly. "I've got pine, poplar, or redwood. I got 2 x 4s, 4 x 4s, 2 x 10s—" She shrugged, bored. "Everything leading up to a 6 x 6. That good enough for you?"

His grin was as wide as he was tall. "That'll do."

"Well? Which do you want then?"

"Some of each." He flashed. "I like variety."

She sneered. "What kind of carpenter shows up to a job without lumber?"

"I don't know." He laughed. "The boss?"

Petey snorted, cramming popcorn into his face.

"The boss?" asked Luke. "What'd you say your name was?"

"I didn't," the big man replied. "But it's Hoot. Hoot Wheeler. Me and my family hail from Toulouse." He ducked his chin in the direction of the four-way stop. "But my dad said business was good here." He winked at Micah. "So here I am."

Chapter Fourteen

The Sprayer And The Smudged Mascara
Meadow

Uncle Wolf rested his elbows on the opened window of my car door. He stuck his head inside and eyed me over the heaps of mail and packages. "I've never understood how you drive in the middle of the seat like that."

"You get used to it." I opened the bag of food, and the aroma of barbeque chicken swamped the stale, dusty smell of old paper products. "Want some?"

Tempted, Uncle Wolf glanced over his shoulder.

"Lenny went back inside. I won't tell." When my uncle regarded me doubtfully, I added, "I didn't poison it, I swear, but I am seriously angry with you." *And with a lot of people, I thought. Especially my daughter.*

"Have you heard from him? Tell me the truth."

"Why? So you can go tell the sheriff?" I glared at him. "You know, there's nothing he can do. It's been over twenty years. Things are different now. Mitch could even turn around and file charges against you and the sheriff for harassing him." I experienced a sliver of satisfaction when my uncle flinched.

"We…I…would just like to talk to him." His tone was measured. "You were a child, Meadow. He needs to account for himself. For what he did. For where he's been. For his total lack of regard and responsibility and—"

I groaned loud enough to bring his rant to a stop. "No," I said. "I haven't seen him. And I doubt I will. He was ambushed. You and your buddies were waiting for him. He probably thinks I set him up. Or that I put Bella up to it."

"Who cares what he thinks? Did he really expect for Shady Gully to welcome him with open arms?"

I wanted to argue and fight with him. To rail against them all. My uncle, the sheriff, and even Bella. Her betrayal hurt the most. How could she have found her father, which was a miracle in itself, and then arrange to see him behind my back? "There's nothing any of you can do, Uncle. It's time you let it go."

"Just like you have, huh? That's rich coming from you." He regarded me. "This man cut your life off at fourteen. Not because of Bella, but because you chose to stop living after he broke your heart. What he did not only defined your life, Meadow, it stole it."

I fielded the low blow. "Will you just please stay out of it. Give me some space? If he does show up, I don't want to—"

"To what? Miss the chance to get back together with him?" My uncle's green eyes sparked.

"I've waited a long time for this, Uncle Wolf. I never thought I'd see him again."

"You're a fool, Meadow." I watched as he stepped away from the car, paced a little. Prayed his frustration away. Or whatever he did.

"Bella's angry too," I stoked. "Even with you."

He grunted. "Well, I'm glad y'all could finally come together on something." He turned as a big guy with a beard pulled his shiny truck to the back of the garden center, dropped his tailgate. "I just want you to be happy, Meadow. That's all I've ever wanted."

I grumbled, annoyed now that he was trying to make me feel guilty.

Just then Lenny and his sons, along with Robin's daughter, Violet, trekked to Lenny and Desi's luxury van. When Violet waved at me, I was reminded of her compassion at the shower. The shaggy haired apostle with the tattoo called out. "Hey, how's our boy?"

He meant Fireman of course, who was in fact coming to terms

with his unrequited love for Bella. While I still wanted to snap at everyone in my path, I couldn't deny Petey's interesting eyes, his authenticity, and his charisma. "I think he actually has a crush on someone new now," I told him. "Another woman. Older."

He grinned. "He's got goals. That's for sure."

As they piled into the vehicle, I eyed my uncle. "I'd better move my car, so they can get out." His expression had dissolved into one of resignation. Disappointment. *How does he do it*, I wondered? He had a knack for absorbing my anger and wearing it like a badge of honor.

He gestured toward Dolly's Diva Dome just beyond JJ Wheeler's tent. "Of all people, you'd think she has an iron in this fire. I wonder what she thinks about her ex-husband showing up after all these years?" He lifted his shoulders in speculation. "Heck, maybe she wants to get back together with him as well."

The thought horrified me. I hadn't even considered the possibility…

No. Surely not. Especially now with Shady Gully's Rhinestone Cowboy back in town and very much in the mix. "I doubt it," I said with more confidence than I felt. "She's probably got other things on her mind these days. With her dad. And all."

"Indeed." Uncle Wolf moved toward his truck. "I can say this much for Dolly. At least she's moved on."

Another low blow.

One that motivated me.

Determined to use my salty mood to my advantage, I picked up my pace. Just before Sacred Heart Catholic Church, I hung a right and quickly delivered mail in a few trailer parks and modest subdivisions. Once done, I took another right and rolled down Opry Lane. With offshoots like Waylon Road and Willie Road, the area was one of the oldest and most established in Shady Gully.

Dolly lived on The Boys Road in an old brick home. Once

upon a time in Dolly's life, she lived with her husband, Mitch, in the beautiful Piney Lake neighborhood along an awesome lake. Fast forward to the present, and Desi and Lenny lived in the beautiful home by the awesome lake, and Dolly dwelled in an outdated brick house most likely given to her by her parents.

The scandal—my shame—had certainly rocked a few boats. Changed a few lives.

As I put mail into Dolly's mailbox, I scanned the dirt driveway. Sure enough, Adam's big silver truck was parked at a slapdash angle along the side of the house, under the shade of a long-established Bradford pear tree.

After I hurriedly delivered flyers, parcels, and packages to the remaining Opry Lane residents, I worked my way back to the main road. Just as I was about to turn into Sacred Heart Catholic Church, I spotted Lenny and Desi's van parked next to an empty lot on the left. Luke, tall and serious with his belted khakis and tucked-in shirt, looked the part of a Realtor as he pointed this way and that. I watched as Petey's and Violet's gazes traveled the length of his fingers.

Interesting, I thought, but not enough to slow me down. Fortunately, the chipper priest was otherwise occupied, so I easily got in and out with his mail and bulky packages. Finally, I headed back toward the four-way, and set out to hand deliver the day's mail to Dolly's Diva Dome.

My argument, accusations, and grievances on the edge of my breath, I climbed the three steps and entered her salon. Alone in the shop, she had her back to me, and rinsed the shampoo sink with a sprayer.

I cleared my throat, but she didn't turn around, apparently not hearing me. Well, this was awkward. I cleared my throat again and added a cough. Finally, she turned, sprayer in hand. I resisted the urge to duck.

Her eyes were more swollen and squinty than usual, and her daily tube of mascara had smudged under her eyes. "Oh. Hey."

"Uh." I stood awkwardly, slightly disoriented by her nonchalant demeanor. "Your mail. I brought it in."

Dolly eyed the two letters, suspicious. "Big haul. You must be exhausted." *There she is,* I thought, *the Dolly we all knew and hated.* "You wanna sit down? Rest?"

"No." I tossed the letters onto the Formica styling station and nearly toppled a can of hairspray. "I think it's time we talked."

"About what?" Her tone held more annoyance than aggression.

Her manner was totally throwing me off my game. "Did you know he was coming?" I blurted.

"Did I know…what?" Her eyes disappeared into slits as she made a face. "You mean Mitch? Shoot, I had no idea, and I could care less." She rifled through her mail, snorting her indifference. "All I know is he better not show his face around here."

Whoa. Taken aback, I eyed the seat next to the styling station. Dolly swiveled it, patted the edge. Knowing I was risking life and limb as there were hot curling irons and flat irons and, God forbid, perm solutions nearby, I reluctantly perched into the seat.

"He ruined my life." She looked at me in the mirror. "Humiliated me. Made me lose my house. All for…" She stopped, wisely changing direction. "I was upset for a long time. Angry, but after seeing her sing—"

"Her? You mean Bella?"

Dolly nodded. "I heard her sing at James's church. She was trying out for the creative team, and my brothers got into this huge fight. Remember?" Her eyebrows bent to a V. "Wait. You weren't there, were you?"

"I've heard her sing," I said defensively.

"Yeah. Well. I don't know. After that, after seeing her, and hearing her great big voice"—she dragged her hands through my hair, absently reaching for a brush—"I stopped caring. Stopped caring about him. Stopped missing him. It…*he*…just seemed so trivial."

"You stopped being angry?" I held my breath as she picked up a flat iron, smoothing a section of my hair.

"No. I didn't say that. I'm still angry." Her fingers found another section, and she repeated the motion. "It's different now though. Now I just feel…" She paused, flat iron in hand. "Relief. Relief that it's behind me. And that he doesn't have power over me anymore." She casually twisted her wrist, and miraculously, my scraggly bangs at once became shiny and full of body. "So much has changed since then. That was when we had two churches. Now we have none."

"Well, some say eating JJ Wheeler's barbeque is a religious experience."

She didn't respond. Either not appreciating my joke or hesitant to go on record about JJ Wheeler."

"Did you know where Mitch was all this time? Did he ever contact you?"

"Shoot no. If anything," she eyed me in the mirror, "I figured he might have tried to get in touch with you." She plucked her fingers lightly through my hair, shaping it in a way that resembled a starlet on a magazine. "Hairspray?"

"Uh…I don't…" I lifted my shoulders.

"Close your eyes." I obeyed and let her have her way with my hair. I smelled the slightly fragrant notes in the aerosol and felt a mist of spray as it hit my hair. "Open."

Whoa.

As I stared at my reflection, a flush crept up my cheeks. Dolly and I marked each other in the mirror. "I'm seeing someone now," she said matter-of-factly. "So, to answer your original question, I didn't know he was coming. And I don't care."

I managed to drag my gaze off myself long enough to wonder. "How much do I—?"

"It's on the house," Dolly said. "Thanks for bringing in my mail."

I pulled to a park in front of Luke's duplex, still reeling over my surreal encounter with Dolly. Encouraged, and weirdly hopeful—*the hair?*—I trekked to Micah's apartment and knocked on the door.

Nothing. I knocked again. Then walked around to the back

of the duplex where Luke had placed picnic tables beneath the looming oak trees and dogwoods. I tapped the apartment's back screen door several times.

"*Humph.*" I turned to watch two robins as they fluttered about in a birdbath. When they abruptly scattered in opposite directions a large reddish flash careened into me, nearly taking me down. Duchess's stocky body bounced in excitement, a tattered leash whipping from side to side in her mouth.

"Are you looking for me?" Bella's voice mingled with the *rat-tat-tat* of Luke's screen door. "Oh my gosh, there it is." She stalked over to Duchess and wrestled the shredded tether from her mouth. "It's all wet. She must have buried it." She nuzzled the dog's head. "Bad girl. Very bad girl."

Finally, she remembered I was there. She considered me a moment.

"I thought we could talk," I said. "I know you think I orchestrated that whole thing at the shower, but—"

"Your hair looks good."

"—but I didn't. I was as shocked as everybody else. Except maybe you."

She turned. "Come inside. I was organizing Luke's files for the upcoming council meeting."

Duchess and I followed Bella into Luke's apartment, and the dog headed directly for an oversized stuffed doggie bed on the floor. We watched for a minute as she wrestled with a blanket, a ridiculous flurry of twisting legs, whiskers, and ears bursting before our eyes. When she finally settled, with only the tip of her snout peeking from the blanket, Bella laughed. "You cute little tattuye!" She glanced at me. "That means fox."

I nodded, amused as always by her fascination with words and their meanings, symbolic and otherwise. "She reminds me a little of Hania."

"That's what Uncle Wolf says too, although Hania was much too dignified for this kind of silliness." Reluctantly, Bella pulled her gaze to the task at hand.

I joined her at the table, where files and agenda sheets sat in careful, precise stacks.

"I saw Luke with his dad earlier. They were looking at an empty lot with Violet and Petey."

"Yeah. Petey told Luke he wanted to invest in some land. For the future."

"Really? He and Violet?"

"He didn't say." She shrugged. "But it doesn't matter. Even if they don't know it yet, they're a couple. I have no clue what the land is for though. The places he wanted to look are in the heart of town. You know, by the four-way stop. Seems a strange place to build a house."

"Maybe you're wrong. About them being a couple. I didn't get that impression from Violet."

"Violet?" Bella asked crossly. "I didn't realize you two were close."

"We're not. She just seems too serious for him."

Bella set down a stack of paper. Glinted at me. "She said she talked to you."

My heart dropped. *Could Violet have told her about my tirade at the church?* I waited.

"She said she sent you a picture of my dress." Bella leaned forward suddenly, intent on my response.

"She did. It's beautiful." Filled with relief, I added, "I'm sorry I couldn't make it to the fitting."

She fiddled with the edges of the printed agendas. "I know you didn't scare him off at the shower. I was just mad. And disappointed. I don't want to fight about this all over again, I really don't. I mean, I sort of understand why you don't want me to meet him, but why can't you try to understand how I feel?"

"I don't know. I guess…I feel threatened." I swallowed thickly, allowing—forcing—myself to be honest. To be vulnerable. "I'm afraid he'll turn you against me. More than you already are."

"I'm not against you, Mama. You're just…"

And there it was. The judgement. I fought the heaviness

behind my eyes. "Do you have any idea how soul crushing it is to have a daughter who makes you feel stupid? Who makes you feel terrible about yourself? You wonder why I don't want to do any of this wedding stuff. Well, that's why."

"What?"

"Everything I say. Everything I do. I can see the disapproval on your face." I tried to temper my growing anger, which I knew through a deeper lens stemmed from fear. "Maybe you'll have a daughter one day, and you'll understand when she oozes contempt every time she looks at you."

Bella puffed up. "Is that what you want? You want me to feel guilty? To be unhappy?"

"Of course not." I backed down. Ashamed. The last thing I wanted was for Bella to be unhappy. "No." I looked away. Turned toward the doggie bed. Focused on the rhythm of Duchess's soft breathing through the rise and fall of the blanket. Once I composed myself, I offered my daughter a rare nugget of truth. "I'm not sure how I feel anymore. I'm tired of being…tired. And mad. And hurt. Seeing him…your father…was not what I expected."

Bella squinted at her files, wavering. Clearly struggling with something. And then, "I think he wants to see you."

Too stunned to consider the note of resentment in her words, I absorbed them in a heart-pounding, chest-aching, cloud of delirium. I asked, "Why do you say that?" When she didn't answer, I changed course. "Would you tell me how you found him? Where he's been."

Bella explained how she stalked friends of his family on social media, forming bonds and fishing for information. While I didn't have the capacity to understand the method, I recognized it took cunning, savvy, and patience.

"I think he lived in Arkansas for a while, and Texas. And just recently he moved to Alabama."

"Did he…did he ever get married? Have kids?"

"Nope. I don't think so. I'd hoped to ask him that, among other things, when we met. I'd hoped to have a friendly, civilized, sit-down talk with my father. One without the sheriff, my future father-in-law, and Uncle Wolf racing in like special forces."

We let that sit for a moment, until the rattling of Bella's cell phone jolted us back to reality. "Hey," she clicked. "What's going on?" Shock lined her face as she listened closely. "Okay. I'll go with you. I'll be ready."

She looked at me when she ended the call. "That was Luke. Father Patrick called from the hospital. Brother Wyatt died. Since Luke is the mayor, we need to go pay our respects." I picked up the note of pride in her voice.

"Of course." I stood.

"Luke said the family already has the funeral planned out and everything. I guess they'd been expecting it."

"Yeah, I guess so."

My thoughts unexpectedly drifted to Dolly...and the sprayer... and the smudged mascara.

I think he wants to see you.

After I crossed the Unity Bridge to The Creek, I wound down the swirly, back roads toward my house. To my *shanty*. Not as nice as Dolly's outdated brick house, of course, but it was my family's home. Repaired and carefully mended by Uncle Wolf after the nightmare two years ago, when the shanty was defiled, his garden was destroyed, and our hearts were broken.

Located only a mile up the road, Uncle Wolf had built his home when he was a younger man. The dwelling was simple, except for the custom-designed shed that contained his herbal supplies and gardening tools. My uncle had picked up where my mama had left off, and now served as a healer to The Creek People.

Mama's animals—chickens, cats, dogs, and an assortment of random misfits—had migrated to Uncle Wolf's when Mama was killed.

Bella had always lived with me, but the older she got and the more fractured our relationship became, the two of us living under the same roof proved impossible. So naturally, when Micah invited her to share an apartment in Luke's duplex, Bella jumped at the chance.

So now, I lived alone. Me. My shanty. And my cigarettes and wine.

And yet, I knew with absolute certainty I wouldn't be alone tonight. I couldn't explain it, but Bella's words sang to me all the way back to The Creek.

I think he wants to see you.

I found myself glancing often in the rearview mirror, my reflection still thrilling as I spied my shiny, luxurious hair. When I pulled into my dirt driveway, everything *looked* the same.

But what had I expected? A Volvo? A BMW? A pumpkin transformed into a magical coach and carriage worthy of a princess? *Now* that *sounds like him,* I thought gayly. *Something grand and flashy.*

I flipped my hair and strutted to the front door like a super model. If only I'd thought to apply a little lipstick.

As I walked inside, my eyes bounced off the walls, into the kitchen, and then the living room. Again, everything looked the same. Nothing out of place, the air still smelling of stale, old cigarettes and soured wine.

The first swell of disappointment tugged, coiling its way into my heart with dreadful familiarity.

I think he wants to see you.

Think? Wants?

How would Bella know that? She'd never even met him! How could she possibly intuit something like that? And even if he'd wanted to see me, why would he take the risk? Especially after what happened at the Recreation Center.

I gulped a lung full of air as devastation cradled me. "No," I mumbled to no one, as tears dragged my eye lids down. "No, no." A guttural sob wracked my body, and I stumbled toward the bedroom, my coiffed hair mocking me as I passed the mirror.

And then the atmosphere shifted. Just like that, the space changed. I gulped. Breathed deeply. Sniffed greedily.

His scent. Him. He was here.

"Mitch…" My voice sounded ragged, distorted to my own ears.

His footsteps fell across the bedroom as he moved toward me.

At last.

Chapter Fifteen

Onward, Amazon Woman!
Violet

Tuesday

Of all the things I crammed into my suitcase, a funeral dress hadn't been one of them. Because of my inability to anticipate the death of Shady Gully's most prominent religious leader, I now found myself standing on a pedestal at Nails and Thread.

Sigourney Sky barked orders through a cluster of pins in her mouth. "Turn this way."

I obediently wobbled in the designated direction, inwardly cursing my obscene size and shape. My peculiar and inappropriate frame made it impossible to borrow a proper dress from anyone. Not my mother or Aunt Desi, who if you stacked one atop the other would barely reach ten feet tall. Bella's figure tended toward the curvy and compact, while Micah weighed a hundred pounds soaking wet, so I was out of luck there as well.

"Do you play sports?" Sigourney muttered. "You are quite statuesque."

That was one way to put it. I was an awkward cross between a towering basketball player and a broad-shouldered swimmer. In school I'd been taunted with the moniker *Amazon Woman*. "Not unless chess counts. That's a sport, right?"

She regarded me oddly as she cinched the excess fabric around my waist and pinned accordingly. "I can make this garment work. A simple let out in the length and a tuck here and there in the frame."

"Great." I looked at the drab gray fabric. "I appreciate it. I know how busy you are, and this isn't what you needed today. I apologize—"

"An emergency is an emergency is an emergency." The seamstress bobbed her head matter-of-factly. "Until today this outfit had been condemned to the moo-moo pile, and now I'm looking forward to making it come alive." She directed me to the dressing area, where I was supposed to carefully remove the dress without losing pins or jabbing myself. "Be quick now."

I'd almost managed to pull the monstrosity over my head when my stringy hair got snagged in the back zipper. Twisting and swiveling at awkward angles, my deranged expressions met me in the mirror at every turn. I gasped aloud when my cell phone rang.

"Need help?" Sigourney called from the other side of the curtain.

I spied the 225 area code. *Baton Rouge.* "Uhhhhh…"

Sigourney surfaced suddenly, and like a graceful apparition armed with scissors and a tape measure, she rescued me from the dress. And a few strands of hair. Once she disappeared in the same fairy-like fashion, I managed to answer the call. "Uh… hello?"

I listened as the recruiter raved about my grades and my potential. "We're all flabbergasted by the dual degrees you've managed to accumulate in such a short period of time. From the early college courses in high school to your master's degrees in Medical Science and Clinical Research, it's clear you're a very focused and hardworking young woman. And the good news is several of your course credits will transfer."

"You mean…?"

"Oh yes, Violet. You are absolutely, a hundred percent, accepted." When she cleared her throat, I could almost picture the thin woman with the choppy pixie haircut. I recognized the moment her tone shifted. "There is one thing though. Because of your late application, we'll need to know right away. I understand you said you needed some time, but—"

"No," I said quickly. "I mean, yes. Yes." Surprisingly, the words tumbled out without hesitation. "I accept. Yes." I grinned at my goofy image in the mirror. "Most definitely, yes."

After I disconnected, I collapsed in the cushioned seat in the fitting area, and my eyes once again drifted to the mirror. A half-dressed combination of wild hair and sheer panic, my red cheeks dappled an otherwise pale canvas.

I'd said yes without consulting my mother. Or talking to Sterling. Or even Petey.

Driven by my own passion, and perhaps selfishness, I'd set a whole new direction for my future. With or without Petey. With or without my mother's blessing. I'd officially pulled the trigger.

Somehow, I managed to keep the news to myself the rest of the day. While Sigourney worked her magic on the heretofore expelled moo-moo, I stayed busy helping Micah and Bella with wedding preparations.

Since most of the day's buzz centered around Brother Wyatt's passing and the details of his funeral, my restlessness went unnoticed. Word was the legendary preacher would be buried tomorrow in the very same cemetery as my father.

Regardless of whether Petey was a part of my future or not, or how and when I told my mother, there was one person who deserved to hear the news. While he'd been strangely unavailable during this trip to Shady Gully, my twin brother, Sterling, was and always would be *my person.*

Even more so now that Daddy was gone.

And there was the ache. The guilt. *The shame.*

And just like that, my joy was tainted.

Wednesday

My brother and I stood over my father's grave.

"I assume Dad knows already, huh?" He indicated the headstone.

"Yeah. First one I told. You're the second."

"Not Petey?" His shocked expression sent a jolt of impatience through me as I still felt wounded over Petey's texting—or sexting—with Tammy Jo. "Well, I for one am not surprised. I knew you'd get in. And I think it's great." He turned his gaze to the flowers we'd set around the headstone.

"I feel like I'm letting him down."

"What?" Sterling squinted at me. "That's ridiculous. You could be a groovy, free-loving hippy traveling the country in a Scooby Doo van and Dad would be over the moon. Violet, you could do no wrong in Dad's eyes." He lowered his own dark eyes. "And you still can't."

I shrugged, not believing him. "What about you? We never talk anymore. How are things at North Lake?"

"Great," he said. "The music is great. The creative team is great. I love leading the worship songs on Sundays. We're experimenting with new styles, doing new copies, and really shaking things up. Plus, the band and I are getting regular gigs on the restaurant-patio scene. Lighting up social media."

"But?"

"I don't know. I'm torn." He considered me a moment, my beautiful brother who, much like Petey, dazzled everyone in his path. Not only was he handsome with his dark hair and muscular build, but being around believers like those at North Lake had solidified his faith. "You're gonna think this is stupid, seeing as how you read algebra textbooks for fun."

"Tell me."

"You remember those whodunits Dad used to read before he died? Remember when Billy, his hospice nurse, got him hooked on them?" Sterling pivoted toward me, becoming animated. "At first, I read them because I missed Dad, and I was trying to get into his head those last few weeks, wondering how he processed those stories and what he thought of them. You know?"

"Sure."

"But then I started reading more. Like whole series. Crime thrillers and procedural cop stories and—"

"You want to be a writer?"

He shrugged. "Maybe. But I'm thinking—I want to be a lawyer."

My mouth fell open as I stared at Sterling, who'd always hated school with a passion. But then I remembered his interjection during the shower debacle, and how he'd challenged the sheriff on the statute of limitations. I chuckled. "Maybe you could be a lawyer who writes legal thrillers? Kind of…the best of both worlds?"

His face lit up. "Like John Grisham? Yeah, that works. Of course, like you, I'm late following my passion. Most people our age are finishing up school now, not starting." He spied me through his hooded eyes. "And then there's us."

We swiveled as the first signs of mourners made their progression toward Brother Wyatt's grave. The funeral home had set up seats around the burial site, and now Jesse and James led the congregation.

Sterling and I discreetly stepped away from Daddy's grave, falling in behind the rest of the funeral-goers. Petey latched onto me with his hazel surveillance and joined us beneath the canopy. "Nice dress, Sable."

My anger was no match for his playful, easy manner, and I naturally fell into step beside him. As we joined his parents, along with my mother and Sheriff Rick, Aunt Desi reached in for a hug. "Sigourney did a beautiful job," she said. "You look like royalty. Like an elegant queen." I laughed at the notion, meanwhile tempering another wave of irritation as my mother wandered over to my daddy's grave with the sheriff in tow.

Uncle Lenny shook Jesse's and James's hands as they passed, and offered his condolences, which they solemnly accepted. Luke followed suit, and then Bella. I couldn't help but think how easily she fit into the role of the politician's wife. With her simple, elegant black dress and her hair swept up in a conservative style, she made the perfect fiancée for the mayor of Shady Gully.

"Excuse me." Aunt Desi stopped Jesse and James. "I just wanted to say how sorry I am about your father. He was a good man. His guidance meant so much to me in my spiritual journey." As usual, when Aunt Desi talked about Jesus her face filled with a profound and deep sense of gratitude.

James said, "Thank you. I remember my brother and I baptized you." James refused to look at his brother while referring to him.

"That's right, my legs were shaking." Desi looked reflective.

"Yes, yes," Jesse added in a clipped voice. "If you need any help with the Lord's Prayer today, it's in the program. Remember it goes, 'thy kingdom come, thy will be done…'"

I felt Petey tense next to me and caught his slight forward movement in my peripheral vision. Instinctively, I brushed his arm. Heard him smother a bolt of fury.

The tense exchange passed and then shifted again when Dolly strolled into the mix. Looming next to her was her new *friend*, a lumbering, red-headed cowboy with tight jeans and a big, buckled belt. "Howdy," he smiled at me, and nodded at the family.

This must be the legendary Adam, who was spoken of only in hushed tones when Aunt Desi was around. Like a purple spectacled flame, my mother appeared, and positioned herself defensively in front of Aunt Desi and Uncle Lenny.

The sheriff followed, but honestly, my half-pint mother seemed scarier than he did, even with a gun strapped around his waist.

"Great to see you, Adam," my mother said. "So sorry for your loss, Dolly." As she urged them forward, another tense scene seemed to have been averted, until Adam glanced over his shoulder and launched a bold, brazen wink straight at Aunt Desi.

She let out a little gasp. Uncle Lenny paled. And time seemed to drag in slow motion as the generation before mine pitched potent, emotionally fueled lasers at one another. Each too heavy and convoluted for Luke, Bella, Sterling, Petey, or me to understand. I didn't think the friction would ever end, or that anyone would ever actually dare to breathe again, until the formidable Wolfheart stalked onto the scene.

He bounded over and muttered to my mother. "Sorry I'm late." He then turned his gaze, which had morphed into a glare, directly at Adam. He nodded at the sheriff out of courtesy, probably because he was the one with the gun.

Eventually, Adam and Dolly moved on, and positioned themselves in the chairs closest to the casket. Once I was able to breathe again, I glanced at Petey. "Are you okay? Want to sit down?"

He shook his head. "I'm fine."

We filed into a line of chairs next to his parents, and Luke and Bella, which completed our row. Meanwhile, Wolfheart, the sheriff, and my mother settled into the row ahead of us.

Micah dashed in then, dressed to the nines in a black sheath dress. After giving me an exaggerated once-over, she mouthed, "Dang, girl," and then scooted in next to my mother. "I closed up the store," she whispered to Uncle Lenny.

Sterling perched on the seat next to Micah.

After a moment, Micah checked her phone, and then swiveled, looking past us. When she waved at someone, we all turned to see who it was, and lo and behold…Tammy Jo headed our way.

Gracious, but funerals were hard.

After fluttering her eyelashes at everyone in greeting, Tammy Jo settled next to Sterling and Micah.

Petey grinned and leaned forward, offering up some witty remark or another. Micah, Sterling, and Tammy Jo all smothered back chuckles. When he sat back, his leg started to twitch. *Bounce. Bounce. Bounce.*

"Petey." I put my hand on his leg to stop the twitching.

"That bothering you?" He sparked in irritation.

I removed my hand.

Bounce. Bounce. Bounce.

He was obviously antsy, presumably keen to get up ahead with the cool kids.

Father Patrick miraculously appeared then, introducing himself and sharing a few kind words about Brother Wyatt. There was an uplifting tone to his words, and the mourners leaned in, clearly enjoying the kind reminisces and recollective stories of the deceased from a *fellow man of God.*

Father Patrick then handed the service over to Jesse.

Jesse, the oldest by a minute or so, began with a prayer. Not just any prayer, but an emotional, overly affected, stage performance complete with tears and the practiced cadence of a TV evangelist.

He ranted for several minutes before slowing to a pregnant pause, which apparently was James's signal to take the stage. James, in turn, set up his own podium on the opposite side and set into his spiel. Back and forth they preached, bouncing scriptures off one another with barely a reference to their father. Or a glance at one another.

Dolly's bleached blonde head swiveled back and forth, and to her credit, she appeared ashamed as the dueling preachers vaulted back and forth.

Out of the corner of my eye I noted Petey fiddle with his phone. My frustration mounted as he pecked away at the keyboard, and grinned as it lit up with a response. Because he held it at a discreet level, however, I couldn't see the sender's name.

But the reaction on the row ahead made it clear. Tammy Jo even risked a glance over her shoulder, eliciting a muted snicker from Petey. I glared at him. He remained oblivious.

Until Jesse mentioned the Lord's Prayer.

Petey's fingers froze mid-tap, and I heard Aunt Desi's breath hitch in anticipation.

Jesse cut an oily glance her way. "If anyone in particular would like to lead us in the Lord's Prayer…?" He held up the program, brandished it about. "We have a cheat sheet, of course." His gaze landed pointedly on Aunt Desi.

Without warning, Petey suddenly burst out of his chair, nearly tumbling it over. His fists were tightly clenched, and his body radiated with pent up fury.

"Son," Uncle Lenny hissed in a stern tone.

"Petey," Luke breathed. "Not the time. Or the place."

Aunt Desi said nothing as she remained frozen in her chair, paralyzed but for the twisting of her hands.

Still Petey stood. Bouncing. Clenching. Trembling.

"Petey," I whispered, reaching up just enough to brush my hand against his fist. "Sit."

He let out a long breath, and then settled back into the chair next to me. Once the funeral-goers had turned their attention back to the pulpit, Petey grabbed my hand.

And bounced his leg.

Despite my calming effect on Petey, he quickly fell back into character as we trekked to our cars. He linked his arm inside his mother's and escorted her to her van with the pomp of a royal chauffeur. "Your chariot, Madam, and do be careful of the grand ditch here."

All along the old country road, pick-ups, SUV's, minivans, and even a few bikes straddled the grass and the ditch in front of Shady Gully's most established graveyard. I watched as Petey settled Aunt Desi in, buckling her seat belt and kissing her on the forehead.

Uncle Lenny cleared his throat hoarsely, offering us a curt, dazed nod. Still visibly upset by the day's events, he steered Aunt Desi's van in the direction of Piney Lake subdivision.

We watched them go, and then at last turned our attention to one another. "Petey, I have to tell you something—"

"Thanks," he said softly.

"What?"

"Only one voice cut through my rage...and it was yours."

My heart pounded inside my chest. This, these words, and the way he said them...it was all I needed to hear. It was everything to me.

But then a round of laughter distracted him, and his interest shifted. Just like that, he'd turned away from me...and toward Sterling, Micah, and Tammy Jo's conversation. Crushed by how carelessly he'd dismissed me, I shriveled in resignation.

And yet, despite myself, I fought one more time to claim a

piece of the smile forming on his bright face. "Guess what?" I tugged his sleeve. "LSU called. I'm in."

His mouth stretched happy and wide. "No kidding? Way to go, Ivory! Woohoo!" He danced a little jig, and my heart swelled once more.

But he pivoted, just a little, but enough to prove his commitment was fleeting. Insubstantial. "Hey, let's tell everybody." He waved at Micah's group, beckoning them over.

"Petey, no. Don't! I haven't even told my mother."

"Well, you'll have to now."

When he once more hurled his attention their way, I lost what remained of my restraint. "You know what? Why don't you just go to her?"

"What?"

"Tammy Jo. Just go. But please don't patronize me and use me as a tool to strike up a conversation."

"What are you talking about?" He seemed genuinely confused.

"And by the way, while we're being honest, can I just say how sick I am of your Ruby-Sable-Jade routine? I have a name—"

"Of course, you do. Look, I don't understand what set you off. I'm sorry—"

I wasn't buying it. "You've been texting her since we got to Shady Gully. Don't try to deny it, Petey. I saw her name pop up on your phone."

"Tammy Jo? But we're just friends—"

I snorted. "Don't lie, Petey. It doesn't suit you." A deeply stricken look flashed across his face. Had I gone too far? I wondered.

But I plowed ahead. "I'm leaving after the wedding. I'm going to Baton Rouge, and I'm getting on with my life. I'm done following you around hoping you'll send a smile of approval my way."

"You've got this wrong. All wrong." He circled me then, lowering his shaggy head to mine, imploring me to understand. "Seriously, Goldie," he tried to be funny.

"It's too late, Petey."

"You're right. I have been texting her. But it's not what you think."

Whatever he said after that I didn't hear. My mission was clear now.

I would find my mother and lay out my plan. Whether she liked it or not wasn't my concern. When I spotted her arm-in-arm with the sheriff, a thrill of angry resolve ran through me.

Just as the female warriors in Greek mythology anchored themselves with swords, daggers, and bows and arrows, I moved forward with renewed determination, finally ready to confront my obstacles.

Onward, Amazon woman!

That Pestilent Rooster
Lenny

Thursday

Desi had barely spoken a word on the way home from Brother Wyatt's burial ceremony. I understood why, of course, as Jesse's despicable attempt to humiliate her had nearly succeeded. Had Petey let his anger hijack a good man's funeral, Desi would have been devastated. She'd have unraveled right there in front of the whole town.

Had that happened, Jesse, James, and Dolly would have had the last *unholy* laugh and reveled in their twisted vindication. The unpleasant scene would have played out to rival all the other scandals in Shady Gully.

And Lord knew there were quite a few of those to choose from.

One in particular stood out for me, involving the infamous Adam, whose portentous return was about as welcome as an outhouse breeze.

Just seeing that hound's face again, still cocky after all this time, delivered me right back to high school. To that bonfire at Desi's, when he'd serenaded her with his lame *Desi, You Make Me Dizzy* song, then to homecoming, when he'd finagled his way into driving her homecoming car around the track, and finally, to the blow-out at Cicada Stadium.

Legendary Cicada Stadium, now known as the Shady Gully Recreation Center, had served as ground zero for generations of Shady Gullians eager to exercise their inner rebel. Before

Luke had transformed the old, abandoned ballpark into a modern, eye-popper of a venue, the hangout had been host to countless iniquities.

I still wondered about the wrongs committed there. Had they been forgiven? Possibly. But doubtful they'd been forgotten.

Definitely not the one on a graduation night years ago, when a celebratory evening had dissolved into an all-out brawl. Adam had shown up with his stinking guitar, determined to stir things up, and by the time the night was over I'd smashed his beloved instrument into a hundred pieces and slugged him into a state of unconsciousness.

Still made me smile.

But then the cops had come, and even worse, Desi had broken up with me that night.

Happy graduation, Lenny. You just ruined your future because you couldn't control your temper. Or your possessiveness. Or your jealousy.

Apparently, not much had changed since then because even though Desi and I had been married for decades, all it had taken was one shameless wink, and I was ready to roll around in the dirt with him all over again.

Even now, my knuckles twitched with the urge to pummel him senseless.

How can he still hold that kind of power over me after all these years? I'm a grown man. What is wrong with me?

My phone chimed. Petey. He wanted to talk and was waiting for me at the Cozy Corner. I'd sensed a restlessness in him lately, a pronounced agitation that robbed him of his otherwise cheerful temperament. *Good,* I thought, encouraged that he sought counsel when feeling unsettled and out of sorts.

Before I left, I texted Father Patrick, as I too was feeling out of sorts.

A spin around Shady Gully's old country roads had done wonders for my mood, and the rugged ride of my Dodge RAM truck had provided a much-needed boost to my old ego. By the time I found Petey sitting at a picnic table at the Cozy Corner, I felt strong enough to give him a leg up, if needed.

He mulled over a menu. "Hey, Dad." He locked onto my truck. "I see you brought out the big guns, eh?"

"Yep."

"Let me guess. Mom has the minivan." He flashed a sly wink. "What? Did she run off to Nashville?"

I gave him a look.

"Too soon?" He tried a grin. "Yeah. Probably so."

"*Humph.*" I sat down heavily. "Who knows lately? After yesterday."

"I'm glad you came. I wasn't sure if you were working today."

"Micah is managing the store today. I swear, she's getting to where she could run it in her sleep. And you? What's up?"

Petey handed me the menu. "Charlie Wayne attempted to put together an official menu."

I pulled my glasses out of my shirt pocket. "It says burger and fries."

"Pretty expansive." Petey pointed. "At the bottom it says you even can add cheese to your burger if you want."

Charlie Wayne huffed as he plodded over with a pencil and a pad in his hand. "What'll you have?"

"I guess I'll go with the burger and fries," Petey deadpanned.

"Cheese?" Charlie Wayne held his pen, on the ready.

"Sure."

"I'll have the same." I turned to Petey. "Are you okay?"

"Yeah." He shrugged. "Seriously, where's Mom today?" His leg bounced up and down in frenetic little movements. "Is she okay after what happened at the funeral?"

"I don't know, son. Honestly, it's really hard to tell anymore. She and Aunt Robin are spending the day at Lake Osprey, and then tomorrow she has an early appointment with a doctor in Belle Maison. Robin's going with her."

"What kind of doctor? Like a *lady* doctor?"

I nodded. "Yep. I figure at this point it's best for me just to step aside and let the ladies go and conquer." I again considered Petey's quivering leg. "So, you had something on your mind?"

"What's the deal with this Adam guy?"

I gaped. "Ah, just a long history." *Where was Charlie Wayne with our food?*

"Did he and Mom have a…thing? Like when she was in school? I feel like I have a right to know, since it seems half of Shady Gully does."

I didn't want to tarnish his mother's image by revealing that Adam and Desi's *thing* came much later in life, so I treaded carefully. "Is that what you wanted to discuss?" When I got no response, I said, "Actually, you *don't* have a right to know, but I'll tell you what you need to know, so that you can distinguish between rumor and truth if you ever have a need to."

Charlie Wayne chose this moment to place our food on the table, and by the hesitant expression on his face, he seemed inclined to linger. "Thanks," I said, quickly turning back to Petey. Once Charlie Wayne had returned to his barren order window, I continued. "Adam flirted with her in school. He was infatuated, which is understandable, but I think he enjoyed the conquest more than anything. He was older than her, and had a reputation for philandering, and Sunny sensed right away that he was bad news. So, thankfully, she presented me to Desi in a positive light."

"Makes sense. Mom would do anything for Nana Sunny." Petey bit into his cheeseburger. "Of course, you were quite the catch." He grinned. "I mean, hey, the quarterback and all."

"Gee, thanks." I dragged some fries through my ketchup. "Anyway, that's all there is to it. Now, back to you—"

"Did they ever get together?"

"Is this really what's on your mind, Petey?"

He waited.

Finally, I yielded. "No. Which is probably why he enjoys tormenting her at every opportunity. Adam has questionable morals, son. Always has. To this day, he bounces between a variety of women, regardless of their marital status. Or his."

"And now he's with Dolly. Wow." Petey polished off his burger and set into his fries.

"Are you done with this volley?" I considered him. "Or are you ready to tell me what's really going on? With you. Why is your leg twitching so much lately? You did that when you were a kid when you were anxious."

"What's with everybody's obsession with my leg twitching lately? Geez." He finally shrugged. "I don't know. Indigo's mad at me."

"Does she have reason to be?"

"Maybe. I mean, she thinks she does, but she doesn't."

"Okay. That's a non-answer." I squinted. "Petey, it's clear to everyone you two have feelings for one another."

"What?" Incredulous. "No. It's not like that. We're really just good friends. Cousins, you know?"

"Okay," I said skeptically. "So, why did your *really good friend* get mad at you?"

He stared at the remnants of food on the red and white checked wrapper. "It doesn't matter anyway. She's got her whole life planned out. *Plan* being the key word. That's something I don't have."

"Well, seeing as how you're *cousins* and *really good friends* and all, seems like you two could coordinate your plans. Right?"

"You don't understand, Dad. She's got really big plans. Impressive plans. She's going to LSU this fall. To Baton Rouge." Forlorn, he wadded up his greasy wrapper. "And I'm not." He tossed the trash into Charlie Wayne's, *Put Trash Here, Morons!* can.

"Well. That's big news. I guess she's off to get another master's degree?" I asked curiously, as this was the first I'd heard about LSU or Baton Rouge. "Or something in cancer research?"

Suddenly evasive, Petey wouldn't meet my eyes. "Not my news to tell, Dad."

"So then," I pressed, "what are you going to do? Is there

something you could do in Baton Rouge? If you wanted to go along with her, that is?"

His leg twitched violently. "I had my shot, Dad, and I blew it."

This time I waited him out, my mind spinning with questions.

Petey sighed heavily. "Timothy pulled some strings. I had an opportunity to talk—to preach—to an auditorium full of kids at LSU, and I…I just couldn't pull it off. If I had, there was a good chance I could have been involved in the student ministry there. Offering counselling, support, spiritual guidance…but I choked." He grunted. "So, I reckon I'm feeling a little lost and aimless these days." He forced out a sarcastic chuckle. "Like Micah."

"I'm sorry, son." My eyes drifted from the pain in his eyes to the cross on his wrist. "I hate that for you, but I don't think you should give up. I believe teaching and ministry is the right path for you. Heck, so does anyone who has ever met you."

"I don't know about that." Petey shrugged, suddenly restless. "Anyway, it looks like I'll be in Shady Gully for a while. Giving Father Patrick a hand. Maybe Luke will give me my old job back at the Auto Parts store."

I chuckled. "There's always the hardware store. Although I'd have to run it by my Human Resources lady."

"Yeah, I hear she's a beast." Petey tried a grin.

"I know one person who will be thrilled to have you back in town." I reached across the table, squeezing his arm. "Might be just the thing she needs right now."

"If I can make Mom feel better, then maybe this is where Jesus wants me to be."

"Exactly," I said. "And who knows, maybe when Violet gets done snagging another degree or whatever she's working on, she'll come back—"

"Shady Gully isn't for her, Dad. I even tried floating that idea when we were fishing." Petey shook his head. "She needs to be in a big city. Besides, she's off to do her thing. Live her life. And she made it clear, I'm not part of it." He stood, stretching his long legs. "Besides, it's not like that with us. We're just friends."

I nodded, concern mounting as I reflected on my normally balanced, untroubled, and self-collected son. "I'm on my way to see Father Patrick in a bit. You should come."

"What for?" He scrutinized me. "Are y'all gonna discuss this mysterious meeting he's trying to set up? For when Timothy gets here? What's up with that?"

"No telling." I shook my head. "Maybe I'll find out more when I see him, but that's not why I'm going today."

"Why then?"

"A spiritual tune up." I placed my hand on his jittery leg, slowing it to a stop. "You should come. He's the best holy man Shady Gully has these days." I tilted my head. "So far, anyway."

"Thanks, Dad, but I can't today."

We turned as gravel skipped across the Cozy Corner's parking lot. Daryl and Bubba climbed out of Bubba's red truck.

"You could have walked," teased Petey. "I can see the auto body shop from here."

Bubba huffed as he carried his heavy frame over to the table. "Yeah we coulda, but then we'd have to smell JJ Wheeler's ribs all the way here." He frowned at the menu. "And then eat this."

"It's just wrong." Daryl—the skinny to Bubba's hefty—shook his head. "Loyalty is one thing, but Charlie Wayne is asking a lot."

Daryl jumped when Charlie Wayne closed in behind him. "What'll you have?" Charlie Wayne sniffed Daryl's shirt suspiciously. "Where've you been? You smell like—"

"Nowhere." Daryl ran his fingers through his neatly trimmed beard. "I swear. I'll have the cheeseburger and fries. You know, something different."

Bubba complained. "How about a pulled chicken today, Charlie Wayne? On some nice French bread—"

"I got cheeseburgers and fries. What'll you have?"

"Guess that's what I'll have then." He glanced wistfully at JJ's tent across the corner.

"Luke stopped by earlier," Charlie Wayne announced. "He

was on his way to the courthouse. Said he found something in the town's bylaws, like restrictions or something, and he thinks we might be able to get rid of that clown with the lady hair."

Daryl smothered a groan.

"That's…great news," Bubba said forlornly.

Petey and I traded glances, watched as Charlie Wayne returned to the order window, a hopeful skip in his cranky step.

Father Patrick wore a dust rag over his shoulder and pushed a mop up and around the nave of the church. Unaware of my presence, he whistled as he worked. He stopped to spray a generous dusting of Pledge along the back pews.

"I wouldn't do that," I cautioned.

Father whipped his head in my direction, his face flooding with cheerful exertion. "It's fresh citrus. Doesn't that sound divine?"

"Your parishioners will just slide right off the seats. Especially the little ones who can hardly sit still."

"Oh, heavens. We can't have that, now can we?" He tossed me a dust rag. "Come, let's quickly wipe away the evidence."

The blend of incense, lemon, and citrus ignited my senses, unexpectedly transporting me to my own boyhood, when I struggled to sit still during Mass. Always trapped in the pew between my parents, my tiny legs—unable to reach the floor—had dangled constantly. When the time came to unfold the kneeler, I'd restlessly grind my heels along the cushion, determined to scrape the morning's chicken coop muck off my shoes.

Inevitably my mother would brace her hand along my thigh to relax my movements—much like I'd done to Petey—but I'd rarely stop until my father gave me *the look*, and only then would I slow to a stop, contrite and repentant.

"Doing a little spring cleaning, Father?"

"I'm afraid my motives aren't that noble, Lenny. I'm a sinner, full of vanity and pride. I'm set on spiffing things up, as I desperately hope to impress the esteemed Kentucky preacher." His eyes rounded. "Shameful, isn't it?" He gawked suddenly at the lights. "I mustn't forget to dust around those fixtures."

I chuckled. "Timothy is pretty easy going, Father. Picture Petey, but older and more seasoned."

"Well, that sounds brilliant. Now I'm even more intimidated."

"Timothy would be one to get on his hands and knees and scrub alongside you. He's not the kind to judge, so don't worry. You two will get along fine."

"We had a splendid call. I'm quite eager to lay eyes on him."

"What exactly are you two cooking up?"

"Oh, just a little tete-a-tete with some of the leaders in the community. Elders of the church, those in good standing, and of course, the outlaws, Jesse and James. Dolly as well. You and Petey. Luke. And Mr. Wolf, to represent those on The Creek.

"Wow," I muttered, my curiosity peaking. "That's quite a gathering."

"Yes, it is," he said. "But that's not important now. Let's discuss you. What's on your mind, my friend? Is wedding planning taking its toll? I hear it's not for the feeble or faint of heart. Perhaps you need a quiet place to retreat. Let's have a seat, shall we?"

I relinquished my dust cloth and followed Father Patrick to the front pew. "Actually, the wedding plans are moving along nicely. Luke is great. Bella is well, despite her father swooping in and trying to steal her big day."

"Any sign of that scoundrel?"

"No. The sheriff—Ricky, is trying to lay low. In all actuality, there's nothing he can do. Especially if Meadow and Bella don't feel threatened."

"Hmmmm." Father looked thoughtful. "And how are you and Desi holding up? All well there?"

Aware that he'd seen what happened at Brother Wyatt's funeral and had probably made his own assumptions, I hesitated. "Yeah, all is fine." The extended silence prompted me. "I'm a little worried about her, to tell you the truth. Robin is taking her to the doctor tomorrow. Hopefully she can get her squared away. I've heard them talking about hormones and what not."

Father shuddered. "A nasty business, that." He confided, "I've counseled a number of women as they approach…a certain age, and I can assure you it's both an emotional and a physical crisis in many cases. I'd urge you to take an interest, Lenny, rather than laying back, as you say. Desi needs to know she's not alone during this…difficult and challenging season."

I considered his words, appreciating his frankness. I cleared my throat, all in now. "I'm also concerned a—certain chicken from the past has come home to roost, as they say."

Father Patrick peered over my head, probably spying another dusty light fixture to wrestle. "Would this chicken happen to be one of those red-headed hippy chickens?"

I swallowed a chuckle, relieved. "You could say that, yes. This… uh…chicken…has caused us problems in the past, and there's a chance…" I trailed off, scrubbing my hand through my thinning hair. "There's a chance this…chicken issue…has never truly been resolved and could actually be the root of a lot of Desi's depression."

"Quite."

"This chicken…" I went on. "Aw, hell, let's just call him a rooster." I genuflected. "Sorry Father. Anyway, this rooster has been a thorn in my side since high school. He chased Desi relentlessly, irreverently, even while we were married. I'm worried…" I hesitated. "I'm worried that part of her depression is because she harbors some…attraction, or chemistry, toward said chicken."

"Rooster."

"Right. Maybe she feels like she made the wrong choice."

"I see. And did…uh…this rooster ever put your marriage at risk?"

"Yes." I swallowed thickly. "Nothing ever happened, but yes. There was a difficult time, right before we lost Dean to cancer. We got some counseling while we were in Lexington. At North Lake, actually."

"Splendid! Another feather in Timothy's cap." He regarded me. "So perhaps more counseling would help. Kind of a preemptive, proactive approach."

"Perhaps. But…sometimes I really struggle, Father."

"With?"

"With my faith. With believing. I'm ashamed to admit that because I was brought up in the church." I glanced around. "I was raised Catholic. And it was good. My parents were believers. And then Desi—"

"Yes?"

"My wife is amazing, and she's been through some really horrible things." I thought of her parents' divorce, Tom's perverse violation, and the ridicule she'd endured because she wasn't well-churched enough for Shady Gully's cliquish community. "Desi wasn't raised in church. She didn't even know the Lord's Prayer until she came to Shady Gully in the eighth grade. All that to say, I've never in my life seen anyone so determined, so dedicated, so intent on realizing her faith. She went searching. She longed for God. And she didn't stop until she found Him. Or He found her."

"Sometimes those of us born into the church get lulled into a false sense of security. We take it for granted, thinking we can hide behind the church instead of running to God."

I breathed deeply. "Catechism, Communion, Mass, all of it. It was handed to me on a platter. And then when Desi came into my life, her strong faith carried me the rest of the way. But I—I'm struggling, Father. With my anger, my jealousy. I feel so threatened by this…rooster. Where is my faith, Father? Have I lost it? Did I squander it?"

"Your faith hasn't left you, Lenny. You're here, aren't you? Just as Desi so doggedly sought out God long ago, you're doing the same thing now. We in the Church don't always get things right. Unfortunately." He seemed suddenly reflective. "But you are God's. He's claimed you, and He's not letting you go." He patted my leg. "Deal with it."

I chuckled, suddenly feeling better. More hopeful.

"And pray. Often." He clasped his hands together. "Why don't we pray now? Let's pray for the grace to trust Him even when we don't see Him. And for the faith to know He's there even when we don't feel Him. Let's pray for Desi's health. And for a lovely, joyous wedding that will remind us that our Lord loves us and wants good for us."

I nodded as he genuflected and bowed his head.

"And let's pray for that pestilent rooster." Father Patrick raised his shoulders in an *it-is-what-it-is* gesture.

Reluctantly, begrudgingly, I bowed my head and prayed.

Chapter Seventeen

Girls Are Fun At That Age
Meadow

Friday

He traced the length of my body with the tips of his fingers. Even, light strokes, along the curve of my hip, and then down into the cave of my waist, and then up again, brushing the side of my breast.

His fingers, uncalloused, lingered there. I lounged on my side, watching his eyes as he explored, trying to guess his impressions. Hoping to interpret his thoughts. But he gave nothing away. He never had.

While he was also on his side, his gaze was drawn to my body rather than my face. His detour gave me a chance to do some exploring of my own. I noted how little he'd changed, how the years had been kind to him. Except for the dashes of gray along his temples, he was the Mitch of years ago.

His eyes, still vibrant and blue, finally dragged themselves away from my naked body and settled on my face. His undivided attention snatched the breath right out of my chest. He laughed.

"What?" I asked shyly.

"Nothing. You look…good," he said. "Older. But good." He kissed my lips, and after a moment I focused on the feel of his mouth, the way his tongue probed mine, and the mounting thunder that promised ahead.

Had it been only days since I'd discovered him waiting for

me in my shanty? We'd hardly left the bedroom since, so it was impossible to tell.

"I've missed you," I said impulsively when he released me. "I wish you hadn't left. We could have figured out a way to be together."

His eyes danced with amusement. "I don't think so, love. You were underage then."

I winced. The way he said it made it sound like an accusation. Like…blame.

"What I mean is, our passion was too big for the world to handle. They wouldn't have understood." He kissed me again, just a quick peck this time, as the mood had shifted.

I watched as he rose from the bed. Naked, he padded toward the kitchen.

I shamelessly considered following him, but instead recovered my robe from the floor and belted it against my exposed body. "I can fix you something to eat if you're hungry." But he was already rummaging through the pantry when I found him.

"We're almost out of food. We're scraping to the back of the cupboard now." He shook his head, disappointed. "Cheetos? Really, love? Do you know what's in those?"

"There's popcorn on the second shelf. The kind in a bag. It's healthier."

At once I recognized his patient expression, the one he'd summoned often during our affair. Always tolerant, he took time to explain things to me, to counsel me in the ways of the world beyond The Creek.

"Just because it's popcorn doesn't mean it's healthy. This crud is full of preservatives." He swiveled to open the refrigerator, giving me a clear view of his lean, sculpted backside.

"You must work out all the time." I sidled over to him, reaching my arms around him from behind.

"Absolutely. Every place I've lived I've had a gym membership. You've got to, love. You should too."

Every place I've lived…

"And where all have you lived?" I asked boldly. "Texas?"

His face clouded with disinterest. "Meh. I didn't stay there long. Too many cowboys and rednecks. I recently moved to Alabama." He eyed me contrarily. "What's with the inquisition?"

I backed off, resisted the temptation to ask more about his life. I didn't want to task him when he had so much on his mind, and we'd have plenty of time to talk about such things. Eventually, I was sure, he'd tell me about his adventures, traveling and otherwise.

"So," I teased, "when are you going to take me for a ride on your motorcycle?" I tilted my head toward the rear of the shanty, near the back steps where he'd stashed his bike. "I like low-key transportation. Is it fun?"

"Yeah. It gets me where I need to go." He frowned as he studied the contents of my refrigerator. "How about this?" He pulled a carton of eggs out of the fridge. "I'll fix us breakfast, and then we can take a walk. Go for a hike or something. You took another day off, right?"

"Yep." I grinned. "I told Cruella Claire I had a stomach virus."

"Boy that one, she's a number, eh? Definitely hasn't aged well." He found a skillet and set about making himself at home in my kitchen. I watched him for a minute, my heart pounding in my chest, still reeling from the very sight of him. Here. In my home. In the flesh. How I'd longed for this!

"Are you concerned someone will see us?" I asked. "Like the sheriff?"

"Nah." He whisked eggs into a bowl, his biceps pulsing with each stroke.

He's braver than me, I thought, as I feared we'd run into my uncle, or God forbid, Bella.

"He's got nothing on me. He can't touch me." Mitch snorted. "I can't believe Ricky became sheriff. What a joke. He was always such a putz in school, you know?" He stopped, ticked my chin with his fingers. "But you were just a babe then. You wouldn't know. Trust me, he and Lenny, all of them really, were absolute nitwits."

I heeded his remark, concerned now that he wouldn't approve of Bella's marrying Lenny's son. "Yeah. I agree. They act like they own the town—"

"Do you have any mushrooms?" His focus had moved to vegetables as he precisely chopped bell peppers and onions. "They'd be great in the omelet."

"Um…let me check." Although I went through the motion of looking in the pantry, I knew I wouldn't find mushrooms. I couldn't stand them. "Looks like I'm out."

"Come on, love. Mushrooms are a staple in everyone's kitchen. Or they should be anyway."

"Yeah, I just ran out. Sorry."

"And who made Lenny and Desi the patriarch and matriarch of Shady Gully? What a joke. And Robin? Man, you should have seen that one in school. Talk about a potate."

"A…po…" I tried to pronounce the word.

Mitch chuckled. "Potate. It's what we called chubby cajun girls."

"Oh." I laughed, although I really didn't get it. Robin was as thin as a rail. I watched as his focus now shifted to his cell phone. He stared at the screen with a mixture of irritation and unease. "Is everything okay?"

"Huh?" He glanced up, squinted, almost as if surprised to see me. "Yeah, yeah. All good. Hey, why don't you go get dressed? I'll have your high-protein-low-carb breakfast ready to go when you're done."

Delighted by the way he wanted to wait on me, to take care of me, I headed off to the bathroom. All of a sudden, I felt the weight of his scrutiny heavy on my backside.

"Oh hey, love."

I turned, now grateful that I'd opted for my robe.

"Fix your hair like the other day. That was smokin' hot."

Twenty minutes later, I stood fretting in front of the vanity.

Although my annoyingly thick hair was now blow-dried, and

the hot iron was primed and ready, I couldn't seem to work the magic the way Dolly had. I did, however, succeed in burning my pointer and middle finger on my right hand while nearly grazing my forehead with 350 degrees of heat.

Discouraged, I blasted my appearance in the mirror. What had Mitch said? That I looked good... but *older*?

I agonized for a few more minutes, and then finally conceded. I unplugged the tools of torture and pulled my raggedy hair into a ponytail.

Mitch's mood dipped as we hiked to Uncle Wolf's place. While only a mile away, the walk was rugged, and mostly uphill. Assuming he was as winded as me, I offered him some water from the thermos.

"Nah. I'm good." When he picked up his pace, I struggled to catch up. "But I sure can hear you huffing and puffing," he added curtly.

"It's hot today."

He stopped. "Sure, it's hot, but it's more likely the cigarettes." He closed in on me. "I found them in your kitchen drawer. When did you start that disgusting habit?" He cut his eyes at my ponytail. "Don't let yourself go, Meadow."

I flinched at the reproach in his tone.

"Those cigarettes are old," I lied. "I quit a long time ago."

He shook his head, hiking on, and I hurried to match his stride.

Finally, thankfully, we came upon Uncle Wolf's place. We were immediately greeted by several squawking chickens, a few stray cats, and Uncle Wolf's dogs, Black and Blue. Mitch inspected the property, taking in the simple, well-built home, as well as the extensive shop. "I see he's still got his garden, huh?"

"He replanted," I answered sulkily, still smarting from his scolding. "After Madhawk set it on fire two years ago."

Mitch scanned the garden. "Does he still grow the good weed? His product was always the best. Kids came from as far out as Toulouse and Naryville for that stuff."

"No. He doesn't do that anymore." I felt this strange need to defend my uncle. "You do know what happened two years ago, don't you?" He looked at me oddly, as if he were struggling to comprehend.

Afraid of exasperating him, I made a point to articulate properly. "Mama's boyfriend, Madhawk, killed her. Didn't you hear?"

"No. I must have missed that. She was The Creek's healer, right?"

I nodded, confounded because she was so much more. Disappointed that Mitch would never get to know her, I explained, "Madhawk beat on her all the time. I'm sure you remember me telling you about that in school. In one of my counseling sessions."

"Oh yeah." He raised one eyebrow seductively. "I loved that job." He stared off into the distance, as if recalling something pleasant.

"He went crazy one night, and Hania was here, with Uncle Wolf, and I was the only one there to protect her. He beat me up too."

"Also."

"Huh?"

"You mean also." He reached for the water thermos. Drank thirstily. "Hania was…?"

"Her dog. A wolf really. She raised him from a pup." I propped my hands on my hips. "How can you not remember what a difficult time I had with Madhawk? I told you all about it when you counseled me. Remember when you asked about the bruises I had all the time?"

"Forgive me, love." He grinned. "I apparently had other things on my mind." He tweaked my breast, and then gently stroked my nipple in a deliberate, precise circle. Without warning, he reached for me, and kissed me with an intensity that both stunned and aroused me.

As the kiss ended, he carefully unzipped his pants. I trembled, my eyes widening in anticipation. And then he peed on Uncle Wolf's tomato plants.

"I'm sorry for your loss, love. Really tragic." Mitch squinted at the sun for an extended moment, allowing the gravity of the remark to linger appropriately. And then, "Let's head out. Maybe you can show me The Creek's fancy new bridge?"

"Okay." After I pulled my disturbed gaze off Uncle Wolf's sullied plants, I followed. I attempted to shoo Black and Blue off as they trotted beside us, but when they persisted, I made a path to the shed. "Just a second. I'll get them some kibble."

Mitch waited patiently as I fed them.

"Aren't they cute?" I asked lightly. "They're strays that landed at the right place. Some kind of lab mixes, I think."

"How do you tell which is which?"

"Black is the black one." I scratched him beneath his chin. "And Blue is the one that looks blue in the sunlight." I positioned Blue toward the sun, exhibiting the way his fur gleamed a velvety bluish-black.

"Nice."

To his credit, Mitch slowed his pace for me as we hiked toward the Unity Bridge. Once there he grew cheerful and affectionate. "Fancy piece of hardware here. How'd y'all rate this?"

"Luke commissioned it. After he became mayor. And Bella… well, she almost died when the old one collapsed." I searched his face. "Would you like to hear a little about her? Your beautiful daughter?" I smiled hopefully.

"Yeah, sure." He scrolled through his phone as he nestled into the shade beneath a giant oak tree. He patted the space beside him. "From what I saw, she's beautiful. Just like you were."

"She's a lot braver than I was at her age. She's courageous and bold." I side-eyed him. "She must have got that from you."

"Must have." He put his phone away.

I thought of the way Bella had snaked her way into the lives of his family and their friends, all for a chance to find him. "Were you shocked to hear from her?"

"I'm surprised she found me."

"She was determined. She wants to get to know you."

He reached again for his phone, seemingly distracted. "Maybe we can do that. At some point."

A heavy sense of foreboding ran through me. "But…when? I thought you came to see her for her wedding."

"Nah, weddings aren't my scene. I make it a point to steer clear of those." He glinted at me. "Does she have a lot of friends? Girls are fun at that age, up for anything. Maybe I can take 'em out for their bachelorette party or something?"

I thought carefully about how to respond. "She has a few, but…I think she's more interested in some time with you. She has a lot of questions—"

"Questions?" Exasperation floated off him. "I'm not…that's not what I'm here for."

"What are you here for then, Mitch?"

"I'm here because she asked me to come." Irritated, he pushed himself to his feet. "I didn't come to get the third degree, that's for sure." He looked at me harshly. "From anyone." He paced and studied his phone intermittently. Restless. Offended. Bored.

I'd messed up by pleading Bella's case. And why? For the life of me, I couldn't understand why I'd ruin my chance to have him all to myself, and for Bella, who didn't even appreciate or approve of me. "Here. Look." And yet I found myself scrolling through my phone for her picture. I tapped on the image of her in her wedding dress. "Isn't she stunning?"

He scanned the photo, enlarging, zooming for a better view. "Nice." He handed it back to me.

"And did you know she sings? She has a beautiful voice."

"We should take a trip," he said impulsively. "Just the two of us. Maybe a beach." He inched closer, tugging my belt loops until our bodies touched.

"What do you have in mind?"

He responded, widening his hands, and pulling me snugly into his groin. "Let's leave today. We could be in Gulf Shores by midnight."

"Well," I grinned favorably, "that would be excellent except the rehearsal dinner is tomorrow night."

"The what?" His expression of distaste made the inside of his mouth snap. "Oh, come on, love. You'd pass up a chance to go to the beach with me for some rubber chicken and a night with Desi and Lenny? If so, you aren't nearly as smart as I thought you were."

"Mitch. This is important to Bella. I'm the mother-of-the-bride, and you're the—"

"I barely even know her!"

Stunned by the vehemence of his statement, I hung back, struggling for the correct response. Finally, I said, "I don't understand. If not for Bella, why did you come?" I held my breath. Hoping he would say *for me*. Afraid he would say *for me*.

"Because I'm an idiot, I guess. Maybe I was just curious about what was going on in Shady Gully these days. I don't know. But I didn't come to be put on the spot, that's for sure." He marched toward the bridge, clearly done with me.

A fire truck approached from the Shady Gully side, heading into The Creek. It looked like Redflyer, the chief of The Creek's fire department, and his buddies, Youngdeer and Moonpipe. As they crossed the bridge with nary a rumble, I felt a strange sense of pride for the way Luke's bridge held sturdy and reliable against the weight of the fire truck.

"We should go." I gestured toward the woods, where we could easily slip away.

"What for?" Mitch frowned at me. "I have every right to be here." He ducked his chin toward the Creeks in the fire truck. "As much as them."

The big, red truck slowed to a stop, and Redflyer, brawny and fierce like a warrior, appeared wary when he set his eyes on Mitch. "Hey, Meadow. Everything alright?"

"Yeah," I answered, although honestly, I wasn't at all sure anymore.

"Of course, she's alright," Mitch snapped at Redflyer. "Why wouldn't she be?"

"I know who you are." Youngdeer stuck his head out the passenger window. "Ain't nobody wants you around here."

Mitch stalked over to the truck. "That's not true, nitwit. My daughter, Bella, wants me here. Meadow wants me here. Isn't that right, love?" Mitch glanced over his shoulder, planting me with a sugary sweet once-over.

Now Bella was his daughter. Now I was his love.

Resignation mingled with acceptance, and just like that, I was once again that young girl in school, a low-life Creek, dazzled to be noticed by the sophisticated guidance counselor. To be seen through his hungry blue eyes, and grateful for his attention, his concern, and his tutelage.

And somewhere, deep down inside, wretched and miserable because of it.

"That's right," I said to my Creek friends. "I'm fine, Redflyer. Really."

Reluctantly, Redflyer cranked the fire truck to a start and chugged toward The Creek's new fire station. As I watched them go, I found myself both dismayed and ashamed by the encounter. Once their truck disappeared into the bowels of The Creek, Mitch gestured us forward. "Come on, love. Let's head back to your shanty." He held my hand. "Do y'all still call them shanties on The Creek?"

I said nothing, finding words impossible, but holding his hand tightly, nonetheless. He chattered incessantly on the walk, topics ranging from vacation plans to what he'd cook for dinner. "Maybe some pasta? With a red sauce?"

Hopeless, depressed, and confused, I longed for a cigarette. A glass of wine.

Perhaps even to be with Bella and the girls as they talked about the rehearsal dinner and the wedding.

Where had that come from?

As we closed in on my shanty, I spotted Luke's truck parked in the dirt driveway.

"Who's that?" Mitch asked.

I held my arm out, urging caution. "It's Luke's truck, Mitch. It's probably Bella. Or the both of them."

"Oh." Mitch's blue eyes darted nervously, obviously scrambling for a passage to escape.

I turned to him, asked, "Would you like to cook dinner for them? I'm sure they'd love a nice pasta and red sauce."

His heels drug to a stop. "Pass."

Despondent, I asked, "Why don't you want to meet her?"

"I do. I do," he lied. "Just not today."

Chapter Eighteen

Nobel Prize
Violet

Micah eyed the monitor critically. "Thank goodness we aren't in the Azalea Room." She swept her gaze around the large event room in the Shady Gully Recreation Center. "That place has bad juju." She lowered her head once again to her laptop, carefully synchronizing each photo to match the crescendos of the music.

We were in the Redbud Room, a gorgeous room with high ceilings and lots of light. In preparing for tomorrow night's rehearsal dinner, Micah handled the logistics of the photo montage while I addressed the convoluted table settings. So far, I'd managed to cover the first table with a white tablecloth. "Where do the centerpiece arrangements go again?" I asked, totally confused.

"Uh…" Micah twisted her petite frame my way. "The center?"

"Well, you never know these days." I carefully set the lavender, pink, and deep purple flowers at the center of the round table. "Each table also includes"—I read from the specific list Aunt Desi had given me—"three candles, a printed menu, a story card, and a framed photo of the bride and groom."

"You're right. They really should have drawn you an illustration." Micah went back to her photos. "Bella should be here soon. She'll know."

"Where are our mothers anyway?" I'd always found Aunt Desi's presence comforting, even if I wasn't overjoyed at the thought of my own mother fluttering about the scene. Moreso, there was still the matter of telling her about my plans. I reasoned, however, that the timing wasn't right now that the wedding was at hand.

"They're in the Dogwood Room, finalizing details with the caterer for the big event. Now that's a fancy room. Have you seen it?"

"No. I heard about it. Floor to ceiling windows. Great view."

"Overlooking the pond. Yeah. The caterer lady, Carly somebody from Naryville, is going all out for the wedding. It's going to be quite elaborate."

"More elaborate than this?" I felt flustered, considering the fancy table arrangements. "I mean, I grew up setting a formal table, but this is complicated."

"I know. Sunday night, for the wedding, there are going to be six settings per table. She's doing tomorrow night's rehearsal dinner too, but it won't be as high pressure." Micah shot me a mischievous grin. "Check it out. It's Petey! Naked!"

I nearly dropped the plate in my hands. I—sort of—averted my eyes as I glanced at the monitor in the center of the room. Petey, as a toddler, running around a kiddie pool, stark naked. Luke, slightly older, seemed to be chasing him with the appropriate swim trunks.

Micah's shoulders shook as she cackled. "Should I use it? I think I should. Do you think he'd be mad?"

"I don't know." I shrugged. "But you'd better prepare for the consequences just in case."

We turned toward the French doors as Bella flew into the room with an easel and an art case. "Hey. Sorry I'm late." She appeared hurried, tense, and very distracted. "Oh, the flowers are beautiful." She held her hair back as she bent to inhale the scent. "That makes me happy."

"And what's not making you happy?" I asked. "Is something wrong?"

Bella placed the easel at the room's entrance and began unloading her calligraphy supplies. Hesitant at first, she elaborated after a cautious glance at the entrance. "I went to Mama's.

I don't know why. That never ends well." She wiped her craft brushes with a cloth. "But we had a semi-decent moment a few days ago at Luke's apartment. It was the day we found out Brother Wyatt passed. Anyway, we talked a little about my Daddy. Gosh, just saying that sounds weird."

"So, what happened?" I asked. "Did you find him?"

"No." She brooded. "I mean, I'm not sure."

Micah moved away from Petey's naked picture, closing in on Bella. "What does that mean?"

"Well, Cruella Claire told me Mama had been sick. Some kind of stomach virus. I thought I'd ride out and check on her, you know, make sure she wasn't trying to get out of coming to the wedding."

"Bella." Micah gaped. "She wouldn't do that."

Bella raised her eyebrows doubtfully. "Nobody was home, but Mama never locks her door, so I went inside just like always. I think…well, I'm sure…he was there. Or else she's hooking up with somebody else."

"What?" Micah's whisper came out like a shout. "How do you know?"

Bella rolled her eyes. "The bed wasn't made. Dishes for two. And dirty underwear."

"That's terrible," Micah hissed.

When Bella blanched, I said evenly, "Look, the sheriff can't arrest him, right? So maybe it's best just to let it be. Let it play out."

"I just don't like them hiding from me. I mean, not to sound self-involved or anything, but this *is* kind of about me, isn't it?"

When dialogue from the outer room grew louder, Bella, Micah, and I flew apart guiltily. My mother and Desi waltzed in carrying boxes filled with lavender candles and silverware. They regarded us curiously.

"What?" Micah insisted. "We're working." She went back to her slide show editing, while Bella turned toward her easel, brush in hand.

Aunt Desi winked at me. "The table is coming along beautifully." She handed me some candles, demonstrating how she wanted them placed. "Perfect. It will be lovely." She wheeled. "What do you think, Bella?"

"I love it," Bella said. "And I'll have the menu done shortly."

"I always wanted to learn calligraphy," my mother said as she moved toward Bella's easel, admiring her long, even strokes. "I don't know why I never learned."

"It's never too late to try something new." This from Aunt Desi, who smiled contentedly as she watched over Bella's shoulder.

Aunt Desi seemed different. More composed, at ease, and certainly less troubled. I considered her poised demeanor, suddenly hopeful that her doctor's visit had gone well. "How did your doctor's appointment go this morning?" I asked brazenly.

Micah looked over her shoulder at her mother while Bella's calligraphy brush froze in midair. While Aunt Desi's condition had been alluded to and whispered about in private conversations, it had never been discussed in great detail, and certainly not before everyone.

"You know, girls," she answered after a beat. "I'm optimistic."

My mom leaned into Aunt Desi then, and they bent their heads together. "She's going to be fine."

As they looked at each other for an extended moment, a lifetime of layers seemed to unfold between them. Their friendship and their history together had always seemed magical and otherworldly to the rest of us, as if their bond transcended the here and now and would eventually extend into the heavens.

"So, Bella." Aunt Desi seemed eager to change the subject. "How is Duchess? Is she feeling any better today?"

"What's wrong with Duchess?" I asked, concerned.

"I don't know." Bella sighed. "She's probably just exhausted with so much going on, but she seems tired lately. Not her usual wild self." We all watched, almost hypnotized, as Bella completed the word *risotto* and rounded off the letter *o* in a sassy swirl.

As she inspected her work critically, she added, "I took her to the vet yesterday, and they did some blood work. She's at home now. Hopefully she'll get some rest." Bella cast her eyes around the room doubtfully. "I'm trying not to worry, but she just doesn't seem right."

I frowned.

"Where do you want these extra tables?" Sheriff Rick's voice boomed from the outer foyer.

"Oh, hold on." My mother dashed over to extend the French doors for him and Uncle Lenny. "Right over there. By Violet."

"Hold the doors open," Uncle Lenny said. "The boys are heading in with another one."

As they carefully set the table down, Sheriff Rick smoothed his mustache and attempted to make eye contact. I busied myself with plates and candles, doing my best to deflect his attention. "Ain't that just as pretty as a picture." He specified my table display. "All the colors and whatnot."

I leaned in the direction of the display, feigning deep concentration as I moved a candle precisely to the left.

"Violet." My mother spoke in that annoying corrective voice that drove me batty. "Ricky is speaking to you."

I glared back, livid. How dare she call me out in front of everyone? With exaggerated deliberation, I removed another candle from the box, defiant as I set it on the table.

"Hurry." Petey's voice teased mischief as he entered the Redbud Room. "Tell Luke where this table goes or he's going to have a hernia on his wedding night." Petey's laughter mingled with Sterling's and Luke's as they lugged the table toward me.

Great.

"Hey, Amber," Petey said in greeting, giving me the eye as they set the table down. "What's up?"

I turned away from him just as I'd turned away from the sheriff.

Aunt Desi distracted everyone with an upbeat inquiry. "So, have we heard from Timothy? Anybody know when his flight is coming in tomorrow?"

"Should be early," Uncle Lenny answered. "It's the first one into

Alexandria in the morning. We've got the thing with Father Patrick at ten, so he'll make it in plenty of time for that." He drifted over to his wife, kissing her forehead. "How did it go this morning?"

As he, my mother, and Aunt Desi began to murmur softly in conference, I observed several encouraging nods and a lot of hopeful head bobbing.

I turned back to the daunting table setting with a sense of resolve.

"Hey." I felt his breath in my ear, and despite myself, my heart flipped with expectation. "Are you still mad at me?"

"No, Petey. I'm done being mad." *Resigned, maybe, but not mad.*

"Seriously, we're a team. We always have been. Just because our plans didn't work out exactly the way we wanted doesn't mean that one day we can't—"

"We can't what, Petey?" I hissed under my breath, growing frustrated as the sheriff struck up a conversation with Sterling a few feet away. "I'm going to do my thing now. Okay? You should do yours."

"What?" He looked stricken. "Why do you keep saying that?"

I rededicated myself to the table placements, hoping I could blink back the tears clouding my eyes. *How dare he act like he cared now?*

"Did you talk to your mom yet?" He moved closer, blocking Sheriff Rick's line of vision. "You need to. She's getting suspicious."

"Suspicious?"

"Just saying. She asked me what was going on with you and why"—his remarks grew softer—"why you didn't like the sheriff."

"What?"

A hush fell over the room as everyone glanced my way. I shifted my focus, tried to decide on a stupid candle.

Petey plucked a deep lavender candle from my hand and set it on the table next to the centerpiece. "Now. Will you at least listen to me?"

Sterling approached and offered in a mocking whisper. "Y'all are strange. Anybody ever tell you that?"

I rolled my eyes, now determined to ignore them both.

When Luke led the sheriff over and the whole lot of them proceeded to inspect my table arrangement, I was brimming over with irritation.

"Really nice," mumbled the sheriff. "Really, really nice."

"I don't know," teased Petey. "Kind of girly, don't you think? I mean, where's the gray? The brown? The blue?"

"Don't worry, Petey." Sterling grinned. "Someday you'll get your turn."

"I doubt it." Luke put in. "Can't imagine who'd have him."

Sheriff Rick, the big oaf, chose this moment to defend my skills, my honor, and more succinctly, me. Not necessary, or even logical seeing as how they were all teasing, but that wasn't the point. The point was my mother was watching, and Mr. Magnanimous was about to put on a show. I wanted to string him up by his mustache.

"Are you boys kidding me? Violet here has bigger things to do than set a table. She's gonna set the world on fire. You'll see her on the cover of *Time* magazine one day, I'd bet on it."

I turned away from him as his exaggerated southern accent and overly affected good ole boy routine grated on my very last nerve.

"She's smart as a whip, I'll tell you that." He went on, "She's got more letters next to her name than's in the alphabet."

"No, I really don't, Sheriff." I pleaded for him to stop. *I needed him to stop.*

"I'm serious. She's gonna be the bread winner in her family. I guarantee." He winked at Petey, who held back a chuckle as he sensed I was on the edge. "Take this to the bank," pronounced the sheriff with overblown bluster, "this woman right here is gonna cure cancer."

The French doors opened on the other side of the room. Regrettably, my head buzzed with such intensity I couldn't turn to see who'd entered. The sheriff's mustache moved up and down, his words coming like tumbleweed in the desert, constant and fast.

I thought I marked my mother moving toward me, but I could have been wrong.

"Ain't no telling how many lives she's gonna save," the sheriff droned on.

It wasn't my mother. It was Tammy Jo. Tight jeans. Raven hair tucked into a ball cap. Glossy lips shining behind a big, inviting smile. "I made it." She beamed at Petey. "I'm ready to help. Y'all just tell me what to do."

They all grinned at her. Petey, Luke, Sterling, Micah, Bella—everyone—welcomed her. Beckoned to her. Invited her into my inner circle. Into my family. Heat rushed through my cheeks, sweat bubbled at my forehead, and I wobbled unsteadily.

"I reckon she'll get a Nobel prize one day," the sheriff still drawled on.

"Tell me what I can do to help," Tammy Jo breathed at me in slow motion through glossy red lips.

"No!" I screamed. "No! No! No!"

My breath felt trapped in my chest as I desperately tried to draw the oxygen out of the air. I needed some space. Some quiet. Out of the corner of my eye I spotted my mother closing in on me. Petey as well. My eyes wobbled, and I could hardly track them in my peripheral vision. I held my hands up. Thankfully, they both stopped.

Everyone stopped. Even the sheriff.

Silence is loud, I thought, as the roaring in my ears continued to rage.

"Honey." It was Uncle Lenny, his soothing tone reminiscent of my daddy's. "It's alright. Let's you and me go get us some air."

Oh, how I loved him, my Uncle Lenny. And how I missed my daddy.

"No," I told Uncle Lenny through thick, garbled tears. "I'm okay." Unconsciously, I reached for his hand, and when he gently tucked it into his own, I raised my head and addressed them all.

"I am only one person. I can't cure cancer. Don't put that on me. Please. I. Can't. Do. It."

When Petey moved toward me, I stopped him with a glare.

"I wish I could, and I'm sorry. I'm sorry I'm letting everyone down. And I'm sorry I'm letting everyone who will ever be sick down. And my daddy." Defeated, and devastated, I wept. "I'm especially sorry I'm letting him down."

As Sterling approached, I placed my other hand in his, now bookended between him and Uncle Lenny. "You all have to stop expecting so much of me," I said thickly. "Putting so much pressure on me. Don't you think I want to be what you all think I am?"

Petey's hazel eyes tugged at mine. He understood. He knew. "I'm not going to be a research physician. I'm not going to run clinical trials on cancer patients." I looked pointedly at the sheriff. "And I'm not going to win a Nobel prize or be on a magazine cover."

My gaze marked Petey. And then Sterling. "I've decided on a different path."

Chapter Nineteen

Game Changer
Lenny

Saturday...Rehearsal Dinner

Luke, Petey, and I presented a united front as we entered Sacred Heart Catholic Church. My attention shifted between Luke as he detailed the eviction and ousting of JJ Wheeler, and Petey as he griped about the possibility of Micah's using a nude photo of him in the family montage at tonight's rehearsal dinner.

"You're not totally nude," Luke insisted. "You had those little flipper thingys on your feet."

"That doesn't make me feel any better." Petey's mood leaned ornery today. No doubt because of Violet's emotional unveiling last evening at the Recreation Center. He refused to talk about it, which concerned me on many levels.

"Alright, boys," I said in my serious-father voice. "Heads up." I led them toward the church hall.

"The hall?" Petey paled. "I thought this was just going to be a few folks."

I shrugged. "I think it's a bit more than that, and this is where Father Patrick instructed us to go, so—"

I opened the door to the sights and sounds of a lively group of Shady Gullians. Competing conversations ricocheted off the walls, and while none of them were decipherable, the urgency was clear.

"Whoa," Petey groaned.

"It'll be fine," Luke assured. "What could go wrong? You've got the mayor with you."

"First off, you should never say that," Petey complained. "And second, why do you have to be in such a good mood? Your pre-wedding euphoria is really getting on my nerves."

Luke laughed brightly, which further irritated his brother.

Charlie Wayne and Sprite from the Quick Stop descended on Luke with enthusiastic, hearty welcomes. "You did it," Sprite said. "You got rid of that scalawag. I saw him packing up his grills on my way here. His man-bun was out to here." Sprite, humming with his daily dose of sugar and caffeine, gestured wildly.

"Yep. I waved to him as he drove off." Charlie Wayne mimed. "And rubbed my belly."

While Charlie Wayne and Sprite collapsed in laughter, Bubba and Daryl looked far from pleased. "Was there really a restriction in the town's by-laws?" Bubba asked as they approached. "Or did you make that one up?"

"There was," Luke insisted. "Plus, he didn't have a license."

As Luke fielded the town's reactions to JJ Wheeler's banishment, I urged Petey aside. While I understood his dispiritedness, I was concerned that his doldrums would run counter to whatever Father Patrick had planned. "I know you're upset about Violet, son. We all are. Especially after the way she ran off in tears yesterday. But—"

"I'm worried, Dad. I burnt her phone up last night, calling and texting, but she never responded."

I nodded. "I don't think she wanted to talk about it. Robin told your mom that she tried to get her to come out to Lake Osprey last night, but she refused. And your mom tried to talk to her this morning before she left, but she wasn't receptive."

"Left? What do you mean?"

"Violet borrowed the minivan this morning. She said she had something important to do in Baton Rouge." I raised my brow pointedly. "Sort of urgent and time sensitive." When Petey looked disturbed, I added, "She said she'd be back in time for the rehearsal tonight."

Father Patrick rounded on us. "While I'm thrilled to lay eyes on you three movers and shakers, I have to ask, where in the world is Timothy?" He stretched his chin toward the door.

"He's stuck in Dallas," I told him heavily. "He considered renting a car and driving, but thought he'd make better time if he waited for the next connecting flight to Alexandria. Desi, Robin, and the sheriff are waiting at the airport for him to arrive. They'll have him here ASAP."

"Let's hope that flight doesn't get delayed." Petey shoved his hands into his pocket. "It would be a shame for him to miss all the fun." He dejectedly scanned the crowd.

"Oh, my word." Father Patrick muttered as he regarded my son, worry stretching his normally cheery face. "Well, heavens. Heavens indeed." He paced. "We must carry on then. He'll get here when he gets here. Are you ready?" He tagged Petey.

"For…what exactly?"

"Never mind. Game on, gentleman." Father Patrick genuflected and clasped his hands in a quick prayer.

As we followed him, Petey turned to me and mouthed, *Game on?*

When we joined the other attendees, they craned their necks in anticipation. Squinted as they searched behind us. "Where is he?" demanded Thaddeus, who sat next to his buddy, Big Al. "Don't tell me I wasted my time coming here today?"

"He didn't show up?" Mrs. Guidry oozed disappointment. "I'm in the middle of a remodel, and I took the time to come." She *tsked*. "I would have expected more from Timothy."

"Have no fear, Mrs. Guidry," Father Patrick said. "Nor you, Mr. Thaddeus, sir. Nor any of you stargazers who'd hoped to catch a glimpse of the mesmerizing Timothy from North Lake."

"I stream every Sunday," muttered Bluejay, who sat next to Redflyer and his pals, Youngdeer and Moonpipe. "My wife wanted me to get his autograph." They turned as one to Wolfheart, who'd dressed in a neatly pressed button-down shirt for the occasion.

After a keen glance at me, Wolfheart concurred. "If he said he'd be here, he'll be here."

I nodded, amused by his careful dress and noticeable eagerness.

"He'll be here shortly," Father Patrick assured the assembly. "Now, is everyone comfy? Have you had your fill of coffee and pastries?"

"I reckon I'll take another one of them bear claws," Big Al said. After Father Patrick neatly placed a pastry on a napkin for him, he dipped his head. "Thank ya, kindly, Father."

"Anyone else?" Father Patrick waved his hand over the refreshments. "I'd have loved to provide a fresh batch of mimosas for the occasion, but time beat me to it."

Granny Lacey, who hailed from The Creek and was known for her skewed recipes, raised her thin eyebrows in complaint. "I must say, the spread is a little sparse. I woulda' gladly made my zucchini bread, if only you'd asked."

A sharp intake of breath slithered throughout the gathering. Patty, Shady Gully's no-nonsense EMT, glanced skeptically at her friend, Denise.

"Well then," Father Patrick addressed Jesse, James, and Dolly, who sat together wearing glum expressions, "I've asked you three to sit in front because you hold a very special place of esteem within our community."

There was a ricochet throughout the room as disbelief triggered forced coughs and exaggerated throat clearing. Once it subsided, Father Patrick began. "First of all, on behalf of everyone here, condolences. Your father was much beloved and respected in Shady Gully."

Jesse, James, and Dolly sat. Stone-faced.

"This morning I got word that Mr. Wheeler, our friend from the four-way stop," Father Patrick paused with mischief in his voice, "decided to take his career in a different direction." He waited until the laughter subsided. "Naturally, we wish him all the best, but the whole, uh, *occupation* of the crossroads, for lack of a better term, got me to thinking."

Cruella Claire slipped behind the priest and filled two coffee mugs. When she returned to her seat, she handed one to Chester, the ornery old coot who hung out at the post office and made sure Claire had a pot full of grudges and contention to stir. I tried to gauge her demeanor, as she would likely be a factor in whatever Father Patrick had up his proverbial robe.

"I've been thinking about the spiritual state of our little town." He presented a somber picture for Brother Wyatt's children. "If I may be honest, and somewhat blunt, the loss of your churches has been devastating for our community."

All at once, the silence became thick with expectancy. While I tried to read the room—and couldn't—I found Petey riveted by Father Patrick's concern and manner of speaking. He and Luke were quite literally leaning forward in their seats.

"It's been two years now"—he looked squarely at Jesse and James—"and while many of your members in good standing join us here for Mass at Sacred Heart, I fear it's because they feel they have no other choice.

"Of course, a large group of your former congregations watch Timothy online, and that's splendid, but I'm not sure taking communion in your jammies on a regular basis provides the reverence the holy sacrament deserves. The internet is a wonder, it truly is, but I fear it can make us lazy and apathetic. My friends, I have come to the conclusion that the spiritual health of Shady Gully is at great risk." His words slowed, which elevated the moment's significance. "We are in dire need of a brick-and-mortar church. Besides Sacred Heart, of course."

Jesse snorted loud enough to draw everyone's attention. "Well, Patrick, you're not going to get that. Not unless my brother sells me his land."

James snapped in return. "Or you sell me yours. That way I can build a nice big church on the corner and get everyone out of their jammies on Sunday, just like the priest said."

Dolly remained quiet, focusing her attention on her stiletto heels and pink toenails as she dangled her foot back and forth.

"You are right on one thing, Patrick," Jesse sniped. "There is no alternative. Yours is the only church in town, and unless my brother gives up his land, there will be no building one either. Ever."

Luke, who'd been listening intently, ventured. "Well actually, there's plenty of land. Perhaps someone else could build one Somewhere else."

James cut off the crowd's mumbling with a stern rebuttal. "And where might they build one? In the boondocks somewhere? Across the creek?" His expression exuded distaste. "That's preposterous."

Wolfheart cleared his throat. "Don't tempt us, James. The community has lost faith in you. We'd be happy to build a church across the creek, and people would come, especially now that we've got the Unity bridge.

Claire *harrumphed*. "I don't think so. That's a long way to drive. However, I agree with Father Patrick, y'all need to come to terms. This has gone on long enough." She bobbed her head with finality. "We need our church at the four-way stop. We demand it."

"I'm not selling," Jesse said stubbornly, his eyes bulging amid his heavy jowls.

"Well, neither am I," echoed James.

"That's it then," Jesse curled his lip in satisfaction. "No land. No church. And certainly, no preacher." He snorted petulantly. "Without us, there's nobody to preach. Unless your pal, Timothy, is moving to Shady Gully, which I highly doubt."

"Oh my." Mrs. Guidry shivered in excitement. "Is that what this is about, Father? Is Timothy leaving Lexington and moving to Shady Gully to preach for us?"

A crescendo of hopeful giggles spread throughout the hall.

"No, no." Father Patrick held his hands up, putting a stop to the dizzy speculation. "I'm afraid not, but—"

James interrupted, highly irritated. "This was a waste of time."

"I disagree." Father Patrick's tone turned plucky. "In fact, I believe there is someone to preach. Someone we all know. Born and raised in Shady Gully. A fine young man who inspired us and prayed for us when the town nearly burned two years ago. He's one of our own."

"Who?" James asked. "Are you talking about…" He cut his eyes at Petey. "*Him?*"

"Yes, I am."

"That's ludicrous. He's never been to Bible College. He has no experience. Our church elders would never allow it." James shrugged.

"The members in good standing would find it laughable," echoed Jesse, his chair creaking with the bulk of his weight.

"Besides, he stays in Kentucky half the time," added James. "What would be the point?"

"I—" Petey stuttered.

"I happen to know he's been looking for land," Father Patrick countered. "Right here in Shady Gully." He winked at Wolfheart. "Perhaps, Mr. Wolf, even along the creek."

Petey paled in his seat beside me.

"And really, James, I hate to ask," Father Patrick went on, "what elders do you have? I wonder, since your church burned, have you kept up with your community members? Checked in and prayed with them regularly? Do you gather weekly in living rooms, back yards, or…anywhere for that matter?"

Uncomfortable, James swallowed deeply, finding himself bound to give his brother an opening.

Jesse scanned the room, making a point of lingering on each of his past church members. "What say you?" A long, awkward silence ensued. "Come on, now. Thaddeus, what about you? Would you feel comfortable with this inexperienced boy telling you what a sinner you are?"

Thaddeus frowned, awkwardly brushing away pastry crumbs as he stood. "Well, I reckon I'd take offense at that, yeah. Just as I would from you Jesse, to be fair." He glanced briefly at Petey. "But no, I'd vote no. I just don't see the kid as an authority."

"Me either," agreed Big Al.

"Me either," added old man Chester in a testy tone.

Claire stood. "I like Petey okay, and I want a new church, but I don't think he has enough experience."

Patty and Denise nodded in accordance.

"I mean," went on Claire, "don't you have to have a degree or something?"

Father Patrick cleared his throat. "I don't know." He turned to Jesse. "Do you have a degree?"

Jesse dissolved in a spit of anger, muttering and biting back curses.

"I've got an associate degree," James said proudly.

As they bickered back and forth, Dolly's pink toenailed foot came to a complete stop. She removed a set of documents from her purse, stood, and ambled to the front of the hall next to Father Patrick. "Actually. I have something to say."

"Whoa," muttered Sprite from the back of the hall. "Game changer."

"I appreciate what you're trying to do here, Father, but…" She stared at her brothers. "You're wasting your time with them. I tried to get them to come to an agreement by paying JJ Wheeler to take over the corner. I thought mocking them would work, but we all know how that ended." She shrugged. "So now, I'm the one you need to be talking to." She held up the papers, looking like the cat that ate way more than the canary. "In one day, the land is going to belong to me. Both lots. All of it."

A hush fell across the church hall, and then rose again in high pitched confusion. Father Patrick spotted Luke, Petey, and me, and raised his shoulders in bewilderment. After an extended moment of chaos, Luke walked to the head of the hall and picked up a sanctuary candlestick. He hammered it against Father Patrick's pulpit. Once he had everyone's attention, he gestured to Dolly. "You were saying."

"Daddy's will. This is it right here." She skewered her brothers with a diabolical glare. "It states that upon his death, Jesse and James have six days to come to terms over the two lots at the four-way stop. And if they can't agree, it reverts to me." She waved the will at her brothers. "And tomorrow is the sixth day."

Again, sheer pandemonium as the reverberations of Dolly's disclosure swept through the room. I watched, stunned, as several folks pecked urgently on their phones, eager to alert their fellow Shady Gullians.

Dolly has certainly outsmarted her dastardly brothers, I thought, but the bigger question was whether she was worse than the both of them put together?

"I'd like to hear from Petey," she said snidely. "The land might be for sale soon."

While Jesse and James were in the midst of a conniption fit, Father Patrick gazed at the ceiling in prayerful praise. I admit, I felt a flutter of exhilaration myself, but when I urged Petey toward the front of the room, he refused to budge.

"This isn't the way it's supposed to be," he mumbled, as if dazed. When Father Patrick, Wolfheart, and Luke closed in, each offering encouragement, he added, "Y'all don't understand. I'm not feeling very…confident today."

"Well, that's a pity, my boy." Father Patrick patted his leg. "It happens to the best of us sometimes. Only one way around it though." He looked squarely at Petey. "Put your game face on and head to centerstage. And trust the Lord, of course."

"Come on, little brother," Luke urged Petey. "This is your big chance. You can do this."

"This isn't the way it's supposed to go," Petey repeated, emotional and wrought-up. "She should be here." He lowered his head.

Distressed by the weight of my son's pain, I was just about to come to his defense when Jesse smirked from across the room.

"Well, there you have it," he snorted. "The kid is clearly not up to it. He can't even work up the nerve to speak in front of a small audience."

"Petey," Father Patrick offered in a soothing voice, "I'm sure you've considered this before, haven't you?"

"Sure, but it's true what they say. I don't have a degree. I've never been to Bible College."

"But you've had two years with Timothy." Wolfheart crouched beside him. "Don't you think that happened for a reason?"

Luke, Father Patrick, Wolfheart, and I watched as Petey's face filled with resolve. We traded looks of relief when he stood and doggedly faced the crowd. "Thank you, Dolly, for this opportunity," he said politely.

"The land's not hers yet," James seethed. "And you'll never preach in my church. I can assure you of that."

"Well, you don't really have a church right now, so…" Dolly said scornfully.

Petey considered the audience and began tentatively. "Jesse and James are right. I don't have a degree, and to be honest with y'all, higher education scares the daylights out of me." A few undecided chuckles traveled throughout the gathering. "I have this friend, well, she's the smartest person in the world, and she…she lights up when talking about cells and tissues, coronal and axial frames." He eyed the crowd. "Yeah. I don't know what any of that means either."

Chuckles spread as folks bobbed their heads in consensus.

"My speech is plain. I have an accent. Sometimes people think I'm…well, they think I'm unsophisticated. And I reckon they'd be right on that. Sometimes I even forget scriptures—"

Charlie Wayne cleared his throat. "Are you trying to convince us or scare us to death?"

"I just want you to know I'm not fancy. But I'm not a pretender either."

The room went quiet as church elders and community leaders watched Petey closely.

"I won't put on any airs or try to be showy with my words. Honestly, I couldn't even if I tried. But if you consider me to be your pastor, we can build a church in Shady Gully." Petey passed a look at Dolly, and then across the assembly. "Whether it's at the four-way, or The Creek, or wherever, I believe that together, we can start a revival like you ain't never seen."

"Amen!"

All heads swiveled to the back of the hall.

Tall. Gangly. Blue-eyed. Arms lined with tattoos.

"Oh, my word," gushed Mrs. Guidry.

Timothy had arrived.

With the notable exception of Jesse, James, and Dolly, Timothy shared coffee and pastries with most of Shady Gully. He heard stories about crops that had come to life, viruses that had disappeared, and tumors that had turned out to be benign. The Shady Gully storytellers insisted it was because of him and his inspirational sermons, but Timothy gave all the credit to God.

He spent some time on the basketball court outside the church hall, shooting hoops with Wolfheart and Father Patrick and then playing horse with Fireman and a gaggle of kids who had appeared out of nowhere. Everyone seemed fascinated with Timothy's tattoos, especially Father Patrick who unabashedly ogled them as the sinewy preacher extended his inked arms to make several layups.

And he did, for the very first time, sign an autograph. "I've never done this before, Mr. Bluejay. I'm not sure I know how." As a circle of heads hung over him as if he were a rock star, Timothy scribbled his name on a pastry napkin, and handed it to the beaming Bluejay. "My *y* is a little unruly, but hopefully your wife can read it."

On and on it went, and I couldn't help but think he was having as much fun as the residents of Shady Gully.

Desi, Robin, and Ricky had done well delivering Timothy to Shady Gully, and now they stood with Sterling, Micah, and Bella along the edges of the crowd. The sheriff even seemed a bit starstruck, repeatedly smoothing his mustache as he lingered amid the throng.

Petey, despite it all, remained disturbingly mournful.

"Have you heard from Violet?" I asked Robin.

She glanced at her watch. "Not yet. She said she'd make it back for the rehearsal tonight."

Eventually, Timothy addressed his audience right there on the edge of the basketball court. When he motioned for Petey to join him, I recognized the downhearted shade in my son's eyes.

"Now, I could share with y'all all the amazing things Petey did while he was interning with me in Kentucky, but it's almost lunch time, and I understand the mayor's rehearsal dinner is tonight. I hear that's kind of a big deal. Am I right?"

A smack of howls spread like wildfire, and Luke's face turned red when Bella stood on her tiptoes and gave him a peck on the cheek.

"So, I won't take the time to go into detail about Petey's four mission trips to Haiti, how he served the poor with compassion and grace. And I won't tell you about the countless teenage boys who turned away from drugs after receiving Petey's counsel. And I won't even mention the number of people who came to visit, and later join, North Lake Christian Church after sharing a mere conversation with Petey at the checkout lane at Kroger.

"What I'd like to do though, is read a letter I received just before boarding the plane to come here. If you'll allow me." Timothy pulled a ragged envelope folded in three out of his pocket, finding a tattered sheet of notebook paper inside. "This letter is from Kenny," he said soberly, "who lives in Opelousas, Louisiana."

As I perused the crowd, I noted the way they moved closer, leaning in with heightened interest.

Timothy read, "Dear North Lake. Sorry, I don't know the pastor's name. Hopefully whoever reads this does."

A few chuckles sounded as Desi tugged my sleeve, and whispered, "Look. Violet just drove up." Sure enough, Violet had zeroed in on Timothy, the crowd, and Petey.

When the sheriff's phone buzzed, I tried to measure the concern in his face as he listened to the caller, but distractedly turned back to Timothy when he continued reading the letter.

"My name is Kenny," Timothy glanced at the crowd, "And I should be dead."

"Oh," Mrs. Guidry gasped, as did her buddy, Mrs. Shanna May, a much beloved secretary who'd retired from Shady Gully High.

"My plan was to jump off the Broussard Bridge as soon as my shift ended at the café. I'd already loaded rocks from the quarry into my backpack, and I had just enough gas to drive out to the bridge. I wasn't scared, but I was in a bad mood, and it got worse when this young couple came in and took forever ordering their breakfast. The guy, he was especially annoying because he kept looking at me. Like, really looking at me. The kind of looking where somebody really sees you, and I didn't want to be seen that day. He kept asking me questions, about how my day was going and stuff, and it was like he somehow *knew...*

"His eyes were weird. Not brown, and not blue, but somewhere in between, with a light that moved around inside them. He had a cross tattooed on his wrist. And when he asked me *how he could pray for me*, it really set me off. I don't believe in God, and I don't pray. But this guy, he wouldn't let up, and I really wanted to get on that bridge. I could almost feel the heaviness of the rocks against my back, and the freedom of nothing but the air below my feet.

"So when his girlfriend went to the bathroom, I don't know why, maybe just to shut him up, I told him everything. I told him about my boy, Jack. About how me and my wife tried for years to have a baby and couldn't. How we did fertility treatments until we went bankrupt, lost our house, and I had to get a second job at the café. And how, just when we gave up trying, she got pregnant. It was like a miracle, only it wasn't, because we lost Jack after only six months. He drowned. In the bathtub. My wife was bathing him, and the phone rang, and..."

Timothy paused in his reading, partly to gather himself, and partly to let the writer's testimony resonate with the community. I put my arm around Desi, who had tears in her eyes. Wolfheart stood off to the side with Father Patrick, trying to look unmoved as he shuffled his feet.

I stole a quick glance at Ricky, who cradled his phone, pacing and looking agitated. Perhaps with the caller, or maybe with what he was reporting.

Timothy went on. "Things went downhill from there. My wife and I started fighting all the time, and she eventually left me. She said I made her feel guilty, and I probably did. But here's the thing, the reason I'm writing today, about the guy with the tattoo and the eyes. As I was telling him all about my Jack, about how he was the greatest little kid in the world, and how he had this funny little smile that would make his mouth go all goofy and lopsided, well, I'm just bawling my eyes out, and when I look up, I see the guy with the tattoo and the eyes, and he's crying too. That's when I knew he wasn't a faker. He gave me his card. He wrote down the names of several churches close to me, but he wrote down so many the ink bled across his name.

"When he and his girl left, I thought about my Jack, about his crooked, lopsided smile, and instead of going to the bridge after my shift, I dumped the rocks out of my backpack, and went home to my apartment. I kept thinking about this guy, how he seemed legit, and how he didn't judge me. The rest of the day I couldn't get this guy out of my head, and at some point, I realized…if he hadn't come into the café, I'd be dead. So I took a chance, and I called one of the numbers on the card. I went right then and talked to somebody. And everything sort of clicked.

"I still hurt. A lot. And I'm sad, especially when I think of Jack. But I don't have the urge to stuff my backpack with rocks anymore. I'm doing better. I'm taking it day by day. Anyway, I'm thinking this guy must work at your church in Kentucky, and I wanted you to know my story, and what he did for me that day. This guy with the tattoo and the light in his eyes…he saved my life.

"Sincerely, Kenny."

After Timothy refolded the letter, he scanned the crowd. "I'd

encourage you to consider this young man with the light of the Lord inside him. He will lead your revival. And he will save lives."

The moving testimony of the grief-stricken man from the café still reverberated, and Desi especially was moved to tears. But happy ones. For the first time in a long while, I felt optimistic.

But then the sheriff crossed the length of the basketball court with an irritated stride, and I prepared myself for bad news. As did Wolfheart. We both tentatively approached him.

"Let's go pick up Mitch," Ricky said.

"What?" Wolfheart's eyes narrowed into slits. "What's happened?"

"Quietdove and Max have been working NCIC. They struck gold today."

"And?" Wolfheart pressed.

"There's a warrant out for Mitch's arrest. Seems he got into trouble in Texas for something very similar, but in this case, the young lady's parents filed charges. We can officially pick him up."

"But we don't know where he is," I said doubtfully.

Wolfheart and Ricky exchanged looks, and then their eyes cut across the crowd toward Redflyer, who watched our conversation closely.

"Actually," Wolfheart said. "We do."

Chapter Twenty

Late Night Gold
Meadow

"You don't have to go to the rehearsal dinner tonight," I told Mitch for the fifth time. "But I'm going." I sifted through another photo album, determined to find the picture Bella had come looking for yesterday.

I faltered as I recalled the way we'd shrunk into the woods behind my shanty, all because Mitch hadn't wanted to rush an introduction with Bella. Why he dawdled over meeting his own daughter was beyond me, but we'd held back, lurking in the brush like common criminals. Once Bella had driven off in Luke's truck, we'd entered the shanty and spotted her note. She'd been desperate to find one of the most treasured photos in our family.

"So, who's this picture of anyway? Me?" Mitch chuckled as I continued my search. "Come on," he said, "I know you have some photos of yours truly stashed away somewhere. Where are they?"

He randomly picked up objects as he walked around my living room, making a production of searching beneath them.

I ignored him as I combed through ragged photos in hopes of finding the lost picture. Taken long ago, the photo was of the three of us; my mother, Peony, Bella as a newborn baby, and me, a young mother of fifteen.

"I don't have any hidden photos of you," I lied.

"Well, okay then." He frowned. "I guess I'll throw away the ones I have of you."

My heartbeat quickened at the thought of him reminiscing over photos of me, perhaps even pining over a missed chance at love.

"I'm joking," he said. "I don't keep old pictures. I focus on what's ahead, not what's behind."

It seemed like every time he spoke, his thoughtless and hurtful words cut me to the core. Or was I simply too sensitive and needy? "Well, I can't find it." I rose, making a conscious effort to appear less needy. "I'm going to go shower and get dressed."

"Whatever." He flopped onto the couch and scrolled through his phone. "If you want to go to some manufactured celebration, go on. I might prowl around Shady Gully and see what I can get up to."

"On your motorcycle? Do you really think that's a good idea?" I panicked at the thought of him leaving. What if he never came back? And just disappeared like he had twenty-four years ago? An overwhelming temptation to get around going tonight bloomed inside me, as thoughts of whatever *Mitch might get up to* teased with foreboding.

"Geez, are you lecturing me about my motorcycle? You sound exactly like my mother, and she's old. Don't be that way, Meadow. If you act old, you'll get old."

I stood, faking nonchalance. "Whatever. You'll just miss all the fun."

He scoffed; his eyes now squarely focused on his phone. The cursed device seemed to dictate his temperament. Whether flippant, cheerful, or uneasy, it apparently held all the riddles to his fickle state of mind. It was constantly with him, and he guarded it with a complex passcode.

"I highly doubt it will be fun." He frowned, dismissing me as he texted away. "More like lame."

As I moped to the bathroom, I considered the irony of my championing an event that I'd dreaded for the past several months. I turned on the hot water in the shower and undressed as I waited for the old plumbing pipes to heat up. I then carefully placed my dress on the bed and set my heels and purse to the side.

I'd just slipped into the warm flow of oscillating water when Mitch opened the shower door. My resolve was no match for his suggestive grin, and I willingly invited him in.

Surprisingly, he pulled me out, dripping wet, and carried me to the bed. "I want you." He kissed me roughly, pushing me onto my back. "Right here." When my damp skin crushed against the pristine and perfectly pressed fabric of my dress, I bucked.

"What?" He scrunched his face angrily. "It'll be fine."

"No." I squirmed from beneath his body. "Stop, Mitch. Let me get dressed."

When he sneered, I suddenly saw him for the ugly, cruel, and unseemly man he'd become. Or maybe he'd always been?

Bang! Bang! Bang!

The front door of my shanty hammered with sounds much too loud to be anything but trouble. Mitch and I traded wide-eyed looks, and he quickly jumped off the bed. When he reached for his underwear, I automatically followed his lead, finding my robe hanging on a hook in the bathroom.

More thunderous whacks. Louder, and more insistent this time. And then, "Sheriff's Department! Open up!"

"Meadow!" I heard Uncle Wolf shout. "Are you okay?"

Mitch cursed as he frantically searched for the nearest exit, zeroing in on the flimsy window in my bedroom. He quickly hobbled into his jeans, one leg in, one out, and somehow managed to raise the window. He then manhandled the screen behind it, and eventually stumbled to a fall outside.

"Greetings, dirtbag." Deputy Max, Robin's little brother, remarked sarcastically. "Fancy meeting you here."

Quietdove posed beside him, one olive-skinned hand resting on his gun.

Mitch let out a vile, multi-worded curse as the deputies jostled him back through the window, essentially dumping him onto my bedroom floor. "Now, now, Mitch." The sheriff ambled in, his mustache looped with satisfaction. "That's no way to talk in front of a lady."

Mitch peered angrily at me, grunting with contempt. His ability to insult me, even without words, spoke volumes. I tightened the belt on my robe as I heard a cacophony of vehicle doors slamming outside.

"You've got nothing on me," Mitch snapped. "I'll sue you and your keystone cops for harassment."

"Au contraire." Sheriff Rick grinned, referring to a document in his hands. "I'm looking at an outstanding warrant for your arrest. Apparently, the authorities in Texas have been looking for you, and they promised me a big, Texas-sized steak if I picked you up."

Uncle Wolf and Lenny entered my bedroom tentatively, positioning themselves on either side of the sheriff. While Lenny looked uncomfortable and a little embarrassed, Uncle Wolf sparked with defiance.

"Texas, huh? Those yahoos have nothing on me either. That warrant is bogus."

Max and Quietdove climbed in from the window, joining the impromptu party in my bedroom. "So, you knew about the warrant then? And you fled to Alabama anyway?" Quietdove shook his head. "That sounds to me like evading arrest."

"Me too." Max bobbed his head. "Really bad move."

The sheriff squinted as he made a show of reading the warrant. "Looks here like they got probable cause, Mitch. You should know by now it's against the law to have sex with a minor."

"She wanted to," Mitch argued. "It was consensual."

When Uncle Wolf cleared his throat, the entire room sank into silence. It was then I noticed Bella peeping around the doorway, confused and tense. A man I didn't know stood next to her, gently reassuring her as she huddled beside him. The man looked vaguely familiar. He was tall and thin, with shaggy, dark hair. His arms were coated with tattoos, which seemed incongruent with his harmless, notably benign demeanor. Nevertheless, I hugged my robe tighter into my body, feeling suddenly exposed.

"How old was she? This girl in Texas?" Uncle Wolf asked. "Does it say?"

"Well let me see here." Sheriff Rick squinted, using his finger to trace the lines on the warrant. "Says here she was fourteen."

Bella's hands flew to her face. "Oh…"

"See, Mitch, even if in your twisted mind you think she *wanted to*, the law says you can't have sex with a minor, so there goes that theory. Surely, you see the problem here." Sheriff Rick gave Max a signal, and the jangle of handcuffs filled the room.

"You're a numbskull, Ricky. Dammit, I'm being railroaded because of an old grudge." Mitch's eyes darted back and forth, finally zeroing in on Bella. "I wish you'd never contacted me." Mitch turned his potent glare on me. "I wish I'd never come. It was hardly worth it."

When Uncle Wolf took a step forward, Bella's arm instinctively flew out to stop him. "I'm glad you came," she said to Mitch. "Because now I know who you are. And I can tell you one thing…" Luke's shadow suddenly filled the doorway behind her, "you're definitely not worth it. *You're* the disappointment."

Luke gently placed his hands on Bella's shoulders, as if to let her know he was present and within reach.

Mitch swiveled, gawking at me. "Seriously? This is the one you've been going on about? Begging me to get to know? To build a relationship with? And God forbid, go to her stupid wedding?"

"Timothy," Uncle Wolf said thickly, "would you pray for me? 'Cause I'm afraid I'm going to have to give in to temptation and pummel this scumbag."

Timothy? *The Church Guy?*

"It would hardly be worth it," he answered lightly. "And you'd ruin the manicure you got for the wedding tomorrow. You want to look your best when you walk Bella down the aisle."

While the sheriff chuckled, Max made a face. "You got a manicure, Wolfheart? Man, your whole image—I can't even look at you anymore."

Lenny's phone rang just as Sheriff Rick and his deputies led Mitch away. "Hello," he answered. "Yeah, she's fine. Everyone is okay. Uh-huh." Lenny paced a distance away, apparently unable to meet my eyes.

"Are you okay?" Bella asked me in a low voice.

"Yeah." But I wasn't. The man I'd been consumed with for decades had just been led away in handcuffs, and I felt like a fool. Here I stood, in the middle of my bedroom wearing nothing but a shorty robe, my hair dripping wet, and my sin laid bare for friends and strangers alike.

"As soon as I heard what was going on," began Bella, "I hopped into Uncle Wolf's truck. I knew he'd have to take me with him then. I even left Luke behind." She side-eyed her fiancé, who like his father, oozed discomfort.

"I'm glad you're okay, Meadow," Luke said. "And that he's… gone." Luke moved toward the TV preacher, and the two began to speak quietly together.

Bella regarded me. "I guess at first I mostly wanted to come because of him. My—father," she said thickly. "But then on the way here I started to worry about you, and even before Uncle Wolf pulled in, I'd decided you were the one that mattered."

I looked away, eyeing the disorder in my room, focusing intently on all the things I'd have to do to get to the rehearsal on time.

"Meadow," Uncle Wolf said. "Listen to your daughter. She's trying to tell you something important."

I started to cry. "I know." I'd have to iron my dress and mop the water from the old wood floors, or they'd warp and buckle—

"I'm sorry he hurt you. Back then. And today."

—and then I'd have to contend with the damaged window screen, so mosquitos wouldn't get in—

"But I'm glad you had me, and loved me, and took care of me. Even though I'm not…always nice to you. You deserve better. You always deserve better than people give you. And that makes me sad."

My daughter padded over, tugging my face toward hers, forcing me to meet her eyes. "I'm sorry, Mama. I love you."

I held her close, greedily breathing in her perfectly unique smell. "I love you too." *My Bella. My beautiful Bella.*

"Ahem, uh, that was Desi." Lenny plodded back into the room. "There are some, uh, wedding matters to deal with, so I'm gonna have to go. Do you need anything, Meadow? Bella?"

Once we convinced him all was well, Uncle Wolf walked Lenny outside. Bella followed soon after, and she and Luke were off to get ready for the rehearsal. I let out a large sigh, grateful to finally be alone with my humiliation and shame.

"So…uh…you excited for tonight?" I nearly jumped out of my skin as the TV preacher seemed to appear out of thin air. "Sorry, I didn't mean to scare you."

I tightened the belt on my measly little robe. "It's okay. It's been that kind of day."

He came closer. "I know, right?" The way he said it made me laugh. Not sure why, maybe because he seemed unaffected by the day's events, and his eyes twirled with an energetic, playful vibe. "I got in late this morning. My flight was delayed, and the airline lost my luggage. Can you believe that?" He waved his hands down the length of his long body. "I got this at Walmart this morning. Really nice folks there."

I chuckled, noticing for the first time that his twirling eyes were blue.

"Sharp dressers. Seriously, a lot of bold fashion statements being made at the Walmart between Belle Maison and Shady Gully." His smile was infectious, and his eyes were very, *very* blue. Way bluer than Mitch's. "We should go sometime. Just hang out and see the sights."

I couldn't hold back then. I tossed my head back and laughed ugly, just an all-out cackle that filled my tummy with butterflies. Was I in shock? Perhaps. Maybe I should have had a paramedic look at me? It didn't make sense to be so easily tickled by this blue-eyed preacher man decked out in his Walmart ensemble. Especially so shortly after my world fell apart.

"You're good at this stuff, I see," I said.

"What stuff? I don't know what you're talking about."

I shrugged. "Preacher man stuff. Coming in and cheering people up when they should be sad."

"Preacher man stuff?" Now *he* was laughing ugly. "That's excellent. Can I use that sometime? Like in a sermon. That's late-night gold, right there."

We fell easily into another round of hilarity, and somewhere between laughing and crying I realized that of all the people today, this strange character seemed to be the only one who hadn't judged me.

Bella had charged in fully expecting me to be the villain. Uncle Wolf had been highly exasperated with me. And the sheriff, as a rule, was generally aggravated with everyone. Even Lenny and Luke had seemed disappointed, almost embarrassed, by my situation.

"Thank you." I used the belt of my robe to wipe my eyes dry. "I guess now I get why Uncle Wolf and Bella like your show so much."

"My show?" His grin loomed, growing wider and wider. "That's classic. Seriously." He held my gaze for a long moment, so long that I might have felt uncomfortable. But I didn't.

"I don't know about myself sometimes," I mused. "I seem to make such bad decisions." I sniffled unattractively.

Again, his eyes held no judgement. Only understanding. "Me too."

We shared another surprisingly long moment, considering one another. When the screen door sounded from the front of the shanty, I muttered awkwardly. "Well…"

"As impressive as that robe of yours is, it sounds like you might have some more company. If you want to go change, I'll distract them." He raised his eyebrows mischievously.

I shook my head, bemused by this tattooed man who presented himself as a spirited simpleton. "Okay, thanks." I pulled a pair of jeans from my dresser drawer and headed to the bathroom.

I'd just shut the door when he called out. "Hey, do you have a hammer?"

Once again, I found myself shaking my head and giggling in the bathroom mirror. "A hammer? What for?" I hollered back.

"The window screen. It's in desperate need of some counsel. Or last rites. But that's Father Patrick's department."

"It's in the drawer in the kitchen," I called out in answer. "Beneath the coffee pot." As I heard him trek toward the front of the house, I gasped. My cigarettes! He'd see them! I held my breath.

But soon the thumping of a hammer filled the room, mingling occasionally with a grunt from Timothy as he wrestled with the mangled screen. After I'd changed into my jeans and T-shirt, I tentatively returned to the bedroom.

The window was tightly closed, and it appeared the screen had been pounded into submission. "Wow."

"Not bad." He turned around to face me. "If my show gets cancelled, maybe I could do construction work."

I nodded. "Or you could work at Walmart."

"Yeah. My people."

I snickered, my heart strangely light after the emotional upheaval of the day.

"Oh, hey, your uncle—great guy by the way—wanted me to give you this." He handed me the photo.

"Oh…" My hands shook as I took it.

"Beautiful family," Timothy said. "That looks like three generations of kick-ass right there." As he continued to gaze at the picture over my shoulder, I thought that he was right.

My mother's fierce face stared back at the camera, her arm tightly around me as I held baby Bella in my arms. I'd only been fifteen then, though I looked much older.

Uncle Wolf's steps slowed as he walked into my room.

"Where'd you find this?" I turned to my uncle.

"I've had it all along. I didn't know y'all were looking for it until Bella told me on the way here. It's my favorite picture. I stole it from Peony's album a long time ago." He turned to Timothy. "I'll drive you back. Whenever you're ready…"

"Sure, thanks." Timothy presented me the hammer as if it were a bouquet of flowers.

"I'll check in with you later." Uncle Wolf glanced at me. "You can ride with me to the Recreation Center if you want."

"Okay."

As Timothy and my uncle filed out of my bedroom, Uncle Wolf gave the door a final pat just before he disappeared. I watched as the door naturally swung to a lazy, slow close. "Oh…" My breath hitched inside my chest.

Apparently, not only had Timothy repaired the window screen, but he'd placed my rehearsal dress on a hanger and hung it neatly on the hook of my door.

My heels and purse positioned perfectly below.

Secrets And Silliness
Violet

Bubba and Daryl had been assigned as ushers, but since there weren't any real guests at the rehearsal, they spent most of their evening at the Magnolia Bar. Fireman, meanwhile, took his ushering job seriously.

He insisted on using me for practice before escorting Bella's mother, Meadow, down the aisle. "You're walking too fast," he complained. "Desi said I was supposed to go slow and come to a complete stop after each step." After two dry runs, he announced with the heavy burden of self-importance. "Okay. This one's for real. I need you to concentrate, Violet."

After strolling me down the aisle at a painstakingly slow pace, my mother and Aunt Desi gave him a round of applause. He seemed pleased, and I was finally released on my own recognizance.

The tall windows in the Dogwood Room allowed a generous amount of light inside, providing a picturesque view of the Recreation Center's pond and the woods beyond.

When I spotted Bella outside, I hoofed it over quickly, lest Fireman summon me back for another spin down the aisle. I found her hovering next to Duchess, who sprawled on a bed of blankets on the veranda.

"Hey," I said lightly, until I noticed the worry in her eyes. "What's wrong? Is it your dad? I heard about his arrest. I'm sorry."

She shook her head forlornly. "No. It's Duchess. Remember I told you I took her to the vet for blood work?"

"Yeah. Did they find anything?"

"No. They just called, and they found nothing unusual. But she doesn't seem to be getting any better, and I've noticed that now when she stands up, her back legs seem wobbly."

I sat on my heels to get a better read on Duchess. She seemed a shadow of the jumper-cable-thief I'd met on our first day in Shady Gully. "Hey girl, let's have a look." While her irises should be clear and white, they were instead cloudy and runny. Her pupils also seemed a bit dilated. "Hmmm. Let's see those ears." The full faced pup lifted her head as I spoke to her but didn't seem inclined to rise. While her ears were normal, with no signs of leakage or noticeable odor, the swelling around her tongue and gums was concerning.

"You see why I'm worried?" Bella said.

"Has she been eating and drinking?"

"Yes, but—"

Fireman scurried over in a tizzy. "Come on. Everyone is looking for you, Bella." He rolled his eyes with the exasperation of a wedding planner. "And you too," he reprimanded me. "You're walking with Petey."

Bella sighed. "Come on," she tugged my arm. "I'll call the vet again after the rehearsal."

Luke met us as we entered the Dogwood room. "How's the patient? Is she doing any better?" He appeared strained with worry.

"No." Bella sniffed, directing him to take his place near the flower lined arch at the head of the room. "Timothy and Father Patrick are waiting for you at the altar." She rose on her tiptoes, kissing him lightly. "Go on, or we'll face the wrath of the wedding planners."

"You mean my mom and Aunt Robin?" Luke asked lightly.

"And Fireman." When Bella flashed her intended an encouraging smile, he dutifully headed to the altar. She then turned to me. "Come on." She put her arm in mine and led me toward the rest of the wedding party at the back of the room.

I avoided Petey, choosing instead to focus on Bella's mom, who'd worn a lovely pink chiffon dress for the occasion. She was unrecognizable, not because of the fancy outfit, or the lipstick, but because her usual woe had been replaced with something else. Some indefinable quality that almost looked like relief. Because of the drama of Mitch's arrest, I'd half expected her not to show up, but remarkably Mitch's arrest seemed to have had the opposite effect on her.

When Sterling playfully swept his fingers up and down the piano keys in an exaggerated fashion, the cue to begin garnered cheers and whistles. The waves of excitement lured even Bubba and Daryl from the Magnolia Bar, drinks in hand, and ready for action.

We all watched as Fireman genteelly guided Meadow to her seat on the bride's side. From the head of the room, Luke smiled at his soon to be mother-in-law, as did Father Patrick who stood next to him. Timothy, who would be co-officiating along with the priest, went a step further and winked at her with surprising familiarity.

A shuffle behind me sounded as Uncle Lenny entwined his arm with Micah's and moved toward the aisle.

"No, honey," Aunt Desi rushed over. "You and Micah go after Petey and Violet." She then jostled Petey and me together, frowning as she found it necessary to smush us even closer. "Okay. And now with the music. Off you go…"

As Petey linked his arm with mine, I felt the heat from his hazel scrutiny as it combed my face, practically begging me to acknowledge him. I fixed my gaze firmly ahead and concentrated on putting one foot ahead of the other.

"Not so fast," my mother said. "Slow down. There. That's better."

I'd agonized over this moment all during the drive to and from Baton Rouge. Could there be anything more awkward than doing the wedding march alongside the man who'd rejected you? Who'd chosen someone else? Someone who—"

Someone who was here! How had I not noticed her before? *Tammy Jo.*

Apparently, there *were* guests, and she sat alongside Quietdove, Max, and Sheriff Rick in the front row. Their heads were cranked back awkwardly, stretching so they could see us better.

Perfect. All I needed now was to reward them with an ungainly stumble down the aisle.

"Hey, Coral," Petey said lowly. "I see you were in your element back there on the veranda. With Bella and Duchess."

I ignored his remark, countering with one of my own. "And you? I hear the elders and members in good standing are holding an official vote later."

"Well." He shot a twinkling grin toward his raven-haired fan in the pew as we walked past. "The unofficial vote this morning was a big fat no, but then Timothy had his say." He shrugged. "So, we'll see." He flashed his eyes at me. "How are you? Did things go okay in Baton Rouge?"

I purposely ignored his question. "If the vote goes your way, it's a good thing. Regardless."

"You'd think." He winked at Luke as we closed in on the beautiful arch festooned with pink, lavender, and deep purple flowers. "But if Jesse and James don't come to an agreement, that means—"

"That Dolly gets the land."

"Yep. And word is she wants to build a beauty boutique. Whatever that is."

We had reached the point where we were supposed to split up and go in opposite directions, him to the groom's side and me to the bride's, but Petey held firm to my arm. "You still mad at me? Because you shouldn't be—"

As I tried to pull away from him, he refused to release his grip.

At the altar, Timothy's eyes widened.

Just moments ago, Aunt Desi had practically forced us together, and now, she furrowed her brows as she marched over and pried my arm free of Petey's. Once liberated, she steered me safely to the bridesmaid's side. "Okay," she pronounced, a tad breathless from the effort. "Now it's your turn, Lenny. You and Micah. Come now." She beamed at the sight of them, even as her melancholy pushed tears from the corners of her eyes.

I felt the same, as the sight of Micah and Uncle Lenny walking down the aisle brought a slew of mournful thoughts to the surface. Somehow though, I managed to get through the rest of the practice ceremony without shedding a tear.

Although at one point, when Tammy Jo mouthed something to Petey as he stood beside his brother at the altar, I glared at her with such intensity Uncle Max got twisty in his seat. He and Quietdove traded glances, as if they feared the situation might escalate.

It could, I thought. It was still early, and I was feeling feisty.

After Timothy pronounced Bella and Luke *almost* man and wife, I beat a path toward the veranda.

"Dinner is this way." Sterling waved me over. "You're sitting at our table."

"*Our* table?" The last thing I wanted was to sit and watch Petey and Tammy Jo make googly eyes at one another all night.

"Violet." My mother's voice resonated behind me, immediately shooting annoyance up my spine. "I think it's time we talk."

"Okay, fine. But first I need to go check on Duchess. Bella was concerned before rehearsal."

"She was eating a few minutes ago, so I think she's feeling better. Come on, let's go get a drink in the Magnolia Bar."

Resentful, I followed the tracks of my mother's bird legs to the bar. She found a table tucked in a corner, and I wondered fleetingly if she'd conspired with the staff to hold it for us on this crowded night. "This isn't the best time, Mom. You know Aunt Desi has the rehearsal dinner timed to the minute."

"Absolutely she does." She glinted smugly. "And we're fine."

Ah. So this *was* a setup, a well-orchestrated conspiracy. I surrendered into the comfortable leather chair, begrudgingly acknowledging my mother's manipulative powers. "I'll have a chardonnay," I told the waiter.

"House?"

"Fine. Thanks."

"I think it's a perfect time. You've been avoiding me. Mad at me for too long. I know we were never especially close, and that your father held that special place in your heart, and probably Sterling as well, but I want us to try. I need us too. You need to"—she stopped, making an effort to rephrase—"I hope you'll tell me what's bothering you, and what this big, mysterious decision in your life is all about."

The waiter brought the wine, and my mother clinked my glass. "To your future." We drank. Her bony fingers massaged the stem of the glass. I thought, not for the first time, how hauntingly thin she was, as I'd always suspected she was anorexic.

"I have secrets too, Violet. Not big ones, not anymore, but I understand how they can be debilitating and destructive."

I stared out the giant window of the Magnolia Bar, marveling at the sun setting over the pond. "Tell me your secret then." I waited as she took another sip of wine. "Is it the sheriff?" My scornful emphasis on the word "*sheriff*" was deliberate. I didn't regret it. In fact, it spurred me on. "Daddy would be appalled. I mean, how can you even be with somebody like that after being married to Daddy. Someone who was…"

"What? Sophisticated? Smart?" She eyed me. "Maybe that's why. How could I live with the constant comparison if I dated a brilliant, shrewd businessman? I simply couldn't do it. Nobody could ever measure up. Everything he did would be held and compared to the way Dean did things, and he'd be doomed. And so would I."

"So, you're dumbing down then? Is that it?" The petulance tripped out of my mouth without effort.

"Violet, is it that you don't like Ricky? Or is it you don't like the idea of my being with someone? It's been seven years now and…" To my horror, my mother sniffled, and swiped a mascara smudge from beneath her purple glasses. "My heart aches. Every. Single. Day. Some days it's all I can do to…" She removed a tissue from her pocket, blotting the offensive tears. "Violet, I wasted so much time with my…silliness, and one thing I've learned about myself is that I tend to overthink and analyze too much. I'm determined not to do that again."

"Silliness? Secrets? Which is it?" My parents had always had a complicated relationship. Ironically, they'd seemed happiest just before he died.

"Silliness and secrets, they're one and the same. Stupid stuff, and I lost so much time because of them." She shook her head, as if trying to shake off the inevitable images that popped up. "Don't do that, honey. Don't be like me. What's your secret? What's dragging you down? If you talk about it, you might find it's not that horrible."

"I just don't get what you see in him." Whether it was a diversionary tactic, or that I really wanted to know, I wasn't quite sure, but I pressed, nonetheless.

But my mother's patience was faltering. "He's not sophisticated," she said sharply. "And he's kind of ornery. He talks like a backwoods dweller, but he's smarter than you think. And he's kind. And he's not trying to take Dean's place. He just wants to spend his life with me."

I gulped the buttery chardonnay and considered ordering another. Especially if forced to sit at Tammy Jo and Petey's table.

"Your turn, Violet."

I swirled the wine, reflecting on its rich golden hue for a moment. And then I told her. "I've decided to take my career in a totally different direction. I don't want to be a physicist, or run clinical trials, or do biological research. I realize I've wasted a lot of time, like you said, taking classes and earning degrees that are essentially useless. I know I've wasted a lot of your money—"

"You haven't. You've had scholarships, Violet. Tell me now. I'm excited to hear what your plan is."

"A lot of the courses will transfer, so it's not as bleak as it sounds, but…" I swirled. And swirled. "I'm afraid— No, I'm ashamed, that I'm letting Daddy down. I feel like if I'd stayed the course, I could have done some good in the world. I could have contributed somehow to eradicating cancer. I could have maybe done something that would have honored him. But I just can't." I scrubbed my face with my hands, surprised when they came away dry.

"But all he ever wanted was for you to be happy—"

A sudden shriek boomed throughout the bar, and everyone turned, searching for the source. "It came from the big room with the windows." A man pointed.

"No. I think it's coming from outside." Another man declared.

I sprang, hurrying out of the bar, down the big hall, and onto the veranda. Bella cried as Luke knelt next to Duchess, desperately trying to rouse her.

"I think she's dead," Bella wept.

She wasn't dead. She was paralyzed. I recognized the symptoms immediately. "Duchess." I knelt beside her. She opened her eyes. They zipped back and forth fearfully, finally landing on me.

"She's alive!" Bella squealed. "Look. She opened her eyes."

"Everybody, hey, everybody, let's move back a little, okay?" Petey, his voice as serious as I'd ever seen it, urged the family back to give me some space. Timothy and Father Patrick, supportive, took his lead and kept the gathering at bay.

"She's panting," Luke said. "She's in distress. And is that—"

A puddle of urine suddenly pooled around her thick, red-ginger body.

"Oh no," Bella sobbed.

"It's okay, girl," I cooed, running my hands down the length of her body, but except for her darting, frantic eyes, Duchess remained absolutely still.

"Here's a towel." Petey squatted next to me, blotting the urine away so it didn't soil her fur.

"Luke," I asked, "could she have gotten into any poison

or anything? You know how she is…maybe some pesticide or something?"

"No. I've got the duplex's shed tightly padlocked."

"Bella, I know you said the vet in Belle Maison did blood work, but did they also do X-rays?"

"Uh…" She ran her hands through her hair, clearly unraveling as she looked to Luke.

"They did," Luke answered. "And they found nothing unusual. Both the X-rays and blood work were totally clear."

"I got the emergency clinic pegged at thirty miles on my map here." The sheriff eyed his phone as he paced on the outer edges of Petey's illusory boundary. "I can get my lights and siren cranked up in half a second."

My mind raced as I ticked through the lists in my head. There had to be an explanation. *This dog was perfectly fine a week ago.*

Suddenly, my heart began to hammer wildly in my chest. "Luke," I said calmly, "didn't you say y'all have been hiking lately? Across the creek?" I glanced at him for confirmation, but it was Bella who answered.

"Yes," she said. "A few days after the shower. Remember Luke? We went on that five-mile hike across the creek. I guess I was trying to find my dad."

My hands plowed through Duchess's thick fur, up and down and in between every crevice. Behind the ears. Under the armpits. In and about her scruff. Her neck.

"What are you looking for?" My mother lifted her voice, her tone suddenly hopeful. "What is it, Violet?"

"I don't know yet," I muttered. "But tick saliva can cause an allergic hypersensitivity in some dogs. And…" I glanced at Petey, "there is such a thing as tick paralysis. Even small children have become paralyzed after being bitten."

"Oh my gosh." Aunt Desi huddled next to my mother. "That's horrible."

"It's usually temporary," I breathed. "But you have to find the—" I drew a giant gulp of air. "I found it!"

"I'll be damned," the sheriff muttered. "Right there between her toes."

"Yep." My heart leapt with promise. "But I have to get it off and kill it immediately." I glanced around the veranda. "I don't suppose anybody has any tweezers. Or rubbing alcohol?"

"I've got tweezers!" Micah unzipped her dainty purse and handed me a bedazzled set of pink tweezers. "Don't have any rubbing alcohol though."

"I got some bourbon," Bubba offered helpfully.

"I'll go get some." Sterling headed toward the front desk, and Tammy Jo followed behind usefully.

In one firm outward pull, I lifted the pest from Duchess's body. I held it closer, inspecting its spindly legs and the destructive hooks in its mouth that latch on and cause such destruction. "Dermacenter variabilis. Gotcha."

"My word." Father Patrick was incredulous. "It sounds quite ghastly. What did you call it again?"

"Dermacenter variabilis. Also known as the American dog tick."

"Nicely done." Petey grinned proudly, and something in his eyes reignited the spark I'd been trying so hard to dilute.

"Is she going to be okay?" Bella glanced at Luke, who hovered close.

"Yeah. If the sheriff's offer still stands." I glanced at the sheriff. "I'll ride with her to Belle Maison. It would be good to monitor her for the night, but yeah, Bella, I think she's going to be fine. This was the culprit."

"Here you go." Tammy Jo and Sterling returned with a container of rubbing alcohol, where I condemned the pest to certain death by drowning. "Can't flush them down the commode. You need the alcohol to totally kill them."

"Okay. Yeah." Bubba hugged his bourbon and coke tighter into his chest. "This was kind of a light one anyway. Probably wouldn't done the job."

Daryl grunted.

Bella's Uncle Wolfheart crouched beside Duchess, grateful

as he rubbed her thick fur. "You have a gift," he said. "Reminds me of my sister, Peony. Her way was with medicinal herbs, an ancient method of healing used by the Creek People for generations."

"It's what you do now, Uncle Wolf." Bella leaned her head against his shoulder. "You're carrying on Mamaw's tradition."

"True." He regarded me for several seconds. "But Violet's gift is different. It's more medically based."

I nodded, respectfully acknowledging his sound intuition. "Yeah, it is."

"And I suspect…"

I stood then, and let my eyes slowly sift through the assorted faces around me.

And all at once, in one shocking and very subtle exchange, my perception shifted. It had been nothing more than a light brushing of the hands, but the glow that erupted between Sterling and Tammy Jo was electric. Never in my life had I seen my twin brother's face emit such raw adoration.

The affection between them was obvious. But I'd been too deep in the muck to see it.

Secrets and silliness. One and the same.

Just like that, my world tilted into an upright position. I considered Petey. And then my mother.

I tilted my head at Wolfheart in acknowledgment. "Yes," I said. "I've always wanted to be a doctor. I just didn't realize I wanted to be an animal doctor."

A few shocked gasps competed with the giddiness of surprise and happiness to create a splattering of cheers. "Now that's a great plan." Uncle Lenny lit me up with one of his best, and most cherished looks of fatherly approval.

I soaked it up, and held it close to me, imagining my daddy standing next to him, his own expression matching Uncle Lenny's exactly.

At last, I fixed my gaze on my mother. "I've been accepted into the LSU School of Veterinary Medicine. I'm going to be a veterinarian." When she flashed with pride, I added, "And I want to open a clinic here in Shady Gully."

Petey's hazel eyes bloomed wide and misty.

Chapter Twenty-Two

The Mayor's Wedding
Lenny

Sunday...Wedding Day

Desi and I sat side by side on the porch swing, sipping our morning coffee while the dogs guarded the perimeter. Ginger's tail climbed like a flag up a pole when a pair of cardinals landed in the bird bath. She pranced, barked, and carried on as if the Taliban had launched an offensive in her backyard.

"Hush, Ginger," Desi fussed. "You'll wake the neighbors."

Ginger showed no signs of having heard, and instead, sent the birds aflutter when she tore down the patio steps like an operator. She trotted back up the steps, and eyed Desi expectantly.

"You're a very bad girl." Desi tickled her beneath her chin.

"The coffee was good." I set my cup down so Mary Ann could lick the last sip. Unlike Ginger, our easy-going cocker spaniel had no taste for war games. "Look. There it is, Desi."

"It's beautiful," she mused at the sunrise over her steamy mug. "The prettiest this week."

I chuckled. "Probably the only one you've seen in a while."

"True. I can't believe our baby is getting married tonight."

"I think he'll be happy. He and Bella have something special. And she comes from a good family."

"*Humph*," Desi teased. "I'll confess that even Meadow seemed unusually pleasant last night at rehearsal. Did you see her chatting with Timothy? What do you think is up with that?"

"I don't know, but it looked to me like Timothy was doing most of the chatting."

"I don't know. Those two seem an unlikely pair. Timothy with his joyous, spirit-led heart, and Meadow with her…heart of stone."

"Stop," I joked, pinching her knee. "You're impossible."

"Perhaps," she admitted with a grin. "And you never know, maybe they're exactly what the other needs. God in His infinite mercy always provides what's best for us, whether it's what we want or not."

I let that sit for a moment, trying not to read too much into it. "It was a strange night, that's for sure. Nobody even ate. I guess after the spectacle with Mitch—"

"And poor Duchess."

The wedding party and rehearsal guests had ended up joining the sheriff's convoy to Belle Maison, his siren blazing a quick trail to the Emergency Animal Clinic. "Have you heard how she's doing this morning?"

"Micah texted," Desi replied. "She said they kept her overnight and gave her an oral flea and tick preventative. She also got a nice, fancy bath in some flea and tick shampoo. Apparently, these cases are very common in Australia, but increasing here. Wasn't Violet simply brilliant? Robin is beside herself, just so proud of her."

"Dean would be as well." I swallowed. "He wouldn't want her fretting over letting him down. She could never do that."

Desi sipped her coffee, her eyes following Ginger as she positioned herself at the edge of the patio, her ears spread like butterfly wings as she listened for errant birds. "She and Petey…I don't know what's taking them so long to figure out they're in love. We're trying to be patient, but—"

"We? You mean you and Robin?"

"Of course. We thought maybe Petey wasn't sure if Violet would be content to settle in Shady Gully. You know he's a homeboy at heart."

"He is," I agreed. "But I think he'd be willing to settle anywhere to make her happy. Even a big city like Lexington. Or Baton Rouge," I added knowingly.

My wife whipped her head in my direction.

"Just saying." I shrugged. "Although it doesn't seem to be an issue now." I patted her leg happily, knowing she was feeling victorious. "Frankly, it doesn't surprise me that Violet likes the low-key life here. Despite her Mensa score, and her huge education, she's very shy. I can see her here. See *them* here. If they ever figure it out."

"They will," Desi said with confidence. "Hopefully sooner rather than later, while I'm still in wedding planner mode."

I chuckled. "Actually, I must say, I'm impressed with y'alls patience. You and Robin aren't usually so indulgent in these matters. Especially when it's personal."

"Part of our strategy. We've been working very hard to maintain an air of indifference."

I considered my empty coffee mug resting at Mary Ann's snout. "I think Petey's issue is more about his own identity. While Violet is focused, and purpose driven, he's not sure where he fits in. That's my take anyway."

"Have you heard anything on the vote?" As Desi finished her coffee, Mary Ann looked up hopefully.

"Not yet. Father Patrick texted early this morning. Like in the wee hours. Did you know he's into social media? Apparently, he uses that early morning time to spread the good news on the internet. Lately he's into something called TikTok." I guffawed, utterly baffled. "He says that's where the young people are." I watched as Desi tilted her cup for Mary Ann to lick clean. "Anyway, he said he'd give it until noon before inquiring."

Desi lazily scratched Mary Ann's head until her back leg kicked in pleasure. Encouraged by the upward curl of my wife's lips, I blurted, "You seem better. Happier lately. Since you and Robin saw the doctor."

"I am. She offered me some hope. It was good to find out I'm not the only one struggling with this—stage in life."

"You mean menopause?"

She looked at me sharply.

"I'm not a complete moron." At least not since my chat with Father Patrick, encouraging me to be a partner in Desi's struggle. "Did she put you on hormone therapy?" I did my research.

Desi opened her mouth, and her eyes crinkled in a full smile. "She did. I've only been on the pills for a few days, but I swear I feel a difference. It could just be the aforementioned hope, of course, but I don't feel as weepy, and I've slept better."

"Do you still love me?" I asked impulsively. "Can those pills do that?"

She blinked. "Lenny? What kind of question is that? You know I do." She squinted at me. "I've never loved anyone more. Not even my mama."

I cleared my throat. "I've spent a lot of time lately thinking about how Sunny pushed us together, and I worry if maybe… well, do you ever regret your choice? You've had a lot of admirers, Desi. Before we were married, and after. I'm talking specifically about Adam, of course." My shoulders heaved with tension. "It wasn't fun seeing him again, I'll tell you that."

"Lenny—"

"And I've even been thinking about Wolfheart lately," I blurted in interruption. "I know y'all are just friends, but it seems like you've always had chemistry with him. Some kind of bond, a connection…something…that I can't break through."

"Stop, Lenny." She frowned. "Just listen. Okay?" She planted her hand firmly on my thigh. "I do have a connection with Brad, you're right, but it's not the way you think. I've done some regrettable things and made a lot of mistakes. I've been to the dark side, so to speak, and I suppose, it's easier to talk to him about those things. Because of his own past, he can relate."

"What? I can relate."

"You can't, Lenny. Because you're so good. And you couldn't possibly understand some of the sordid, evil things I've experienced. And you know what? I wouldn't want you to. I wouldn't want to taint you like that."

"But I'm your husband. I want you to taint me." Laughter suddenly bubbled between us. "I'm serious." But I couldn't keep a straight face.

"And as far as Adam…" Desi scoffed. "He's the biggest mistake I *almost* made. Almost being the key word. Trust me, my love." She moved her hand down the length of my leg. "I'm all yours. You're stuck with me. Menopause and all."

We clasped hands, our feet automatically setting the swing to rocking. After a moment, I said, "I want to know how to reach you when you're sad, is all. I want you to know you can share that with me."

She regarded me a long moment. "It's hard to explain. I drive around Shady Gully and see all the old, familiar landmarks. The school. The Cozy Corner. The same oak trees. All bigger now. All older. And now a new generation travels those roads, consuming all the things that were once ours, so sure they've got it all figured out."

"And they don't," I said somberly. "And neither did we."

She nodded. "In a blink they'll be us, and those landmarks, the trees, all of it, will be all that remains." She wiped a tear from the corner of her eyes. "We're all just passing through. It's not terrible really, because death is just a doorway to something better of course, but…"

"But it's sobering to think how fleeting it all is."

Desi nodded. "And your child getting married is a milestone that brings that truth to light."

"Indeed, it does," I conceded, deciding that now that things were going so well, I'd tip the affection needle even further in my favor. "Okay. I have a little surprise."

"A surprise?"

"Yep." I reached behind the swing, retrieving the plastic bag I'd stashed earlier. "We've been married a long time, Desi, and if I know anything, it's the one true way to your heart."

The edges of her lips turned up in her impossibly singular smile. "But how…?"

I dropped the plastic bag into her lap, and she dug into it greedily. "Okra? My goodness!" She sniffed the small, hairy-based green pods. "They're fresh. Where did you get these?" She sniffed them again.

"They're still tiny because they weren't ready to be picked yet, but I wanted to show you. I grew them at my silly store. I tilled up that little patch behind the garden center, and I rigged up a greenhouse so I could plant early. They get just the right amount of sun."

Desi wrapped her arms around me and buried her head in my chest. "You are the best man I've ever known, Lenny. You are so good to me." Tears sprung out of her eyes.

I kissed the top of her head, more content than a man had a right to be. "Maybe I'll try planting some of those pickling cucumbers you like next."

"Maybe so." She leaned back, just enough to lay eyes on me. "I'll help you lay out a nice garden. I've been wanting to come and see that silly store anyway." She kissed me on the lips. "In fact, I was thinking, it could do with a nice little women's area. You know?"

"That's an idea. You've been talking to Micah?"

"No, but I think we could lure the ladies in with some crock pots and pressure cookers and such."

My heart flipped as she used the word, *we*. I was just moving in for another, more substantial kiss when a sudden *rat-a-tat-tat* at the door jolted us from our reverie. We turned to find a very flustered Robin storm onto the patio.

"Oh no," Desi gasped. "What's happened? Is it Duchess?"

"No," Robin answered. "It's Carly. As in the caterer. She and her staff are all bent over, quite literally, with the stomach flu. Or food poisoning. Nothing they prepared for tonight is edible. And the emergency with Duchess probably saved us all from being sick." She stalked to the edge of the porch, and a swell of birds scattered in terror.

Ginger wagged her glamorous tail, gazing up at Robin with respect.

"We're in a bit of a pickle," she said as she turned to face us. "And Lord help me but I'm fresh out of ideas."

The despairing mood at Lenny's Tool Shed equaled the sense of calamity at home. "Did Micah make that?" I pointed at the sheriff's coffee mug.

"No, that's why it's good," he answered. "And fully leaded."

"Excellent." I poured myself a cup of coffee, adding a few forbidden spoonfuls of sugar. "That's just what this situation calls for."

Micah slammed the phone down. "There's nothing in Azalealand either. They said it's too short a notice."

"I'll say," muttered Ricky.

Micah glared at the sheriff, and then turned back to Luke, who anxiously paced the aisles of the hardware store. "This is a total disaster. First Duchess. And now this. I don't even have the heart to tell Bella."

"Don't you dare tell Bella," Micah hissed. "She's got enough to deal with right now."

"Micah's right. We'll get this ironed out, son. Don't worry." I spoke with a confidence I didn't possess. "I promised your mother I'd fix it, so I'm gonna fix it. Everybody got that?"

"Aye-aye, Captain." Ricky removed his hat. "Just tell me what to do. This morning my woman was madder than a three-legged dog trying to bury a turd on an icy pond."

Luke squinted at the sheriff. "There are so many disturbing things about that." He clawed his hands through his hair and glanced at his watch. "We're running out of time, and we've called everywhere."

Micah pushed a pad of paper toward him. "Try this one. Just found it online."

The door chimed and Daryl and Bubba trooped in. "Hey,

did y'all hear about the food last night being wonky?" Bubba shook his head dramatically. "And I almost snuck one of them chicken wings too."

"It's my wedding," Luke snapped as he clicked his phone. "I've heard, trust me." He told Micah. "No answer. Message said they're closed until Monday."

"Why are you here?" Bubba asked Luke. "Shouldn't you be with Bella? Trying to comfort her about her dog? And the fact that there ain't gonna be food at the wedding?"

"Bubba, it's bad luck for the groom to see the bride the day of the wedding," Micah explained. "And you should know that, as many times as you've been married."

Bubba looked stricken. "What? Are you kidding me? Maybe that's why ain't none of 'em worked out."

"Okay," I reordered everyone's attention, "everybody. Let's just think. Maybe we're looking at this all wrong. We're trying to find caterers. Maybe we should just be calling people and asking them to bring a dish. That's what small towns do. We come together in times of crisis."

"Oh my gosh, Dad!" Micah was appalled. "A potluck wedding? Seriously? If you fix it like that Mama is gonna have your head on a platter."

Luke sighed hopelessly. "I don't know. Maybe we should ask Violet and Petey to pick up pizza on their way back from picking up Duchess. That may be as good as it gets."

"You could do worse than pepperoni pizza," the sheriff recollected.

"What vehicle did they go in?" Bubba asked. "I bet they could fit a lot of pies in Desi's van—"

"Okay." I chugged my sugar and caffeine. "Let me think. How many cars did they go in, Luke?"

"Dad!" Micah huffed.

"Only one." Luke, despondent, sat on the stool by the cash register. "Violet and Petey went, and I think Sterling and Tammy Jo were going to ride along as well."

"We are *not* having pizza. Red sauce doesn't blend with lavender and deep purple. It's wrong, wrong, wrong!" Micah waved her hands about. "We are supposed to be getting manicures and makeovers right now." She stormed to the door, flipped the open sign to closed and lowered the shade. "We are not ordering fast food for the mayor's wedding!"

Bubba peered at Micah. "Geez, I hate to say it, Lenny, but you're in for trouble when that one gets married."

"Good grief." Luke's head fell into his hands. "Bella's going to divorce me before we even get married."

"How many guests you got coming?" asked Daryl.

"Two hundred."

Bubba whistled. "Impressive. I landed a little over a hundred at my last wedding, but never made it to that level. Congratulations."

We all turned when the door rattled noisily. A persistent bang followed. I could just make out a large, looming shadow as someone cupped his hands and peered inside. Impatient now, the banger continued. When I opened the door, I came face to face with Hoot Wheeler, full of venom and spitting mad.

"Oh my gosh, not you again," Micah snarled. "We're closed. Didn't you see the sign? Or do you think you're special or something?"

"Micah, that's no way to treat a customer," I reprimanded my daughter, even as the inkling of a solution began to take shape in my head.

Hoot meandered over to the cash register and eyed us all curiously. Dipped his large hand into the sheriff's taffy bowl. "First of all, I am special." He winked at Micah. "Second of all, it's after church hours, so why in the world would y'all be closed? And finally, who died?"

Ricky cut his eyes toward me, his mustache twitching shrewdly.

Daryl and Bubba exchanged glances, flashing pointedly in my direction.

Luke rose from the stool, wandering over to take measure of Hoot.

Hoot said to Daryl, "Why aren't you at the work site today? Mrs. Guidry said you were off. What's up?"

"Well…" Daryl shuffled, imploring me with his spot-on look. "Uh… it's Sunday. And there's a wedding."

The sheriff cleared his throat, muttering nonsensically.

"Uh, Micah," I said, "why don't you see if you can help the gentleman?"

"Gentleman? Are you serious? No way. I have to go get my manicure—" When she took note of my expression, she acquiesced.

As she led the big brawny son of JJ Wheeler to the paint center, Bubba, Daryl, Luke, and the sheriff closed in on me.

"I couldn't," I said. "Charlie Wayne would kill me."

"Desperate times call for desperate measures," Ricky said flatly. "And whose wrath are you more worried about? Charlie Wayne's or Desi's?"

"Lenny," Bubba whispered, "JJ Wheeler made the best food we ever had in this town. And how do we show our appreciation? We run him out of town. I'll never understand that." He glared accusingly at Luke.

"Bubba's right," Daryl backed up his buddy. "Just take the man-bun out of the picture for a second. Although, I never really understood why you'd have a man-bun *and* a beard."

"Yeah." Bubba looked thoughtful. "Don't they kinda cross each other out?"

"Right." Daryl bobbed his head. "Kinda like a double negative."

"Let's focus," Ricky broke in mercifully. "Time is of the essence."

"Just sayin'," Bubba finished his point. "It's kind of a no brainer."

"It kind of is," Ricky agreed. "Although you'd have to have the mayor's approval, seeing as how he did run JJ Wheeler out of town."

"Banished him completely." Bubba shook his head, filled with a sense of injustice.

"Man," Daryl said in a watery voice, "I can almost taste the ribs."

I ambled over to the window and stared past the big blue rocking chair and toward the desolate four-way stop. "Luke," I turned to my son, "your call."

"We'd have to contend with Charlie Wayne," he deliberated slowly, "but…that barbecue."

"It'd be legendary." Bubba jigged hopefully. "Come on, Luke. Pull the trigger."

"Let's do it."

I moseyed over to the paint center, and found Micah glaring up at the big, strapping man with barely contained fury.

"Say, Hoot," I said. "What's your Daddy up to today?"

Chapter Twenty-Three

The Best Revenge
Meadow

"**M**ama." Bella's tone was leaden with reverence, reflecting the significance of the moment. "Timothy's here. It's time."

She reminded me of her fourteen-year-old self. Her hair bunched in a ponytail and drawn through a baseball cap, with nary a stitch of makeup, not even ChapStick.

"Are you excited?" she asked.

"Yeah. Sure, I guess." I wasn't, but in the interest of extending this newfound harmony with my daughter, I behaved respectfully.

As this was a renowned and sacred ritual for her, I deferred to her recommendation on dress. We both wore flipflops, shorts, and old T-shirts. I noticed Bella's toes were rough and imperfect, spotted with cracked nail polish.

"Is everything all set for the wedding?" I asked. "Any last minute issues?"

"Nope," she said. "All going according to schedule."

"And Duchess?"

"She's much improved. Petey and Violet are picking her up today, and she's going to stay with her Auntie Micah while we're on our honeymoon in Santa Fe." She ruminated, "Or if she feels better and gets too rowdy, she'll maybe stay with Uncle Wolf. Or her grands."

Lenny and Desi. The grands. Ready or not, the reality of my new life was upon me, complete with in-laws and grand-dog duties.

"But now isn't about me," she said. "Hurry." Excited, she reached for my hand. Our flipflops smacked behind us as we padded outside to meet Timothy and my uncle.

They stood off in the distance at the top of my dirt driveway, heads bent together, deep in conversation. A stab of emotion ran through me as I noted my Uncle Wolf's skinny, pale legs. He wore a T-shirt and blue jean shorts. Not the fashionable kind you buy, but the kind that country folks literally cut to make use of old, tattered jeans.

Timothy's legs were sun-deprived as well, and I glimpsed an indistinct tattoo on his lower calf. His shorts were sports driven, and stylish, and his T-shirt said *Forgiven.* As Uncle Wolf turned toward us, I identified the same shirt, but with the words *New Creation* across the chest.

As my heart chugged faster, I recognized Bella's interpretation of the event as poignant, and possibly even dramatic, but what did I know about such things? I only knew that as we closed in on them, I felt both anxious and eager.

"Nice wedding duds," Timothy teased us as we set off for the creek bed. "It's beautiful out here. Your uncle was telling me y'all got a fancy new bridge a few years ago."

"You can thank me for that," Bella quipped. "I was on it when it collapsed."

Uncle Wolf pulled Bella toward him as they plodded ahead. "My beautiful, brave niece," he said with genuine affection. He turned to Timothy. "Have you ever heard her sing?"

"Actually, Sterling had the whole North Lake Creative Team listen to her version of Bethel Music's "Raise a Hallelujah". We were quite impressed." Timothy paused to pick a swatch of swamp mallow, or hibiscus moscheutos. "Whenever y'all visit Lexington, we'd love to have you sing at our services." He handed Bella the flowers.

"What? Are you kidding?" Bella blushed. "That's like…thousands of people."

"Your rendition is deeply moving. They'll love it." Timothy

turned, handing me my own pseudo bouquet. "There," he pronounced. "Really brings your outfit together."

I suspected I'd forever be leery of a man with blue eyes, as I felt suddenly uncomfortable, my uneasiness increasing the longer he held my gaze.

"There it is." Uncle Wolf pointed to the bridge connecting Shady Gully proper to The Creek. "I was thinking of an area in a small gully to the left. Not too deep, not too shallow. And not too many alligators."

Bella laughed as Timothy's eyes widened. "He's messin' with ya. There aren't any alligators in the gully."

"Lots of snakes though," I chipped.

Uncle Wolf chuckled, leading us to a peaceful dip in the creek, the water soothing as it rushed past us at a steady pace. "What do you think?"

"I think it's perfect," Timothy answered. "Snakes and all." As he slipped off his flipflops, I noted the tattoo on his lower leg appeared to be that of a name, although it was impossible to make out. Unless I was willing to tackle him and make a spectacle of myself. Which I was not.

Uncle Wolf treaded into the gully with Timothy, and Bella followed. "Are we…are we supposed to go with them?" I asked her in a whisper.

"I am."

Skeptical, I removed my flip flops and joined them in the middle of the gully.

While Timothy whispered softly to Uncle Wolf, my uncle nodded repeatedly, his eyes closed in concentration. Bella, despite her boldness, remained a few feet away, allowing them intimacy. Privacy. Or whatever was called for in these circumstances.

I aligned myself with my daughter, deciding to do whatever she did. Within reason.

"Brad, as we've talked about and studied, this is the best decision you'll ever make. You'll never regret your decision to follow Jesus. Will you repeat after me?"

Uncle Wolf's face softened before my eyes. He nodded emphatically, eager for what would happen next. I glanced at Bella, who swiped a tear away. When she reached for my hand, I held it tight.

"I believe," Timothy began, "with all my heart."

"I believe," Uncle Wolf repeated, "with all my heart."

"That Jesus is the Christ. The son of the living God."

"That Jesus is the Christ." Uncle Wolf's voice mounted thickly. "The son of the living God."

"He's my savior. And my friend…" Timothy patted Uncle Wolf's shoulder encouragingly.

"He's my savior," Uncle Wolf said with conviction. "And my friend."

"Based on that confession, I now baptize you," Timothy said reverently. "In the name of the Father, the Son, and the Holy Spirit." He positioned my uncle's hand to hold his nose, and proclaimed, "Death." He gently dipped him back into the water. "Burial." And as he lifted Uncle Wolf out of the water, he proclaimed, "Resurrection!"

I watched, as mesmerized as I'd ever been, as my quiet, somber, and normally scowling uncle raised his arms into the air. Triumphant. Joyful. *And new.*

He embraced Timothy, and to my surprise I saw tears slip from the blue-eyed TV preacher's eyes. Bella rushed over to them, happily joining in their embrace. I stood still, unsure—

"Meadow." Timothy offered me his hand. "Come."

When I moved forward and entered their circle, I felt an inkling of belonging like I'd never felt before. As if my world was once again tilting, and perhaps, finally…righting itself.

As if Uncle Wolf's baptism hadn't been emotionally charged enough, I now found myself the queen diva in Dolly's dome. Offering myself up like a Thanksgiving turkey, I sat buttered with foiled highlights and seasoned with textured layers.

I'd given her the power to either make me beautiful or become the laughingstock at my daughter's wedding. "Thanks for coming in today," I said amiably, hoping for mercy. "I know it's your day off."

"No problem. I did Mrs. Shanna May's hair earlier. And I've got Mrs. Guidry coming in after you. It seems like everybody in Shady Gully is going to the wedding."

My heart teetered. Had Dolly been invited? Probably not. I could almost feel my head beginning to itch, the formula in the foil liners frying my hair with each passing minute. Dolly set the timer on her phone and plopped into the swiveling chair next to me. "Have you heard what's going to become of Mitch?"

Whoa. I hadn't seen that one coming. How was it that Dolly always seemed to blindside me this way? "Uh, not really. I just know that Sheriff Rick delivered him back to Texas, where he'll face charges for…whatever he did with that young girl."

"Good," she said.

I glanced at my watch, wondering how long it would take to fry my hair to the roots? When I scratched the skin around my ears, Dolly toweled off the damp spots around my face. "He definitely had a type. A pattern." She eyed me. "I should have seen it. We were both fools. You know that, don't you?"

"I guess I'm starting to realize that." Since Mitch's arrest, I'd been mulling over how much time I'd wasted on him. Throughout the prime of my life, I'd been consumed with him. I'd needed him. I'd been in love with him. Angry with him. Just…*with him.*

"Well, no matter," Dolly said. "The best revenge is to be happy, right?" She smiled as she scrolled through her phone.

"Are you happy? I mean, with Adam? Are y'all…" I shook my head apologetically. "I'm sorry. That's none of my business."

"No, it's okay. Yeah, we're together. I know he's got a terrible reputation, and people think he's a player, but I really like him." She sought my eyes in the mirror. "And I really think he likes me." She tapped the timer on her phone, taking several moments to inspect my hair—or what was left of it—inside the foils. "Perfect. Let's wash and condition."

I relaxed as Dolly massaged my scalp, and when she finally settled me back into the styling chair, I was downright exuberant. "Wow," I exclaimed in both relief—that I still had hair—and delight as artful highlights glimmered back at me in the mirrored lights.

"So, do you like Luke?" Dolly asked as she towel dried my hair. "And his family?"

"They're growing on me. I think Luke will be good for Bella, and Lenny is as good as gold, and there's something about Petey. Have you met him?"

"Yeah. I know all of them." Her inflection was impossible to interpret.

"Petey seems genuine to me. He doesn't appear to have an agenda, and he's kind to everyone he meets. He helped Fireman overcome his broken heart, and I didn't think that was possible."

Without a word she dried my hair, elaborately flipping and lifting with a big round brush. "Nice, huh? Now, are we going for a sophisticated updo? Or do you want to wear it loose and sexy?"

The fact that Dolly was even asking me this question seemed surreal. Since I was totally out of my element, I deferred to her, and after describing my dress, Dolly suggested a loose, sexy updo—whatever that was.

"One of the ladies in the shop earlier was repeating the story about Petey and the waiter in Opelousas," she said.

"Yeah, I'm not surprised. He has a way about him. He's seriously religious, but he doesn't come off as judgmental."

When Dolly crossed the room to choose hair accessories, her phone lit up. Amused by the pulsing moniker illuminating her screen, I smothered a snicker. *Cain*, it flashed, likely announcing the caller as either Jesse or James.

She picked up her phone when she returned, grunted as she listened intently to the message. Afterward, she rolled her eyes in what appeared to be astonishment.

It suddenly occurred to me that I was at the epicenter of the highly anticipated church vote and land news in Shady Gully.

Since I didn't relish that position, I made an effort to be invisible and neutral. "Did your brothers come to an agreement?"

Or not.

I gasped as the words spilled out of my mouth. "I'm sorry, Dolly. I don't know what's going on with me today."

Dolly raised her eyebrows as she moussed and fluffed accordingly. I marveled at my transformation, finding myself strangely indebted to this inscrutable woman I'd despised most of my life.

"Of course not." Dolly twisted my hair this way and that, precisely placing a strand of hair like an artist, making it appear as if it had just fallen astray. "Yes." She stepped back, as if examining a rare sculpture. "The land at the corner belongs to yours truly. All three lots. Mine, Jesse's, and James's."

"Oh…well, that's great. Congratulations."

"Thanks. They are madder than mules chewing on bumble bees, but it is what it is."

I chuckled, giddy over my hair, and tickled over Dolly's imagery. "What are you going to do with it?"

"I don't know. I might build a big old beauty center. I've got the Diva Dome here, so I could do a spa on James's lot, and I don't know… maybe a nail salon on Jesse's." She cackled. "Wouldn't they just love that?"

I tried to think of something positive to say and came up short. "I guess Shady Gully could always use more…beauty…places."

She paused, marking me in the mirror. "I know Sigourney has her little cottage kingdom next door, but that would be part of the fun. I could outdo her and take all of her business."

Oh boy. There she is.

I noted the lines around her lips as she placed a pearl studded comb into my hair. The gray around her temples. The bags under her eyes. I took a deep breath and tried to summon the tranquility I'd felt just after my uncle's baptism.

"Or…maybe you could sell their two lots. You could take the money and do something nice for yourself. Maybe build a nice house."

She appeared thoughtful. "I used to have a big, beautiful house"— she stopped, gawked at me— "but you know that though, don't you?"

I shrugged. "Like you said, being happy is the best revenge. You enjoy your work. I can see that. So why not build a beautiful house to go home to every night?" I let that notion linger, and then said, "Rather than exhausting yourself trying to compete with Sigourney Sky?"

She studied me in the lighted mirror. As always, inscrutable.

Because of the tall ceilings in the Shady Gully Recreation Center, my high heels echoed noisily throughout the hall. While each click increased my anxiety, I eventually found my way to the bougie room where Bella and her bridesmaids were dressing.

I knocked lightly on the door. And then nearly jumped out of my skin when my eyes flitted past a mirror as I waited. Who was this out of place woman in a dress and high heels? I hardly recognized myself. I fought the urge to run.

But when the door flew open, and Desi's mouth formed a giant O, my window of escape had passed. "Meadow," she gushed. "You're stunning."

"My goodness," Robin added as she sashayed to the door in a chic purple pants suit. "Your hair jewelry is lovely. So elegant."

"Mama…" Bella said softly as she approached. "You're so beautiful." She, Micah, and Violet wore matching robes in a clingy, lavender material, and when they all gathered around me my embarrassment jumped by a mile.

"You could be on a cover of a magazine." Micah grinned. "Who did your hair?" She swiveled to the girls. "We should have done ours up like that."

They'd all had makeovers and donned false eyelashes to accentuate their loveliness. Even their nails and toes were beautifully manicured and glistening in the light of the bright room. I marveled at their youth, at their complete beauty. And then I answered Micah's question. "Actually, Dolly did my hair. And speaking of Dolly, there's something I have to tell—"

"Dolly? No way?" Desi's eyes tripled in size. Like Robin, she'd gone with a version of purple, but presented in a sophisticated dress cut at the knee. The flared bottom complemented her petite figure.

Shamefully, I realized I'd allowed all the fuss to become one-sided. "You look nice," I said to Desi, and then turned to Robin. "Both of you do."

They each pointedly linked their arms into mine, almost as if they'd made a decision to take me into their coven. For the first time I started to relax. "Come see her dress." Desi led me to a dressing room within the fancy room. "It's hanging on the door. Waiting for her."

"Speaking of that," Robin glanced at her watch, "it's time."

Micah and Bella squealed, and while Violet did not, she hurried to the dress and began the practical and painstaking task of unbuttoning the copious buttons. Micah helped her along, and Desi snapped pictures.

Bella squeezed me around the waist and ran her fingers lightly along my arm. "I'm so happy you're here, Mama."

"Of course. Why wouldn't I be?" I swallowed thickly, pierced with the regrettable fact that I'd fought tooth and nail for months to deny this day, to reject this exquisitely profound moment. Guilt swept through me then, followed by an image of Uncle Wolf in the creek and the joy he'd exuded as his body rose triumphant from the water.

My uncle. My Bella. My family. *I must get myself together,* I thought. *I dreaded so much of life…and perhaps, if I gave it a chance, it really wasn't so bad.*

Just as we shimmied Bella into the lovely gown, we heard a steady tapping at the door, accompanied by a clear, male voice. When Bella shrieked, Desi hurried the girls into hiding places. "Nobody can see her!" Micah warned. "It's bad luck!"

Once everyone was safely hidden away in the dressing room,

Desi opened the door a crack. She turned and looked directly at me. "It's Timothy. For you, Meadow."

My heart fluttered, first out of fear, and then with something else entirely.

"Hey," he said as I slipped out into the hallway. "I just thought I'd drop by. You know, hang out, see what's new, talk about the weather—" He stopped. Suddenly at a loss. "Whoa. You…you really clean up nice."

I laughed, extremely amused, but also pleased that my appearance had brought his inane chatter to a halt. "Thanks. You as well." His eyes crinkled as he looked down at me. He was a formidable sight in his sharply fitted gray suit and violet tie. His blue eyes appeared even more inviting, and brighter after a fresh shave.

"Uh…I came…what did I come for?" He chuckled in a self-deprecating manner. "Oh, I came to give this letter to Bella."

I stood firm at the door. "Well, you'd be taking your life into your hands if you tried to cross this threshold. Trust me."

He handed me the letter. "It's from Luke. For Bella. He read it to me. It's quite touching. Heartfelt."

I took the note, inexplicably disappointed when our hands didn't touch. When he lingered, I added awkwardly, "Thanks. I'll give it to her."

"There you are." Father Patrick and Lenny dashed over, Father in his clerical jacket and collar, and Lenny in a suit similar to Timothy's. Father Patrick paused, bending over to catch his breath.

"You look magnificent," Lenny said sweetly. "Is Desi in there? And Robin?" He lightly tapped on the door.

"Thanks. Yeah, they're guarding the girls so y'all don't see them."

Just then Desi and Robin peeked out the door. "Well, aren't you handsome?" Desi moved eagerly toward her husband, and I swear the man blushed.

"I have news." Father Patrick finally caught his breath.

As Robin and Desi fully joined us in the hall, a rush of squeals echoed from inside the dressing suite.

"The vote is in," Father Patrick said. "And it's good."

"I never had any doubt." Timothy beamed.

Lenny nodded. "The Shady Gully community overwhelmingly voted for Petey. A complete vote of confidence. They accept that he hasn't had any official schooling, but they have faith in him. They want him to lead the church."

"Oh," Desi gushed, leaning into her husband, "now all we have to do is build him one. You should make Dolly an offer for the land."

"You should," Robin concurred. "Do it ASAP. Strike while the iron is hot."

"Agreed," Father Patrick echoed. "In person is best, and a festive occasion such as a wedding is the perfect time."

"She wasn't invited, Father." Desi paled.

I cleared my throat. "Well…I started to tell you earlier, but I was a little nervous because I wasn't sure how you'd take it." I had their full attention now. "I invited her. Today, when she was doing my hair. I know it wasn't my place, but I felt sorry for her—"

"Meadow," Desi exclaimed. "You're the mother-of-the-bride. You can invite anyone you want."

Trusting my instincts, I added, "And after talking to her today, I actually think she might be receptive to an offer. I wouldn't under bid though."

Timothy laughed aloud.

"Brilliant!" Father Patrick exclaimed. "Splendid!"

When Sheriff Rick approached, Lenny, Desi, Robin, and Father Patrick fell into an intense conversation about the offer, so it seemed only natural for Timothy and me to move together and chat among ourselves.

"So, uh…" he started, "I can tell by the sound of high-pitched squeals that time is of the essence, but I've been meaning to ask you something."

I steeled myself and met his eyes with as much confidence as I could muster.

"How do you feel about basketball, bourbon, and horses?"

As usual with him, I laughed big. And then I studied his eyes. *So blue, so much like Mitch's…*

"Bourbon and horses, maybe," I quipped. "But basketball, really?

"Well…okay." He blushed, much like Lenny had with Desi. "Basketball isn't a dealbreaker." His blue eyes crinkled along the edges. Kind. Gentle.

And yet, so very different from Mitch's…

The Feisty One
Violet

Whether it was the bridesmaid's dress or my dreadful, shapeless figure, I bore a striking resemblance to an elongated grape. Seriously. I was like the overripened berry destined for the bottom of the bag, impaired and unappealing, pushed aside to make way for the crisper, more sublime grape that glistened ahead.

That grape would be Micah. Perky and bright, and blooming with freshness. And Bella…well, Bella would be that rare, exotic fruit on a tropical island, one so exquisite it was yet to be named, a work of art so divine its design was constantly evolving, moving closer and closer toward perfection.

She sat perched on a stool, reading Luke's letter while the long train of her white satin gown surrounded her like a plush cloud on the edge of heaven. Despite her tears, Aunt Desi managed to snap several pictures before my mother took possession of the camera.

"Violet, Micah, why don't you go stand behind her?" my mother suggested. "The lighting in this room is incredible." She glanced around. "You as well, Desi. Get in there. And where did Meadow run off to?"

"She was chatting with Timothy the last time I saw her." Micah flashed a wily grin.

"Luke named this the Illumination Room," Bella said.

I could see why. With the over-the-top amenities and superb lighting, it was perfect for wedding parties. It was also a makeup artist's and a photographer's dream because of the natural light the windows provided.

"They do a lot of family portraits here—" Aunt Desi turned when there was a cautious tap at the door. A vertical slant widened to reveal an impeccably coiffed Tammy Jo. Dressed in a wine-colored cocktail dress, her gorgeous raven hair fell over her shoulders in waves.

A day ago, I'd have withered in jealousy at the very sight of her, but because a crucial piece of data hadn't been entered into the program, I'd processed incorrectly. It had been my own brother, Sterling, who Tammy Jo had been pursuing, and Petey had served as nothing more than a tool.

*It's not what you think…*Petey had said.

I should feel silly, and I did, but mostly I felt relief. Even though Petey and I had simply fallen back into our usual pattern, and there'd been no outward expression of anything more, at least I didn't have to compete with the alluring Tammy Jo.

This revelation, along with my mother's favorable reaction to my career change, had greatly shifted my perspective. *Why not Shady Gully?* I thought. My extended family lived here. My daddy was buried here. And Lord knew, the town could do with a local veterinarian.

Bella sniffled as she folded Luke's letter. When she brushed her finger underneath her lashes, Tammy Jo made for her purse. "Wait. Don't do that." She rifled until she found a tissue. "I just wanted to drop in for a minute," she said while helping Bella fix her makeup.

"How is Duchess?" Bella asked her. "I miss her under my feet."

"I just checked, and she's doing great," Tammy Jo reported. "She's in the kitchen right now hanging out with your Uncle Wolfheart, Charlie Wayne, and that…that *dude* with the hair."

"Good to know they're working together." Desi raised her eyebrow emphatically. "Luke made that a condition. He warned them that if they ruined his wedding with their feud, he'd banish them both."

"They seemed fine," Tammy Jo said. "You look gorgeous, Bella." She nodded at Micah and me. "And so do your bridesmaids."

"So Duchess is eating and drinking okay?" Bella pressed. "And walking alright?"

"Yep. Just a little slow on her back legs, but much better. She'll be up causing trouble in no time."

"You know," I said lightly, "I've been thinking about her mischievous temperament, and I have a suggestion." It felt strange to have everyone in the room turn to me as if I were an authority. "I think Duchess might settle down if she had a friend. Y'all might consider getting another dog."

"Violet!" Aunt Desi exclaimed. "Don't say that. Two of them? Really?"

"It works sometimes." I considered my mother. "Look how well Mama's cat Buford and the sheriff's cat get along."

"It's true," Mom confirmed. "Buford and Gerty have become fast friends. They keep each other entertained and out of mischief."

"I love that idea," Bella exclaimed. "We'll get a boy dog, and we'll name him Duke."

"Ladies!" An adolescent voice sounded in pace with the banging door. "It's time."

We all turned as Meadow and Fireman entered the Illumination Room. "We'd better go," Meadow cut her eyes at Fireman, "or our pint-sized wedding planner here will have a hissy fit."

My mother winked at Meadow as we filed out into the hall. "We missed you while we were taking pictures. I hear you've been chatting with Timothy?" It was a question, and although Meadow didn't answer, the way she colored proved telling.

As we passed the kitchen, the rich scent of honey sweetened barbecue sauce mingled with the spicy seasonings in jambalaya to make my mouth water.

"I smell shrimp. And crawfish," Micah said moistly. "And buttery crust. Is that…?"

"Yes, it's Glenda's shrimp and crawfish pie," Desi answered. "She made individual mini-pies for all the guests. Can you imagine?"

"That was so nice." Robin shook her head. "I miss her, haven't seen her since school."

"She's fabulous. Said she wanted to contribute something seeing as how our catering situation fell apart."

"Oh, those pies are so good." Micah practically drooled. "I'm starving. None of us got to eat last night."

"Probably a good thing," I remarked as we sneaked past the kitchen.

While Bubba and Daryl looked to be doing more eating and drinking than ushering, they did make a point to step out and whistle as we clicked by in our formal wear. Charlie Wayne and JJ Wheeler stretched their necks out as well, and set to clapping as they set eyes on Bella.

"All of you! Just get!" Micah fussed. "Nobody is supposed to see her!"

Hoot Wheeler appeared then, casually leaning against the frame of the door, towering over them all. He nimbly sipped a beer as he goaded Micah. "Make me."

Quietdove frowned hard from his position at the swinging doors to the Dogwood Room. "Is he giving you trouble?" he asked Micah. When she didn't answer, he shot Hoot a glare before checking his watch. "Alright, I'm supposed to send the mothers on their way."

And just like that, the procession began. Fireman, newly confident, delivered the moms to their seats with much aplomb, and before I could think too much about my debut as an overripened grape, Petey was beside me, smiling with his whole face.

"Did you hear?" he whispered just below the ceremonial music. "I got the votes. No doubt it was Timothy's influence, but—"

"I never had any doubt."

"Mom and Dad are going to talk to Dolly tonight. And if she won't sell, we'll find another place in Shady Gully to build. Maybe even The Creek. I feel like people will come."

"They will. And just so you know, I heard Dolly might be open to an offer."

"Seriously? That's awesome! We could get the community involved and have an actual church raising. That's like a barn raising. It's what we do here in the country."

I smiled, watching for Quietdove's cue to move forward. "I know what a church raising is, Petey."

He took my arm into his, squeezing ever so lightly. "Are you serious about opening your clinic here someday?"

I met his eyes. "Yes."

"I'll find you some land and we'll get Daryl to build you something nice. Only the best for you and the little critters of Shady Gully." He added, "I'll be waiting for you when you finish school."

A long beat, meaningful and unspoken, resonated between us.

"Okay. Let's go." Quietdove signaled, holding the double doors open for us.

"You ready, Crystal?" Petey tugged my arm, moving it closer against his body.

As we moved into the beautiful Dogwood Room, I was keenly aware of all the faces as they twisted back to watch us. No longer feeling like a smushed, discarded grape, I savored the stroll down the aisle with Petey. I was always better with him by my side.

I saw Dolly sitting a few pews behind Desi, on the groom's side, as well as Uncle Max and his wife, Danielle. Behind them were Big Al and Thaddeus, Claire from the post office, and Mrs. Guidry. I also caught a glimpse of Mrs. Guidry's friend, Mrs. Shanna May, and her husband.

I spied Sterling and Tammy Jo snuggled up on the pew behind my mother, looking very much the couple, and of course, the sheriff was glued to my mother's side. While I still wasn't completely sold on Mr. Mustache, I begrudgingly admitted he and his blazing sirens had come through for Duchess.

He'd also seemed particularly interested in my future as a Shady Gully veterinarian. Throughout the ride to Belle Maison, he'd regaled me with tales of his cat, Gerty. The thought of the mustached redneck being a cat lover seemed weirdly comical, but time would tell.

Meadow perched elegantly on the front pew of the bride's side, while a number of folks from The Creek were in attendance behind her. Redflyer, Moonpipe, Youngdeer, and old man Bluejay and his wife, appeared festive as they watched the wedding procession.

After Petey parked me on Bella's side of the stage, he took his position on the groom's side of the altar. I glanced at Luke, who seemed giddy; Father Patrick, who exuded reverence; and Timothy, who appeared utterly enchanted. When I followed his gaze, I found it trained on Meadow.

I considered the single status of Lexington, Kentucky's, most eligible pastor, newly curious as to his long-standing bachelorhood. He must be just over forty now, and I found it curious that he'd yet to find a wife. Especially as single women in Kentucky boldly vied for his attention. Had someone hurt him? Broken his heart? Or had he just not found *the one?* Either way, there was definitely a story there.

Just after Micah and Uncle Lenny sauntered up and took their places, the wedding march began. As everyone stood, my heart fluttered. What was it about that music? That sound? Much like the national anthem, it evoked veneration and sometimes, even tears.

Like now.

When the doors swung open and at last Bella appeared, a swell of praise rose as the guests, unable to smother their *oohs* and *aahs*, sent a lively buzz straight to the top of the lofty ceilings of the Dogwood Room. None were more taken by the bride's spectacular beauty than her betrothed, who looked spellbound as he realized the significance of what he was being given. Tears streamed down Luke's face, his demonstration of emotion only rivaled by Bella's Uncle Wolfheart.

Dapper in his gray suit and violet tie, Wolfheart towered over Bella. He was surefooted, and light on his feet, and like a wolf his gait flowed effortlessly. When they reached the end of the aisle, he stood before the groom and the two holy men at the center of the arch. When asked, *who gives this bride away*, he answered, "Her mother and I."

He kissed Bella, and with tears streaming down his face, he settled next to his niece, Meadow. Since I was facing them, I gulped back a wave of emotion when Meadow tenderly stretched her arm around her uncle and pulled him closer as he wept.

Timothy and Father Patrick tag-teamed the ceremony, which was both lighthearted and humorous, and somber and reverent. Just before they recited their vows, Bella presented Luke with a gift of her own, in exchange for his letter.

Sterling rose and took his seat at the grand piano to the right of the arch, and Bella moved to join him, clutching a microphone to her chest. As if the audience weren't emotionally gutted already, when Bella belted out "Bridge Over Troubled Waters" the audience completely unraveled.

Muffled sobs and discreet sniffles reverberated throughout the Dogwood Room, but I couldn't see who wept or who wiped away tears, because throughout the poignant love song, my focus was drawn to only one person.

And to my absolute astonishment, I found my scrutiny reflected in his extraordinary hazel gaze.

I rushed past the kitchen toward the reception hall, resolved to make sure the tables were exactly as Aunt Desi wanted them. She and Uncle Lenny had slipped off to talk to Dolly privately after the ceremony, so it was up to me to make sure Charlie Wayne and JJ Wheeler hadn't made a mockery of their carefully planned vision.

Aunt Desi and my mother had commissioned Luke's staff to oversee the two ornery competitors, and had even set one table as a precise template. Still, I wouldn't relax until I laid eyes on the reception hall myself.

If it was a disaster, I'd have ten minutes—tops—before the guests filed in for dinner and toasts.

As I turned the corner and pushed the doors open, I breathed in the sweet air of relief. Lilac, lavender, pink, and deep purple displayed beautifully on each table, each with a subtle sprinkling of greenery. Bella's wedding colors presented a stunning success.

The flowers smelled fragrant. Even the silverware and the wine flutes were bright and spotless. I ambled between tables to reassure myself, my mind drifting to the ceremony, to the moving pageantry of it all.

"There you are," Petey said. "I've been looking all over for you."

"Did you hear something?" I asked. "Did Dolly agree?"

He shrugged, his dress shoes clicking along the hickory floor toward the table. He'd unbuttoned his suit jacket, and now shuffled over easily with his hands planted deep in his pockets. "No, nothing yet. It'll be fine though, either way."

I nodded, turning my attention back to the tables, scanning for anything amiss. "Aren't these lovely?" I twisted one of the candles to better enhance the foliage draped across the white tablecloth.

He leaned toward the table, his shoulder lightly brushing mine as he picked up a flower. "There's a lot going on here, I'll say that."

I chuckled, plucking the flower he'd taken and setting it right. "They're all so beautiful. I can't decide which ones I like the best. The deep purple, the lavender, or the—"

"Violet."

I whipped my head at him.

"Definitely the violet."

I drew in a giant rush of air, quite literally unable to speak.

His eyes flashed, and he slowly bent his head toward mine. When our foreheads touched, he whispered, "I love you."

I could feel his breath against my mouth as he said the words, *I love you.*

"Always have," he said. "Always will." He kissed me.

This man, this *boy* I'd fallen in love with so many years ago, had finally opened his heart and invited me into his extraordinary light. I returned his kiss. And we didn't stop until we heard footsteps track into the reception hall.

Dinner was a roaring success. The drinks flowed, Glenda's shrimp and crawfish pies were divine, and according to JJ Wheeler, the barbecue was *elevated*. Upon this pronouncement Charlie Wayne resisted the eye roll loitering just behind his coke bottle glasses. He clearly understood that with one false move he'd be *banished* by the mayor of Shady Gully.

As dinner wound to an end, Luke stood, and clinked his glass with his fork a few times. Once he had everyone's attention, he thanked the guests for joining him and Bella on their special night. "Before we head to the dance floor to bust a move, kick up our heels, or…whatever people say these days—"

"Party hardy!" Bubba and Daryl chanted.

Duchess, who sat demurely in a doggie bed beneath Bella's feet, pounded her tail until the guffaws subsided.

"I don't even know what *party hardy* means." Luke chuckled. "Anyway, I'd like to thank my parents for tonight. And for raising me to have enough sense to recognize an angel of a woman like my Bella. And for Micah, who coached away some of my nerdy tendencies so I could fool Bella into falling in love with me."

Micah raised her wine glass. "New Tip. Don't ever say *kick up your heels*."

Luke nodded, and then addressed Meadow with a raised glass. "To Bella's mom, for bringing Bella into the world, and for allowing me into your heart. And to Mr.…uh…*Uncle* Wolf, you're an inspirational and noble man. Welcome to the family." He grinned. "I apologize in advance."

After much laughter, Luke cleared his throat and looked at Petey. "And now, I'd like my brother, who's my very best friend, the most fun at a party, and one of the Godliest men I've ever known, to say a few words.

Petey lightly squeezed my thigh underneath the table before heading to the microphone. He paused at *the grown-up table* long enough to high-five Father Patrick, fist bump Timothy, shake hands with his father and Sheriff Rick, and kiss his mother and mine on top of the head.

"Suck up," someone who sounded very much like Bubba teased from several seats away.

"Hey everybody." Petey slowly spread his gaze from table to table, and I could practically hear the sequential swish of lips turning upward to meet his infectious smile. "Everybody happy?" A scattering of cheers, clinking glasses, and whoops ran through the crowd. "Me too! We've got a beautiful bride and a…so-so groom." Laughter erupted. "Great food, plenty of wine, and soon-to-be song. Don't worry, we'll try to keep Luke off the dance floor.

"But you know what? It's easy to be happy right now. Weddings bring hope, and promise, and our senses and appetites are sated with fun, laughter, and barbeque. Right?"

This is where he paused, and while I didn't know what would come next, I knew he did, and as always with Petey, I knew it would be provocative. "But joy? Well, I believe that's something else entirely. I don't think joy and happiness are the same thing at all. Now, they could be synonyms. I don't know for sure." He shrugged. "I'd have to defer to the smart people in the room for that." He looked pointedly at me. "People like Violet."

A surge of swoons and giggles mingled with surprise as Petey had finally said my name in public.

"You see, spiritually, there's a huge distinction between joy and happiness. For example, one of the most joyful people I know…is my mama."

A rowdy and pronounced round of applause exploded throughout the room, and Petey raised his own fists in a tribute to Aunt Desi. "Yep. Let me tell you a story about my mama. A long time ago, some mean kids made fun of her because she didn't know the Lord's Prayer. Can you imagine? They ridiculed her. Embarrassed her. Reveled in her humiliation." He stopped, letting that sink in. "But some good things came out of it, you know? Because that's what our Lord does, He takes something bad, and He turns it for good. And you know what He did? He gave her a best friend that day. And that would be my Aunt Robin."

Another rambunctious whoop-whoop erupted. "And guess what else He did? My mama's shame pushed her to go deeper, to read the Bible, to seek Him out, and eventually, to accept Him as her Lord and Savior." Petey's eyes swept through the crowd, landing squarely on Dolly. "And you can bet she knows the words to the Lord's Prayer now."

Land be damned, I thought, *Petey wasn't holding back.*

"And my mama, well, she's the most joyful person I know. Seriously. Even when she's not happy. When she doesn't feel good. When she's sad and missing her parents. Or when she's mad at my dad…"

Father Patrick's hearty chuckle drowned out all the others.

"But I swear to you, my friends, she is always, always, joyful. Do you know why?" Once the room settled into complete silence, Petey said, "Because happiness is good food and a wedding. Happiness is falling in love." Again, he looked directly at me. "But joy…joy is a gift, it's the fruit of the Holy Spirit. Philippians, chapter four, verses eleven and twelve say, 'Not that I am speaking of need, for I have learned in whatever situation I am to be content. I know how to be brought low, and I know how to abound. In any and every circumstance, I have learned the secret of facing plenty and hunger, abundance and need.'"

"Amen," Timothy said reverently.

Petey concluded, "You see, my friends, while happiness is built on circumstances, joy is anchored in faith, in the confidence that our Lord Jesus Christ loves us. Always. Not just when we're victorious and celebrating, but when we're down. And sad. And defeated. And hopeless." The room went pitch quiet. "And He will never, *ever* let us down."

He waited, purposely extending the silence, and then he grinned. "Anybody here want that?" Cheers rose. "I know I do! Y'all want some joy? You wanna be content in all your circumstances?"

"I do!" someone in the back called out.

When Petey raised his glass, the gathering matched his motion by lifting their own crystal high in the air. "To my brother, Luke, and his lovely bride, Bella," Petey smiled, the light shimmering brightly in his eyes, "I wish you the fruit of the Holy Spirit. I wish you a lifetime of joy."

An explosion of cheers and amens reverberated throughout the room. Forks clinked against glasses to bring the celebration to a rowdy crescendo. When the cheers eventually landed quietly, Petey said, "For any of you who don't know me, I'm Petey. My mama named me after the great apostle, Peter." Petey flashed his signature grin. "He was the feisty one."

Just as the DJ cranked up the dance music, I felt Petey's hand slip into mine.

"Violet," he whispered, and the feel of his breath against my ear sent an electric jolt through my body. "I'm kind of liking the sound of that. Violet. Violet," he teased. "I want to say it over and over. Just think how much catching up I have to do. Violet. Violet."

The lights were dim, and only the spectacle of lavender, pink, and violet strobes flashed across our faces. "You wanna dance? Or we could go into the kitchen and hang out with Duchess. Word is her mischievous spark is back in full force."

I laughed. "Bella must be thrilled. A perfect night for her."

Petey cringed as he checked the dance floor. "Except for the fact that her husband can't dance. I'm embarrassed for him. It's painful to watch."

"He could learn some moves from Fireman." We watched as Fireman shook his hips and bobbed his head, frolicking in the middle of the stage as several women surrounded him in a celebratory shimmy.

"He's gonna break a lot of hearts, that one," Petey said, and then frowned as he tucked his head toward Hoot Wheeler. "Now that guy…" Hoot removed his suit jacket and flirtatiously began to serenade Micah, swaying and grinding his way over to her in an invitation to dance. "That guy is gonna be trouble."

We moved to the bar, where Petey ordered us both a glass of wine. Charlie Wayne sulked along with Quietdove, who glared furiously at Hoot.

When Micah finally gave in to Hoot's foolishness and agreed to dance, Quietdove turned away from the dance floor, shaking his head in disappointment. "What could she possibly see in that clown?" Disgusted, he ordered a double bourbon.

Charlie Wayne commiserated, patting Quietdove's shoulder supportively. "Dang Wheelers…the whole lot of 'em is rotten to the core."

Petey buried his amusement as he reached for our wine.

"Hey, Petey," a female voice moved us to pivot. We exchanged stunned looks as Dolly led us away from the bar and the loud music. We followed her to a quiet area where Father Patrick served generous dollops of pink and purple ice cream to the guests. The jolly, red-bearded priest was in his element as he chatted vociferously with the guests and slurped his own cone.

"How you doing, Dolly?" Petey plucked an ice cream cone from Father Patrick's hand and presented it to Dolly with flourish. "Ever had violet ice cream?" He sent me a playful wink. "I hear it's delicious."

"Thanks." Dolly awkwardly took the ice cream cone. "Actually, I wanted to talk to you before I told your mom and dad. It's about the offer…"

While Petey seemed relaxed, giving Dolly his full attention, my heart pounded in anticipation.

"I was one of those kids. The mean ones you were talking about earlier."

He nodded somberly.

"I'm ashamed of that. I don't know why I did it. To prop myself up I guess, to present myself as better than her. I don't know. I was a stupid kid." She studied the purple ice cream as it melted down the cone. "But I also behaved—dishonorably in the way I left the house when your mom and dad bought it."

Petey found a napkin, and gently took the cone from her, wiping the edges and wrapping it firmly before handing it back.

"I'm sorry for what I did. The way I acted," she said. "And I plan to tell her that tonight." Dolly's mascaraed eyes flitted between us. "The land is yours, Petey. I plan to accept the very generous offer your parents made. I hope you build a big ole church and make Shady Gully joyous again." She considered the ice cream. "I think it would make my daddy happy."

"Thank you, Dolly. Your father, Brother Wyatt, is the one who introduced my mama to the Lord. I'll do everything in my power to honor him."

After she walked off with her dripping cone, Petey signaled Father Patrick with a thumbs up. The priest rejoiced cheerily. "Really? That's brilliant!" He joined us. "And I practically had a front row seat for the moment. What luck!" he gushed.

The red headed priest took a generous lick of his ice cream cone. "Your words were truly inspired tonight, my boy. Timothy and I sat there like proud papas watching you stir up the audience. Well done, indeed." After another lick, he added keenly, "Speaking of Timothy, he certainly has some impressive ink along his arms, doesn't he? That Philippians verse is quite exquisite. Perhaps I'll get one. Although I think Psalm twenty-seven is more my style. What do you think?"

Petey nodded, his face full of amusement. "I say it all the time. You and Wolfheart. The coolest cats in Shady Gully."

Father Patrick glanced at the growing line at the ice cream station, which appeared to be mostly children going in for their second round. "Well, I'm off to serve the hungry." He waved, his eyes already twinkling in anticipation of his next delightful conversation.

When Petey turned back to me, he bundled me into his arms, and I could feel the relief spilling off him in ripples. He hugged me tightly, murmuring a prayer of thanks. "Wow. Things have certainly turned around for us, haven't they?" After he kissed me fully, he said, "Alright, I'm ready now."

"For what?" I asked.

"Let's go kick up our heels. Don't tell Micah I said that."

As he led me onto the dance floor, all the angst I'd felt over my grape dress now seemed trivial and senseless. My place next to him felt natural. Even when we were younger, Petey always had a way of lifting me up and making me feel… *seen*.

We joined Sterling and Tammy Jo, who seemed oblivious to everything going on around them. My sweet, enigmatic brother whose aspirations jumped from musician to lawyer to writer—how I hoped he'd someday find his calling. And his special someone.

"Look, y'all!" Bella, who remained gorgeous even with her dress pinned in a bustle and her hair in disarray, squealed with delight. "Look at JJ!"

Petey and I watched, stunned, as JJ Wheeler spun around the dance floor, mimicking the moves of Wolfheart, Bubba, and Daryl as they led a line dance to a popular song. At first, I was so completely blown away by Wolfheart's sexy dance moves that I didn't realize JJ was the one everyone was egging on.

"Take it off," whooped Bubba.

"All the way," echoed Daryl. "Come on!"

JJ twisted and dipped, moving his head in elaborate circles, performing a striptease—of sorts—with his hair. Beside me, Petey cackled loudly. "He's taking off that bun thingy."

The crowd had moved to form a circle around Wheeler, and clapped to the beat of the music, roaring into a frenzy when he finally freed his long hair from the notorious man-bun. As it fell to his shoulders, Wheeler grew emboldened, his movements electric as he shook his head round and round, his hair spinning wildly in all directions.

Petey nudged me with a grin, pointing to the bar where Quietdove and Charlie Wayne continued to brood in solidarity.

"Finally," he said as the music switched to a slow ballad. "I've been waiting for this all night.

Never a graceful dancer, Petey made me feel coordinated and elegant as he rocked me from side to side, moving closer and closer with each chorus. Surprised by the intimacy of the moment, I closed my eyes and rested my head on his shoulder.

"Hey," he whispered, pressing his hands tighter around my waist, "check it out."

I followed his line of vision, catching Timothy and Meadow in a similar position of intimacy, as well as Uncle Lenny and Aunt Desi, and—my mother and Sheriff Rick.

"Come on," he teased. "I think they're kind of cute."

"*Humph*," I grunted noncommittally.

"Be nice."

While I hated to admit it, the relief I'd felt after sharing my plans with my mother had been redemptive. Her approval—and her enthusiasm—had been affirming.

Likewise, my begrudging consent over her relationship with Sheriff Rick seemed to alleviate her anxiety, serving as a balm to her fragile spirit. Had she needed my support as much as I'd apparently needed hers? I'd always known, intuitively, how much a daughter needed her mother's approval, but the thought that the mother needed the daughter's was unfathomable to me.

And yet, after getting to know Meadow and witnessing her anguish over her broken relationship with Bella, it was clear that the mother-daughter relationship was fraught with challenges. How was it possible, I wondered, that two people who loved each other, who were made from the same mold, inside and out, could get so bogged down in misguided perceptions and stubborn communication?

The inclination to find fault and slash away at the ones we loved—in fact, the very ones we needed the most—seemed as regrettable as ever.

And yet, as I saw my mom's head dip back in laughter, obviously tickled over something Sheriff Rick had said, I realized I *wanted* her to be happy. Her happiness wouldn't taint Daddy's memory, nor would it diminish our love for him.

"God loves you both, you know?" Petey pulled away from me suddenly, almost as if he could read my thoughts. "He wants you both to be happy."

And there he was again, always making me a better person. "Okay, I'll try."

"We do have one very important issue to discuss. It's kind of significant."

"Okay." His tone was ominous.

"It's about our household."

Our household? I squinted at him, confused.

"We need to decide right now," he said. "Before we go any further."

"Okay," I repeated, my heart pounding.

"University of Kentucky or LSU?"

I laughed at him, this crazy boy with the light inside him. "I think as long as we've got two license plate holders, we're good."

The Matriarchs & Their Families

Desi – married to Lenny, best friends with Robin, mother of Luke, Petey, and Micah

Lenny – married to Desi, father of Luke, Petey, and Micah

Luke – Desi & Lenny's oldest son, mayor of Shady Gully, engaged to Bella

Petey – Desi & Lenny's son, charismatic, loved by all, spiritually driven

Micah – Desi & Lenny's daughter, dental hygienist, baby of the family

Robin – widow of Dean, best friends with Desi, mother of twins, Sterling and Violet

Sterling – Robin's son, handsome, creative, musically inclined

Violet – Robin's daughter, brilliant, driven, well educated

Shady Gullians

Sheriff Rick – the sheriff of Shady Gully, graduated with Desi, Lenny, and Robin. In love with Robin

Max – Robin's baby brother, deputy in Shady Gully

"Cruella" Claire – graduated with Desi and Robin, gossip, head of Shady Gully's post office

Charlie Wayne - ornery owner of The Cozy Corner, Shady Gully's favorite eatery

Sprite – owner of Sprite's Quick Stop, a gas station & general store at one of the corners of Shady Gully's fabled four way stop

Bubba – graduated with Desi, Lenny, Robin, works at Luke's Auto Body Shop

Daryl – graduated with Desi, Lenny, Robin, works at Luke's Auto Body Shop, also does construction work

Patty – Shady Gully's favorite EMT, friends with Denise, a classmate of Desi and Robin's

Tammy Jo – Petey's ex-girlfriend, nurse

Jesse & James – twin sons of Brother Wyatt, who was a pillar in the Church community

Dolly – daughter of Brother Wyatt, owns Dolly's Diva Dome, and once married to Mitch

Chester – ornery old coot who hangs out with Claire at the Post Office

Big Al – outspoken resident of Shady Gully

Thaddeus – Big Al's sidekick

Across The Creek

Wolfheart – born & raised on The Creek, devoted to his niece, Meadow, and her daughter, Bella. Friends with Desi & Robin

Meadow – Lives on The Creek, delivers mail in Shady Gully, mother of Bella

Bella – daughter of Meadow, Wolfheart's great-niece, engaged to Luke

Quietdove – hails from The Creek, handsome, deputy sheriff in Shady Gully

Sigourney Sky – A Creek woman who opened Nails & Thread, a successful salon, at the four way stop in Shady Gully

Redflyer – hails from across the creek, now heads the fire station there

Youngdeer – Redflyer's friend, works at The Creek's fire station

Moonpipe – Redflyer and Youngdeer's buddy, works at the fire station

Fireman – twelve-year-old Creek boy who accidentally set a church on fire, has a crush on Bella, and wants to be a fireman when he grows up

Granny Lacey – Fireman's elderly grandmother, notorious for her bad cooking

Bluejay – hails from across the creek, reserved, a staple in The Creek community

The Shepherds

Father Patrick – popular priest at Sacred Heart Catholic Church, Irish ancestry, jolly, loves food and wine and the people of Shady Gully

Timothy – pastor of the mega church, North Lake Christian Church, in Lexington, Kentucky

Shady Characters

Mitch – graduated with Desi, Lenny, Robin, became guidance counselor at Shady Gully High. Briefly married to Dolly, but eventually left Shady Gully after scandal involving a young student

Tom – Desi's stepdad who sexually abused her

Adam – pursued Desi in high school, and even after she married Lenny, an aspiring country music singer, a womanizer

Deceased

Dean – Lenny, Sheriff Rick's friend, brilliant businessman, was married to Robin, father to Sterling and Violet

Sunny – Desi's flamboyant mother, artist, loved by all

Acknowledgements

This book is fiction. That means I made it all up. For real. Thank you to Mike Parker and Wordcrafts Press.

I'm extremely grateful to Scott Rambo, Lead Pastor at Abundant Grace Church in Deville, Louisiana, as well as Matt McNeeley, Associate Pastor. Your expertise—and your honesty—on a variety of issues helped frame Petey's journey. Your stories and anecdotes set my fictional town of Shady Gully on the right path, and your real-life community is blessed to have you.

I would be lost without Rachel Dodge, who is blessed with genius when it comes to all things technical. Even more notable is her ability to present all this unpleasantness in a way a mature creative like me can understand. And if I can't, she just fixes things with her magic fairy dust. Thank you, Rachel.

A special thank you, as always, to my first readers, and I'm especially happy to add the esteemed Kathy Fox Vancil to the club. Not only does Kathy narrate the *Shady Gully Series*, but her advice is invaluable to me. And as always, thank you to my best author buddy and treasured friend, Charly Cox.

Speaking of early assessment, I'm indebted to my new friend and cherished editor, Jennifer Jakes of the Killion Agency. Thank you for your expertise, your patience, and your friendship.

And to the wonderful Dr. Shelly Kirkland of the Animal Clinic at Equestrian Woods in Nicholasville, Kentucky, thanks for jumping on board with this storyline. Your help hammering out the details of this premise was crucial, and I'm grateful for your time and knowledge.

This novel, even more than books 1 and 2 in the series, truly became an interactive experience with my readers. My readers are such a fun, creative bunch, and they really rose to the occasion when I asked for suggestions on a fun dog breed and a great name.

Thank you, Barbara Shoemaker, for introducing me to Shiba Inus. How is it possible I'd never heard of these mischievous dogs with their big, toothy smiles? I'm absolutely besotted now! Google "Shiba Inu smiles" and you'll see why.

And Matt Tarver, Duchess was the perfect name for Shady Gully's newest bundle of trouble. In fact, I think Duchess needs a friend. A Shiba Inu friend. We'll call him Duke! Stay tuned!

Glenda Jolly Hathorn, your recipe for shrimp and crawfish pies will surely have readers drooling as they peruse the menu at Luke and Bella's wedding. Thank you for your contribution, and don't worry, Shady Gully fans, you can get the recipe on my website: **https://www.hallielee.com/recipes.html**

And finally, we all have one of those friends, right? You know, the one that dares you to put him in one of your books?

"Don't tempt me," I teased Jason Adams. "I'll do it."

"Do it," he insisted. "And make me a villain."

And with that, JJ Wheeler was born. Man-bun and all.

This book was so much fun to write. I loved all the contributions and suggestions as much as I loved the way they moved the series forward.

Finally, I'm forever grateful for my husband, Bruce, and my beautiful daughter, Bree. This one is for you, my sweet daughter. I love you.

Note to Readers

Thank you for spending time with me in Shady Gully. I hope you enjoyed Luke and Bella's wedding as well as the new characters and critters.

If you enjoyed *Paint Me Fearless*, *Wolfheart*, and *Shades of Violet*—and look forward to Book 4 in the *Shady Gully Series*, please take a few minutes to leave a review on your favorite book retailer's or reviewer's website. Your reviews *really do matter*!

And please, mosey on over to my website, and sign up for my blog and newsletter. When you become a FRIEND OF HALLIE, you'll get all my book news FIRST, including release dates, cover reveals, contests, giveaways, recipes, and more!

https://www.hallielee.com/

I'll see y'all back at the Cozy Corner in Book 4. Until then… Stay Fearless!

Born and raised in Louisiana, Hallie's screenplays and books are inspired by the southern landscape, which she says is "rich with cantankerous, salt of the earth folks destined to be on the page."

Paint Me Fearless, *Wolfheart*, and *Shades of Violet* are the first three volumes in the *Shady Gully Series*, a series which promises thought-provoking, relatable journeys, and a cast of characters who tend to be ornery—but loveable, dramatic—but kind, and quirky—but smarter than they appear.

Hallie and her family, furry kids included, now live in the hills of Kentucky, near Lexington.

Connect with Hallie online at:

www.HallieLee.com